FORCE OF NATURE

SUZANNE BROCKMANN

FORCE OF NATURE

A NOVEL

BALLANTINE BOOKS • NEW YORK

Copyright © 2007 by Suzanne Brockmann ✓

Published in the United States by Ballantine Books, an imprint of The Random House Publishing Group, a division of Random House, Inc., New York.

BALLANTINE and colophon are registered trademarks of Random House, Inc.

LIBRARY OF CONGRESS CATALOGING-IN-PUBLICATION DATA

Brockmann, Suzanne.
  Force of nature : a novel / Suzanne Brockmann.
    p. cm.
  ISBN 978-0-345-48016-3 (acid-free paper)
 1. Private investigators—Fiction.   I. Title.

  PS3552.R61455F66 2007
  813'.54—dc22   2007013642

Printed in the United States of America on acid-free paper

www.ballantinebooks.com

9 8 7 6 5 4 3 2 1

First Edition

Fic.

To the multitude of readers across America who wrote to tell me about their GLBT friends and family members who, like Jules Cassidy, proudly celebrate who they are while walking in the sunlight.

To the reader who matter-of-factly told me how, at age sixteen, she left home forever in loving support of her brother when their parents kicked him out because he was gay.

To the teenaged reader who wrote to say, after reading *Hot Target*, she told her brother, "If you were gay, I wouldn't care—why should I? I love you," and he cried and then said, "Oh, by the way . . ."

To the father who thought his son was gay and wasn't sure how to start that conversation, so he left a copy of *Hot Target* on his kitchen counter, open to the book's dedication, so that his son would read it and understand that his love, too, was unconditional. (A few days later, much to both of their relief, his son came out to him.)

To all the parents who love and accept their sons and daughters, and marvel with pride at the variety of ways they are their own unique selves.

And again, always, to my own son, Jason, who inspires me not just to change the world, but to change it *now*.

This one's for you.

ACKNOWLEDGMENTS

First of all, *thank you* to everyone at Ballantine Books—especially Gina Centrello, Jennifer Hershey, Porscha Burke, and Kim Hovey. Thank you for being such a tremendously supportive team.

Mega-thanks, as well, to my rockin' agent, Steve Axelrod.

Super snaps to the home team, who gets to see me in all my most outrageous craziness—Ed Gaffney, Eric Ruben, and my parents, Fred and Lee Brockmann. And a standing ovation to my son, Jason Gaffney, for introducing us to his amazing and talented friend Apolonia Davalos, who spent a month with us in the dead of winter and warmed our lives with her sunshine and high spirits. And thank *you*, Apple, for brightening our days. Please come back soon—it's just not the same watching *Buffy* without you.

Thank you, too, to my first-draft readers: Deede Bergeron, Lee Brockmann, and Patricia McMahon.

Thank you to the incredible Tom Rancich, for being available to answer my questions about underwater explosives, as well as for his insightful posts on my bulletin board. Tom, you always make us think and you usually make us laugh. Thank you for your awesome stories. (And finish writing your book, will you?!)

Thank you to the real-life Lora Newsom, for donating her name for an incredibly worthy cause—the Southern Poverty Law Center's Teaching Tolerance program. You rock, woman!

And thank you, too, to Ann Schauffler (and her hero of a husband, Stan Griffith) for your wonderful donation to Greater Boston PFLAG.

Thank you to my crew of brave volunteers, who are currently helping me plan my next reader weekend: Elizabeth and Lee Benjamin, Suzie Bernhardt, Stephanie Hyacinth, Beki and Jim Keene, Laura Luke, Jeanne Mangano, Heather McHugh, Peggy Mitchell, Dorbert Ogle, Gail Reddin, Erika Schutte (yay!), and Sue Smallwood.

Check my website at www.suzannebrockmann.com/appearances.htm

for information about my next reader weekend, and information about my *Force of Nature* book tour.

I've got to share a story about something truly amazing that happened while I was on tour for my last book, *Into the Storm*. Literally a week before I left for Atlanta to hold a reader event to promote this book, I was made aware of a young Navy SEAL named Justin who had cancer and needed to find a bone marrow donor for a life-saving transplant. The odds of his finding a match were one in twenty-five thousand, yet he was optimistic and undaunted.

I tried, via my e-mail newsletter, to help spread word of his situation, and of the need to register as a bone marrow donor, and one of my readers, Deborah DeVane, stepped up and hit the ball out of the park. Deborah organized an impromptu bone marrow donor registration drive for my Atlanta reader event. It was amazing—in record time, she made it happen.

Another incredible reader, Paulette Smith, created a blog at www .imaswabbie.blogspot.com, to provide people with information about bone marrow donor registration drives, as well as to provide reports on Justin's progress. Plus, she also helped organize drives at many of the bookstores during my *Into the Storm* book tour. She found volunteers to man the tables, and even arranged for bone marrow donor test kits to be sent to the participating stores. (And she did this as her husband got ready to leave for Iraq.)

Other readers set up drives across the country, too—including the amazing Jan Albertie, who seems to have become something of a force of nature, herself.

Here comes the good news: On September 11, 2006, we received word that Justin had found a bone marrow match. He had a willing donor—and finally a fighting chance to survive his cancer. At last report from his parents, I'm happy to say that he is doing well. (You can check out his progress at the blog listed above!)

For more information about how to register as a bone marrow donor (It's easy—and imagine being *the* one person in 25,000 who could save another's life!), please visit www.marrow.org.

Last but not least, thank *you*. For reading my books, for clamoring to see more of the recurring characters in my Troubleshooters world—especially FBI agent Jules Cassidy. Jules first appeared ten books ago, in *The Defiant Hero*, and has appeared in nearly every book since. I hope you enjoy this installment of his ongoing story.

As always, any mistakes I've made or liberties I've taken are completely my own.

FORCE OF NATURE

PROLOGUE

I t was a hot, humid night. A sweaty night.

A night exactly like hundreds of other hot, sweaty Saturday nights in Sarasota, Florida.

The moon was nearly full and it made the Gulf sparkle. The beautiful, fine white sand of Crescent Beach seemed to glow.

As he walked toward the crowd gathered at the southernmost lifeguard station on the public beach, some of that sand shifted into one of Detective Ric Alvarado's black dress shoes, where it was significantly less beautiful.

"Over here," Bobby Donofrio called, as if Ric could've missed his bald head gleaming in the searchlights that had been set to illuminate the crime scene. He was standing with wiry Johnny Olson, who could've been the department's best detective if he'd cut back on his drinking. " 'Bout time you showed up."

It had been only fifteen minutes since Ric got the call. He'd made good time on the road. But there was never any point in arguing with Donofrio. "Any witnesses?" he asked.

"None so far," Johnny said, turning toward him. He whistled. "Nice suit, kid."

"We caught you in the middle of a hot date or something, huh?" Donofrio asked.

"Or something," Ric responded, unwilling to rub their noses in the fact that they, unlike the other members of the detective squad, *hadn't* been invited to Martell Griffin's party for passing the bar exam, at the Columbia Restaurant out on St. Armand's Circle.

Which was where Ric had been just fifteen—sixteen—minutes ago. Listening to the salsa band his own father put together with only a few hours' notice when the club's regular musicians got stranded at the Key West airport. Flirting with a pretty blond teacher on vacation from Ohio. Celebrating his best friend's well-deserved success.

It was where Ric had been enjoying himself—before Donofrio had called him in to translate, even though Lora Newsom, who spoke fluent Spanish, was among the uniformed officers on the scene.

"Why am I here?" Ric kept his voice even as he gazed at the heavy-set detective, but he knew his annoyance showed in his eyes.

"Because the victim's sister don't speak bueno English and the last thing we need is another weeping female." Donofrio rolled his eyes toward a woman who was, no doubt, the sister. She'd collapsed in the sand, several of the uniforms keeping her back so that the crime-scene photographer could finish taking pictures of the body sprawled on the beach. "One is bad enough."

That was crap. Newsom was one of the few women on the force, which meant she'd worked twenty times harder to get there than any of the men. Compassionate yet firm, capable of kicking ass when she had to— she was a rock in a crisis. But ever since she'd broken down in the locker room at the news that her mother-in-law had died in a car accident, she'd been getting all kinds of grief. Especially from Stan and Ollie here.

One incident, one time, and now it was all these clowns could remember.

Thanks to his famous father, Ric knew that he stood on that same shaky ground.

"You don't think the sister has the right to cry?" Ric asked. He should have just ignored Donofrio, but he was pissed. One of these days, this son of a bitch was going to push him past his breaking point. And Christ, as he got closer, he could see that the victim looked to be no more than eleven or twelve years old. He knew the gangs were initiating 'em younger these days, but this kid was an infant.

"Guess we blew your chances at getting lucky." Skinny Johnny O would not let go of the fact that Ric was out of his usual uniform of sneakers and jeans.

"Not necessarily," Donofrio quipped. "The sister's a mamacita. You could still make time if you play your cards right. Make her think it's about comfort."

He wasn't kidding. Ric had to turn away. One of these days . . .

It was then that he saw them.

Two kids. Older than the dead boy, but not by much. They were separated from the rest of the onlookers by a good forty feet, standing in the
shadows outside of the light from the spots.

There was little for him to do until the photographer finished her mor-
bid task. Ric could tell just from looking that the sister wouldn't be good
for questions until after she was allowed to approach the victim. Even
then, she probably wouldn't be up for a police interview until the body was
sent to the morgue.

If then.

So Ric sauntered down the beach, careful not to head directly toward
the pair of kids. His intention was to flank 'em, to put them between him
and the crowd of police officers and detectives, but he didn't get far before
Donofrio spotted them, too.

"Hey! You kids! Come 'ere!" he shouted.

Of course they turned and ran.

Johnny and Bobby D took off after them, but even in his dress shoes,
Ric was faster.

He chased them up into the dunes—ecologically fragile areas that
were off-limits to the public. They were running full out, and Ric scrambled after them, through the brush that divided the beach from a poorly lit
parking area.

He was finally starting to gain on the boys, his lungs burning as he
pushed himself even harder, faster, when one of them—the taller one—
tripped.

He went down hard, but came up almost immediately, moonlight
glinting off of metal in his hand.

The kid had a handgun.

Ric could see it clearly, the stainless-steel slide gleaming. It was a
Smith & Wesson nine-millimeter, tiny but deadly.

He had his own weapon out as he shouted, "Drop it! *Suelte el arma!*"

But the kid didn't drop it and the world went into high-def slo-mo.

Details stood out in sharp relief. The black grip of the pistol. The
tightness and fear on the perp's face.

He was older than Ric had first thought, probably more like eighteen
or nineteen, but small for his age.

The other kid was long gone.

"*Suelte el arma,*" Ric shouted again, the words stretched out long and
loud as it took an eternity and then another eternity for his heart to pump
his blood through his body, roaring in his ears.

But the kid didn't drop it and still didn't drop it and Ric's weapon was up and he had a clear, easy shot, but God damn it, hadn't one dead boy on the beach been enough?

Apparently not, because the kid fired twice—a quick double pop—and a hot slap to both his side and his left arm spun Ric around. So much for his new suit.

The kid fired again, this time missing him, giving Ric enough stretched out endless fractions of a second to re-steady his own weapon and take the kid down.

He pulled the trigger, and the kid hit the sand, his weapon flying out of his hand.

But damn, Ric couldn't keep himself standing and he, too, fell heavily to his knees just as Johnny and Bobby D crested the dune.

"Officer down," Johnny shouted as Donofrio fired.

"No," Ric said, but they didn't hear him, couldn't possibly hear him as Donofrio unloaded most of his magazine into the scrawny kid. Two, three, four, five, six, seven shots, and the night's body count was doubled.

Son of a bitch.

"Hang on, kid," Johnny told Ric, leaning close, his breath smelling like lower-shelf whiskey and cigarettes. "Help's coming. Just hang on."

On a scale of one—mere nausea—to ten—curled in a fetal position, weeping in a darkened room for hours—today's hangover was a solid eight.

Coffee took the teeniest edge off of his skull-splitting headache, but increased the nausea factor a hundredfold. It didn't help that he couldn't remember the night before. How he'd gotten home. Whom he'd been with.

As if he couldn't guess.

Still, Robin Chadwick had thrown himself into the shower. He'd gotten dressed, organized his day pack, lathered himself up with sunblock, found his hat, and stumbled out the door.

His brother-in-law had gone to a lot of trouble to set up today's activities. How often was it that an actor got to train with a team of Navy SEALs?

Sure Demi had spent some time at Coronado before filming *G.I. Jane.* But she went through channels, through the Navy's public relations department. She didn't have the kind of access to the real team members that Robin did.

No, his situation was pretty unique. His sister, Jane, had married a SEAL chief named Cosmo Richter.

Seriously. The guy's given name was Cosmo.

It wasn't some meaning-laden handle bestowed upon him by his BUD/S instructors, the way Robin's latest character had been nicknamed "Crash."

No, apparently his brother-in-law's slightly crazy mother had given birth to him, looked into his little red face, and declared that he was to be called Cosmo.

And there he-with-the-funny-name was, leaning against his truck out in the driveway, watching as Robin winced when the bright sunlight hit him like a pickax to the head.

Holy Jesus, and he already had his sunglasses on.

Robin fumbled for his keys with shaking hands, rushing back inside, where he surrendered his coffee in an attempt to appease the porcelain god. The sacrifice was apparently accepted, because the pounding in his head lessened almost immediately. After splashing his face with water, he looked almost human again.

Almost.

Luck and genetics had given him one of those launch-a-thousand-ships faces, and as he moved more solidly into his midtwenties, he was losing the boyishness and gaining something more rugged and even elegant. He was definitely one of the lucky ones—as he got older, he was getting even more handsome.

But this morning there was a grayness to his skin. Unattractive purple shadows around his blue eyes.

Harve, a friend in the makeup department and a fellow hearty-partier, often quipped that the secret to looking great was all in the hair. As long as you were having a good hair day, no one would notice the little imperfections that any self-respecting makeup person could easily hide.

Ever since he'd turned thirteen, Robin's life had been one giant, continuous good hair day.

He leaned in closer to the mirror. Today he could definitely benefit from thirty minutes in Harve's chair, though. A little foundation, some cover-up on the bags beneath his eyes . . .

And yeah—like he was going to hang out with Navy SEALs while wearing theatrical makeup. Way to get them to open up and talk to him.

The eyes could be kept hidden behind sunglasses. The pallor would improve when he got some fresh air. The shaking hands could also be concealed—although that one was easier said than done, especially where Cosmo was concerned.

Still, Robin was an actor. Fooling people was his job.

Exit from the house, take two.

"Sorry about that," Robin called to his brother-in-law. Hey now, he *was* one hell of an actor. He actually managed to sound cheery. Light-hearted. As if he hadn't just puked his guts out. "Forgot my cell phone. And then I couldn't find it. I had to call myself, except I had it set on vibrate. Long story short, I finally found it. So." He even smiled as he pocketed his keys. "I'm all set to go, Chief."

Cosmo hadn't moved. Unlike Robin, who found it hard to stay in one place for too long, Cosmo had a stillness to him that could be unnerving. He also had a BS meter that was infallible.

As Robin approached his truck, Cos still didn't move. He also didn't say anything. He just looked at Robin expressionlessly, his eyes hidden behind his trademark mirrored shades.

"Yeah, okay, great." Robin cracked under the pressure. "I don't know why I always try to bullshit you."

"Y'look like shit," Cosmo finally said. At times, he spoke as if he were charged a hefty fee for every word he used, creating contractions that didn't really exist.

"Cos, believe me, I *feel* like shit," Robin admitted as he climbed into the truck, setting his pack on the floor at his feet.

"Sure you want to do this?" Cosmo got in behind the wheel.

"Yes. Shooting starts in just a few months." A fact that scared the crap out of him. Was he really ready to open a movie? A lot of people were counting on the fact that Robin Chadwick could be a bankable box-office draw.

Cosmo sat there, on the other side of the truck's cab, just looking at him.

Holy crap, that made him uncomfortable. Dude should have been a priest or a CIA operative. His mind-reading ability—or at least his ability to make it seem as if he could read minds—was off the charts. How the hell did he do that?

Finally, Cos looked away. He put his truck in gear and pulled out onto the street. He didn't say anything else, not for a good long while. It wasn't until he was signaling for the turnoff into the navy base that he even glanced over at Robin again. "Janey's worried about you."

Robin sighed. "Janey's always worried about—"

"I am, too." Cosmo broke the bank, putting forth two entire sentences. "I'm not sure you should take this role, Rob."

Robin bristled. "You don't think I can play a SEAL?"

"This training is intense. You're not in the kind of physical condition you need to be in, to—"

"I can do this," Robin said. "I'm going to do this." Like he was going to turn down half a million dollars and a chance to work with Oscar-winning director Victor Strauss? "This movie puts me onto an entirely new level. After this, I'm a star."

"You're already a star."

"No, I'm not. I'm a flavor. Yeah, I've lasted longer than a month, but *Riptide* puts me on the map."

Cosmo glanced at him. "*Riptide?*"

"Yeah. That's the new title they're going with—this week, anyway," Robin told him. "My character gets framed for a botched assassination attempt on the U.S. President. I pretty much get caught up in this situation that I can't escape from. Riptide—get it? But the bad guys have no idea who I am or what I'm capable of doing. I pretty much kick their asses and clear my name and save POTUS from a second assassination attempt. Plus I get the girl." There was always a girl—a love interest—in a movie like this.

Cosmo shot him another look, but said nothing.

"It's a popcorn movie," Robin continued. "It'll be my face on the one sheets. If I do it right and it opens big, I'm a star." And if it didn't open big, or if he somehow screwed it up by being indiscreet . . .

"So that's what you want," Cosmo said with another of those penetrating looks. "To be a star."

"Yes," Robin said, gazing out the window so he didn't have to see Cosmo's disbelief. But he didn't need to see it to feel it. "It's what I want that I can have, okay? So just . . . zip it. Not everyone gets to have the kind of relationship you have with Janey. So just . . . don't go there. Please."

Cosmo, of course, wasn't about to say anything. In fact, he didn't speak again until he'd parked in the lot outside a single-story building, among a variety of cars, trucks, and SUVs that screamed alpha male.

As they both got out of Cos's truck, he gave Robin the most matter-of-fact warning in history. "This training is going to break your balls."

"Well, gee golly," Robin said, hefting the strap of his pack up onto his shoulder. "Whatever are we waiting for?"

Annie Dugan was sick and tired of late-night emergency phone calls.

For months she'd lived on the brink of disaster, cursing the inevitable.

She was a prisoner of the specter of approaching death, trapped in a corner yet still fighting like hell against the odds—for someone who, in the end, had gone and quit on her.

Pam's funeral was lovely, of course. Pam had made all the arrangements herself, in advance, and her parents were there to see that it went off without a glitch. Annie had sat in the back of the church, too tired and still too angry at her best friend to cry.

The house—a rustic New Hampshire farmhouse that Pam had renovated with her artistic flair two years before she was diagnosed as inoperable—sold almost immediately, mere hours after the hospice bed was removed from the front parlor.

It had felt as if it were all happening too quickly to Annie, but in her heart she knew it was a good thing. As much as she'd loved that house, as much as she thought of it as a home, it wasn't *her* home and she didn't want to stay.

Annie had gone back to Boston. Templar, Brick and Smith hired her back, just as they said they would. Eunice Templar, known throughout the business world as the Dragonlady, had gotten tears in her eyes when Annie had explained she couldn't just take a month's leave of absence, that she was moving to New Hampshire for an indeterminate amount of time so that her best friend, Pam, could live out her last months at home, instead of in a hospital, surrounded by strangers.

After Pam died, Annie went back to work at the accounting firm. She found an apartment in Newton, and took her furniture and business suits and shoes out of storage.

This was when, the hospice coordinator and the grief counselors had all said, she would slowly but surely find her life returning to normal. It would take time, though. She should be patient. Expect bumps in the road.

It would feel strange at first, going back to work in a cubicle, after spending so much time outside. It would feel surreal, even. Almost as if she'd never left, as if the past few months hadn't happened.

She should continue with counseling, they'd told her, so she dutifully went. Once a week, as part of her new/old routine.

But it had been months now, and still none of it seemed even remotely familiar—at least not until the phone rang tonight, interrupting Jon Stewart, at a quarter after eleven.

It was Celeste Harris, the woman who had bought Pam's house, and she was clearly distressed. Pam's dog, Pierre, a tiny mutt, part poodle, part mystery, had run away from his new home with Pam's mom and had shown up again, in Celeste's backyard. She'd tried to coax him inside, tempting him with food, but he'd shied away. It was cold out and getting colder. She'd called the town dogcatcher, but he couldn't make it out there until the morning.

Celeste was afraid that would be too late—that Pierre would freeze to death by then.

So she'd called Annie, hoping she could help.

And here Annie was. Heading to the rescue. North on Route 3. Shivering as her car took forever to warm up in the cold New England night.

She'd called Pam's mother, who reported Pierre had run away a full week ago—she hadn't wanted to bother Annie with that bad news. That dog was such a trial. Always hiding under the desk in the kitchen. Refusing food. Pooping at night on the dining-room floor.

Pam, who'd arranged every detail before she'd done the unspeakable, had made sure Pierre would go to live with her cousin Clive, of whom the little dog had grudgingly approved. But when Clive was offered a promotion and a move to his firm's London office, Pierre went to live with Pam's mom.

It was nearly 1 A.M. when Annie turned off the road and onto the crushed gravel of the drive that led back to Pam's house. Pam's former house.

The lights were still on, both porches lit up. The kitchen windows glowed, too, and the back screen opened with a familiar screech as Annie parked and got out of her car.

"Thank you for coming." Celeste came out onto the back porch, followed by her two daughters.

Pam would've loved the fact that children were living in her house. She wouldn't have loved the hatchet job they'd done on her beloved mountain laurels, though.

"He's over by the garbage pails," the younger girl announced. "Alongside the garage."

"It's a barn, dimwit," her older sister loftily corrected her.

"Yeah, but we keep our car there, so it's also a garage, *stupid*."

"Girls," their mother chastised.

Annie was already heading—slowly, carefully—around the side of the barn. "Pierre," she whispered, very softly.

Pierre had had a painful past, Pam had once told Annie as she snuggled the little dog in her arms, his head possessively on her shoulder. Long before Pam had met Pierre at the animal shelter, someone had neglected and even beaten him. It was hard for him to trust anyone, but he'd finally bonded with Pam. She'd told him, every day, that no one was going to hurt him, not ever again.

"Pierre, it's me," Annie whispered now. Not that he'd ever deigned to give her his attention before. Of course, back then, Pam was always there— his goddess, his all.

She heard him before she saw him—the tinkling of his tags as he shifted and then . . . He poked his head out into the dim light, wariness in his brown eyes.

He was almost unrecognizable. His hair was matted and dirty. And he was skinny. Skinnier. And shivering from the cold.

"Hey, puppy boy," Annie said softly, using Pam's pet names for him as she crouched down and held out her hand for him to sniff. "Hey, good dog. Everything's okay. No one's going to hurt you . . ."

To her complete surprise, he didn't hesitate. His tail even wagged slightly as he came out of his hiding place and licked her outstretched hand. Looking over his shoulder, as if to make sure that she was going to follow him, he trotted out onto the driveway and over to her car.

Annie stopped short. Did he really want . . . ?

"Wow, she likes you," the littler girl said, admiration in her voice. "She doesn't like us very much."

"*He* doesn't like *you*," her older sister pointed out. "Probably because you can't tell the difference between a girl dog and a boy dog."

Pierre looked at Annie, looked at the car, and then back at Annie, as if to say, *What are you waiting for?*

"I can't have a dog in my apartment," Annie said, as if he could actually understand her words. "Plus, I work full-time . . ."

Celeste opened the screen door. "Why don't you come inside?" she invited Annie. "Both of you. It's too late to drive back to Boston tonight. You can stay over on the couch and we can figure out a plan of action in the morning."

The thought of going into Pam's house was both appealing and dreadful. But it *was* late, and Annie was exhausted. "Thanks," she said.

Amazingly, Pierre didn't protest as she scooped him up. She followed the smaller of the girls inside, and . . . It was beyond weird.

Because it wasn't even remotely Pam's house anymore.

They'd repainted the walls, muting Pam's bright colors. And their furniture was vastly different from Pam's wicker and white painted wood. It was faux Colonial now—all dark veneers and copper drawer-pulls.

It smelled different, too.

"Bathroom's down the hall, second door on the left," Celeste said. "Of course, you know that. I'll be right back with some blankets."

She disappeared, shooing her daughters along to bed, leaving Annie and Pierre alone in the living room.

"I can't have a dog," Annie told him again, but he put his head down, right on her shoulder, the way he used to do with Pam, and he sighed. His entire little body shook with his exhale, and the crazy thing was that Annie felt what he was feeling, too.

If it wasn't quite contentment, it was pretty darn close.

It was oddly familiar.

Vaguely normal and very right, in spite of the freaky abnormality of their surroundings, in spite of Pierre's unfortunate aroma.

It was far more normal and right than she'd ever felt in her cubicle in Templar, Brick and Smith. Even before Pam got sick.

Celeste came back with an armload of bedding. "Worse come to worst, the dogcatcher'll be here in the morning. I know it's not the best solution, but at least the dog'll be warm in the pound. He'll have food . . ."

"I'm keeping him," Annie told her.

"But you said your apartment—"

"I didn't really like it there," she admitted. She didn't particularly like her job, either. Or Boston's relentless cold—the winters that lasted for nearly half the year. "Thanks for your hospitality, but I'm awake enough to drive. We're going home."

"Are you sure?" Celeste asked, following her to the kitchen door. "Because it's really not an imposition—"

"I'm sure," Annie told her. "Thanks again."

The gravel crunched under her boots as she took Pierre to her car. He didn't seem anxious as she set him down on the passenger seat. He just made himself comfortable, watching her expectantly.

Annie sat behind the wheel, started the engine. "Well," she said to the dog as she backed into the turnaround and headed down the drive, "now we just have to figure out where exactly home is."

His team leader, Peggy Ryan, hated him.

It was an inane thing for FBI agent Jules Cassidy to be thinking, considering that a shooter had suddenly opened fire on the crowd of law enforcement personnel, all of whom had just rushed out from their protective cover behind half a dozen police cars.

But to be fair, this entire situation was drenched in extra crazy. It reeked of some serious what-the-fuck, too, starting with the cozy-looking little Cape-style house, located here on what should have been a peaceful suburban D.C. street.

The catastrophuck began ten hours ago, when the report of a hostage situation first came in. Jules's counterterrorist team had gotten a call because the hostage taker was a well-known bubba—a wanted terrorist of the homegrown variety.

They were told that—as best they could allege—there were three hostages being held by that lone HT in this unassuming little house with its flower gardens and white picket fence. As a full variety of police and FBI teams arrived on the scene, surrounding the structure and setting up the cars as a barricade to keep them all safely outside of Bubba's rifle range, negotiations had been started.

After hours of standoff, to Jules's complete and utter surprise, the bubba had surrendered.

He came out of the house and into the yard with his hands up and empty—no weapon in sight.

At which point, Peggy gave the order to take him into custody. She and the local police chief—a bear of a man named Peeler—led the charge into the yard as Jules and the rest of the team headed for the house to see to the safety of the hostages.

The game was finally over.

Except, not so fast there, you.

Apparently, the *real* game was just beginning.

Because no, that wasn't just *one* shooter firing at them from that Cape, making them scatter. There were at least two. Crap, make that three. As Jules looked up at the house, he counted, yes, three different shooters—all firing rifles from the second-story dormer windows.

"What the hell . . . ?" Jules's FBI team member Deb Erlanger said it all as she and Yashi and George scrambled, pulling Jules with them, back behind one of the state police cruisers.

"Our radio's hit," Yashi announced.

Of course it was.

It was times like this that reinforced the importance of law enforcement personnel giving heavier weight to the presence of the word *allegedly* in the facts surrounding the decision-making process. *Allegedly* was a lot like *assume*, but in this case it didn't just make asses out of their team leaders, it made people dead.

Apparently, there wasn't one hostage taker and three hostages. Instead there were at least three hostile gunmen, apparently all determined to commit suicide-by-SWAT-team, while taking as many FBI and police with them as possible.

From Jules's new proximity, he could see that Chief Peeler had been shot. How badly he was wounded, Jules didn't know, but Peeler lay motionless in the Cape's front yard, protected only marginally by the garden's flimsy picket fence.

All but one of the shooters had what looked to be terrible aim—a clue that probably meant two of the three were amateurs.

Most of the FBI and police had made it safely back to cover behind the cars, with limited casualties—except for Peggy Ryan, who hated Jules and was pinned down in the yard, behind a small outcropping of rocks. She was plastered flat against the ground, weapon drawn, halfway between Peeler's sprawled body and the full cover of a neighbor's garden shed.

She'd dropped her radio. Jules could see it near Peeler's leg.

"Center window," Jules told Yashi, Deb, and George as he reached into the cruiser and grabbed the medical kit. He was going to take it with him just in case he and Peeler got pinned behind Peggy's rock. "Whoever's up there's the only one who can shoot worth shit. Focus your fire there. Keep it up until I get the chief back behind that shed."

George expressed his incredulity. "*You're* going to move Peeler?"

Yashi had a far more pertinent question. He held up his regulation sidearm. "Range on this thing's too short. It won't—"

"Just do it," Jules ordered. With luck, it would cause the shooters to take cover. It was hard to aim and shoot to kill whilst ducking.

"Yessir."

"Now!" Jules said, and medical kit slung over his shoulder, his own weapon out, he ran out into the street, toward the yard. Deb and Yashi and George's sidearms roared behind him, and as he headed straight into what could potentially be a hail of bullets from the holed-up gunmen, he realized he'd blown the perfect opportunity to say, *Cover me, I'm going in.*

Bullets from the shooters in the house hit the ground around him, sending puffs of dirt into the air. But there was no turning back now.

Jules fired his own weapon—not easy to do while running full out— aiming as best he could for that center window. He slid to a stop in the grass near Chief Peeler, tearing out the knee of his pants. Dang, this was his favorite suit, but perspective was important here. Last time he'd looked, Men's Wearhouse didn't sell internal organs.

The chief, however, hadn't been as lucky. He was lying with his head in a pool of blood. Expecting the worst, Jules felt for a pulse. To his surprise, he found it, steady and strong—and he realized that the chief had merely been grazed. A bullet had creased his hairline, over his left ear, hence the copious bleeding. It had knocked him out, but the man was alive.

For now, anyway.

Jules covered Peeler with his own body as a new rain of bullets pinged the ground around them.

He grabbed the radio that Peggy had dropped. "Cover me," he ordered whoever was listening on the other end. "I need some weapons with real range aiming for those windows. Keep it going while I pull the chief to the shed."

He didn't wait for confirmation—he pitched the radio over to Peggy and grabbed Peeler beneath his massive arms.

Jules may have been small of stature, but he was strong. He dug in his heels and dragged, but sweet Jesus, why couldn't the chief have taken a trip or two to the salad bar over the past few years instead of relentlessly supersizing the cheese fries?

But then Peggy was there, helping him, and together they pulled the chief all the way to that shed, where a medical team was already standing by.

"You hit?" one of the medics, a woman with her hair swept back into a tight ponytail, asked him.

Jules shook his head no. Miraculously, he wasn't. "Peg, you okay?"

She was already barking orders into the radio, calling in the SWAT team. If she was bleeding, she wasn't letting it slow her down.

"Man, you got balls," the other medic said. "*And* a shitload of luck. You know, Channel 4 news got it all on camera. You're going to be a hero. People 'round here love Chief Peeler, and you saved his life."

Great. Jules was going to have to call Laronda—the boss's assistant— and get her on top of smothering *that* merde cream pie as quickly as possible. Last thing he needed was his face on the evening news.

But it wasn't until later, until after the SWAT team sang and the dust had settled around the body bags being carried out of the newly secured house, that Jules was finally able to reintroduce himself to his cell phone. And even then, he had to pocket it, when Peggy Ryan approached him.

Peggy Ryan—who hated him. Who probably wouldn't give a hoot if his name and likeness were plastered all over the national news.

In fact, she would use it as reason number 4,367 why he should quit.

It was then, as she was heading toward him, wearing her official business face, that Jules realized that by saving Morgan Peeler, he'd been saving Peggy Ryan.

"This doesn't change anything," she told him, trying to wipe the ground-in dirt from her starched white blouse. Her helmet-hair was messed up, too, but her eyes were just as they'd always been. Cold and distant. "Between us, I mean. I still don't think you belong in the Bureau."

"Gosh," Jules said, unable to keep his temper under check. Not that he'd expected a total change of heart, but was a simple "Good job" too much to ask? Or how about "Thank you"? "In *that* case, I guess I just should have let Chief Peeler die." He shook his head in disgust. "Believe it or not, *ma'am*, I didn't help him because I thought you would approve. I did it because someone had to help Peeler. Until I went out there, you didn't seem to be concerned with much more than saving your own ass."

She flushed. "How dare you!"

Okay, so maybe that was a little harsh. Things had happened fast, and she *had* been pinned down. But he was sick of her crap, of her refusing to admit—even now—that he was an important player on their team. He'd tried winning her over with humor, but that hadn't worked. He'd hoped that today's heroics would at least gain him her grudging respect, but now he finally had to admit it. She was never going to accept him.

"I don't give a shit whether or not you think I belong here," he told her quietly. "The only two opinions I care about are mine, and the boss's. And we both think I'm doing fine. If you don't want to work with me, lady, *you're* going to have to put in for the transfer. Because I'm not going anywhere."

She wasn't listening. She never did. "If you think—"

Jules cut her off, got even farther up in her face. "I saved your soul today. You were team leader. You gave the order. If Peeler had died, you'd have had to live with that forever. That must really gall you, huh, Peg? The gay guy rescued you. That must really grate."

She spun on her heels—or heel, rather. One of them had broken off in the brouhaha. As Jules watched, she stalked away.

"You're welcome," he called after her, but she didn't even so much as look back.

"Whoa. I didn't expect to see *you* today." Steven was manning the front desk at the police station. "I mean, welcome back."

"Thanks." Ric was still moving gingerly, his left arm in a sling. For a pair of wounds that weren't particularly life threatening, they sure hurt like a bitch. The stitches in his side pulled with every step he took.

The younger man stood up uncertainly. "Should you really be back so soon?"

The doctor had told him to take some time before returning to work. But he'd meant *work* work. "I'm just going to file some reports," Ric said. "Nothing strenuous. What are you doing back there, anyway?" Steven's usual shift was in the morning.

He rolled his eyes. "Too many losing hands of poker."

"Don't play with Camp or Lora, man. Didn't I tell you that? What, have you got their shifts up front from now until Halloween?"

"Christmas," Steve said morosely. "You know, Ric, you don't look so good."

"I'm fine," Ric said, heading down the hall. "I just need some coffee."

The phone rang, and Steve had to pick it up, ending their conversation. "First precinct. Hey. Yeah, he's here . . ."

Ric ducked into the coffee room—where Bobby Donofrio and Johnny Olson were having an early lunch.

"Hey, hey, hey," Bobby D said through his cheeseburger. "Look who's up and around. I thought you weren't going to be discharged from the hospital until tomorrow."

Johnny came over to help him with the coffeepot. "Sure you don't want to take another day?"

"I wanted to get that report done," Ric said as Johnny poured the steaming coffee into a mug. "Thanks. I'm sure the family would appreciate the closure."

"A tough guy, huh? Well, rest easy, the case is closed. The perp was the victim's cousin," Donofrio reported, leaning back in his chair. "The other cousin—a younger kid—came forward. Apparently there was an argument over some guy—or guys—that the sister was screwing—you saw her, there was probably a list as long as my arm. The victim wouldn't give up the info, there was a tussle, and the gun went off accidentally. Yeah, like anyone whose head isn't up their ass would believe *that*."

"Ballistic report matched," Johnny told Ric. "The perp's nine-millimeter was also the murder weapon. No question."

"Everything's neat and tidy. So we—lucky bastards—don't have to dick around with a trial." Donofrio tossed his McDonald's bag into the garbage, leaving a streak of ketchup on the table. "The surviving cousin's a juvie. He's confessed to being an accessory—they've already put him into the system. The perp's dead—you took care of that. Very nicely, I might add."

"*I* did?" Ric said. Coming in today was definitely a mistake, because now his head was starting to hurt almost as badly as his arm and his side.

"Dude." Donofrio gave him a big smile that was almost as disconcerting as his use of the word *dude*. "I may have shut out the lights a little more quickly, but your shot to the perp's groin . . . It was perfect. Crushed the artery. He was already dead when I hit him—he just didn't know it yet."

Ric had shot to wound. Only to wound. He'd aimed for the kid's leg, not . . .

"Hey, Martell," Johnny said, turning to the door. "Long time, no see. How's the legal world treating you?"

"Well enough." Martell Griffin's basso profundo was unmistakable. Ric looked over and saw his friend leaning in the doorway, dressed like the lawyer he now was, in a dark suit and power tie. The look he shot Ric was full of reproach. "You should be home, in bed," he scolded.

But Donofrio wasn't finished. "So congratulations, Alvarado," the heavy-set detective continued. "I've got to let you claim the kill."

Claim the *kill . . . ?* Was he serious?

Across the room, Martell straightened up. "This probably isn't a conversation Ric should be having while he's on pain meds," he pointed out.

"It's a big one, too." Bobby D just kept on going, grinning that shit-eating grin. *Neat and tidy . . .* Mother of God. "The year's tenth."

He said it like it was some kind of honor, some kind of badge for them all to wear with pride—their having reached double digits in the number of perpetrators who hadn't survived an altercation with Sarasota's finest.

"Ricky, man, come on. Let me drive you home," Martell said.

"I don't want it," Ric told Donofrio.

"No, no, you don't comprend-ay," Donofrio said. "The kid was nineteen and there's no question that he was armed and dangerous. It's already been cleared by internal affairs. It's yours, Detective, and it's squeaky-clean. That's not something to throw away."

Ric didn't even realize he was moving. One second he was standing there, and the next he had Bobby Donofrio up against the wall, his right arm pressed hard against the son of a bitch's throat. "But the dead kids—Francisco and Jorge Flores," Ric heard himself snarl as the prick struggled to get free. He held him even tighter. "Them you can throw away. Who the fuck cares—they're just two more Hispanics who won't grow up and go to jail, clog the system, right?"

"Ricky, hey. Hey, hey. You're choking him, man."

It was true. Bobby D's face was turning even more red than usual.

And Martell was right behind him. "Ric, come on, brother. This isn't you. Let him go."

Ric exhaled hard. And stepped back.

Donofrio sucked in a breath and then shoved him hard, pushing him into the lunch table, knocking over chairs. "I'll kill you, you fuck!"

Ow. Ric felt his stitches rip as he rolled away, avoiding a full body slam from big boy Bob.

Johnny had run to get the lieutenant, and she exploded into the room, clapping her hands together as if they were misbehaving lapdogs. "Stop this. Right this minute!"

"He fucking jumped me," Bobby D shouted, letting Johnny help him up and hold him back, "out of the fucking blue!"

"Lieutenant," Martell said smoothly as Ric pulled himself to his feet. "Ric shouldn't even be here. He's on pain meds and his judgment is a little—"

"I'm not on pain meds," Ric said.

Martell shot him an exasperated look. "So much for our defense strategy."

"I'm not going to lie," Ric told his friend.

"I would never ask you to lie." Martell was offended. "Although, I suspect that if you took a blood test, we'd find—"

Donofrio chimed in again: "The cholo fucking jumped me!"

Martell got big. "Oh, *that's* nice! You gonna nigger me now, *dude*?"

"You!" The lieutenant pointed at Ric and Martell. "Out in the hall. You, Donofrio. Do yourself a huge favor and be silent!"

Martell pulled Ric out of the coffee room. "Ah, man—you're bleeding."

"Yeah, my stitches were . . . whoa." The entire side of his T-shirt was soaked with blood. That wasn't good. Still it was going to have to wait. He had to talk to the lieutenant. "I'm done here," Ric told his friend.

"I'll say." Martell was looking for something to wipe his hands on, so Ric offered him the clean side of his shirt. "We need to get you back to the hospital and—"

"No, Martell, I'm done here. Like, done forever."

"You know, it's possible we can argue extenuating circumstances. How long have I known you? Ten years? And how many times have I ever seen you lose it like that? I can probably count 'em on my thumbs, so—"

"No," Ric interrupted again. "I mean I'm done. *I'm* done." *Claim the kill . . . Jesus God.*

Martell finally got it. "Wow. This is . . . new."

Ric shook his head. "No, actually, it's not. It's been coming for a while."

Martell laughed his exasperation. "Did you, like, tell me and I missed it? Studying for the bar exam—I know I was pretty self-absorbed, but . . ."

"No," Ric said. "I didn't tell you. I didn't tell anyone. It's just . . ." He shook his head. How do you bring up a topic like that? *Hey, man. Wanna beer? Your softball team's looking good this year. And oh, by the way, I'm feeling more and more dissatisfied with my life and I don't know why. On the surface, everything looks perfect, but I'm thinking about shaking things up. Quitting the job that I supposedly love . . .*

The lieutenant emerged from the coffee room, closing the door tightly behind her, looking none too pleased. "Alvarado, what is wrong with you? Get out of here. I don't want to see you for a full week. And when you do come back, you better be ready to apologize to Bob. That's the only way you'll be able to . . . What's this?"

Ric held out his sidearm and badge.

She took it. Shook her head. "I'm not suspending you."

"He's done," Martell told her, and took Ric back to the hospital.

CHAPTER
ONE

"I'm going in."

Ric laughed out loud, which was probably not the best thing to do, given the circumstances. "No, you're not."

But Annie only narrowed her eyes at his amusement instead of delivering a smack to the side of his head.

Which, he realized, was something she hadn't done to him since she was thirteen. Still, he could tell that she was tempted.

"Look," he tried reason. "I said you could ride along. There's an unspoken understanding there that you'll stay in the car." Of course, they were both already out of the car, standing in this suckhole of a parking lot on the crap side of Sarasota.

At least they were standing in the shade.

Annie, too, tried reason. But hers was laced with attitude. "*You* can't go in. And unless Hutch is on his way over . . ."

Damn, but he hated when she called him Starsky, even by omission like that. But this time he clenched his teeth and kept his mouth shut. This was definitely not the time or place to get into The Argument, which went something like: "Oh, that's right, Ric, you don't *have* a Hutch. You don't want one, don't need one, even though I'm standing right here, volunteering for the job. No, you prefer to believe—despite years of police work that proved otherwise—that you don't need any backup whatsoever. You'd prefer to end up lying in an alley again, with the shit kicked out of you. You'd prefer to pee blood. Again."

Annie's second day of work as his new office assistant at Alvarado Private Investigations hadn't been a particularly good day for Ric.

Her third day, however, had included his successful apprehension and delivery to the FBI of the shitkicker's brother, who was wanted in four states for a variety of violent crimes. Ric had received a twenty-thousand-dollar reward for his diligent, but not particularly brilliant detective work. Twenty thousand. After adding up the time he'd put in, plus expenses, it worked out to just over four hundred dollars an hour, which was sweet. Well, sweet, with the exception of those particularly nasty twenty minutes during which he'd allowed himself to get stomped in order to gain possession of the kicker's cell phone—which subsequently revealed the location of his even nastier older brother's girlfriend. And again, it wasn't Ric's skill as a detective, but rather the fact that Nasty the elder had just broken the woman's nose, that had worked to Ric's advantage. For a slim five percent share of the reward, plus a truckload of revenge, she'd eagerly divulged the wanted man's whereabouts.

Still, four hundred dollars an hour, however he'd earned it, wasn't something to sneeze at. And the fact that he'd finally worked a lucrative case that didn't involve bored, wealthy suburbanites cheating on each other was another reason to cheer.

Yet it was the getting-beaten-up-and-peeing-blood part that Annie brought up over and over again.

Along with the fact that she had been sorely misled by her own asshole-of-a-brother-Bruce—her name for him, not his—to believe that Ric needed an assistant rather than a receptionist. Annie had taken this position, she'd told him, not merely because she needed a job where she could bring along her separation-anxiety-suffering little rat-dog, but because she didn't want to sit behind a desk all day. Yet all Ric wanted her to do was sit in his office behind a desk, take phone calls, and create—again, her words—stupid office forms.

Of course, the most recent stupid office form Annie had created—in under ten minutes—was an exceptionally well-organized client interview sheet. It was precisely what he'd needed—possibly with the exception of those two little boxes, one that said yes, one that said no, next to the words *This client wants to do me.*

He'd used her interview sheet with his current client, an extremely well-put-together older woman named Lillian Lavelle, who'd come to his office just this morning.

As Ric now watched, Annie got ready to go inside of Screech's, the so-called gentleman's club where a young dancer named Brenda Quinn had last been employed. They had been hired—*he* had been hired—to find Brenda, who was Ms. Lavelle's recently deceased daughter's former roommate. Ms. Lavelle apparently had a photo album that she wanted to give to the young woman.

The entire case was proving to be slightly more difficult than he'd first imagined. He'd taken it just this morning, expecting to be filing it in the "case closed" drawer long before noon.

It was now sunset, pink and orange clouds streaking the western sky, as a cooling breeze blew in off the Gulf of Mexico.

As Ric watched, Annie took off her jacket, tossed it in the back of her car, and ran her fingers through her light brown curls.

"Maybe he won't recognize me," Ric said as she fished in her shoulder bag for something.

He deserved the look of scorn that she shot him, because it *was* a stupid thing to say. There was zero chance in hell that Screech's bouncer, Tommy Fista, *wouldn't* recognize him. Seven years ago, almost to this very day, Ric had jammed his knee into the middle of Tommy's gargantuan back as he'd cuffed him and read him his Miranda rights. Fista had gone to Raiford Maximum Security for five to seven for assault and battery with a dangerous weapon.

Ric tried again. "I heard he found God in jail."

As he watched, Annie glanced around the corner at the bouncer. Clearly Fista hadn't found Jenny Craig in the lockup. The huge man was standing at the door to Screech's, which was a fairly new establishment, having opened since Ric had left the police department last year.

Still, it hadn't taken Ric much effort to learn that it was owned and operated by Vitardo Co. Strip clubs in this part of Florida were usually owned either by local scumbag Gordon Burns or his main rival, Miami-based Bernie Vitardo.

"So what's the best-case scenario?" Annie asked as she applied lip gloss with one finger, leaning down to see herself in her little car's side mirror. "Tony-the-bouncer takes you by the hand, leads you inside for a joyful hymn and prayer session before sharing—willingly—everything he knows about Brenda Quinn?" She straightened up, smacking her lips together as she put the container back in her bag.

"It's *Tommy* the bouncer," Ric corrected her. This was possibly the first time he'd ever seen Annie with makeup on, and he searched his memory, trying to prove himself wrong. But no. Aside from Halloween back when she was little, he couldn't think of a single time that she'd gotten dressed up. She hadn't gone to her school prom. And she'd worn one of Bruce's suits and ties to her high school graduation. Although, as far as makeup went, what she had on now wasn't much. It just made her full lips look shiny. More moist.

If that was possible.

Annie Dugan wasn't traditionally pretty, at least not in a helpless-and-fragile delicate female sense. She did, however, have the fresh-faced, Irish American peasant-girl thing down pat, with big gray eyes and freckles, naturally curly hair, and a wide smile that could, at times, be incredibly sweet.

Her attitude, however, was pure twenty-first-century kick-ass domina-trix.

With the exception, perhaps, of her attachment to her ridiculous little dog, Pierre. Ric would've expected a woman like Annie to have a golden Lab. Something large and outdoorsy, capable of playing ultimate Frisbee in the park. Something that galloped. Something friendly named Pal or Lucky.

Not this glorified fuzzball of a quivering rodent named Pierre, that she now hugged and kissed and gave a doggy treat to, all while reassuring it that she'd be right back.

"So what's the worst-case scenario here?" she asked, plopping the rat-thing back onto the front seat of her car, making sure his travel bowl of water was full before turning her attention back to Ric. "A trip to the den-tist with your two front teeth on ice in a Ziploc baggie? Or maybe another few days of pink urine? Gee, that's always so much fun. Setting my watch alarm to go off every ten minutes so I can check to make sure you haven't gone into shock from excessive hemorrhaging . . . ?"

Yeah, telling her about the internal-injury thing had definitely been a mistake. At the time Ric had thought it would invoke a little sympathy, maybe make her extend the two-week notice that she'd given him back when she'd quit—on day one of her employment—when she found out she'd be sitting behind a desk.

Time was running out. He had only a few days left to replace her or convince her to stay.

And it was there that she had the unfair advantage.

He wanted her to stay. Rather badly.

"It wasn't days, it was *day*," he pointed out now.

"I'm going in to find Brenda Quinn's last known address," Annie told him with that hint of bitch-queen, do-not-cross-me, I-am-determined, you-are-toast that he'd first heard in her voice back when he'd met her, when she was eleven and he was fifteen. Almost twenty years ago. Damn, had they really been friends for nearly two decades? Although he hadn't seen very much of her in the last ten years . . .

Still, it occurred to him that now, just as when she was little, the best way to deal with her might be simply to let her try. Just hang close to pick her up and dust her off in case she failed miserably.

It wasn't as if there were any real danger hiding in that strip club.

It was, however, filled with relentless apathy, seedy despair, and un-ending depression. Spending some time in Screech's might well make Annie decide against a career path as a private investigator.

"Okay," Ric said.

She looked up at him with a mix of wariness and disbelief.

Ric nodded. "Go for it. Go find Brenda."

"You don't think I can do this," she accused him.

"What does it matter what I think?" he countered. "It only matters what you do. Or don't do." Which was more likely going to be the case. But she'd find that out soon enough.

"Thank you, Yoda." She gave a tug on the bottom of her T-shirt, as if that would somehow provide the illusion that she had real breasts.

And thank *you*, Mary Mother of God, for keeping him from saying that aloud, because he definitely hadn't meant to be insulting, just realis-tic. Not that her breasts *weren't* real. They just weren't stripper-sized.

They were extremely nice, actually. And now that he was thinking about it, it was really her waist that wasn't stripper size, which was good, because women who had that creepy, tiny-waisted wasp thing going on just didn't do it for him. No, Annie was curvy and soft in a way that Ric truly appreciated. She was no skinny twig who might snap if you held her too tightly and he was *so* screwed because he was standing here, staring at her body, thinking about sex.

And that was a serious violation of rules one through about two thou-sand and twenty-seven in the male employer/female employee relation-ship handbook. It came right before rule number two thousand and twenty-eight: Never, never, *never* employ family or friends—because how the hell do you go from twenty years of friendship to employment without completely screwing things up?

Cursing Annie's brother, Bruce, and his brilliant ideas—Bruce who was going to be mad as hell when he found out that Ric had actually let Annie go into that strip club, so he better never find out—Ric looked slightly more northward, and found himself meeting Annie's gray gaze.

Her very cool gray gaze.

It was disconcerting as hell. If she wore heels, she'd be at least as tall as he was, and he was not a short man.

"You're such a jerk," she said, clearly able to read his mind all the way back to his real-breasts thought. "What, do you think I'm going to pretend I'm here to apply for a job as an exotic dancer?"

Well, yeah, that *was* what he'd thought. But sometimes it was best to keep one's mouth firmly shut.

"I'm not stupid, Alvarado," Annie continued. "Nor am I deluded. I know what I look like." She laughed her disbelief. "Who'd pay to see me strip?"

With that, she turned and walked away, across the parking lot, around the edge of the building that kept Ric out of Tommy's line of sight, toward Screech's front entrance.

Pierre stood up in the front seat of Annie's car, paws on the steering wheel so that he could watch her go.

Ric watched her, too—watched her T-shirt stretching across her back as she moved. Bruce had told him that one of her last jobs, after she quit the accounting firm, was assisting a woman who built stone walls. She was clearly strong and very . . . healthy. Very. With those long denim-clad legs leading up to a posterior that was . . . definitely healthy.

And in a flash, he could picture her, in motorcycle leather, sexy as hell, with seven-inch platform heels that would turn her into a total Amazon, strutting the stage with a whip, hooking her leg around a pole as she writhed to the pulsating music.

God save him.

She was out of sight now, and he peeked around the corner, far less patient than Pierre, who'd settled in for a nap as he waited for Annie's promised return.

Across the parking lot, she'd stopped to speak to Tommy Fista, who not only let her pass, but actually held the door for her. When Tommy's head was turned, she sent a quick grin and a thumbs-up in Ric's direction, before vanishing into the club.

Max Bhagat, the head of the FBI's most elite counterterrorist division, had a huge stain on his tie.

He was standing in the waiting area just outside of the Oval Office, and as Jules Cassidy approached this man who was both his boss and his friend, he saw that it was Emma-goo that marred the fine blue silk. It looked as if it might be oatmeal, with traces of Max's one-year-old daughter's favorite, mashed sweet potatoes.

"Here's the file, sir." Jules handed the sealed envelope over. "The news is bad." He couldn't say more than that out here, but he didn't need to.

Max knew what they were dealing with. This was just confirmation. "Thanks," he said, sticking the envelope into his briefcase.

The man had also missed a spot while shaving—a small patch near his left ear. No one else would notice it—at least those who didn't know Max as the meticulously, obsessively well-groomed person that he was.

To Jules, who'd worked with him for years, he looked practically slovenly.

And yet his hands were steady, his eyes clear. He no longer seemed as if his head were on the verge of exploding, despite the gravity of the news he was here to share with the President.

"President Bryant will see you now, Mr. Bhagat."

"Sir." Jules had his own tie off and held out to Max before noting that it was, because of its pattern of teensy, barely recognizable SpongeBobs, perhaps even more inappropriate for a meeting with the U.S. President than that tie stained from Emma's epicurean euphoria.

And sure enough, Max waved him off. "Put it back on. You're coming in with me."

"Excuse me?" His voice actually cracked.

But Max had already disappeared into the Oval Office, leaving Jules standing there under the impatient and somewhat disdainful gaze of the President's secretary.

So he put his tie back on, straightened his collar, brushed the invisible dust from his jacket, and walked . . . onto the set of *The West Wing*. Except this was the real thing.

And the bald-headed man with his shirtsleeves rolled up and tie loosened was the real U.S. President.

Who probably wouldn't even remember that phone call Jules had made to him on his private line—the number somewhat illegaly obtained—during an international crisis a few years back.

There was a meeting already in progress—several members of the President's staff were sitting in a circular grouping of couches and chairs.

"How're Gina and the baby?" Alan Bryant was asking as he shook Max's hand. "Emma, right?"

"Thank you, sir," Max said. "They're both doing well."

"Mr. Cassidy, how's the leg?" Bryant shook Jules's hand just as warmly. "Sit, please sit."

So much for his not remembering. "Fully healed, sir," Jules reported as he and Max both sat down. "I'm back to speed."

"Nice tie," the President said, squinting at it more closely. "I've got a granddaughter who adores that show. I've watched it with her—funny stuff."

"Yes, it is." Was he really discussing SpongeBob with the leader of the free world?

"I've gotta get me a tie like that. Where'd you get yours?" the President asked.

Jules glanced at Max, who was busy opening the sealed file—no help was coming from him.

So okay. His President had asked him a question, he was just going to have to answer it truthfully. "I was on vacation in Provincetown," Jules admitted. "In Massachusetts. Cape Cod. There're stores there with . . . campy stuff." To hell with that. If he was really out, then he was out in the Oval Office, too. He explained. "Gay-friendly stores."

Max glanced up at that, but Jules didn't look at him. It was entirely possible that, after this meeting ended, Max would inform him that he'd just exploded his career.

If so, so be it. Jules was who he was.

But Bryant was smiling. "Oh yeah," he said as he reached down and opened one of the drawers of a nearby cabinet. "I'm familiar with Provincetown. My favorite nephew and his partner—spouse now—have a summer place there." He took out a mahogany tray that turned out to be filled with a colorful array of new ties, and held it out to Max, as if he were offering hors d'oeuvres. "I've got a pack of granddaughters. One's about the same age as your Emma. Her aim, too, is unerring."

"Thank you, sir." Max took a tie and put it on, slipping his soiled one into his pocket.

Jules took one, too, replacing it with his. "I'm happy to donate Sponge-Bob to a good cause," he told the President.

"Unnecessary, but sincerely appreciated," Bryant told him with a smile, but then morphed into the man Jules had seen on TV—gravely serious. "You've got bad news for me, I gather."

"I'm afraid so," Max said, handing him the contents of that file.

"Let's have Mr. Cassidy give the report," Bryant said, "since you're obviously grooming him as your replacement."

What the . . . ? Was Max really?

Jesus yikes.

Again, no eye contact from his boss, the bastard, who told the President, "Cassidy'll also be in charge of this investigation."

Another piece of breaking news that left Jules speechless.

Of course, now Max did look at him, but only because he was passing him the proverbial microphone.

Not that this wasn't completely typical behavior from his legendary boss—surprise the leaping bejeezus out of him, then make him give an impromptu presentation—his first in front of the U.S. President and his staff.

Jules cleared his throat. "The photo you've been given, sir, is that of Yazid al-Rashid al-Hasan. Our code name for him is Tango Two, due to the amount of time he'd spent as Osama bin Laden's right-hand man back in the late 1990s. We believe he's heading to the United States, with the intention of carrying out a major attack on an East Coast city, probably New York, possibly Atlanta.

"We believe his point of entry will be the Gulf coast of Florida via South America. We've been watching a mob boss named Gordon Burns, who's based in Sarasota—we believe his organization may have been responsible for smuggling another al Qaeda operative into the country, although we've uncovered no hard evidence to date. We're working to find out the logistics—where, when, how.

"We have an agent inside," Jules continued. "Peggy Ryan has been working as a live-in housekeeper at the Burns estate for the past two months." And wasn't she going to love it when she found out that Jules had just been assigned agent-in-charge of an investigation she was working, when just last year he'd been working for her? Especially when she'd transferred down to Florida to get away from him. "As of yet, she's found nothing, but she's one of our best and—"

"Cassidy doesn't know this yet, but I was notified about an hour ago"—Max interrupted him—"that Agent Ryan missed her last check-in."

And *that* was not good news. Peggy may have been homophobic, but she was a good agent—always meticulous with safety procedures such as check-ins. Although, good agents missed check-ins all the time, for a variety of reasons. Support staff generally waited to panic until an agent failed to file two consecutive reports.

"Under other circumstances," Max continued, "we'd obtain the necessary warrants and shut Burns's operation down. But apprehending Tango Two is a higher priority." He was still addressing the President, but his message was also aimed at Jules. "As much as we would like to provide assistance to our missing agent, we can't risk doing so at this time."

Those words weren't easy for Max to say. Jules knew that. Although he and Peggy had never gotten along, she and Max were friends.

"If we merely shut down Burns's operation," Jules added, "it's likely that Tango Two will find a different route into the country—a route we may not know about."

"Can't we just continue to track him?" the President's chief of staff asked.

"Well, we could, sir," Jules said, "provided we knew where he was. Last report had him heading for Spain."

Due to its proximity to Algeria, Spain had been, in the past, one of the jumping-off points for terrorists heading into the United States—a fact that the President and his staff knew well.

Jules stood. "If there are no other questions, please excuse me. I need to get to work, locating my missing agent."

As Annie went into the dank darkness of Screech's, she said a silent prayer of thanks to the unlikeliest pair of patron saints—Tommy Fista and, yes, Lillian Lavelle.

Alvarado Private Investigations' newest client had swayed into the outer office early this morning, like some kind of stereotypical private-eye film noir fantasy.

Auburn hair surrounded a heart-shaped face with full lips. Predatory heat simmered in cat-green eyes. Painted nails, do-me shoes, and matching condom-size handbag—she had all her accessories in order. As for that skintight dress from Cleavage "R" Us . . . It was almost too funny for words.

Almost.

Ric, the big dick, didn't exactly laugh as Annie showed Lillian—if that was really her name—into his office. In fact, his eyes appeared to have glazed over.

And Lillian, upon first sight of Ric rising to his feet to greet her, had actually gasped.

And okay. Yeah. With his tie loosened and the top button of his white shirt undone, long sleeves rolled halfway up his forearms, Annie's new boss—and her brother's best friend from their high school days—was scary handsome. With his thick dark hair, deep brown eyes, and that face like a movie star, he was TDH to the max. But he was also about twenty years too young for someone as overripe as Lillian Lavelle.

Ric offered the woman his hand, they shook, and of course she held on way too long. Not that he particularly seemed to mind. Annie settled in, leaning against the filing cabinet in the corner, ready to take notes, but Lillian aimed her artfully made up eyes in her direction.

"This problem I've come to discuss—it's a very delicate matter," she told Ric in her hint-of-Southern-honey voice, focusing now on her hands, clasped demurely in her lap. "If you don't mind, I'd prefer at least the illusion of privacy."

And instead of giving the woman his usual speech about how Annie was an essential part of his team, how she'd be taking the notes that she'd type up for him later, Ric gave Annie a dismissing nod.

So Annie had left.

Twenty-seven and a half minutes later—not that she'd been counting seconds—he'd buzzed her back into his office.

Where Lillian was using a rhinestone-studded compact mirror to reapply her bloodred lipstick.

She smacked her perfect lips together, murmuring "I can't thank you enough." She leaned forward in her copious sincerity, which gave her captive audience—Ric, seated behind his desk—a perfect view of that world-class cleavage.

The woman's lack of subtlety was audacious, and again Annie almost laughed out loud.

She coughed instead, covering her mouth with her fist.

Ric shot her a glance—amazing that he could drag his gaze away from the hypnotic feast of plenty in front of him. He politely rose as Lillian, too, ascended from her seat.

Her every movement was graceful, fluid, hinting of perfectly choreographed sex.

"We've already discussed payment," Ric told Annie as he handed her a file marked *Lavelle* in his ridiculously messy handwriting. "And I've taken her contact information."

She bet he had.

There was nothing to do then but show the woman to the door.

But Lillian Lavelle was not to be hurried. Annie felt like a Mack truck next to her as she swayed her way out of Ric's office.

Always observant, Ric was paying close attention—no doubt in an attempt to solve the mystery of exactly how Ms. Lavelle could be forty-something years old, yet still have such a freakishly perfect ass.

As Annie watched, the older woman turned to give Ric one last smile before she left his line of sight.

She then sped up, thank God, leaving only a trace of her perfume in the outer office as the front door closed behind her. Pierre had lifted his head as she'd passed his dog bed, and he now watched Annie, his brown eyes anxious.

"It's all right, puppy boy," she told him. "The mean lady is gone."

With a sigh, he settled back down. All was right in his world.

Annie lowered the temperature on the window air conditioner, making it kick on, getting the air moving as she took the file to the receptionist's desk.

"She was . . . rather dramatic," Ric said, and she glanced up to see him in his favorite position—leaning against the door frame, thumbs in the front pockets of his faded jeans, left foot crossed over his right.

"Was she?" Annie asked, forcing herself to look down at the file folder, scanning the ridiculously sparse notes he'd taken during their twenty-seven-minute interview.

The case was a relatively easy one. A simple locate-the-whereabouts of Lillian's deceased daughter's former roommate, Brenda Quinn. Brenda most likely wasn't trying to stay hidden. She'd merely dropped out of Lillian's life, leaving no forwarding address, when Lillian's daughter, Marcy, had died. According to Ric's chicken-scratches, the client had made several cursory searches via the Internet, and come up cold.

She'd given them a photo of two young women on what looked to be the local public beach, out on Siesta Key. They were both in their early twenties, dressed in bathing-suit tops and shorts, hair pulled back into ponytails. Both were pretty—one dark, one fair. They were mugging for the camera, looking over their shoulders, showing off what looked to be matching tattoos—some mystical-looking Chinese characters that probably said *kick me*—on the small of their backs.

"Which one is Brenda?" Annie asked.

"On the left," Ric told her. "The blonde."

Annie looked at the photo more closely, trying to see any trace of Lillian in her dark-haired daughter's face. Maybe a little around the mouth and chin . . .

As for the blonde, she had another tattoo on her right arm—three intricately drawn, intertwined calligraphy-style letters—a *G*, a *B*, and a *J*.

According to Ric's notes, Marcy had died just about eighteen months ago. And okay, the final comment he'd scribbled was *daughter dead from drug overdose*. That had to suck.

But then Annie spotted the rate of pay for which Ric had agreed to take this case. "A hundred dollars a day? Are you out of your mind?"

He turned and went back into his office, obviously unable to meet her accusing stare. "Her daughter's dead, she's on a limited budget, it's going to take me fifteen minutes on the Internet to find Brenda . . ."

Annie followed him. She'd spent some time over the past week that she'd been here trying to talk him into taking her on as a partner—paying her with a percentage of the money that she helped him bring in. Currently, she was on salary, and aside from that reward he'd gotten along with the excess blood in his urine, he hadn't earned nearly a quarter as much as he'd paid her last week.

"I'm not sure this is going to work," she told him now. "This partnership thing. But you probably have more experience than I do. So maybe you can tell me, how exactly would you give me a percentage of a blow job?"

Ric looked up from straightening the papers and files on his desk and laughed. And then he stopped laughing. "You don't really think . . . ?"

"Twenty-seven minutes for a basic locate-the-whereabouts interview . . . ?"

It was possible that she'd rendered him speechless.

"It complicates things," Annie told him, perching on the edge of his desk. "I mean, if we're partners and you get a blow job, what do I get?"

"I didn't get a . . . She didn't . . . I wouldn't . . ." Ric was actually flustered, but then he laughed his exasperation as he shooed her off his desk and sat down in his chair. He adjusted his computer monitor and pulled his keyboard drawer out. "What kind of scumbag do you think I am?"

"The male kind?" Annie countered, sinking into the seat that Lillian Lavelle had recently occupied.

"And, by the way, this partnership," Ric pointed out, literally, with a finger in her direction. "You're right. It's not going to work. Because it's not going to happen."

"Well, duh," Annie said. "Because the blow-job thing's a deal breaker. I mean, unless you can guarantee that every time you get one, I get one, too . . . Although I'm not sure exactly how to work that into the contract. *If the party of the first part receives fellatio, then the party of the second part—*"

"Not funny."

"Yeah, actually it is," she countered. "You're laughing."

He tried to stop. "No, I'm not."

"Yeah, you are."

"I'm laughing," he practically shouted at her, "because I can't believe we're having a conversation about . . . this."

"I can't help but notice," she said, keeping her voice a normal volume, "that you haven't actually denied it. There's been a lot of blustering and outrage, but—"

"I assure you that I have never had sex of any kind as payment offered for services rendered. Not with Lillian Lavelle or with anyone else." There was a dangerously hot glint in his eyes as he looked at her. "Although if you really do want me to pay *you* that way . . ."

The Annie she'd been ten years ago would have flushed with embarrassment at that heat, even though she was well aware it was meaningless. Ric looked at all women like that. With genuine appreciation. Regardless of the woman's shape or size or age.

Yeah, Ric Alvarado didn't just look at women. He smoldered at them.

The Annie of ten years ago would've rolled her own eyes and backed away. Even the Annie of last year would have mumbled that he was a jerk, before slinking to her desk.

But the Annie that she was today was braver. Bolder. She'd stared down death, so she could certainly hold this mere mortal's gaze.

And, in fact, he looked away first, closing his eyes and rubbing his forehead, muttering something in Spanish. "I shouldn't have said that," he told her, back to English as he glanced at her through his fingers. "I'm sorry. It was improper. Look, it's going to take both of us some time. To establish an appropriate employer/employee relationship."

"But see, we wouldn't have to," Annie pointed out, "if we were partners—"

"Stop."

And there they sat, on opposite sides of his big wooden desk. Staring at each other. Ric was studying her face, as if trying to read her mind. He finally spoke. "You really thought that I would . . . do that with a client, with you in the outer office, on the other side of that door?"

It was entirely possible that she'd not only offended him, but also hurt his feelings. Except this *was* Ric Alvarado, Annie reminded herself. Unless he'd radically changed since he was in high school . . . "It's been years since we've spent time together," she told him. "I don't really know you, you know, as an adult, any more than you know me."

"I haven't changed that much," Ric protested.

Yeah, that was what she was afraid of. "I've changed a lot," she countered.

He nodded. "I kind of noticed." He pulled his computer keyboard even closer to him. "I should get to work."

"May I ask one more question?"

"Yeah," he said, even though his body language screamed no.

"Why did Lillian—who's basically robbing you by getting you to agree to take her case for a hundred dollars a day. A woman with shoes like those is *not* on a limited budget, by the way—"

"*One* more question?" he reminded her.

"Why do you suppose this client wanted *me* to think that she'd paid the other part of her bill with her mouth?" Annie flipped through the file to the final page—a photocopy of both Lillian's driver's license and her credit card. Her date of birth was . . . "Her *elderly* mouth."

"She's not that old."

"Born in '60. That makes her . . . forty-seven."

"Fifty's the new thirty," he pointed out. "And she was . . . extremely well maintained. Prototypical MILF." At her blank look, he added, "Like Stiffler's mom? From *American Pie.* You know, a *mother I'd love to* . . ." He left the *F* to Annie's imagination.

"Ew."

He shrugged. "I didn't make up the acronym."

"But you used it." She caught herself. "Sorry. She just . . . creeped me out. Everything she did seemed . . . calculated."

"Yeah," Ric agreed. "And I think you're right. After you came back into the room, she turned her volume up to about thirteen. I noticed it, too."

"It feels to me as if she enjoys screwing with people," Annie said. "And call me crazy, but it seems to be pretty rudimentary deductive reasoning that if she's screwing with me, she's probably screwing with you, too. Although, with you, she might give literally a try, along with the figurative stuff."

"I'll consider myself warned," he told her, trying not to smile but failing.

And yeah, it was a stupid thing to have said—warning him that Lillian wanted to jump his bones, like that was something out of the ordinary. It was probably rare for Ric to meet a female client who *didn't* want to get naked with him.

"If I come off sounding judgmental," Annie tried to apologize, "I don't mean to. If you really want to let Lillian use you shamelessly, it's not my place to criticize or disapprove."

Ric laughed. "Yeah, *that* didn't sound judgmental at all."

"You know what I mean," she said, rolling her eyes. "If you want to be a dog, you go be a dog, Ick-Ray. I don't want my presence here to cramp your style."

"For your information," he told her quietly, "I don't have sex—of any kind—with women I've only known for twenty-seven minutes. I prefer more meaningful relationships."

And okay. This time, she looked away first. This time, she couldn't speak past the sudden dryness in her throat.

He wasn't done. "But it's not my intention to cramp your style, either. I'm, um, aware of, um . . . Well, I'm just . . . glad you came home to Sarasota even though your mom and Bruce aren't here anymore and . . . My year wasn't half as rough as yours, but . . . I'm glad you're here."

Annie couldn't keep tears from flooding her eyes. "I'm glad I'm here, too," she said, forcing them back. "I just wish . . . Well, you know what I wish."

Ric nodded. "You've communicated that effectively over the past week."

She actually managed a smile. Stood up. "I'll let you get to it. Finding Brenda Quinn." She pulled the door shut behind her, but then stopped. Looked back at him. "How long will it take? You said . . . fifteen minutes?"

"Give or take a few."

"And if it doesn't?"

"It will. Believe me. This is not going to be a difficult one."

Annie nodded. "But if it does turn out to be difficult . . . Will you let me ride along when you go out to look for her?"

Ric sat there, behind his desk, his face expressionless. "If I let you ride along," he finally said, "will you promise never to discuss blow jobs with me again?"

Annie laughed. "I promise." She shut his door behind her.

It was just shy of two hours after that, after finding nothing on Brenda Quinn except cold information—the most recent dated eighteen months ago—that Ric had actually let Annie drive. He didn't want to get dog hair in his car. Not that Pierre shedded. His poodle genes were dominant.

The more traditional, feet-on-the-street, Q&A method of sleuthing had finally brought them to Screech's, where Brenda had worked as an exotic dancer as recently as one month ago.

And so it was thus, with the help of Saint Lillian of the Over-Endowed sparking that remarkable conversation in which Ric had confessed he was glad she was here, Annie was in Screech's right now, showing him that she was capable of being more than a mere office assistant.

True, she hadn't worked as a police officer, or even a security guard. Her total law enforcement background was limited to the shelves of books she'd recently read, and to a handful of courses she'd taken in college. But she'd always been a detail person, noticing things, remembering what she'd seen or heard or read. She was smart and a quick learner.

She wanted—badly—to work not for this man, but *with* him. Although, truth be told, as the clock ticked closer to the end of her two weeks of notice, Annie found herself coming up with excuses to stay—even if he didn't immediately see the light.

Because as much as she bitched about sitting behind a desk, she actually liked spending time in Ric's little office, provided Ric was there, too. She particularly liked the way he smelled, but okay, he was *Ric*, for the love of God. She was the kid sister he'd never had. Plus, he had a girlfriend.

Some blonde who lived in Ohio, and came into town twice a year on vacation.

Funny, though, how her name hadn't come up during their blow-job conversation. As in, *Gee, Annie, I would never cheat on my perfect blond girlfriend from Ohio by messing around with a client.*

"Can I help you?" The woman who was approaching Annie from the back of Screech's was clearly management. A few major clues were that she was in her sixties, and unlike most of the other women in the room, she had all of her clothes on.

What kind of woman would choose to manage a strip club over, say, a Bath & Body Works? Aside from a heavy smoker with perfume allergies?

Maybe a woman who'd started as a dancer herself to feed her kids when her husband bailed—maybe she would go on to manage this type of place. Or a woman who believed fiercely in the importance of her own independence . . .

Or maybe she was just a woman who didn't care what happened, as long as she got her share of the pie.

While Annie wouldn't have chosen to come here for dinner, the food that went past her on heavily laden trays looked and smelled good. And the tables and floors were clean.

Someone in here obviously cared about *some* things.

So Annie took a gamble. She held out her hand. "Hi. My name's Louellen Jones. I work for a local private investigator. He hired me as his assistant, and I thought he meant *assistant* assistant, but I'm really just his secretary. This is my big chance to impress him, so I'm hoping you can help me . . ."

Robin's sister, Jane, always got a little crazy when her husband went, in macho-SEAL-lingo, *wheels up.* All of SEAL Team Sixteen had gone overseas this time, their destination kept secret even from their long-suffering wives.

Janey was pretty convinced that her husband was heading to Afghanistan, where support from the other branches of the military was not always available, thanks to the unending fiasco in Iraq. She was never a happy camper when Cosmo was gone, but this time she was even less happy.

Robin sat in his sister's kitchen, watching her go through contortions to find child care for tonight for his nephew, Billy, who sat in his high chair, happily drooling on a tray filled with Cheerios, chewing his own tiny fist.

Jane was a movie producer, and tonight she was being given an award by the director's guild. It was some kind of Important Women in Hollywood thing that she really couldn't miss. But Cosmo's mom, who lived not too far away in Laguna Beach and usually sat for Billy, had tickets to a touring-company production of *Aïda*.

"I don't have to go," Robin told her as she scrolled through the address book on her cell phone. "I can stay with Bill."

Jane looked surprised. "You were planning to go?" she asked. "I thought you were still doing press junkets for *Riptide*."

"No," he told her. "I'm done. We did the last of this round before noon. I actually have a night off. Tomorrow, I start the film-festival appearances. It's crazy, but a lot of them picked us for their lineup."

"That's because you're good. Even when you sell out and do a popcorn movie." She went back to searching through her address book.

"Seriously, Jane," he said. "I can sit for Billy tonight." How hard could it be? He smiled at the baby, who was a total clone of his sister. Same dark hair, same green eyes, same Mediterranean complexion. He was going to be a good-looking kid, a drop-dead handsome man.

The baby gave him a very soggy, toothless grin.

Of course, Jane looked nothing like Robin—they'd had different mothers. Their father had liked variety in his women. Jane's mother was Greek, his own was Irish. Robin had darker hair than Jane, but much paler skin and blue eyes. Black Irish, it was called. Although for *Riptide*, makeup had once again dyed his hair and eyebrows blond. He'd been blond in four out of the five pictures he'd done. This time, after the film had wrapped, he hadn't bothered to get his hair dyed back.

"I'm not going to do that to you," his sister told him. "Not on your one night off."

"I really don't mind."

"Really, Robin, I'll find someone else."

And suddenly dawn broke. "You don't want me to babysit for Billy," Robin realized.

Jane closed her cell phone. Exhaled. "You're right, I don't. *We* don't. Cos and me. We've talked about it, Robbie and . . ." She shook her head.

The kitchen tilted. "Are you serious?"

She was. It was obvious that she was. She finally looked at him. "I'm sorry, but . . ."

Robin stood up. This was surreal. "Wow, so much for the diatribes about tolerance that I'm always hearing when I come over. *Gay, straight, or bi, you're my brother and I love you. But I don't want you near my kid.*"

Janey actually laughed. "This isn't about your being gay, you idiot."

"Shhh," he said. It was an automatic reflex, which was stupid, because there was no one here to overhear them.

"You drink too much," Janey told him. "Cos and I don't want you to sit for Billy because you *drink* too much."

"Yeah." He felt sick to his stomach. "Right. Good excuse, Jane."

"It's not an excuse." She was mad now, too. "Don't be a fool. You were sitting right here when I left a message asking Scotty to sit."

Scotty, as in their mutual friend Scott, who lived with his longtime companion, Jack . . .

"Look at you, you're drunk right now." Jane's anger morphed into thorough disgust.

"I am not," he protested.

"You're always extra stupid when you drink," she informed him.

He'd offended her, and he knew he should apologize, but . . . Robin got mad all over again. Because this was ridiculous. Did she and Cosmo actually think . . . ? "I mean, yeah, I had a few with lunch, to celebrate the end of the press junkets, but I'm not *drunk.*"

"There's always something to celebrate, isn't there?" Jane asked, crossing the kitchen to pick up Billy, who was starting to get freaked by their raised voices.

"Yeah," Robin agreed. "Yes. There is. Life is good, Janey. This movie's going to be huge—I'm a *star.* I've finally made it. I'm allowed to celebrate."

"And *I'm* allowed to say that I don't want you *celebrating* around Billy," she shot back. "You of all people should understand why."

What was she saying? "I'm nothing like my mother," he whispered. He'd spent the first part of his childhood in an ever-widening black hole of neglect. Neglect that Janey had rescued him from. No doubt about it, his ethereally beautiful mother had loved him, her only child, but she'd loved her gin and tonics more.

"Yeah, well. I think you got way more than your blue eyes from her."

Jane had never been one to hold back. She covered Billy's ears. "I think it's time you stopped bullshitting yourself, Robin."

"And maybe you should take your own advice." He could play this way—unsheathe his claws. "You're just jealous because I'm the success."

She laughed in his face, because they both knew the truth. *He* was the one who was jealous—of her happiness. "Yeah," she said. "Congratulations. Your agent, your manager, and your accountant all really, *really* love you. That must make you feel great."

Robin kept his mouth shut over words he didn't want to say, words he'd never be able to take back. Instead, he went out the door, slamming it behind him.

Jesus, he needed a drink.

CHAPTER TWO

"Louellen Jones?" Ric had to laugh as he searched for the switch that would turn on the headlights in Annie's car. He was driving so she could sit with needy little Pierre in her lap.

She reached across him, around the steering wheel, her shoulder brushing his chest as she flipped the lights on. "Go ahead and mock me, Dick Tracy. So I panicked and made up a name. I also got the job done."

"Maybe," Ric pointed out. "There's no guarantee that Brenda still lives in Palm Gardens. It's a pretty high-end address for an exotic dancer. Particularly one who's out of work."

Annie flipped open her little leather-bound pad, pushing on the overhead light so she could read her notes. "The manager—her name was Mary Allen—she told me that Brenda was given a severance package—of sorts—after her ex-boyfriend showed up at the strip club, looking for her. Apparently, he and his friends tore the place up. Brenda injured her back in the melee—" She glanced up. "That's a direct quote from Mary, and apparently it was quite the mother of all bar fights. When the dust settled, Brenda signed off on some kind of 'I will not sue' agreement, which included a financial incentive—and a provision that neither Brenda nor her ex ever again darken Screech's door."

"Mary give you the name of the ex?" Ric asked, signaling to make a left turn.

"Nope," Annie reported, clicking off the light. "When I asked, she said *Satan.* I said, *seriously* . . . But then my phone rang, and she used that as an excuse to end our conversation."

It was Ric who'd called her, interrupting her interview. "Sorry. You were in there so long, Pierre was getting anxious."

She kissed the top of her dog's tiny head. "Poor baby. But I always come back. Don't I? Yes, I do." She glanced at Ric. "I should probably get him his own cell phone so you don't have to use up your minutes making calls for him."

"Obviously," Ric said, "I was worried, too. Annie, really, you've had no training—"

"So train me." She turned in her seat, toward him. "Please, Ric. You don't even have to pay me while you're doing it. I've got some money saved."

"Annie," he started, but she cut him off.

"I'm good at this. I actually had fun tonight. More fun that I've had since Pam died, if you want to know the truth."

Annie Dugan had been a master manipulator back when she was eleven years old. The fact that she was out here tonight, working this case with him, was proof that she hadn't yet lost her skill. Back in his office, when she'd gotten those tears in her eyes . . . Ric had known right then that he was screwed. Whatever she asked for, he'd try to deliver. And sure enough, here they were.

But now, with her face lit by the headlights of the oncoming traffic, her gray eyes were wide and guileless.

She *had* done a good job tonight. Although . . .

"So you just walked into Screech's, walked up to Mary Allen, and she just . . . willingly answered your questions?" Ric asked her.

"Yup," Annie said.

He glanced at her and the guilelessness was gone from her eyes. Yeah, there was a little more to the story than she was telling him. "After you gave her . . . how much? A hundred bucks?"

"Are you kidding?" she scoffed. "That would be, oh, let's see if I can figure out *that* math—a hundred percent of our take for this entire case? Not too smart a move. No, she obviously wanted to talk to me about Brenda—I don't think she liked her very much. A twenty gave her reason enough to vent."

So okay. Annie was thrifty as well as smart. And as long as he limited her to the easy cases—the ones where she couldn't possibly get hurt . . . Man, was he really considering doing this?

"Plus, she seemed to like me," Annie continued. "We bonded. So if you decide that today's just a fluke, and that from now on you're going to chain me to the reception desk, I've always got an in at Screech's. Who knew? Apparently there's a place there for dancers who are zaftig."

"Zaftig," Ric repeated. No way.

"That's a polite way of saying larger," she told him.

"I know what it means." Apparently his definition of *zaftig* was different from Mary's. "I wouldn't call you zaftig. You're . . ." Damn. Now that he'd started that sentence, he had to finish it. "Nicely put together."

Thankfully, they had arrived at Palm Gardens, so he focused on pulling into the private drive for the apartment complex, pausing at the signs just inside the front gate.

"Building five," Annie told him, consulting her pad in the street light. "Mary said Brenda's apartment number is 508C."

A sign for buildings three, four, and five pointed him around to the right, back toward the lake with the fountains. He slowly headed over the speed-bump-laden route.

The complex was set up in a series of three-story-buildings with outside stairways going up to balcony-style walkways, which led to the various apartments. A place like this, though, had to have elevators, too—probably in some sort of central lobby.

As they passed buildings three and four, Ric saw that C meant a third-floor unit. The penthouse, so to speak.

Annie was silent, looking around, no doubt taking note of the expensive cars in the lot. The grounds were well groomed, the swimming pool enormous. A sign pointed the way to the tennis courts and clubhouse. There was no doubt about it. Money lived here.

As if a punctuation mark to that fact, a sleek black limo was idling near building five, in a no-standing zone.

It wasn't until Ric parked and they got out of the car, leaving the windows open for Pierre, that Annie spoke.

"Nicely put together," she mused, and Ric realized his earlier relief had been premature. "Generally, people say that when they don't want to be mean. When they can't think of anything positive to say without lying. It's the equivalent of saying *You looked like you were having fun up there* to a friend who was in a show that you thought sucked."

"Third floor," Ric told her. "Door closest to us. Don't look straight at it."

The door was clearly marked 508C, with ornate gold numbers and letters. The windows surrounding it were brightly lit, but just at that moment, the lights went out and the door opened. Someone was coming out.

Three someones. One of them was female and blond.

The limo moved closer, surely not by accident as Annie exclaimed, "Would you look at that moon?"

"Looks like Brenda's got herself a sugar daddy," Ric murmured, pulling Annie against him, her back pressed to his front, his arms encircling her.

"Are you sure it's her?" she whispered, playing along, covering his arms with her own, leaning her head against his shoulder, as if they were lovers looking at the stars.

Well, okay, so this was Florida and the haze factor usually eliminated most starlight. Tonight was no exception. They were lucky, though. The moon was shining through the clouds.

"No," he whispered back. He wasn't sure it was Brenda—she was still too far away. And yeah, Annie was a solid, comfortable armful, but zaftig? Come on. "Let's let her come closer." They were standing on the path, directly between the exit from the building and the limo. She'd have to go right past them.

Assuming that this was her gentleman friend's limo.

Except, up on the third floor, the trio had turned around and trooped back to the apartment.

One of the men unlocked the door, and the blonde went back inside.

"Hurry the fuck up," a disgruntled male voice carried down to them.

"Charming as well as wealthy," Annie murmured. "How long can we get away with standing here like a pair of idiots?"

As if on cue, the moon disappeared behind a cloud, leaving them staring up into the nothingness of the night sky.

"Uh-oh," Annie said.

On the third floor, the two men lit cigarettes, leaning against the railing, still waiting for the blonde.

Their options were pretty limited; still, Ric ran through them in his mind. They could do this overtly—just walk up those stairs, approach the two men, inquire as to whether Brenda Quinn lived in apartment 508C.

That approach was simple and to the point, and would be easier than this undercover investigation they were attempting.

Problem was, every instinct he had was screaming that there would be trouble if Brenda and Co. found out they were looking for her. Keeping this covert seemed ridiculously important.

Of course, maybe he just wanted an excuse to kiss his best friend's little sister.

Annie turned in his arms to face him. "Maybe we could pretend we're reciting poetry to each other. 'There once was a girl from France, who wanted to learn how to dance . . .' "

Ric laughed. "That's not poetry."

"Cut me some slack. I'm thinking on my feet here. I don't see you doing much of anything—"

He kissed her.

He felt her surprise for only a fraction of a second before she caught on, and she kissed him back. Man, she was good at making it look real—anyone watching them would have to look away to avoid getting scorched from the emanating heat.

Her mouth was as sweet as he'd always imagined, her body as soft, as she molded herself against him. Her hands were in his hair, down his back, and—Mother of God—cupping his ass, pulling him closer. She angled her head to kiss him more deeply, going so far as to wrap one leg around him, shifting her hips until her heat was rubbing him and there was no way she could miss knowing that he was already inappropriately aroused.

Although, damn. It was surely more inappropriate *not* to get turned on while getting dry-humped by a sexy woman who had her tongue in his mouth and her hands all over his butt. And okay, if she touched him *there* again, he was going to embarrass himself.

He grabbed her hands and pulled away and found himself staring down at her upturned face, into her amazing-colored eyes.

"Here they come," she whispered, and for several endless seconds, he had absolutely no clue what she meant. And then he remembered.

Brenda Quinn.

Right.

Annie was breathing as hard as he was, but she still managed to speak. "They've locked the door and they're heading for the stairs," she told him, her hands back in his hair. "We just need to stall for a few more seconds . . ."

No way was he kissing her again, but she was up on her toes, pulling his head down to her mouth.

Ric knew only one definite way to stop her. "We're going to do this on a trial basis," he said. His voice sounded raspy, thick, and he had to clear his throat. "This training thing, okay? I'll continue to pay your salary and you'll continue to do the secretarial work that I need done. You won't get to work on everything. If I say it's too dangerous, you don't argue. If I tell you to duck, you duck and you ask any questions later. I'll test you constantly, and if you fail, just once, the deal's off—are we clear?"

She nodded, her eyes wide.

"Good," he said. "And this—you know—kind of thing . . . That we're doing here? It won't happen again. Because it's just . . . too weird."

But Annie's attention was over his shoulder. "I'm not sure if it's her," she whispered, and he turned just as she called out, "Excuse me . . ."

If this was Brenda, she'd cut her hair Halle Berry short. She was much skinnier than the girl in Lillian's photos, too. Any chance of IDing her via her tattoos was eliminated by the jacket she wore, despite the heat of the night.

Heroin addict, anyone?

She was walking just behind the two men, both of whom were young—maybe midtwenties—and white, with shaved heads and a variety of tats and piercings. They both moved as if their balls were too big for their pants. The shorter one wore a T-shirt that bore the number 88. The other had on a leather jacket. He kept his left arm slightly out from his side—which was a pretty sure sign that he was carrying a weapon.

Annie, of course, didn't know that, and when the blonde didn't slow down, she tried to follow.

Ric grabbed her hand, but he couldn't muzzle her without drawing undue attention, and she called out again. "Excuse me. Hi. I'm Louellen, 408C? I think I got a package of yours. Are you Brenda?"

All three of them turned, and it was then that Ric saw her—a slight figure, moving toward them across the grass, in a dark raincoat with a grim-reaper-deep hood that covered the wearer's hair and concealed her face.

Most of the time.

The woman—and it had to be a woman with that shape and height—seemed to look right at him. It was when she turned away—exactly as a car approached, headlights flashing across them all—that he caught a glimpse of her face.

It was none other than Lillian Lavelle.

She must've come from the parking lot. He hadn't seen her approach, but then again, he hadn't seen much of anything with his eyes closed as he'd attempted to touch Annie's tonsils with his tongue. Damn it. As Ric watched his client now, she was sticking to the shadows, moving closer still.

"Who the fuck you getting packages from?" the thug with the concealed weapon asked Brenda, who shook her head.

"I don't know." She looked to Annie for help. "You're sure it's for me? Brenda Quinn?"

"Quinn," Annie repeated. "Quinn . . . No. It was Brenda Johnson or Jackson or . . . Something with a J. Wrong Brenda, sorry."

"It's not mine," Brenda said, talking more to the thug than Annie.

"Sorry to bother you," Ric said, trying to tug Annie away. Whatever was going to happen when Lillian got closer was not going to be good. People didn't dress in hooded trench coats and creep around in the shadows, simply to return a photo album.

He had to get Annie out of there, and Brenda and gang safely into their limo and on their way. As quickly as possible. At which point he would tackle his client to the ground if need be. He'd demand to know why the cloak-and-dagger. Why, really, was she so intent upon finding Brenda Quinn that she would have followed him here?

That she'd managed to follow him without his being aware of her was pretty remarkable. As distracting as Annie was, she hadn't had her hands on his ass all afternoon long.

Ric took his keys from his pocket and held them out to Annie. "Sweetheart, we left the ice cream in the car. Would you mind running back to get it? Hurry, hon, before it melts."

She didn't understand why he was intent upon getting her out of there, but he knew she was remembering his words. *I'll be testing you.*

She took his keys and ran. Thank God.

Which allowed him to focus more fully on Lillian, whose right hand was now in her pocket.

Brenda and the armed troglodyte, however, were still glued to the sidewalk, in the middle of a heated discussion.

"Every other fucking day," her loving boyfriend accused her, "it's another fucking package from eBay."

"It wasn't my package," Brenda implored him.

"Just get in the fucking car."

They were too late, too late . . . Ric found himself reaching for his sidearm, which of course he wasn't wearing, because this was supposed to be a simple case, an easy locate-the-whereabouts.

Brenda and her friends were still about ten steps from the limo when Lillian pulled her hand free from her coat. The moon stayed hidden behind the clouds, and the streetlights didn't work to Ric's advantage either, because he could not see what it was that she held in her hand. He could only see that she was holding something.

Something about the size of a handgun.

"Get down!" he shouted as she raised her arm, and he charged toward Brenda, taking her to the ground, knocking aside the skinhead duo while he was at it.

Both of Brenda's gentlemen friends hit and kicked at him, fighting off what they surely imagined was his sudden unprovoked attack. But almost simultaneous with the elbow slamming the side of his head and the knee crushing the air from his lungs, he heard one gunshot and then another. A bullet smashed into the panel above his head, ripping the metal and shaking the limo.

He heard the car doors open, heard heavy boots hit the ground—more than just the limo driver's.

"We got a shooter," a male voice shouted through the ringing in his ears. "Kill the lights!"

"Shooter's running," someone else reported as the car lights went out.

"Let 'em go," that first voice responded—deep, authoritative. "Just get Gordie Junior—get 'em *all* inside."

Ric felt himself being picked up and tossed into the pitch darkness of the limo. He hit the far door, felt himself wrestled up into a seat and slapped down for weapons.

Gordie Junior. He'd heard that name before.

But his head was ringing and damn, his leg hurt like a bitch, and someone was crying—a woman. Not Annie—Brenda. Annie was safe. Thank you, Jesus.

Ric heard the door slam closed as he felt his wallet yanked from his back pocket, and then the interior lights went back on.

He was looking down the barrels of two very deadly-looking handguns—one held by the skinhead with the leather jacket, the other in the grip of a professional. A second bodyguard started going through his wallet.

"Who is he, Foley?" the skinhead—no doubt Gordie Junior—asked.

"Enrique Alvarado," that second guard—Foley—reported. "He's a private dick." He looked at Ric with eyes that were dead. "Who you working for?"

They were starting to roll. There was so much about this that was not good. With two skinheads and two bodyguards here in the back, Ric was sorely outnumbered—forget about the driver up front and the still-weeping girl. But all Ric could think was *thank God he'd sent Annie to the car. Thank God she'd done as he'd asked.*

Before he could come up with a fabricated answer to *who are you working for*—God knows telling them the truth, that he'd virtually led the shooter right to them, would get him very dead very fast—the skinnier kid with the 88 on his shirt knocked on the window.

"That big chick," he said, from his seat with his arm around Brenda in the back of the limo. "She's with him."

No.

But, yes, the limo braked to a stop. The door opened and Foley scrambled out. He was back in a flash, dragging Annie into the car.

She didn't try to fight him, didn't protest at all, as the man's hands swept over her, as he searched her as roughly as he'd searched Ric.

She just looked over at Ric, concern in her eyes. "Are you all right?" *She* was worried about *him.*

No doubt he looked like shit. He could feel blood from a scrape on the side of his face trickling down past his ear into the collar of his shirt. His *torn* shirt. And his elbow was trashed. His head still hadn't cleared, and his leg . . . He couldn't remember getting kicked in the calf, but he must've been. It still hurt like hell.

Gordie Junior aimed his weapon at Annie now, damn him. "Shut up, bitch," he ordered her.

Ric must've sat forward, because Foley's extra-large partner pushed him back, jamming his own sidearm into Ric's throat. He looked over at Annie, who was looking back at him. "Do what they say," he told her.

"No ID on the girl," Foley reported. He turned his attention back to Ric. "Who're you working for?"

Again, Gordie Junior's little friend interrupted from the back. "Yo, Frankie man, where the fuck you going? Club's out on Longboat Key, and . . . *shit,* dude. Junior, come on. Don't let him do this to us. Bren's jonesing. Bad."

"Gotta take you home, Junior," the limo driver—Frankie—said, an apology in his voice. "You know the drill. If someone's gunning for you, we take you to your father's. Straightaway. No exceptions."

"Dad'll take care of her," Gordie Junior reassured his friend.

"I don't suppose you could just let us out at the next red light," Ric asked Foley, who made a sound that might've passed for laughter in some circles.

Because *that* was where he'd heard the name Gordie Junior before. Gordie Junior was the eldest son of local crime lord Gordon Burns.

Alleged local crime lord Gordon Burns. The man's organization was incredibly tight and ridiculously loyal. As a result, despite all the nasty things Burns had done—from running a prostitution ring to drug smuggling to murder for hire—he'd never gone to trial, let alone been convicted.

Which didn't mean he wasn't guilty as hell. Or any less dangerous than the sharks in the tank at Mote Marine Aquarium.

This was supposed to have been an easy case. A safe case. A case that Annie could work on without putting herself into danger.

Ric couldn't have been more wrong.

"Who do you work for?" Foley asked for a third time.

Ric looked at Annie and shook his head. He would have said or done anything to get her out of there, but their best shot lay in getting a chance to speak to the man in charge. "We'll wait," he told Foley—told Annie, too, by using that we instead of an I—"to speak directly to Mr. Burns."

Peggy Ryan was missing. It was official.

And there was nothing Jules could do about it. Nothing he could do to help her.

It was one of the nightmare scenarios every FBI team leader dreaded. An operative deep undercover vanishing at a time when continuing the investigation was vital to national security.

If Peggy were still alive, she was surely under duress. Held prisoner. Probably being tortured so that she'd divulge details of the case.

She would be asked which of a variety of illegal activities was being investigated. What evidence had been collected and how damning was it? Who else was she working with?

Jules sat at his desk, his insides tied in knots, long after most of the others in the office had gone home, reading and rereading the check-in reports Peggy had sent—in particular the last two.

She'd always been aware of the possibility of interception, and she'd made each report sound like postcards to loved ones. *Weather's been great. Enjoying both Sarasota and the job—same old routine, no news about vacation plans.*

Although, in her last two communications, she had mentioned— almost identically word for word—watching the sunset from the window of her room in the servants' wing at Burns Point. *Mine's the only room with such a glorious view,* she'd written. *Although it's cold in there, colder even than the rest of the house, with the air-conditioning always running. I confess to missing the fresh air.*

Their experts had analyzed her word choices—the message wasn't in code—and had come up with nothing, aside from the obvious clue as to the location of her room. It was frustrating as hell because that was it. After sending those last two reports, Peggy had disappeared.

If she were dead, it was because of him.

And wasn't *that* the biggest crock of crap? Jules hadn't forced Peggy to transfer to Florida. She'd left because of her own inflexibility—her own inability to accept diversity in the workplace.

And yet Jules still felt guilty.

He reached for the phone. Picked it up. Put it back down.

His best friends, Alyssa and Sam, were out of the country on an assignment for Troubleshooters Incorporated—a private security team that was currently assisting the CIA. They were helping out in the hunt for a new arms dealer who'd shoved his way to the head of the international "most wanted" list by claiming to have a suitcase nuke for sale.

It was probably just a distraction—some fiction devised by Osama or some other Big Bad—meant to tie up teams of agents and operatives. Keep 'em from beating the brush in the mountains of Pakistan, where most of al Qaeda was still hiding. Which was kind of overkill, considering that the disaster in Iraq was already getting *that* job done quite nicely for bin Laden. Still, the threat of a suitcase nuke couldn't be ignored, despite the improbability of its existence.

And so Alyssa—Jules's former partner in the FBI—and her ex-SEAL husband, Sam, were somewhere overseas. Jules could call her on her cell, sure, and leave a message, but it'd probably be days before she'd be able to call back.

Plus, God knows he'd already filled his yearly quota of whiny messages left on Alyssa's voicemail.

About Paolo. About gleaming, shiny, perfect Captain Ben Webster, and his latest freaking e-mail, sent from some computer tent in a Marine encampment on the outskirts of Baghdad.

About . . . everything that Jules couldn't have, but wanted.

Like someone to talk to, when he was feeling like roadkill.

As if on cue, there was a soft knock on his door.

"Yeah," Jules called. Maybe if he closed his eyes and wished really hard, it would be Ben, looking resplendent in his Marine uniform, echoing some of the words he'd written to Jules in that epic e-mail, just a few days ago. *I haven't been sleeping, and it's more than just the increased casualties, the kids going home missing arms and legs. I was lying on my cot, staring at the tent above me, and I suddenly thought "What am I doing?"*

"Hey. Mind if I come in?"

Max?

The door opened and it was definitely Max poking his head in.

"What are you still doing here?" Jules asked his boss. "I thought you had some sort of thing tonight."

"I did. I stayed with Em while Gina went to a lecture over at the Smithsonian. Some author she likes. It was over early, so . . ." Max came all the way into the room, and Jules saw that he was dressed down in jeans and a T-shirt, his dark hair casually messed. "When she got home, I told her about Peggy and . . . She thought I should see if you wanted to go get a beer. Actually, what she said was *go get drunk*, but . . ."

Jules laughed. God, he loved Max's wife. "Yeah, that'll help." He shook his head. "Tell her thanks, but no. I've still got a lot to do and . . ."

Max sighed and closed Jules's office door, leaning on it so that it latched with a click. He sat down on the sofa beneath the window and sighed again.

Jules found himself sighing, too. "You know, you really don't have to—" he said just as Max said, "I used to think . . ." But Max repeated himself, loudly enough to be heard over Jules, which kind of forced Jules to stop talking.

"I used to think I had to stay in the office, too," Max said, "when an agent went missing. Or was killed. It's likely that Peggy's dead."

"I know," Jules said.

"It's . . . hard not to feel responsible," Max continued, "if not for the loss, then for . . . I guess I always want it to have some real meaning— when someone like Peggy gives her life—there should be something we get in return. Someone dangerous gets caught, a sleeper cell is eliminated, a bomb doesn't go off and thousands of lives are saved . . . There should be some measurable reward for the sacrifice. It's bad enough when you lose someone toward the end of an investigation, but we're still at the beginning of this one, so . . . Right now her death doesn't seem to have much meaning."

"We've gained nothing." Jules told him what they both already damn well knew. Peggy had been undercover for months, and they'd gained no new information. Except for the fact that she'd gotten close to something or someone and, because of that, had disappeared. Unless she'd left a message—somehow, somewhere . . . "I've got to figure out a way to get inside Burns's compound. I've been going through Peggy's reports—"

"Reports that will still be here tomorrow," Max interrupted. "You can sleep here." He patted the cushions of the sofa on either side of himself. "You can give this case 24/7 attention, but there's going to come a point when you're going to *have* to do that, and if you're already burned out—"

"Oh, this is nice," Jules said. "These words coming out of *your* mouth?"

"I get twice as much done these days," Max told him. "Because I'm actually getting some rest at night, instead of pacing the halls."

"How many times did you go home between 9/11 and the summer of 2005?" Jules asked. "Was it five times or six?"

"Back then . . . I didn't have anyone to go home to," Max said.

"Well, ditto," Jules said. "Ben's in Iraq, and even if he weren't . . ." He exhaled hard. Even though his boss had met Ben a time or two, talking about Jules's love life—or lack thereof—was surely not something Max had signed on for when his wife had urged him to come check up on Jules. "Just . . . thank you for the advice. I appreciate your concern, but—"

"Sam Starrett called me just a few days ago—before he and Alyssa went overseas," Max said. "He, uh, told me about the e-mail you got from Ben. He just . . . thought I should know about it."

Jules couldn't believe this. He could understand Alyssa telling Sam, but . . . "As my boss or—"

"As your friend," Max corrected him. "I just wanted to make sure that you understood, despite what the President said in our meeting—"

"Grooming me as your replacement," Jules remembered. With everything going on in the search for Peggy Ryan, he'd actually forgotten *that* giant anvil that had dropped on his head from out of the blue. Max actually thought that when he moved onward and upward, *Jules* would be able to fill his gigantic shoes. It was almost too much to assimilate, not without bursting into tears—which could well make Max change his mind.

"You're not going to disappoint me if you decide to take a different path," Max told him quietly. "If you and Ben—"

"Whoa," Jules said. "Whoa. Yikes. The man sent me an *e-mail.* I haven't seen him in months. It's crazy to think . . . I mean, God, even when we were together, it was only for a week. It was just an extended one-night stand. It was sex, all right?"

Ben was incredibly good-looking, and even though as a Marine he had to be in the closet, they had hooked up for a while because, well . . . Because Jules was human. But it wasn't worth it—it drove him nuts to have to hide, to sneak around . . . They'd broken up, and Ben went to Iraq. End of story.

Except they'd started exchanging e-mail a few months ago. As friends. Just friends—Jules had made that very clear.

The idea that Ben was suddenly talking long-term commitment was absurd.

Wasn't it?

Although, with Ben in Iraq, their relationship had been whittled down to words, thoughts, feelings — in the form of those near-daily e-mails. Jules had found it oddly enjoyable. Ben was a good writer — a skill that Jules appreciated and even shared. They'd gotten to know each quite well over the past four months — something that was much easier to do without Ben constantly pressuring him to make their friendship physical again.

But this latest e-mail had caught Jules by surprise.

"He's willing to give up his career. You won't have to hide anymore. Isn't that what you wanted?" Max asked Jules now.

Jules nodded. First yes, then no. "I don't know what I want," he admitted. "I honestly don't."

No way was he torturing Max by telling him this, but the sex hadn't been all that great, shadowed as it was by the knowledge that Jules was getting intimate with someone who would never even dare to hold his hand at a Pride parade. Not that Ben wasn't plenty affectionate in private. Jules just found it hard to invest a hundred percent in a relationship that could never be permanent — not without Ben giving up his career.

God, the thought of Ben throwing everything away for Jules — for something that had never been real — made him feel claustrophobic. As if his tie were tightening around his neck as water closed around his head.

Which was probably close to the way Max was feeling right about now, too.

"You sure you don't want a beer?" Max asked.

Jules stood up. Because Max was right — it would all be here tomorrow. Peggy's reports. Ben's e-mail. His future trying to fill Max's shoes as the leader of the most elite counterterrorist team in the entire FBI.

"Yeah," Jules told his friend. "Let's go get a beer."

CHAPTER
THREE

Annie didn't understand much of what was going on inside this limousine, but she did learn one thing pretty fast: Speaking would get them hit.

"Who's Mr. Burns?" Annie had asked Ric, and the goon named Foley had slapped her.

And *that* had made Ric lunge for him, which was totally insane, considering that the second bodyguard—the one built like a refrigerator—was holding a gun on him.

Thankfully, he didn't shoot Ric with his gun, but he did hit him with it, opening up a nasty-looking cut on the arm that Ric had thrown up to block it. But despite that, Ric still bristled. "Don't you dare hit her! I fucking saved your boy, and you *hit* her?"

The skinhead named Gordie Junior, the one with the leather jacket and the foul mouth and the enormous gun that screamed of compensation for feelings of physical inadequacy, was looking at Annie now, disgust in his eyes. "Who's Mr. Burns?" He repeated her question as if she were an idiot. "What rock you been living under, bitch?"

Ric answered for her. "She's new in town. She works for me." He wasn't talking to Junior, he was focusing his words on Foley and Refrigerator, who were both significantly older than Junior and his friends, and seemed to be in charge. "If you let her out at the corner, she'll go back and get her car from the Gardens. She'll go to my office and wait for me to—"

"Shut up," Foley said.

But Ric wasn't done trying to get Annie out of that limo. "Just let her go, and Mr. Burns doesn't have to know that you treated us like this, after we—"

"Ow!"

Foley slapped Annie. It wasn't particularly hard, but her head knocked into the side of the car, which rattled her teeth.

"Now shut the fuck up," he told Ric, "or I hit her again."

Ric fell silent, shooting her a look of apology and misery that was almost as palpable as that kiss he'd given her, back in the Palm Gardens parking lot.

God, but Ric Alvarado knew how to kiss—no big surprise there. Annie let herself think about it, about his mouth, his hands, his incredible body beneath *her* hands. God knows it was better to do something more positive with her time than soiling her pants as they drove north on Route 41, curving around past the festive lights of the harbor.

She held Ric's gaze across the spacious expanse of the limo, remembering the look in his eyes just before he kissed her. She'd made him laugh with her silly rhyme, but his smile had faded until there was only heat. And for that instant, as he gazed down at her with the vertigo-inspiring bottomless midnight of his dark-chocolate eyes, she'd actually felt . . . beautiful.

And okay, yeah, it was all just pretend. Annie knew that. He'd kissed her because they'd needed to stall.

But there was pretending, and there was the kind of pretending that was inspired by the reality of living out a longtime fantasy—and she was not the only one who'd been doing that. They'd both gotten undeniably lost in the moment.

And that look in his eyes, when he'd pulled away from her . . . ?

He'd been shaken up. Scared to death. Conflicted.

And despite stammering something about a kiss like that never happening again, he'd definitely wanted more. If they survived this meeting with this mysterious Mr. Burns, Annie was going to kiss Ric again. She was just going to do it. Just grab him and . . .

The limo was slowing, turning down a side street, heading toward the water. Most of the properties in this area were in the filthy-rich price range, many of them gated estates. They turned again, indeed, waiting for an electronic gate to open, then continued down a brick driveway, through lushly landscaped grounds lit by pretty solar lanterns.

Ric, too, was looking out the window, trying to get a glimpse of the house—a garishly baroque palace, right on the bay.

The limo stopped. Someone from the outside opened the door nearest Ric, and light poured in.

"I want to talk to Mr. Burns," Annie heard Ric demand as he was dragged out, onto the well-lit driveway.

Junior had Annie roughly by the arm, and he pulled her toward the same side of the limo. He swore at her as she skidded before she reached the door. She went down, hard, on her knee.

"I'm sorry," she gasped, sharp pain mixing with fear. But then she pushed herself back up and realized that it was blood that she'd slipped in. It was on her sneaker and all over her jeans and both her hands and oh, dear God, it was *Ric's* blood.

He'd been shot, back at Palm Gardens.

He'd been shot, and he'd just sat there in the limo, bleeding, and he hadn't said a freaking thing.

"Get off of me." Annie yanked her arm free when Gordie Junior tried to grab her again. Instead he grabbed her by the hair. "Ow, ow, ow!" The ungrateful son of a bitch!

"What did you do to her?" Ric fought to get away from the refrigerator who was holding him. His elbow must've connected with some tender part of the big man's face, because he got himself free and scrambled toward her as she was dumped unceremoniously onto the bricks. "Annie, Jesus! Where were you hit?"

He thought *she* was bleeding. He thought *she'd* been shot.

"Get away from her," Foley ordered.

Ric either didn't see or didn't give a crap about the arsenal of weaponry that was now pointed in their direction as he searched her for a bullet wound that didn't exist. "Call for an ambulance," he ordered their captors even as she tried to tell him she wasn't hurt.

"Get away from her," Foley ordered again.

"It's not me," Annie told Ric. "It's you. It's you! *Ric.*" There was an entire army surrounding them—he was going to get them both shot. Although, in his case, it was going to be *shot again.* "Look at your sneaker!"

He finally looked down at his own blood-soaked shoe, at the hole in his jeans that still oozed. "Whoa," he breathed. "It's me?"

She nodded as Foley's voice got even louder. "Get. Away. From her."

"What's going on here?" A man's voice rang out. "Are we *trying* to get the police to visit us tonight?"

The crowd parted for him. He was slight of stature, with thick salt-and-pepper hair, but he walked like royalty and wore a very expensive suit. He looked at Gordie Junior. "Get inside. To a safe room," he ordered.

The kid holstered his gun, heavy on the attitude. "I can fucking take care of myself." What a way for a son to talk to his father.

"We'll discuss this later," Burns said. "For now, take care of your . . . friends."

Junior, his skinhead friend, and Brenda all trooped inside.

"Mr. Burns," Ric said, taking advantage of the sudden silence. "There's been a misunderstanding. My name is Ric Alvarado—I'm a private investigator. I was hired by Florida State Insurance to check out a back-injury claim made by Screech's Nightclub on behalf of Brenda Quinn."

What? Why would he lie? But the look Ric shot her was filled with warning, and Annie kept her mouth tightly shut.

"The case was a simple identify and verify the injury," Ric continued. "Very straightforward. I assure you, I wouldn't have brought my assistant into the field if I believed otherwise. I had no idea of Miss Quinn's connection to your son, sir—not before tonight."

All this talking was taking way too long. Yes, Burns appeared to be listening, but Ric had already been bleeding for too much time.

"I'm sorry, sir," Annie interrupted, "but my boss, here? He needs to go to the hospital. He happens to be bleeding, maybe to death, if he doesn't get some medical help, STAT. The fact is that someone tried to kill your son tonight, Mr. Burns. Ric spotted the gunman and threw himself between the gun and your son, taking a bullet in his leg. So will you *please* call us an ambulance?"

Burns glanced at Foley, who came toward Ric and Annie. "Mr. Foley used to be a paramedic."

Foley crouched next to Ric, giving him a cursory but apparently none-too-gentle examination. He used a deadly-looking knife that the limo driver handed him, to cut open the lower leg of Ric's jeans.

"Ow, shit!"

"Easy," Annie admonished the man, but he was already done.

"Small-caliber bullet," Foley reported, wiping his hands on a handkerchief. "No exit wound. It's still in there, but not too deep. I'm guessing it was pretty much spent." But then he frowned at the limo, crossing over to finger the bullet hole that marred the side of the vehicle. "But this is from at least a .44." He looked at Ric. "Were there two weapons?"

Ric shook his head. "I saw only one. And just a glimpse of it, too. I didn't get a good look at the shooter. He was in the shadows. Best I can tell you is he seemed shorter than average height. I think he was wearing some kind of overcoat. Other than that . . ." He shrugged.

"Can we *please*—" Annie started.

Foley cut her off. "He's not going to bleed to death. He *will* need a tetanus shot, though. If there was only one weapon—a .44—your boyfriend's injury is probably a result of a ricochet. If I were a betting man, I'd put money on the doctor digging a chunk of rock outta there." He looked at Ric. "You're lucky. If that had been a bullet from a .44, you'd be minus a leg."

"I'm lucky, too," Burns said. "If you hadn't been there, Mr. Alvarado, I'd be minus a son." He turned to Foley. "Let's have our men stand down, and invite our guests inside, shall we?"

Annie opened her mouth, but Burns anticipated her request.

"My personal physician is on his way over," he told her. "It'll be faster—and far more discreet—than calling for an ambulance, Miss . . . ?"

It was clearly an invitation for her to provide her name, but Ric beat her to it. "Jones," he said as the larger bodyguard helped him to his feet.

"Of course," Burns said. "Miss . . . Jones." He didn't buy her a.k.a. for a second, but seemed more amused than annoyed. "You look as if you'd enjoy a chance to get cleaned up."

Enjoy. What an interesting word choice after the evening they'd had. Annie quickly moved to help Ric on his other side, but he wrapped his arm around her shoulders and held on tight, more as if he were protecting her than receiving her support.

"Stay close," he murmured as they followed Burns into the house. That is, the palace.

Or rather, the castle. There were actually suits of armor in the marble-tiled foyer. And palm trees. Tall ones. And mirrors.

Annie caught sight of herself—no wonder Ric had flipped when he saw her. She'd managed to smear the front of her shirt with the blood that she'd gotten on her hands when she'd slipped. There was even some on her chin.

His blood.

Burns raised his voice. "Maria! Will you take Miss Jones to a guest room, so she can shower? Oh, and find her something to wear."

"Yes, sir." An older woman, dressed more like the hostess of a posh restaurant than a household servant, smiled at Annie. "This way, miss."

"She'll stay with me," Ric said, at the exact same time Annie said, "I'll wait for the doctor, with Ric."

"Show them both to a guest room," Burns ordered Maria. He smiled at Ric and Annie, every inch the gracious host. "I'll send the doctor up as soon as he arrives."

Ric lay on the doctor's portable examination table with his eyes closed, soaked with sweat as the doctor finished stitching him up. It *had* been a piece of rock, not a bullet, that had lodged in his leg. Foley had been right.

But damn, *that* was thirty minutes of his life that he never wanted to revisit, ever again.

"Next time, don't refuse the anesthesia," the doctor told him, taking his gloves off with a snap. "For your information, local anesthesia only affects—"

"I know," Ric interrupted. "I didn't want it." He didn't trust anyone in Burns's lair, particularly not Dr. Midnight Housecall, here.

"I'm giving you a ten-day course of antibiotics."

There was a rattling sound, and Ric opened his eyes to see him holding out a plastic pill bottle. "Just write me a prescription."

The doctor shook his head. He set the bottle down on the desk, near a pile of clothes that someone—the woman named Maria—had brought for Ric to change into, after he'd showered. "You know I can't do that."

Because this entire procedure had been illegal. Gunshot wounds had to be reported, but information about this one wasn't going to get anywhere near the DA's office. Not via a report from this doctor, anyway.

"What's he got on you?" Ric asked. The doctor was an older man, surely well established in his career. "Gambling debts?"

"One pill, three times a day," the doctor ordered. "Any sign of infection, redness, swelling—call the number on the bottle." He gathered up his things. "Mr. Foley'll put the bandage on, after you shower. Take your time, though. Don't stand up until you're ready."

"To whom do I address the thank-you note?"

The doctor stopped. Turned to look at him. "Don't ask too many questions, asshole. Even I'm not good enough to suture a throat that's been slit. Neither of us are here because we're angels. Just do your job and keep your mouth shut—the way I do."

And with that, he was gone.

Ric let his head drop back on the pillow.

Voices—one male, one female—and the sound of ice clinking in glasses made him turn toward the sliders, which led out onto a deck overlooking a patio.

Annie was out there. She'd swiftly showered and changed before the doctor arrived, pulling her curls up into a bun-thing atop her head, which, with the brightly patterned sarong that Burns's servant had brought, made her look like some kind of sacrificial virgin, about to be thrown into a volcano.

Ric had sent her out of the room, figuring it was the lesser of two evils, about three minutes after he'd refused Dr. Gloom's local anesthesia. She'd resisted his demand, but he'd insisted, refusing treatment until she went outside, onto the patio.

And now, from the sound of laughter, it appeared she was no longer alone. And apparently she was pretending to enjoy herself, which had to be no easy task.

Ric sat up, gripping the edge of the table until his dizziness passed. He slid down onto the floor, catching himself with his left leg—his good leg. Cautiously, he tested his right leg and . . .

Okay. So that hurt. But he could walk. He could even run if he had to. That was a plus.

He hobbled to the deck, looking out onto the pink brick patio below.

It was a courtyard, really, surrounded on three sides by the house. A pool glistened off to the bay side, and the entire enormous two-story area was screened in, to keep both bugs and gators out.

Annie sat in a chair, her back to Ric.

Burns was across a glass-topped table from her, sipping a drink. On that table was Ric's wallet and cell phone, and Annie's cell phone, too.

Burns glanced up and spotted Ric. "Ah, you're up and about."

Annie turned, rising to her feet, holding tightly to . . . Pierre?

Ric came farther out onto the balcony, well aware that, in only his briefs and T-shirt, still soaked with perspiration, he wasn't exactly dressed for a garden party.

"Are you all right?" Annie came toward Ric, climbing the stairs that led up to the deck.

He nodded. "Coupla stitches." He raised his hands to warn her not to come too close. "I still need to shower." He gestured to Pierre. "I'm assuming he didn't pull another Milo and Otis."

The idea of Pierre tracking her here made her smile, but it didn't completely mask the worry in her eyes. "Mr. Burns sent his men to get my car," Annie told him. "They ended up towing it because Pierre wouldn't let them in. It's out front, so we can . . . just leave without having to get a ride back to Palm Gardens."

"How considerate," Ric said, wishing now that he hadn't suggested she keep her distance. He was going to have to warn her not to speak too freely. Local rumor had it that Burns kept his house under intense surveillance—with mics and minicams recording every conversation and tracking every visitor's move. Ric didn't know whether it was truth or urban legend—but he wasn't going to take any risks with Annie's life.

"Mr. Alvarado," Burns called. "What can I get you to drink?"

"Rum and coke," he called back. "Thank you, sir."

Annie looked at him as if he'd lost his mind. "We can leave," she stepped closer to whisper.

"No we can't," he told her, not bothering to lower his voice.

"Why not?"

Ric shook his head. He couldn't risk a lengthy explanation. If Burns had this place bugged, he was using state-of-the-art equipment. Their whispers would be easily picked up. "Because I say so," he said loudly. Sharply even.

Annie actually flinched.

"Why do you always question me?" he added, reaching up to scratch his ear, hoping she'd catch on.

"I'm sorry," she said, instantly and so non-Annie-ishly contrite. She even lowered her gaze. But when she finally looked up at him, she nodded, almost imperceptibly. And she, too, touched her ear, pretending to loop a stray piece of hair around it.

Then, there they stood, just staring at each other.

"It's all right," Ric finally said. "I know you were pretty upset tonight. And I am so, so sorry that you got hit."

"I'm okay," she said, but she unconsciously touched the inside of her lip with her tongue—no doubt where her own teeth had cut her when Foley slapped her.

Ric felt sick. "Annie," he said, wishing he could rewind this entire day, back to this morning when he'd told her she could ride along with him. He should have checked Lillian Lavelle out more thoroughly. He should have known the woman was lying to him. He should have been more cautious. As soon as they got out of here—*if* they got out of here—he was going to track her down and find out what the hell was going on. Was she trying to kill Brenda or Gordie Junior? She was damn lucky she hadn't hit Ric. Or Annie.

God *damn*.

"I'm really okay. I just . . . want to go home." Annie forced a smile. "Whenever you're ready, though."

Ric was more than ready to go. But they had to stay.

If they tried to book it out of there, if they were in too big of a hurry to run away, Burns might well decide that they were a threat to his organization. God knows what they'd seen or overheard while they were here at Burns Point, not to mention while in Gordie Junior's company in the limo.

In addition, that is, to the information that Burns had a private supply of cocaine or heroin or whatever illegal substance for which Brenda Quinn had been jonesing.

Burns hadn't gone to get Annie's car because he was kind and considerate. No, he was cleaning up. Erasing all evidence that they'd ever been to Palm Gardens.

Just in case he decided he needed to disappear them both, after he evaluated what they did or didn't know.

Ric's best chance at getting Annie safely home lay in his convincing Mr. Burns that he wanted to join his team. "How often do I get a chance to do business with someone like Gordon Burns," he told her now—told the microphones and everyone who was listening in. He raised his voice, calling across the patio, "I'm just going to take a quick shower and change. I'll be right out, sir."

"Take your time," Burns called, an easygoing, generous host, with nothing better to do. Yeah, right.

"What were you talking about?" Ric asked Annie. "Before I came out?"

"Movies," she told him. *"Key Largo. Bringing Up Baby. Ocean's Eleven.* He's a movie buff."

"Keep it up," Ric told her. "He seems to like you. I know you're not convinced, but it's great that we're here."

Across the patio, Burns was watching them.

So Ric kissed her. Just briefly on the lips. Gently—aware of the damage she'd suffered from those slaps. But maybe a little more briefly and gently than he would have done had Pierre not growled at him. Because it couldn't hurt to let the organized-crime boss think that Annie did more than work for him—that her loyalty exceeded a business relationship or even mere friendship. "Trust me," Ric told her quietly. "Do you trust me, baby?"

She nodded, but gave him a look for that *baby.*

Ric took Pierre out of her arms, set the rat on the deck, and kissed her again.

Just for show.

But this time Annie kissed him back—apparently her lip didn't hurt her too badly. It was a toned-down version of that blistering Palm Gardens kiss—Burns *was* watching, after all. Still, Ric was suddenly very aware that he was without his jeans.

"Ric." He'd already turned to go inside, but Annie stopped him with a hand on his arm, her fingers cool against his skin. "In a weird way," she told him, "I think it's great that we're here, too." Her sarong was slipping, and she had to let go of him to give it a hike north before she turned and went back to Burns.

"How about *Palm Beach Story,*" Ric heard her say as he limped toward the opulent bathroom where she'd taken her shower earlier. "That's one of my favorites . . ."

CHAPTER FOUR

Annie kept her mouth shut as Ric shook Gordon Burns's hand, promising he'd be in touch regarding that employment opportunity they'd discussed.

It was kind of obvious that Ric would have promised to build a colony on Venus, provided it would have left Burns smiling and giving the order to open the gate for them, as they climbed back into Annie's car and drove away.

Earlier, out by the pool, Burns had told them that he had two sons—Gordie Junior and Stratton. Although Stratton was younger, he was the far more disciplined of the two. He'd moved across the state, and was on track to becoming a well-respected member of the Orlando business community.

Business community, Annie's ass. Still, she'd managed to sit there, smiling. Hugging Pierre. Still worrying about Ric, who'd lost quite a bit of blood and looked exhausted.

But Burns had a lot to say while sipping his drink. Gordie, he'd told them, was a challenge—a perpetual child, dressing and acting like a twenty-year-old, despite his approaching thirtieth birthday. Tonight's shooting hadn't been the first hit attempt on him. There'd been numerous others, starting back when he was seventeen.

It was, Burns declared, long past time for Gordie to grow up.

He wanted to hire Ric and Annie to get into his son's good graces. Befriend Gordie. Find out what was going on in his life, with whom he did business, with whom he spent his time—besides his junkie of a girlfriend and her waste of a brother.

What Gordie really needed, Burns had told them, was a woman in his life more like Annie—and didn't *that* totally creep her out.

He hoped, Burns told them, that they'd also discover who it was who'd tried to kill Gordie tonight. There would, of course, be a bonus for that information.

As Annie sat by, Ric agreed to take the case, offering to fax over his standard client agreement that very night. Burns, however, informed him that he never signed contracts. He worked on the honor system, with a handshake. That, plus a huge retainer—fifty thousand dollars in cash, of course—and they were in business.

Pierre sat in the back, snuggling up to the soft leather bag that held the money, as Annie now drove.

Ric was silent and tense as they approached the still-closed gates. It wasn't until they slowly swung open, until Annie was out on the other side, heading down the street, that he began to breathe again.

But when she glanced at him, he put his finger on his lips.

In the same way that he'd thought they were being listened to at Burns's house, he now obviously thought that her car had been bugged. Or maybe that there was a listening device in the bag of money. Or attached to the clean clothes that they'd been given.

"This is incredible," he said, reaching over and turning on her radio, turning the volume up much too loud. The oldies station blasted "Lola" as, twisting in his seat, he reached into the back, rummaging for . . . her Red Sox cap? He put it on, first sweeping his hair back, off his forehead. "Working for Gordon Burns . . . I've always wanted to live in a house on the bay."

When she glanced at him again, he mouthed the words *Are you really all right?*

Annie nodded. *Are you? And what's with the hat?*

But his head was already down, his focus on his cell phone. He was sending a text message to someone. Of course she couldn't ask to whom.

Hopefully, though, it was to the police.

His attention was still on his phone as she reached the intersection with Route 41. "Your place or mine?" she asked over the music that he'd no doubt turned on to mask the sounds of his cell phone.

It was what she'd be expected to say—after all, they'd pretended all night that they were together. A couple. Still, Ric sent her a look as he put away his phone. She could only guess what he was thinking—and hope that he, too, was reminded of the kisses they'd shared. They didn't just have to pretend to go home together tonight, but wow, did she really want that?

Yes.

But also maybe no.

Talk about weird dynamics in the office until the end of time . . .

What Annie wanted, more than anything, was to talk to him. Look him in the eye and ask him, *You don't really intend to work for Gordon Burns, do you?* and *You do intend to see a real doctor about that wound in your leg, don't you?*

"Yours," Ric finally decided, so she headed south, toward her little place on Siesta Key.

She'd rented a tiny furnished beach house for the summer. When the winter season started, though, the rent would skyrocket and she'd have to find something more permanent off-island.

For now, though, she was steps from the beach.

The romantic, moon-drenched beach. The perfect location for long walks, stolen kisses, and discussions of what exactly had happened tonight and who the hell was Gordon Burns, anyway?

Right now, though, Ric had his phone out again, sending another text message.

If someone was listening in via car bug, money-bag bug or sarong bug, wasn't their lack of conversation going to raise red flags? "So . . . tell me about Gordon Burns," Annie asked as Ric slipped his phone back into his pocket. "He's . . . very impressive. Beautiful house."

Ric met her gaze, nodding slightly. God, but she loved his approval. She loved that they were on the same wavelength, that he could communicate with her so easily with just a flash of his eyes, a nod of his head.

"He's been a major player in southwest Florida for about thirty years," Ric told her. "About twenty years ago, he moved to Sarasota from Venice Beach. He's got a reputation for being a Renaissance man—cultured. Movies, art, theater, classical music—he's a big supporter of the Sarasota Opera. People assume he's related to Owen Burns, who was one of John Ringling's business partners, and one of the earliest property owners in town, back in the early 1900s. But he's not. I think he moved here because of that, though—because the name still carries respect."

"So, this current Burns," Annie asked. "How did he make his money?"

"By not getting caught," Ric told her. "You name it, he's involved in it, but he's never once even been charged with a crime."

Great.

"You need gas," Ric pointed out.

Annie squinted at the dashboard. "I've got plenty."

"I want to fill your tank," he insisted. "We've been driving all night on your dime." He pointed to the Shell station on the corner of Siesta Drive. "Stop here."

And *that* was not a request, so Annie pulled over. She maneuvered next to the self-serve pump. "You really don't have to—"

"Stay in the car," Ric ordered, when she started to get out. He forced a smile to counter the abruptness of his words and tone. "Please. I got it."

But he took forever to pump the gas. What was he doing out there? Annie rolled down her window to look at him.

"Sorry," he said. "This pump is freaking slow. Almost done."

But then he washed and squeegeed the windows—all of them. Not just the front and back, but the sides, too—making her put her window back up.

When he finally opened the passenger-side door, it was to tell her that he had to go inside the little convenience store and use the men's room.

"Are you okay?" Annie asked.

Ric nodded. Closed the door. Opened it again. "You were great tonight," he leaned in and told her. "I just . . . wanted to make sure you knew that."

"Thanks."

But he was gone before she'd even gotten the word out.

Annie watched him walk—he was limping only a little—across the parking lot and into the store. She watched, through the big glass windows, as he wove his way through the racks of snack foods until all she could see was his red ball cap. And then it, too, disappeared from view.

She sat and waited. And waited.

This place was busy for the middle of the night—mostly with college-age kids stopping in to buy beer.

After about five minutes, Ric finally came out, carrying a paper bag, the collar of his jacket up, the bill of his cap pulled down low. She started the car before she realized that it wasn't Ric. It was someone else in a similar jacket and hat. This guy was wearing sneakers—Ric's had been trashed, so he'd traded them for sandals back at Burns Point.

This man was also African American.

Annie had to smile—what were the odds of two men going into a Sarasota convenience store in the middle of the night, both wearing Boston Red Sox ballcaps?

Slim to none.

Or . . . maybe just plain none.

Because the man in the red cap headed straight to her car, as if he *were* Ric. He opened up the door, and even sat down next to her, setting his bag on the floor between his feet.

In the back, Pierre stood up and started to bark.

"Hush your dog," the man ordered her as he reached into his bag and pulled out . . . a gun.

Oh, shit. "Pierre, quiet," she said, and for once he actually listened to her. "Where's R—"

"Hush," the man said again, hefting his weapon for emphasis. "Drive," he commanded.

Annie put the car into gear and took her foot off the clutch, and they jerked forward, out from under the lights, out onto Siesta Drive.

This couldn't be happening. And yet it was. Who was this man and what had he done to Ric? Was he another of Gordon Burns's goons? Had they only thought they'd gotten away?

"Turn here," the man ordered as they approached a side street, rummaging in his bag for . . . what? Some sort of cylindrical metal thing that he turned on and . . . "Pull over."

There were no streetlights here, and as Annie parked along the side of the road, she ran through her options. She had to get out of there, that much was clear. She could turn off the lights as she bolted from the car, and he'd have that much more trouble chasing her—or shooting her.

But she was still wearing this ridiculous dress, which wasn't made for speed. Plus, her feet were bare. She'd been given a pair of sandals at Burns Point, but unlike Ric's, hers had precarious three-inch heels. She'd tossed them into the back when she'd first gotten into the car, preferring to drive barefoot.

As she pulled up the parking brake, the man had turned toward the backseat, running the metal thing across the leather bag, and even Pierre and . . .

"We're clear," he announced. "No bugs."

No . . . bugs? His words didn't make sense at first, probably because her entire focus was on his gun—and the fact that he was now holstering it . . . ?

"We can speak freely now," he told her. "Sorry about the gun-in-your-face thing, particularly after the night you've already had, but we needed to get out from under the lights as quickly as possible. My complexion's not as fair as Enrique's. I can pass for him in the shadows, but—"

"Where's Ric?" Annie asked, trying to process all this information at once.

"He's safe, he's fine. I know you must be worried, but . . . We're friends. I'm former Sarasota PD. He texted me, and I swung past his place and picked up his sidearm and this thing." He held out the electronic device. "It's a bug sweeper. I checked him out in the gas station's store—he was clean, too."

"Where did he go?" Annie asked.

"I'm not sure exactly," the man told her. Beneath her Red Sox cap, his dark brown eyes were apologetic. "He borrowed my car, said it was urgent. Asked me to hang with you until he checked back in. From what he told me, you've had a rough night and probably don't want a babysitter, but he insisted. He was pretty sure your car's being followed—in fact, someone's turning down this way right now, and at the risk of completely offending you before we've even been properly introduced, you should probably put your head down. Over this way." He gently pulled Annie down, and sure enough, car headlights swept over them as another vehicle slowly went past.

To the other driver, with Annie out of sight, and Ric—or this self-described darker-complexioned Ric substitute—sitting up, it would look as if they'd stopped for a quickie. And how ironically appropriate. This day had started with the pretense of a blow job, it was only fitting that it end this way.

"Again, I'm sorry I scared you," Ric's nameless friend told her again, his voice a rich rumble in the darkness above her. "Ric wanted to write you a note, explaining who I was, but neither of us had any paper and the checkout line was too long, and we'd already drawn *way* too much attention to ourselves, swapping clothes, locked in together in the men's room." In the back, Pierre was growling. "Dog's not going to bite me, is he?"

"It's okay, Pierre," Annie said, her cheek against the linen pants Ric had been wearing just minutes ago.

"Pierre, huh?"

"He came with the name."

"He a poodle?"

"Part," she told him.

"This is awkward, huh? Just another sec, that car's turning around at the cul-de-sac, gonna swing past us again. Now that they know this is a dead end, they'll wait for us on the main road."

"Who's following us?" Annie asked, fear tightening her throat. "Gordon Burns's men?"

"That's what Ric thinks," he told her as the lights passed them again. "Okay, we're good."

They were good. Except for the fact that a car full of thugs was waiting for them out on the main road. And God only knew where Ric was.

She sat up, pushing her hair back from her face, forcing a smile, holding out her hand. "I'm Annie."

"I know," he said, shaking her hand. "Ric said you're Bruce's little sister. How do you do? I'm Martell Griffin. Although Ric said to make sure to tell you that you can call me Hutch."

Annie laughed—it was either that or burst into tears.

"He *also* said to tell you that you're fired," Martell continued, "but I told him I wouldn't do that. But, see, I *did* because I wanted to give you a warning—because now that we've been introduced, I see what's going on here. Little sister, my ass. I've never seen that boy so bullshit, you know, angry? Like, chew people in half with his teeth? He's pissed as hell—but mostly at himself for putting you in danger."

CHAPTER
FIVE

J ust because he was home didn't mean he was going to get any sleep.

Jules got out of bed and woke up his computer, because he had to do something to distract himself from thoughts of Peggy Ryan, who, if still alive, was probably being water-boarded right this very second.

It was the torture-to-death of choice being used these days against federal agents. Peggy wouldn't be the first, and she sure as hell wouldn't be the last, and damn it, he had to stop thinking about her.

A quick check to his e-mail and . . . Nope. Nothing more from Ben.

Jules hadn't heard from him since The E-mail.

Understandably. It was Jules who owed Ben an answer. Sure, he'd sent him a quick acknowledgment last week. *Wow. Email received. Lots to think about. J.*

He was still thinking. Because, jeez, what do you say to someone who was willing to give up their dreams and ambitions for you?

Wow, thanks?

Or maybe . . . *No, thanks?*

Because what if Ben was wrong? What if this was all a giant mistake? What if he made this huge, life-altering decision and regretted it?

What if *Jules* regretted it? Would Ben expect him to make a similar sacrifice in return?

Like giving up the chance to take over Max's team.

Or promising never to watch another Robin Chadwick movie.

Jules scrolled through his e-mail in-box, because thinking about Ben and — God help him, Robin — wasn't going to help him get to sleep, either.

There was a brief e-mail from his mother. She ran into his middle school music teacher in the grocery store. Did he remember Ann Schauffler? She remembered Jules—wanted to know if he was still playing the clarinet.

Oh, and by the way, Ms. Schauffler's son is gay, too. An architect. Single. Looks kind of like Nate Berkus. Lives in Manhattan, which isn't *that* far from Jules's condo in D.C. Not that she was trying to set them up or anything—she knew how Jules hated it when she did that . . .

His cell phone rang, saving him from eye-rolling himself into a migraine. "Cassidy."

"Hey, Jules. It's Yash. We got a call from Sarasota."

Jules braced himself. "Good news or bad?"

"Could be good, but probably not." FBI agent Joe Hirabayashi was an eternal pessimist. "We've had movement tonight at Burns Point. Apparently there was an earlier hit attempt on Gordon Junior—which pretty much happens every two to three weeks. End result is two new players in the game. Neither have been inside the fortress before, at least not since our surveillance started."

Which, according to the reports Jules had read just that afternoon, was approaching the two-year mark. He stood up. Started to pace.

"They've been inside for a coupla hours," Yashi continued. "Male and a female. Male's been ID'd as Enrique Alvarado, a local PI, been in business for about a year. Female's still unknown, but we're working on it."

"Why is that name familiar to me?" Jules asked him. *Enrique Alvarado . . .*

"Dunno," Yash said helpfully. "Although, he's former Sarasota Police. Detective squad. He might've been involved in the Warren Canton case."

A few years back, Jules and Yashi had both spent time in Sarasota, tracking the man responsible for an assassination attempt on the U.S. President. There'd been a huge task force set up—a combination of local police, FBI, and even the military. It was possible Jules had met Enrique Alvarado then.

"E-mail me with whatever info you've got on Alvarado," Jules ordered. "And let's get surveillance in place. I want his home and office watched, 24/7. I want a complete file on this guy, and I want it yesterday."

"You got it," Yashi promised. "Although don't get your hopes up. He may have been in Burns's pocket, even when he was on the force."

"Or he might be the break we need." Jules was eternally optimistic, which made Yashi a good match for him, as a teammate.

"Maybe." Yashi sounded doubtful. "FYI, it'll take about ten minutes for that file to download."

"I'm not going anywhere," Jules said. But as soon as he got off the phone with Yashi, he dialed American Airlines. "I need a seat on your next flight to Sarasota, Florida, out of Baltimore-Washington . . ."

"Don't stop," Martell said. "Don't stop don't stop don't stop!"

"But that's my house," Annie protested.

"It's lit up like the surface of the sun," Martell told her as they rolled on past. "Did you leave that spotlight on when you left for work today?"

"It's not mine," Annie said. "It must be the neighbors'—we share the driveway. They must've just put it in." It definitely hadn't been that bright last night.

"Your neighbors drive a black Olds?" he asked.

"Who, Kathy and Mike?" Annie laughed. "They have a Prius that's covered with bumper stickers about global warming and equal marriage rights."

"How about the neighbors across the way?" Martell asked.

"Pickup truck," Annie said, her heart sinking as she looked in her rearview to see a dark sedan parked in that driveway, too.

"Your house is being watched," Martell told her. "Plus we still got that car on our tail—although it's not a dark sedan, which makes me wonder. Bottom line—no way am I letting you go home."

"If they're watching me . . ." Annie started.

Martell was already dialing his cell phone. But he shook his head. "Ric's not picking up." He left a message. "Yo. Starsky. Call me, ASAP." He tried to give Annie a reassuring smile. "I'm a little broader than he is, you know, around the waist? Those shorts I was wearing were loose on him. He was probably afraid if he put his phone in the pocket, he'll end up pantsing himself, so . . . He probably left it in the car. And remember, everyone thinks I'm him, that he's right here, with you. He's safe."

"I hope so." Annie made up her mind. "I still want to drive by his place."

Martell nodded. "Let's do it."

Lillian Lavelle picked up her cell phone on the first ring. "About time," she said. "I've been waiting for hours."

Unbelievable. "Sorry," Ric said as he drove Martell's car north, toward the string of cheap motels by the airport, where she was staying. "I was busy getting the crap kicked out of me and then being held at gunpoint."

"You should've just let me shoot him."

Him. So her target wasn't Brenda. "I have this problem—with my clients using me to help them kill people?"

"I owe you . . . an explanation."

If Annie were here, she'd be all over that hesitation that came after *owe you*. She'd be rolling her eyes, insisting it was carefully added innuendo, certain that Lillian was going to try to buy Ric's continued silence with high-intensity sex.

"How do you know it's not too late for explanations?" he asked her. "How do you know I haven't made a deal with Gordon Burns—to deliver you to him, for trying to kill his son?"

"Because I'm willing to bet that a former cop hates Gordon Burns almost as much as I do," Lillian countered. "Can we meet?"

"You tell me where," Ric said. "As long as when is right now." He was tired, his leg hurt, and he wanted to get back to Annie's to make sure she was okay.

Yeah, right. Like he wasn't in a rush to get back to Annie because he had a full-blown, zero-gravity, raging-hard-on, heart-in-his-throat thing for her. For sweet little Annie Dugan.

How the hell had that happened?

For starters, he'd kissed her.

He'd finally freaking kissed her, like he'd wanted to kiss her for years. And everything he'd been denying for most of his adult life had come rushing to the surface. And/or to his dick.

Man, he was so screwed. Because this was a relationship that was not going to happen. He knew that. She loved him like a brother—she was the little sister he'd never had. Bottom line, he and Annie were friends. They had been for years—and that was all it was ever going to be between them—even though she'd kissed him the way she had.

It was called acting.

Wasn't it?

Damn, it scared him to death.

"I'm two minutes from your office," Lillian told him.

He was even closer. "I'll meet you there," he said, taking a right turn from the left lane. "Leave your weapons locked in your car. I'll leave the office door ajar, approach it with both hands in the air, open it with your foot."

"That seems a little overdramatic." Lillian laughed.

"Ms. Lavelle, you fired two shots from a .44 into a crowd tonight," Ric reminded her as he pulled into his driveway. "You either do it my way, or I go directly to the police."

Except, here she was, too, pulling up right behind him, making a lot of noise into the phone at his mention of the authorities. He drew the sidearm that Martell had brought to the Shell station for him.

"Change of plans," he interrupted her. "Get out of the car, put your hands on your head, and stand there. No sudden moves."

"I assure you," she said, "unless you're Gordie Burns, I'm not dangerous."

Ric had a dozen stitches in his leg that said otherwise, but she'd already hung up her phone. As he watched, she got out of her car and put her hands on her head. She wore the same full-length raincoat that she'd had on earlier, and she was carrying some kind of pocketbook over her right shoulder.

He kept his weapon on her, herding her in front of him, to his office door. He unlocked it with his eyes on her, and she laughed. "I promise, I'm not—" she said again, but he didn't let her finish.

"Inside."

"Ooh, I love a forceful man."

"Cut the crap." He turned on the lights and the AC, locked the door behind them. He put his cell phone on Annie's desk, because these stupid surfer shorts that Martell had been wearing didn't have real pockets. He steadied his gun hand, his barrel pointed directly at Lillian. "Drop your bag on the floor. No fast moves."

She complied. "You want me to take off my coat?"

"No. Step back from the bag," he ordered. "Keep your hands on your head."

When she'd moved far enough away, he scooped up her handbag, emptying it out onto Annie's desk. Wallet, makeup, tin of Altoids, makeup, makeup, a bunch of loose change, about a dozen store receipts, a pair of . . . handcuffs? A whole lot more makeup, a best of Charlie Parker CD, a pack of photos of Marcy and Brenda with Gordie Junior, still more makeup, but no gun.

Ric felt the bag to make sure there was nothing else inside, but it was empty. He tossed it, too, on Annie's desk.

"Okay, now the coat," he said. "Take it off and drop it onto the floor. Move slowly, keep your hands open and . . ."

Ah, Christ, he'd walked right into this one.

Annie was right—about everything. Beneath her raincoat, Lillian was wearing only underwear—if you could call it that. Maybe a more accurate word was *lingerie*. A black merry widow that barely contained her full breasts, satin-and-lace panties . . . She actually had a garter belt holding up thigh-high fishnet stockings, which with the high heels was quite the look.

She was kidding, right?

Nope.

She walked into his private office and sat down where he could see her from Annie's desk—on his take-a-nap sofa, her arms up and across the back cushions, her long legs gracefully crossed. "You seemed intent upon my not being armed while we talk. This way you can see that I'm not armed."

She wasn't armed. She was . . . incredibly unarmed. She was undeniably attractive in a meaningless, mind-numbing, sex-for-the-fuck-of-it way. And she'd planned this. She knew he'd call her, and had been dressed and ready for him.

She was clearly a woman—a very beautiful one—who'd been around the block a time or twelve. She was comfortable with her body, and she obviously knew what men liked.

Most men. Ric put his sidearm within easy reach on Annie's desk, then picked up Lillian's coat and searched it. The only thing in Lillian's pockets was her key ring. There was nothing hidden in the lining.

He picked up his weapon, took both it and the coat into his office, tossed the coat back to her. "You can put it back on."

"It's warm in here." She set it to the side.

Fine. Let her think she was tempting him. Fancy lingerie just wasn't his thing. He preferred no underwear at all beneath an oversize T-shirt, bare feet, hair a tousled mop of curls, gray eyes wide in surprise at finding Ric camped out on her brother's sofa at the crack of dawn on New Year's Day in the winter of her freshman year of college, and damn, but he had to stop thinking about Annie, with or without her underwear.

"Why didn't you tell me Brenda Quinn was Gordie Burns's girlfriend?" Ric asked Lillian, after turning on his office version of Maxwell Smart's Cone of Silence—a device that would jam all electronic frequencies. If Burns had already come in and bugged his office, or if one of the cars Ric had spotted parked out on the street had a long-range microphone intended for eavesdropping, it would turn this conversation into a scrambled, static-filled mess.

"Would you have taken the case if I had?" she answered.

"No."

"Well, that's why I didn't tell you."

Ric leaned against his desk. His leg was really hurting and he wanted to sit down somewhere soft, but it was kind of obvious that Lillian wanted him to sit next to her, and no way was he doing that. "You said you hated Gordon Burns."

She nodded. "He killed my daughter."

"I thought she died of an overdose."

"That was the official cause of death," Lillian said. "Yes. He made it look like a drug overdose, but it wasn't. It was murder."

"So you just . . . go vigilante," Ric said. "Take the law into your own hands . . . ?"

"First I went to the police," she told him, a trifle defensively. "But they did nothing. They took my statement, sure. But there was no investigation. As far as they were concerned—which was not at all—Marcy was just another body to send to the morgue." Her voice broke convincingly. "Another troubled girl permanently off the streets."

Ric took the box of tissues off of his desk. He brought it to the sofa, setting it down on the cushion next to Lillian. "Do you have any proof? Any evidence that Burns intentionally—"

"She was just out of rehab," she told him, reaching out and catching his wrist. She had one hell of a grip. "I spoke to her on the phone that day, and she was doing everything right. She was doing fine." She looked up at him beseechingly, her eyes filled with tears, her bosom actually heaving with her distress. It was a nice touch. "She told me she was afraid of Gordie Junior—that she'd seen him beat a man to death. She was there when he disposed of the body, and it was awful. She wanted to move to California, but . . . She didn't want to go without Brenda. They were best friends."

"Ms. Lavelle," Ric interrupted. She was determined that he sit on the sofa, so he sat. But he sat as far from her as possible, with the box of tissues between them. "Brenda's a junkie. She's probably more to blame for your daughter's death than—"

"Gordon Burns purposely gave Marcy an overdose," Lillian insisted. "She knew things. She'd seen things. She could send his son to jail."

"Marcy wasn't doing everything right," Ric pointed out. "If she was just out of rehab, the last thing she should have done was start hanging out with her drug buddies again. She wasn't doing fine—I think you probably know that."

Lillian even cried beautifully, one tear, and then another slowly traveling down her perfect face. "He killed her," she told him. "He killed my child—I'm going to kill his."

Ric nodded. "That's not something I can help you with."

"I have money," she said.

"That's not what you told me yesterday," he countered.

"I thought I could . . . get you on my side in other ways." She wiped her eyes with a Kleenex, careful of her makeup, then looked down at herself, and laughed—a hopeless burst of despair. "I guess I'm too old for this approach."

Ric laughed, too. "You know damn well what you look like, so don't even try to play the pity card."

She held his gaze. "And yet there you sit, all the way over there."

"I don't get intimate with clients." What was she hoping to gain here?

Lillian leaned closer, her hand on his knee. "You're fired."

He picked up her hand and put it back on her own lap. "We still have more to discuss."

"The bandage on your leg," she said. "Was that where . . . ?"

"You shot me," Ric finished for her. "And, yeah, it hurts. You've got two choices. You either get on a plane and go back to St. Louis or wherever you're from. First thing in the morning. I'll escort you to the airport myself. If you come back to Sarasota, I'll go to the authorities and tell them everything, and you *will* be arrested. Or you can go with me and talk to them today. I have some contacts with the FBI—good people who I know haven't sold out to Gordon Burns. It's possible they'll be able to get him on some kind of conspiracy charge—he did cover up a murder attempt tonight, but I don't know if that can stick. I have a friend who's a lawyer, but I haven't been able to discuss this with him, not in detail."

"Or we could lie low," she said. "Wait to see what Burns does next."

What Burns had done was hire Ric and Annie to protect Gordie Junior.

Damn it. How the hell was he going to keep Annie safe, short of driving her back to Boston? And yeah, like she'd willingly go . . .

"There's no we," Ric told Lillian, whose hand was back on his thigh, traveling northward. He stopped her, holding her wrist. "I'm not going to kill Gordie Junior for you, and I'm not going to allow you to hire someone else to do it. Yeah, I think Burns is scum, but *I'm* not—and *you're* not, either. I know you're devastated by your daughter's death, but this isn't the answer. Invest your money in grief counseling, Ms. Lavelle. Because here's a truth that you cannot change: Killing Gordon Burns's son won't bring Marcy back."

"Maybe I am scum," she told him through the tears that she could turn off and on like a faucet. They were back in force. "Because it's all that I want."

He didn't see her move, and he sure as hell didn't lean forward, but somehow she was in his arms, crying on his shoulder.

Christ.

And okay. It was definitely easier to be objective about the lingerie when she was on the other side of the room, or even the other side of the sofa. Up close she was all soft skin and softer body. She smelled nice—a little strong, like walking past a department store's perfume counters, but nice. Nothing like Annie, but no one smelled as good as Annie, which was such a pathetic thing for him to be thinking that when Lillian kissed him, he then found himself thinking *fuck it*, and he kissed her back.

The tears shut instantly off, he noted. She'd also popped out of the left side of her bustier as she took his kiss as an invitation to straddle him. Damn, but the woman knew what she wanted, and she took hold of him, right through his shorts—Martell's shorts. Martell was wearing the drawstring linen pants that Ric had been given by Gordon Burns. Martell, who was with Annie right now . . .

And damn it, he shouldn't be doing this. This wasn't just casual sex with some beautiful stranger, which, okay, yeah, under other circumstances he probably would've done because why the hell not, since he couldn't have Annie? But Lillian was kill-the-bunny crazy. There was nothing good that could come of this.

Nothing at all.

When they got to Ric's everything happened too damn fast.

To start with, there were three dark sedans parked outside of the building—which surely meant trouble.

Martell was driving. He'd wanted to show off his badass shake-the-tail driving skills to Ricky's new girlfriend, because despite what the man had said—or more accurately *hadn't* said—this Annie was it. Martell knew this because Ric hadn't told him a freaking thing about her, other than the fact that she was his friend Bruce's little sister—and not so little anymore.

Ric hadn't even invited Martell over to the office to meet her—and she'd been working there for nearly two weeks. This was something that, back when Martell had worked in law enforcement, he would've called a big-ass clue.

The girl looked kind of like that actress, Kate Winslet. The one that Ric liked so much, although it was hard to say which was the chicken and which was the egg. Ric had, after all, known Bruce's little sister for nearly twenty years—long before he'd seen *Titanic*.

Annie Dugan had a softly beautiful face, with ocean-gray eyes that danced with both humor and intellect. Plus she'd looked like she might actually order more than a salad if you took her out to dinner. She also looked as if she wouldn't break in two if you got a little rambunctious with the naked bedtime games.

It was more than obvious that Ric was afraid Martell would take one look at his precious Annie, and steal her away, and keep her for his selfish, selfish self.

The fool really shouldn't have worried, because the admiration society was mutual. The girl was his—the deal done with some serious cement. Annie Dugan was the President for Life of the Ric Alvarado Fan Club— anyone who couldn't see that was blind.

As Martell pulled past Ric's place, a two-story building in an older Sarasota neighborhood that was part residential, part business, he made the mistake of pointing out that his own car—the one Ric had been driving—was parked in front of the garage. It was there along with another—a rental, it looked like, due to the Enterprise sticker on the bumper.

It was times like this, when the clues were so damn obvious, that Martell actually missed being a cop.

"He's still not picking up." Annie hung up her cell phone, looking anxiously at the lights shining through the closed blinds on the first floor. That was Ric's office down there—his apartment on the second floor was dark.

"I'm going in," she said, and opened the door, despite the fact that the car was still moving.

Martell stupidly hit the brakes instead of speeding up and getting the girl the hell out of there. "Annie, wait—"

"Pierre, stay," she ordered her dog, and bolted.

If there was any doubt at all in Martell's mind regarding her attachment to Ric, it was now gone. There was an element of special attitude that could not be feigned in the body language of a woman marching off to rescue her man, and Annie was walking that walk right down the sidewalk to Ric's office door.

There was nothing to do but park her car out front, wave howdy to the folks in the dark sedans lurking down the street, and follow her inside.

She saw Martell coming, and had the good sense to wait for him at the door.

Or maybe sense had nothing to do with it. "It's locked," she said. "I need my keys."

Martell's choices were either to hand her the keys or grab her and throw her back into the car, but the truth was, he was worried about Ric, too. He unlocked the door for her. "I'm going in first."

He put his hand on his sidearm—no point in waving it around in front of the sedan squad, whoever they were—drawing it from its holster only after Annie quietly closed and locked the door behind her.

The outer office was empty.

The inner office was . . . whoa. Martell took a step backward, and bumped into Annie, who was right on his heels.

"Ric?" she said, disbelief dripping from her voice.

Ric stood up fast, all but tossing into the air the Victoria's Secret model who'd been riding him. She bounced on the sofa, titties flying, arms and legs akimbo. It would have been funny, if there hadn't been a healthy load of hurt mixed in with that scathing disbelief in Annie's voice.

At least Ricky's dick wasn't hanging out—that would've fallen under the heading Too Much To Bear—at least for Martell. Annie appeared to have already crossed that particularly ugly line, because even though they hadn't quite walked in on Ric playing hide the salami, it was kind of obvious that they damn well might have if they'd caught a few more traffic lights on Route 41.

Ouch.

What the fuck was the idiot doing? No doubt about it, Martell was going to have to kick his stupid white ass down the street and back.

The redhead on the sofa put her raincoat on, tying the belt around her waist. "This is . . . awkward," she said.

"Yeah," Annie told her, looking at Ric and shaking her head. "It's been one of those extra awkward nights."

CHAPTER
SIX

"Just . . . stop looking at me like that," Ric said to Annie as Martell ushered Lillian Lavelle into the outer office, closing Ric's door tightly behind him.

"Like what?" Annie asked. "Like you're a shit?" She imitated him badly, making her voice sound deep and stupid. "I don't have sex with women I've only known for twenty-seven minutes. I prefer waiting twenty-eight minutes. And oh, yeah. I really dig the babes who are homicidal—particularly the ones *who've already shot me.*"

He sighed—a weary-sounding exhale of long-suffering. "I didn't have sex with her."

"Because we came in. You know, I was actually worried about you. What a joke." Annie sat on the couch before she realized that this was where Ric and Ms. Underwear 1960 had been about to do the nasty. God. But she was too tired to stand up. Too tired, too hurt, and too angry—not just at Ric, but at herself for foolishly thinking that the kisses they'd shared meant anything. Her own brother had warned her about him.

But seeing him with Lillian, and then finding out that *she* was the gunperson who'd tried to kill Gordie Junior at Palm Gardens . . .

Annie crossed her arms. "So is there a reason you protected her from Burns—I mean, other than because you're screwing her?"

"I'm not . . ." He exhaled, hard. "Look, you work for me. I don't have to—"

"Not anymore."

"—explain myself to you and . . . Good, then I assume you'll be open to a twenty-thousand-dollar severance package." Ric sat behind his desk and unlocked the drawer that held his checkbook. "On the condition that you return to Boston immediately."

What?

"And you don't come back," he added. "Without clearing it first with me."

Annie sat back, feeling as completely deflated as she would have been had Ric just kicked her in the stomach. But then she leaned forward. "If you really think Gordon Burns is that dangerous . . ."

"I do."

"Then you should leave, too," she told him.

But he was shaking his head. "I'm not running away."

"Then I'm not, either. I retract my resignation."

"Annie—"

"I'm not leaving you to face this alone," she told him. "You may be a real turd—but it's not like I agreed to work for you in the first place because I thought you'd suddenly turned into Gandhi. You've always been a man-ho—"

"I'm not a man-ho," he protested. "And I'm also not alone. I've got Martell and—"

"Lillian?" she finished for him. "You guys make a real awesome Mod Squad. I mean, assuming Julie wore crotchless panties and carried a .44— with which she accidentally shot Pete. You know, Martell told me he's a lawyer. Did you know he's got to be in court at eight tomorrow morning? It's nearly four A.M. How much longer is he going to be able to stay here, watching your back? *And* as far as you being a man-ho? Look me in the eye and tell me that if we hadn't come in when we did, you wouldn't have had sex with her. Or—and this is where I get the stupid award—that if we'd been alone when you kissed me the way you did in the Palm Gardens parking lot, that you wouldn't have had sex with *me*."

He couldn't do it. Ric couldn't meet her gaze more than briefly. "I'm sorry about that. I am."

He took a deep breath and seemed to brace himself, as if he were on the verge of doing something really painful, like purposely hitting himself on the thumb with a hammer. He also finally forced himself to look at her—to hold her gaze.

"I've always . . . been attracted to you." He said it with the tone and inflection of someone confessing that they got their jollies from squashing baby bunnies. And he wasn't done. "I know it must've freaked you out when I kissed you, because it really . . . freaked me out. I know that you're . . . who you are, and that you . . . wouldn't. Want to. But . . . I do.

Did. Do. *Do*, okay? Damn it, I'm not going to sit here and lie to you." He looked at her as if he'd just made some big important point that she should somehow understand. "So there's another really good reason for you to just . . . pack up and go back to Boston, okay?"

Annie stared at him. "I have no idea what you just thought you told me. I'm . . . Will you please start over. From the part that went: You've always been attracted to . . . me. To *me?*"

"Yeah, I know." He rubbed his forehead as if he had a massive headache. "It's crazy."

She struggled to understand. "Because . . . I'm Bruce's sister?"

He looked up at her as if she were the one who was suddenly making no sense. "Because you're . . . you know."

But she didn't know. "Fat?" she tried.

That obviously pissed him off. "You're not fat. You're just . . . not skinny. You've got . . . curves. Which, yeah, I happen to find . . . very attractive and . . ." He closed his eyes, his head in his hands. "Christ, I'm screwing this up even more than I have already. Just . . . please go back to Boston. Please."

"Because I'm . . . what?" she asked. Wasn't it just this morning that he'd had such trouble uttering the words *blow job* in front of her? What was it that he couldn't say now?

"I'll give you thirty thousand dollars as severance." Ric tried to sweeten the pot. "With that and the money you've got saved, you can go back to school—"

"For the love of God," Annie exploded. "Will you just finish your fricking sentence? Because I'm *what*, Ric? Too tall? Too short? Too smart? Too attached to my dog? A liberal? An athlete? Not feminine enough? *What?*"

"You're gay," he said, and at her total, openmouthed surprise, he asked, "Aren't you?" He answered it himself. "No, you're not. Okay, then. That's . . . great."

"Who told you—" she asked, but he was already answering that one.

"Bruce told me you were, you know, a lesbian," Ric said. "The *son* of a *bitch*."

"Bruce." Her brother.

Ric nodded. "At that party, after your college graduation . . . Mother . . . of God. It was . . . Yeah. It was right after I told him how beautiful I thought you looked and . . . Some detective, huh? I didn't even do the simple math. I'm going to kill him."

"I can't believe you believed him." She, too, was going to kill Bruce next time she saw him.

"Why would he lie?" Again Ric answered his own question. "Because he didn't want me anywhere near you."

"Yeah, but you *believed* him?"

"You were always with what's-her-name," Ric pointed out. "Cindy."

"She was my roommate," Annie told him. "We were friends. We're still friends."

"And then there was Pam," Ric said. "You moved in with Pam."

"Yeah—because I didn't want my best friend from fourth grade to die alone," Annie told him. Which, in the end, she'd failed to do—some friend she'd turned out to be. She had to blink back tears, because she was damned if she was going to cry in front of Ric and have him think she was crying over him.

He didn't say anything. He just looked at her, so there they sat, staring at each other, across his desk.

He finally spoke. "Please go home to Boston."

"Boston's not home anymore," she told him.

He nodded, the muscle jumping in his jaw as he clenched and un-clenched his teeth. "You know you were right about Lillian," he told her. "I was seconds from drilling her."

Annie just looked at him.

"And it's actually kind of funny," he said. "Now that I know that you're not a lesbian, I really don't find you that attractive anymore."

She had to laugh. "Are you done?" she asked. "Because if you are, I'd like to make it clear that I'm not sticking around because I think you're great boyfriend material. On the contrary. I know who you are, Ricky. You find me attractive? Big whoop—because I happen to know that you find every female on the planet attractive. You don't have to lay it on thick to convince me. I've seen that notebook you and Bruce kept during high school—yes, that one," she added at his horrified reaction. "You're as much of a dog as he is. I thought maybe you changed, mellowed with age, I don't know—maybe learned to control your urge to hump everything that moves, but apparently you haven't. Fine. You suck—but I still love you. We're friends—it doesn't really matter to me who you *drill*. Just know that it's not going to be me, okay?"

"That notebook," Ric said. "It was Bruce's. I didn't—"

"There was a list of girls," she reminded him. "Written in your hand-writing. You called it your *Wish List*. It was pretty clear that you weren't aiming really high. I mean, God, Betsy Bouvette was like number two." Slightly rotund, with glasses the size of a car windshield, Betsy had been the president of the Future Microbiologists Club. She'd lived on the same street as Annie and Bruce. "Did the little picture of a soccer goal next to her name mean that you scored?"

Ric just sighed. He shook his head, but it was kind of hard not to notice that he didn't deny it.

"You really suck. She was nice."

"Yeah, she was," Ric agreed. "And apparently you *do* care who I drill. Anyone else I should steer clear of, besides you and Betsy Bouvette? Of course, you could just avoid me altogether by *going* to *Boston*."

"You're going to need my statement when we go to the police," Annie told him. "Plus Burns specifically hired both you and me. He liked me, remember?"

"We're not going to the police," he informed her. "Burns has too many local people in his pocket—I don't want to risk it. We're going to the feds—you can give your statement from out of town."

"Ric—"

"I'll give you forty thousand," he said.

"What if Burns gets suspicious because I've disappeared?" she asked. "What if he decides that you're too much of a risk, because you can't even keep your alleged girlfriend—me—in line? And if you come back with an offer of fifty, I'm going to scream."

"You're worried about me," he clarified.

"Yes," she told him.

"Well, I'm worried about you. You know when Foley hit you, in the limo? And then, when I saw you covered with all that blood . . . ? God damn it, Annie." Ric's voice actually broke. "I don't ever want to be that scared again."

"Me neither," she told him quietly. "Imagine how I felt, knowing that the blood in the car really *was* yours."

He was silent then, for a long time. And when he finally met Annie's eyes again, his face was resigned. "So. You're not going to let me die alone either, huh?"

"Wow," Annie said. "That was really mean."

But Ric's reaction was clearly confused—he wasn't being mean, he was just ignorant. He didn't know. So Annie told him.

"Pam killed herself," she said quietly. "She asked me to help her do it, and I wouldn't, and she . . ." She cleared her throat. "So I'm zero for one when it comes to not letting friends die alone."

"I'm so sorry," he said, clearly stricken. "Annie, I swear, I had no idea."

"Yeah," she said. "I get that."

And there they sat, Ric still looking at her with his heart in his eyes, like he wanted to climb across his desk and pull her into his arms.

But he didn't move, which was good, because it meant that she didn't have to push him away. The last thing she needed tonight was his arms around her. Although she'd no doubt found the perfect antidote to falling under his spell. From now on, whenever she started thinking about how good-looking he was, or how funny, or smart . . . All she had to do was picture him on this very couch, sucking face with Lillian Lavelle.

There was a knock on the door.

"Yeah," Ric called.

"This a good time for an update?" Martell pushed the door open, and Pierre came trotting inside. He jumped up onto the couch next to Annie, settling possessively against her thigh, as Martell dumped the leather bag with Burns's money next to Ric's desk.

"I figure it's better not to leave this out there with Crazy McNightmare," he continued. "And as far as that shit goes . . . ? Bro, you and I need to *talk*."

"Where is she now?" Ric stood up. "You've got to stay with her."

"She was starting to piss me off, so I cuffed her to the conference table. She's not going anywhere."

"Did you make that call?" Ric asked.

"I did," Martell said. "And I was put on hold, for nearly all that time. When they finally came back on the line, I was careful not to mention your name. But as soon as I said that I was the attorney of an individual who'd had a recent altercation with Gordon Burns in Sarasota, Florida, things moved at warp speed. I had a lengthy conversation with one Mr. Cassidy, who seemed very happy that we called. He knew exactly who you were, and probably even what you had for breakfast—the both of you." He included Annie in that. "He didn't say it in so many words, but I'd bet my Aunt LaKisha that you have walked into the middle of a very high-priority FBI investigation. He's coming here, first thing tomorrow, to talk to you."

"Did you warn him about the cars?" Annie asked. "Here and at my place? If Burns is watching us . . ."

"That's actually the biggest news flash of all," Martell told them. "Those cars? They aren't Burns's men. They're the FB freakin' I."

CHAPTER
SEVEN

Robin should have been ecstatic.

Riptide was dominating the buzz at every film festival they attended. His team of wranglers—publicists and agents and God knows who all they were—had just informed him that he'd received an invitation to appear on *Oprah*, the day the movie was set to open wide.

But the best news of all was the mention of that other big O-word—Oscar. The Oscar rumblings were deafening—as was the barrage of phone calls, e-mails, and huge floral arrangements sent to his hotel room from a wide variety of Hollywood actors, directors, and agents, most of whom wouldn't have returned his call last week.

His own agent, Don, had phoned with an offer for a three-picture deal. No way were they going to take it, he'd told Robin. They were going to wait—and they were going to get a whole lot more.

This was what he'd always wanted, what he'd worked for.

So why did he feel like shit?

It was partly Janey's fault. Robin hadn't spoken to his sister or her towering hulk of a husband since he'd left L.A.—since she'd told him she didn't want him watching Billy. Like what? He was going to get plowed, strap the kid on the hood of his Speedster, and drive a hundred miles an hour down the Pacific Coast Highway?

Robin knew his limit. He could hold his liquor. He wasn't even close to being an alcoholic. There were entire stretches of time during which he kept his intake to a meager drink or two with lunch and dinner. Maybe a nightcap after that. But yes, there were also times like these, where his sole purpose was to attend festivals and parties—some in the homes of backers or potential backers. His job was to be eye candy—to stand around and get gaped at and brushed up against, whispered about, photographed, and sometimes even hit on.

It was definitely easier to endure those events with a very solid swerve on.

Plus, it gave him something to do in the morning, when he woke up in yet another hotel room, with nothing on his agenda until the evening's screenings and parties.

He'd lie in bed, nursing his hangover, trying to remember where the hell he was today.

Tonight's party had included an unscheduled interview with a kid writing a story for his college newspaper, a local theater director who wanted to cast him in his upcoming production of *Oliver!*—it was hard not to run screaming from that one—and a seriously cool discussion about *American Hero*, the movie that had put him on the map as an actor, with a group of older women who were clearly movie literate.

That was different. It was amazing how many of these parties he went to, only to find that the attending Richie Riches didn't have any interest in movies beyond the stock market.

As he waited at the bar for another rum and Coke, he saw Dolphina navigating her way through the crowd, toward him.

She was one of his wranglers—the staff hired by HeartBeat Studios to see that he was comfortable, got from point A to point B on time, and yes, behaved himself along the way. Unlike the others, this new girl, Dolphina, didn't even try to pretend that she liked him.

"Time to go," she announced grimly. Gorgeous, with long dark hair, a willowy dancer's body, and the face of an angel, she could outscowl the Grinch. "Limo's waiting, Mr. Chadwick."

Whoa. "I haven't been into the kitchen yet," Robin told her. He'd asked the entire staff to call him Robin—she was the only one who refused.

"Sorry, we're out of time." She intercepted his drink, pushing it back toward the bartender. "He won't be needing that."

"You're going to have to give me at least ten more minutes," Robin said, his patience starting to fray. He could live without the drink, but he *was* going into the kitchen before he left.

Tonight's old ladies had been a giant exception. Usually when he attended one of these things, the people who really wanted to meet him were hard at work in the kitchen, or serving hors d'oeuvres or drinks—one of the reasons he always made a point to hit each and every bar station around the room.

"I've asked—repeatedly," Robin told Dolphina—and who the hell named their daughter after a fish, anyway?—"for a ten-minute warning. If you're unable to get that straight, maybe you should find a different job."

"I knew it." The amount of drama in her voice was usually reserved for Spanish-language soap operas or thirteen-year-olds. "I knew it was just a matter of time before you had me fired."

People were starting to look. Robin leaned closer and lowered his voice. "I'm not going to have you fired. I just want ten minutes to say hello to the serving staff and the caterers. Sign a few autographs. I really don't think that's too much to ask."

She blinked up at him. "That's . . . why you want to go into the kitchen?" she asked, her disbelief heavy in her voice. "To sign autographs?"

"Yeah," he said. "What did you think I would be doing in there?"

"Lining up your next one-night stand," she accused him. "Giving some hardworking girl your key card, so she can meet you later. I know all about you—how you take advantage of women—how all you want is sex—and how easy it is for you to get it."

Oh, angel cake. If you only knew . . .

Dolphina squared her shoulders. "It's not going to be so easy for you anymore. Not on *my* watch."

Robin stared down at her. She really was quite lovely, with those big, dark brown eyes. And up close like this, it was obvious that part of her anger came from her own attraction to him. Oh yes, he'd been around long enough to recognize it in all shapes and forms. It was part of his appeal, his success—and nothing he could really take credit for. He was just the right amount of handsome—not too pretty, nor too rugged either. And his face combined with his generally upbeat, friendly attitude and his willingness to get the party started, had always drawn women to him.

Of course now, with his genuine Navy SEAL-toned body, his attractiveness quotient had spiked off the charts.

A few years back, he would have charmed Dolphina's pants off—literally. In a mere matter of hours, he could have wrapped her around his little finger and taken her to his hotel room. Where she would have soon been naked and willing.

And completely convinced that she would be the one woman who had what it took to tame his inner bad boy. And for a while—a very short while—he'd get just drunk enough to convince himself that she might be what he was searching for so desperately.

A few years back, they'd have had sex. And it would've been disappointing. For both of them.

Sex had become far less disappointing for Robin ever since he'd started having it with men. Which was not to say he'd had a lot of sex with a lot of different men. On the contrary.

For the past few years, he'd had a now-and-then relationship of sorts with a fellow actor named Adam, but Robin had ended it months ago when it became clear that the other man was becoming too attached. Robin didn't love him. Hell, at first he didn't even like the son of a bitch.

But when Adam considered turning down a really great role in a movie, merely because his on-location shoot wouldn't line up with Robin's schedule and they wouldn't see each other for four months . . .

Robin knew it was time to say goodbye.

Since then, he'd had sex exactly zero times—at least as far as he could remember.

It wasn't that he hadn't had the opportunity—because he had.

He just . . . hadn't wanted to start something new with someone else that he didn't and would never love.

His problem was that he was a hopeless romantic. Even though he'd broken a lot of hearts through the years, his intentions had always been good. He'd begun each new relationship with a spark of hope that this would be it—that this would be the one.

His problem now was that he'd already met his "one."

His problem was that the one man Robin wanted to be with—the one person on the planet that he hadn't been able to forget—didn't deserve to be jammed into Robin's closet with him. He didn't deserve a relationship that would have to be kept hidden. He deserved better than that, better than Robin.

So Robin didn't call him. He didn't even e-mail. He just spent a lot of time drinking to stop thinking about him. And thinking about him anyway.

He spent a lot of time *not* having sex.

"Come into the kitchen with me," Robin told Dolphina now, "and I'll show you the best part of being a movie star."

She followed him warily, still unconvinced.

It happened the way it usually always did—at least at parties outside of Hollywood. As soon as he opened the kitchen door, people started to laugh and even scream. His arms were almost immediately filled with two hundred pounds of excited pastry chef.

There were about twenty apron-clad women and three men in the kitchen. He shook hands with them all. He signed aprons, signed menus, signed arms. He gave them his full attention, listening as they spoke, laughing and chatting with them.

Until Dolphina tapped him on the shoulder. "We should find the host and hostess—say good night."

He let her drag him away, back down the hall, toward the room where the so-called real party was still going strong.

"It sort of makes up for it," Robin told Dolphina. "You know, the sleeping alone."

She was looking at him now—really looking, and for one heart-stopping moment, Robin was afraid that she understood the subtext of what he'd just told her. But she didn't say more than "I'm sorry" as she forced a smile, a genuine apology in her eyes.

And no, she just wanted to comfort him. By going back to his room with him and rubbing her naked body against his—an experience intended to be life altering and extraordinarily special, which would, she no doubt believed, bind them together for the rest of their lives.

And if she were a man named Jules Cassidy, she damn well might have been right.

"Poor me," Robin said as he turned to wave goodbye to the still-hyperventilating pastry chef, who stood watching him go from the kitchen door, adoration in her eyes. "Poor, pitiful, movie-star me."

Something wasn't right.

Ric sat behind his desk, listening as Martell recounted his phone conversation with the FBI agent.

"This Cassidy guy said he'd take care of the overabundance of surveillance vehicles," Martell told Annie and Ric. "He apologized if they drew too much attention—he's very aware of how dangerous Burns can be."

No kidding. Ric looked pointedly at Annie, but she purposely gave Martell her full attention.

"He said to open up the office as usual," Martell told them. "Just . . . have a regular day. He expects to get here sometime in the early afternoon—which is great because I'm available then, too. You know, as your attorney."

Wait a minute. Now something *really* wasn't right. What was that sound he'd just heard? Over on the couch, next to Annie, Pierre lifted his little mutant head, ears up, and looked over at Ric.

Martell kept going. "I've got a court appearance first thing this morning, but I should be back by then. If I'm not, don't start without—"

"Wait a minute. Shhh." Ric quieted his friend, and sure enough, from out in the driveway came the sound of a car being started. "Damn it!" He slapped his forehead. "Handcuffs!"

He bolted from his office, and sure enough, the conference room was empty.

"How the hell . . . ?" Martell couldn't believe it. "I locked her up—"

"With her own handcuffs," Ric finished for him. "The ones on Annie's desk, right?"

"Yeah. Those were . . . ?"

"Hers." And her keys were in her coat pocket. Ric threw open the door, and sure enough, Lillian was in her car, backing out of the drive. She floored it when she saw him, screeching to a stop as she pulled out onto the street. "Annie, give me your keys." He caught the ring that she tossed to him, and ran for Annie's car, which was parked on the street, facing the right direction for a hot pursuit. "Martell, stay with Annie," he shouted. "Get inside, lock the door."

Boom. Crash!

Shit! The windshield of Annie's car had shattered.

Lillian was shooting at them. "Get down!" Ric shouted, praying that Martell would grab Annie and take her to the floor.

Boom. Her second shot took out the back windshield of Martell's car with an equally resounding crash.

Boom. His front office window exploded as, with a squeal of tires, Lillian sped away.

Where was the legion of dark sedans when he needed them? Apparently Cassidy had done his job a little too well, and sent them all home.

All over the neighborhood, dogs were barking and lights were going on. But no men in dark suits and sunglasses jumped out from behind the bushes to pursue the woman who, for the second time in one day, had unloaded a .44 in Ric and Annie's direction.

"Ric!" That was Martell, shouting from inside the house. Martell, not Annie.

He'd more than expected her to blast out of the door, ready to come to his rescue, or at least make sure that he was okay.

"Ric, you all right?" Martell shouted again.

He raced back to the house, and threw open the door.

For a moment, his heart stopped, because Annie and Martell were on the floor, directly between the broken window and the crater in the plaster wall where the bullet had struck. Martell was kneeling over Annie, and the tension in his body language scared the hell out of Ric.

"Just stay down," Martell was telling her, but she struggled even harder to sit up when she saw Ric.

"Are you all right?" Ric asked it at the same time she did, and answered in unison, too. "Yeah."

There was no blood. Not on her, not anywhere.

"She hit her head," Martell told him. "That was my fault, too. I tackled her. We landed pretty hard."

Annie looked up at the hole in the wall. "I think you probably saved my life," she said.

"Man, I am *so* sorry." Martell's eyes were filled with self-recrimination. "I assumed the handcuffs were—"

"It's not your fault," Ric told him. "I should have realized."

Annie winced as she touched the back of her head, using her other hand to drag up the top of that sarong Burns had given her.

"I'll get some ice," Martell said, standing up. They'd been far enough away from the window to not have glass all over them. That, at least, was a plus.

"Go upstairs," Ric told him. "Into my apartment. In my freezer. There's a bag of frozen peas."

"What I could really use are some clothes that actually stay on," Annie called to Martell, who was already heading up the stairs. "Particularly before the police get here."

And, indeed, there were sirens in the distance, getting louder.

"Damn it," Ric said. He raised his voice so Martell could hear him, too. "Okay, here's the story we give to the locals . . ."

"She told me her name was Lillian Lavelle. I have a copy of her driver's license, and no, now it doesn't surprise me at all that it was a fake. At the time it never occurred to me to check to see if she was who she said she was." Ric told the story for what had to be the tenth time to police detective Bobby Donofrio. "It was a simple assignment. Locate the whereabouts of a friend of her daughter—the only name she had was Brenda, no last name, which was not a lot to go on. But hey, if she wanted to pay . . . ? Like I said, I didn't find the friend—I'm not sure she existed."

Naturally Bobby D was tonight's detective on duty. Martell inwardly shook his head at Ric's bad luck. This entire evening had to be one of the most bullfuck-filled of his friend's entire life. Although why the boy genius would mess around with Bizarrina McAxmurderess when Annie was so clearly in the on-deck circle . . . He could *not* figure that one out.

And okay, yeah, the lingerie thing had a certain appeal. And the woman was put together in a very yes-there-is-a-God way. But the waves of crazy coming off of her were so strong, they were visible to the human eye. That kind of shit was an instant soft-on in Martell's book.

Of course, Ricky had proved time and again that, as far as intimate relationships went, he sure knew how to choose 'em.

His last girlfriend was some little blond Spanish teacher from Ohio. Yes, children, you heard that right. Oh. Hi. Oh. As in, she lived a thousand miles away. Apparently she enjoyed conjugating her verbs with Enrrrique, so she flew down for the weekend every few months or so. As for Ric, Martell suspected that, for him, the relationship was similar in nature to those of women who hooked up with lifers in prison. Ricky had the illusion of having a girlfriend, with relatively no-strings if not quite regular sex, without any of the day-to-day work.

Of course, it *was* possible that Ric had really liked the girl. When she sent him that Dear John e-mail, he'd been pissed enough to tell Martell about it.

Beeyotch actually wrote to tell him that she was going to be coming down to Sarasota with her brand-new fiancé, Vern—just like that. No *Hello, how are you? I've been thinking hard lately and fear we've grown apart . . .*

Just *Vern's kind of old-fashioned,* and *Would Ric please get his things out of Daddy's waterfront condo before she arrived?* She didn't want to freak ol' Vern out.

Of course, Ric being Ric, he didn't plaster the walls of the place with poster-size reprints of the two of them doing the musicless mambo. He just quietly got his bathing suit and what-all, and left the key with the super.

And then didn't bother to tell anyone that he and Blondie broke up—at least no one besides Martell.

As the clock on Annie's desk flipped from 5:11 to 5:12 A.M., as this marathon of a night refused to end, Ric now expounded to Detective Dickhead that his relationship with Lillian Lavelle had gone from business to very personal—as was often the case with Ric and beautiful women. Next thing he knew, she showed up with a gun and started shooting at him.

Both statements were mostly true—he just left out the parts about her gunning for Gordie Burns Junior, and her wanting to get away so that she could try to shoot Gordie again.

The woman was obsessed, armed, and dangerous. She hadn't shot at

Ric to kill him—merely to keep him from chasing her. Still, that shot she'd fired through the office window could've left someone very dead.

"I don't know," Ric said now in response to Donofrio's question about motive. No way was he going to bring Gordie's name into this conversation with the locals. He'd give that info only to the FBI.

As Martell watched, Ric glanced over at Annie, who was curled up with her poodle in the corner of the sofa, sipping a cup of some kind of freaky herbal tea, bag of frozen peas still pressed against her head. She had on one of Ric's T-shirts—advertising the New Orleans Jazz Festival—and a pair of his jeans. Truth be told, the entire ensemble had never before looked quite so good.

"Maybe Lillian was jealous," Ric continued. "Although I never claimed to be exclusive."

Martell sat down next to Annie. "Do me a favor and give Ricky an I-can't-wait-till-this-asshole-leaves-so-I-can-do-you look."

She didn't. She chose, instead, to give Martell an evil eye of withering disbelief.

"No," Martell said quietly. "Come on. It'll drive Donofrio crazy. This is the guy Ric threw against the wall, by the way, the day he quit the force."

"Really?" That got her interest. She looked over at the heavy-set police detective. "It's hard to imagine Ric throwing anyone against a wall." She laughed, disgusted. "It's hard to imagine him with Lillian, even after I saw it with my own eyes. He's good at presenting this nice-guy image—a real Boy Scout. He's so laid-back and charming, and he pretends to listen when you talk. He's funny, and . . . a total jerk. As least as far as women are concerned. He was like that in high school, too."

"No shit?" Martell looked over at Ric, too. "Because, I've known him for years, and he's never been a player. I should know because I'm a player. Stay away from me. I *will* break your heart."

She laughed, and damn. Even exhausted, with her head clearly still hurting, she lit up the room. "Thanks for the tip, Don Juan."

"Ric had this one girlfriend—Carrie Stark. They were together for four years," Martell told her. "It seemed really serious—at least from Ric's end."

"What happened?" Annie asked.

"She got back with an ex," he said. "Ric even went to the wedding. When I asked him, you know, what he was thinking, he told me he was happy for her—that he always knew he was her second choice—that he was glad she finally got what she really wanted." He shook his head. "I don't know. If I'm going to spend four long years with just one woman, it's going to be someone I can't live without. And I'm going to be weeping and clinging to her legs as she tries to walk away. I'm going to be screaming *don't leave me*—not dancing at her wedding."

Annie was looking over at Ric again. "Do you know his current girlfriend—which really gives the whole thing with Lillian an even higher ick rating. God."

"You mean . . . Miss Ohio?"

"I don't know her name," Annie admitted. "My brother said Ric was seeing some teacher, yeah, I think she's from Ohio."

"They were over months ago," Martell told her.

"Really," Annie said.

"It's possible Ric didn't tell Bruce," Martell suggested. "I think his own father still thinks he's seeing this girl."

"Really," Annie said again.

Pierre lifted his head from her thigh. He had this way of looking at Annie with pure adoration, as if she were the High Priestess of Alpo.

Probably because she didn't talk down to him.

"Hi," she told him now. "What do you need?"

The dog stood up. Stretched. Looked at her expectantly.

"You need to go out," Annie concluded, giving him a kiss on the top of his ugly little head. "Good boy." She put her mug on the end table, the pack of frozen peas beside it, and stood up. "Let's go."

Ric looked over at them. "Where are you—"

"Nature calls," she said, gesturing to Pierre, who was already waiting by the door.

Ric looked pointedly at Martell.

"Hey, I know, maybe I'll go, too," he said, pushing himself to his feet.

Dawn was streaking the sky as he joined Annie and Pierre out on the lawn in front of Ric's building. In the light, the broken car windshields—the front of Annie's car and the back of Martell's—along with the shattered office window, made the place look like something of a war zone.

"What was it the FBI agent said?" Annie mused. *"Just have a regular day."*

Martell nodded slowly as he surveyed the mess. "So far so good."

CHAPTER
EIGHT

Jules sat at Ric Alvarado's conference table, listening as the former police detective filled him in on the events of the past few days.

He made notes on a legal pad, to help him keep the cast of characters straight. Lillian Lavelle, Brenda Quinn, Gordon Burns and his son Gordie Junior. A henchman named Foley, the doctor—a local surgeon—who wouldn't reveal his name, but whom the FBI had already identified as one Dr. Kyle Givens.

Ric sat across the table from Jules, next to his gal Friday, a freshly pretty young woman named Annie Dugan, and his frowning lawyer, another former Sarasota cop named Martell Griffin.

Annie was obviously intelligent, and extremely capable-looking—no fragile flower she—but, as Ric emphasized for about the twelfth time, she was a complete novice in terms of law enforcement experience. She hadn't even so much as held a handgun, let alone fired one.

Her response to that? So teach me.

She and Alvarado had been friends for years. That much had been clear from the moment Jules walked in. They finished each other's sentences and obviously exchanged boatloads of information with the briefest of eye contact.

Jules would've guessed that they were romantically involved as well—until Ric told him about Lillian Lavelle's seduction attempt, and their decision to keep Burns's name out of the police report by identifying Lavelle not as a woman looking to kill Gordon Burns's son, but as one of Ric's many jilted lovers.

At that point in the tale, Griffin kind of casually leaned over and draped his arm around the back of Annie's chair. What was *that* about? Ric noticed it, too, giving Griffin a look that Jules couldn't quite read. Griffin's response was an extremely nonsubtle *So?*

Big and black, with his shaved head gleaming, Martell Griffin was dangerous-looking in spite of—or maybe because of—his nicely tailored suit.

The two men were longtime friends as well—the info in Jules's report had them working together in the Sarasota Police Department for quite a few years. Martell left first, to get his law degree. Ric had resigned more recently, after a deadly shoot-out with a teenager, in which the teen had not survived.

It was interesting, actually, to watch just how protective both men were of Annie. It was no accident that she was sitting in between them.

And when she chimed in with the fact that Gordon Burns had thought she'd be good girlfriend material for his crazy-ass psycho of a son, the tension level of both men went through the roof.

Jules half expected Annie's little dog to start growling, too, from his spot on the floor, next to Jules's feet. And *that* was apparently something of an aberration—the fact that Pierre was so taken with Jules. Apparently the dog didn't bond like this with everyone.

It was something of a dubious honor, due to Pierre's not quite daisy-fresh dog-breath.

Ric wrapped up his story by telling Jules that Gordon Burns wanted to hire Ric—and Annie, she'd chimed in—to befriend and protect Gordie Junior. Oh, yeah, and spy on him, too. Of course, if Gordie found out about the spying part, he'd be pissed.

And when he got pissed, he got violent. And when he got violent, people disappeared.

Talk about an impossible—and dangerous—job. One that it was clear Ric didn't want Annie to have any part of.

Of course, there was also Lillian Lavelle. She was out there, a loose cannon, still gunning—literally—for Gordie Junior. Anyone near him was in danger of being caught in her apparently less-than-careful cross fire.

Jules immediately called Yashi and set the wheels in motion for the FBI to find Lillian Lavelle first.

And then it was his turn to talk.

"As you've probably figured out," Jules told them, choosing his words carefully, "the FBI's been investigating Gordon Burns for quite some time. We believe his organization is involved in smuggling al Qaeda operatives into the United States." No doubt about it, he now had their full and undivided attention. "We believe that sometime soon, Burns will receive a 'shipment' that will contain a high-ranking terrorist—Yazid al-Rashid al-Hasan—whom we do not want inside our borders. But we don't just want to keep him out—we want him in custody. We're currently at a serious disadvantage, because our agent inside Burns Point, who was monitoring the situation, has disappeared."

He took a photo from his briefcase and slid it across the table to Ric and Annie.

"Her name is Peggy—Margaret—Ryan," Jules told them, and they both looked at the picture. "She was working at Burns Point as a housekeeping assistant."

Ric picked it up, looking at it even more closely. But he shook his head as he passed it to Annie. "I didn't see her last night. Did you?"

Annie shook her head, too.

"The only female servant I saw was an older woman," Ric told Jules. "Puerto Rican. Graying hair. Her name was Maria."

"That's right," Annie agreed. "Maria. I didn't see any other women, either. I'm sorry."

It was funny, actually, how much Jules had hoped that one or the other of them would look at the photo and say, *Hey, I saw her there. She was serving drinks out by the pool. She's fine—definitely healthy and very much alive.*

He put the photo away—and laid everything else out on the table. "You're currently my best way in," he told Ric, told them. "Into Burns Point, into Burns's organization. I know it's dangerous, and, yes, as you've said, Annie's got no experience, but—"

"I'm up for it," she said. "I want to help. I'll do whatever I can."

Ric was not happy. "Great, you can go be Gordie's new girlfriend. Christ, Annie."

She looked at him in a way that only an old friend could, to convey her total conviction that he was an idiot. "Like *that* would work. Since when have *you* ever gone out with a woman that your father wanted you to date?"

"I don't want you near either of them. Gordie or his father." Ric turned to Jules. "If we do this, how will you ensure Annie's safety?"

And wasn't *that* the million-dollar question? Jules met Ric's eyes and gave him an honest answer. "I can't."

Ric laughed. "Well, that's great."

"What, you want me to bullshit you?" Jules asked. "I'm not going to do that. This is a highly dangerous situation, and I can't ensure your safety any more than I could Peggy Ryan's. But my hope is to go in with you—provide backup by being as close at hand as possible."

"Go in how?" Ric asked. He was not happy, but Jules had read him right and won some serious points by being point-blank honest.

"The strategy I've chosen is to have you introduce me to Burns as a silent partner in Alvarado Private Investigations," Jules told him. They were working right now on obtaining Gordon Burns's social calendar—the idea was to have Ric, Annie, and Jules "accidentally" run into Burns in a social setting. "The hope is to pique his interest by telling him that I've made some lucrative investments in movies as well, and that I've even got producer credit for several upcoming big-name films. My team is building me a page on the imdb—the Internet Movie Database—as we speak. Burns is a huge movie fan—"

"We know," Ric said.

"Our story will be that you and I met through your father," Jules told him.

"Oh, good," Martell said, who was far less impressed by everything Jules had said, "let's bring Ric's father into this *highly dangerous situation, too.*"

"—who did the score for one of my soon-to-be-released films," Jules continued. "We're making a webpage for that, too. And we *won't* actually be bringing your father into it, although if we did, he'd probably be the first—after Annie—to volunteer to help."

"Oh yeah," Martell was indignant. "I'm sure you know Teo Alvarado real well."

"I'm a fan of his music," Jules said. "I know he volunteered to serve in Vietnam. I know he risked a lot to come to Florida from Cuba, back before you were born." He also knew that Karen Valdez, of Valdez Imports out of Miami, had been disowned by her family when she married Ric's father. Risk taking ran in both sides of Ric's family. He looked from Ric to Annie and back. "Some things are worth the risk."

"I agree," Annie said, but the look in Ric's eyes was pure *easy for you to say—what are you risking?*

"We'll try to phase Annie out as soon as possible," Jules tried to reassure him, "but at this point it sounds as if she's a major part of the reason Burns wants to establish a business relationship with you. We'll have to play it by ear. If it looks as if he won't want anything to do with you if you break up"—that was the cover they'd already put into place, that Ric and Annie were more than business associates—"then we're going to need to keep her around."

"I should also point out that this assignment could take a great deal of time," Jules continued. "Yes, we believe al-Hasan will be entering the U.S. in the near future. But plans change—particularly when an FBI agent disappears. If Peggy Ryan was compromised, if her identity as a federal agent was discovered, the entire operation may have been temporarily shut down, and al-Hasan's mission delayed. It could take months. Or longer." His cell phone was vibrating in his pocket. It stopped, but then started shaking again, so he took it out. It was Yashi. "I'm sorry, I have to take this call."

Jules stood up and left the room as he punched his phone on. "Yeah, Yash." He closed the conference-room door behind him—actually behind Pierre, who'd followed him into the outer office.

"Hang on a sec, sir," Yashi said, and put Jules on hold.

The dog was standing there, looking at him expectantly, so he crouched down next to it and scratched its endearingly silly ears.

Yashi, Deb, and George had all flown down with him, from D.C. They'd spent the afternoon wooing the locals at the Sarasota FBI office—making sure they'd get the computers, telephones, fax machines, desks, and, yes, the full cooperation that they'd need.

Feelings often got ruffled when higher-ranking agents from D.C. swooped in to take control of an ongoing investigation.

Jules would have been over at the local office himself, singing and dancing his way into their hearts if he had to—had it not been so vital to move forward as quickly as possible with this new connection to Gordon Burns.

"Sorry about that." Yashi apologized as he came back on the line. "Got some info re Burns's schedule," he told Jules, sounding, as always, as if he were about to fall asleep. "Thought you'd like it ASAP," he said about as slowly as was humanly possible.

"Yes, I would," Jules confirmed, standing up and moving into Ric's office to better hear him. It sounded as if Ric, Martell, and Annie were arguing in the conference room. Something about *The Odd Couple*?

"Sarasota Film Festival starts tonight," Yashi reported as Pierre followed Jules over to the couch and jumped up onto it. He stood there, looking at Jules, his head cocked. So Jules sat down, and the dog plopped next to him, his head on his leg. "Burns is attending an opening-night star-studded extravaganza at the Bijou Café—I'm reading this right out of something called the Pelican Press. Tickets are five hundred bucks a pop, yowser, guess *I* won't be attending—all proceeds going to support the festival. Open bar courtesy of . . . drumroll please . . . Gordon Burns."

"Get me tickets," Jules said, scrunching Pierre's ears.

"Consider it done," Yashi told him. "So what are you going to wear, boss? And do you think Tom and Katie'll be there?"

Jules laughed, because Yashi, with his perpetually bored-sounding, nearly monotone delivery was the furthest thing from a gushing fan that he'd ever heard. But then he stopped laughing. Because what if . . . ? No. No way. Robin Chadwick didn't have a new film out. Did he?

And *that* was the dead last thing he should've been worrying about.

"We'll need electronics." Jules refocused. "Mics. Minicams. A surveillance van—"

"Deb and George are already on it," Yashi reported. "I'm handling the, uh, important stuff."

Jules had worked with Yashi before. He was, no doubt, printing out local take-out menus and MapQuesting every Starbucks within city limits. "What time does this thing start tonight?" he asked.

"Twenty hundred," Yashi said—military-speak for eight o'clock. "You got the Scooby Gang on our side?"

"Yeah," Jules said. "They're in." He looked down at the little dog, who was leaning against his leg, gazing up at him lovingly. "Including Scooby."

"As your attorney," Martell said, after Jules Cassidy left the room, "I can't recommend that you do this. No offense to the little FBI guy, but *he's* your backup? What's he gonna do, bite Burns on the ankle?"

"I like him," Annie said. And Pierre obviously did, too, the little traitor. She stretched in her seat. God, but she was exhausted.

"I like him, too, but he's so . . ." Martell searched for the word.

"Gay?" Ric supplied.

Annie looked at him in scathing disbelief.

"What?" he said. "I'm not saying there's anything wrong with it. I'm just saying that he sets my . . . what's it called—gaydar clacking. That's all."

"No, he's not exactly gay," Martell mused. "More like . . . precise."

"The same way I set it off?" Annie asked Ric.

"But it's not like he's fussy," Martell continued, "like Felix on *The Odd Couple*. More like . . . careful. A brainiac instead of an ass-kicker, but maybe that's a good thing." He frowned at Annie as what she'd said finally penetrated. "The same way *what*?"

She turned to him. "Bruce told Ric that I was gay. And he believed him."

Martell laughed. "No way." He looked from Ric to Annie and back. "Really?"

"Yes really," she confirmed. "And by the way—Felix? Totally gay."

"Dude was married," Martell pointed out.

"Yeah, and his wife threw him out because *she* at least figured out that he was totally gay."

"Can we please talk about our potential impending deaths?" Ric implored.

"You know . . ." Martell leaned closer to Annie. "If you're into women, I have this friend, Brandi? And I'm thinking if you and she and I all got together—"

"Stop," Ric said. He sounded annoyed.

"Martell's kidding," Annie told him.

"About the three-way," Ric said. "But he's moving in on you. I see him—I'm watching him—and he's moving in." He looked at Martell. "So just fucking stop."

"Boy Scout dropped the F-bomb," Martell whispered to Annie.

She nodded. She'd heard. Ric didn't like to say that word in front of women, which was kind of funny, considering how much he apparently liked doing it, as a verb, with them.

"This is what I mean." Ric bit off each word, his mouth a grim line. Was it possible that he was actually jealous? After last night's sex show starring Lillian Lavelle and her giant boobs?

"Although, okay. Fine," Ric continued. "Maybe we can create a triple-win scenario." He looked past Annie to Martell. "You want her? You got her—but it's got to be for as long as this investigation lasts, and I know even a week is long for you. But I'll give you fifty thousand dollars to help you suffer through."

"Oh, this is nice," Annie exhaled. "I knew I hadn't seen the last of that bribe."

"It's not a bribe, it's payment." Ric's volume increased. "You can take her to Europe, take her on a cruise—I don't care—just *take* her. Get her out of here. Cuff her and throw a bag over her head if you need to—just fucking keep her fucking safe."

In the silence that immediately followed Ric's outburst, Annie realized that the FBI agent had opened the conference-room door and was standing there—looking as if he wished he'd waited outside.

But no way was Annie going to let Ric's crap go. "You have a hell of a lot of nerve," she lit into him. "Offering to pay Martell to *kidnap* me in front of a federal agent?"

"Bad time to come back in," Cassidy decided, starting to back out the door.

Martell stood up. "I was just going to go out, too, give 'em a little space—"

But Annie didn't want space. She didn't want to sit here with Ric and rehash everything they'd already said last night. They were both running on empty—they'd had about two hours of sleep this morning, after the police had finally left and before the various window- and windshield-replacement trucks had arrived.

"I'm doing this," she told him.

Ric nodded. "I know. I'm sorry. I'm . . ." He rubbed his forehead, pressed the bridge of his nose. Annie could relate. She had one hell of a headache, too. "Sorry," he repeated. He turned to Jules. "Here are my terms. She's never alone. If she's not with me, she's with Martell or you. Or one of your other agents, but I want to meet them first."

Jules sat back down at the table. "Is your apartment big enough for a roommate?" he asked Annie, taking his pad out of his briefcase, so he could make notes.

"No." Ric answered for her.

"Yeah, actually it is," Annie said, but Ric wasn't listening.

"She moves in here," he told Jules. "That's nonnegotiable."

"Do you know how much I hate it when you talk over me?" Annie asked.

Ric didn't even bother to look at her. "This is a deal I'm making with Cassidy. It's his job to figure out how to make you comply. I want to be compensated appropriately for our time," he told the FBI agent, "both Annie and me. And Martell, too, if we need him. I don't know what the going rate is for consultants or contractors or whatever you call this, but I'll check it out and let you know."

"I'll check as well."

"I'm not looking to get rich here," Ric stressed. "Just fairly compensated."

"I understand."

"I want Annie to go to a firing range sometime in the very near future. I want her to get a look—up close—at the weapons that Burns and his men will probably use to shoot her."

That was meant to scare her, but Annie didn't have to protest. Jules did it for her. He looked up at Ric. "We're going to do our best to prevent anyone from—"

"Yeah, and how'd your best work out for Peggy Ryan?" Ric countered.

The mention of the missing agent was clearly a sore spot for the FBI agent. The two men stared at each other for several long seconds before Jules answered. "Not well," he admitted. He looked back down at his list of Ric's demands. "What else?"

Ric glanced at her. "I want Annie to be able to walk away at any point in this investigation. Just pack up and leave, if she wants to."

Jules nodded.

"And witness protection, if necessary. Regardless of whether or not Burns is convicted. Regardless of whether or not he's even charged, or whether she stays through to the end. Monetary compensation in the event of death. A guarantee of covered medical and physical therapy expenses in the event of injury."

"You want health insurance," Jules concluded. "Where do you think you are, Canada?"

It was clearly a joke, but Ric didn't laugh. "I want a guarantee of covered—" he started again.

"Thank you," Jules cut him off. "I got it."

"That's it," Ric said.

The FBI agent looked at the list, reading through it again, flipping back a page to where his notes started. When he was finally done, he looked up at Annie. "Is this all right with you?"

She nodded.

"Good," he said. "Because we start tonight."

CHAPTER
NINE

Robin was dressed and pouring himself the evening's first drink when someone knocked on his hotel-room door.

It probably wasn't Dolphina or another of his handlers—there was still a solid hour before he had to leave for . . . whatever event was happening tonight.

Well, maybe it was Dolphina, who'd recently decided she no longer hated him and that she'd rather be his mother. Over the past few days, she'd made sure he ate right, found time to exercise, and if he drank a little too much, she got him safely back to his room—all without ending up in his bed.

Although, that might no longer be true. Last night he'd been particularly shit-faced, and as he'd stumbled over the seam between the suite's living-room tile and the bedroom carpeting, she'd caught him and kept him from breaking his nose. He'd repaid her by dragging her back with him onto his bed, because she was not unattractive, and when he got skunked, sex of any kind seemed better than no sex at all.

As so often was the case with him when he drank too much, that was where his memory went from murky to dark.

So yes, it was probably Dolphina a-knockin' on his door. She knocked again—louder this time.

Robin looked through the fish-eyed lens of the peephole and . . .

Holy dancing Jesus. He almost dropped his drink. He looked again.

He took off the chain and opened the door, and yes, it definitely was Jules Cassidy standing in the hotel corridor.

Dressed in eveningwear similar to the tuxedo that Robin himself had on.

Other than the tux, Jules hadn't changed at all in the past few years. Same short dark hair, same trim, compact body, same handsome face, same warm brown eyes.

Same molten attraction in those eyes that didn't fade even when he smiled.

The man had a ridiculously sweet smile, even when it was tentative, as it was now.

"Sorry to surprise you," Jules said. "I called your cell, but you didn't pick up."

Robin didn't answer. He couldn't. He no longer spoke English—it had been flabbergasted out of him. Instead, he stepped back and gestured for Jules to come inside.

Jules, of course, hesitated. "I was actually thinking we could go down to the bar."

A stiff drink would be great right about now. But then Robin realized he was holding a glass of rum in his hand. He hadn't yet added the Coke, but what the hell. He took a healthy sip, and his ability to speak returned. "I'll be mobbed. Down there. I can't just go to a bar anymore. Well, I can, if I grunge up, but not on the opening night of a festival like this."

Jules nodded. "I should've realized. I'm sorry, I'm . . . Congratulations. I've heard great things about the movie and . . . Your career's really . . . Congratulations."

He was as flustered as Robin was. Maybe even more so. And he'd known who was going to be on the other side of the door before it had opened.

"Please come in," Robin managed.

Jules looked past him and into the suite. It was huge—and set up as a living room. Sofa and chairs, and even a full-size dining table. No king-size bed for them to have to pretend not to notice. That was on the other side of French doors that Robin kept tightly shut, mostly due to the fact that he was a slob.

"Thanks," Jules said as he came inside, as Robin shut the door behind him, putting the chain back on—which Jules noticed. Of course, FBI agents tended to notice everything.

But God, he still smelled exactly the same. And suddenly Robin went from just barely able to speak to unable to shut the fuck up. "Jesus, I've missed you," came spewing out just as Jules said, "I'm here on business."

And that wasn't just disappointing, it was also awkward as shit.

"I guess that means you don't need a drink." Robin filled the silence with social noise as he crossed to the bar, desperate for a refill. "How about a soda? Water? Juice?"

"I'm fine." Of course, Jules being Jules, he was unable to ignore difficult things. He closed his eyes briefly. "So, okay, I'm not fine. I'm as thrown by this as you are, and I'm sorry that I came up here because seeing you is . . . You look good. You look . . . too good. So I should just say what I came to say, so I can leave."

No doubt about it, this elephant-size attraction they once shared hadn't died a natural death over the past careful years of zero contact. It was here in the room with them, looming large, as if absolutely no time had passed.

Except it had. A lot of time. "Am I allowed to ask how you are?" Robin found himself a bigger glass. "How you've been, what you've been up to?" He glanced over to where Jules was standing, still over by the door. "You still seeing what's-his-name, the Marine?"

"Ben." Jules supplied the man's name, but no other information. "Look, I'm going to the party tonight—the same party you are. I checked on the Internet and saw you were in town and . . . I'm here because I didn't want to do this in public—see you for the first time after so long. Especially not while I'm working undercover."

"You're undercover," Robin repeated, bringing his drink over to the leather sofa. He'd first met Jules nearly two years earlier, when the FBI agent was part of a team protecting Robin's sister. Janey had received death threats when they were filming *American Hero*, her award-winning biopic that outed a popular World War II hero. It was Robin's portrayal of the gay war hero that had first put him on Hollywood's map.

The death threats had turned out to be real, and people had gotten shot. Including Robin.

A woman—one of the bodyguards' wives—had actually died.

"Undercover doing what?" Robin asked as he sat down.

"My job," Jules told him.

No shit, Sherlock. "How dangerous is it this time? Is it—"

"I need you to pretend you don't know me," Jules interrupted. "I'm using a different name, but . . . Just keep your distance. Please. You have no reason to approach me, so . . . Don't."

"So on a scale from one to ten, where one is *not at all*, and ten is *very*, it's a, what? Eight? Nine?" Robin sipped his drink, trying to act as if the idea of Jules putting his life on the line didn't make him want to throw up. Of course, it wasn't as if Jules had spent the past few years sitting behind a desk, out of harm's way. In fact, Cosmo had told him—apparently the Spec Ops and Intel communities were closely knit—that Jules had been badly injured not too long ago. That was how he'd met Ben-the-Marine—in the sick bay of an aircraft carrier after helping to save the world.

Again.

"I'll be there with several other people," Jules told him now. "Stay far away from them, too. Plus, there's a local man? Gordon Burns. He's got a son, Gordie Junior. Stay away from both of them."

When Jules was dealing with dangerous people, he was one serious son of a bitch. And right now his grimness level was off the scale.

"What have they done?" Robin asked. "Burns and son."

Jules shook his head. "I've already told you too much."

"What's the name you're using?"

Jules was getting pissed, but he wasn't as good as Robin was at disguising it. His exasperation leaked out of him. Or maybe he just wasn't trying to hide it.

"I'm curious. Do you go for something simple? Bob Smith? John Jones?" Robin said, because it was easier to talk about this than admit the truth—that if he could, he'd go back in time to that day when he'd let Jules walk out of his life. Because despite what Jules had said, he was not here merely on business. No. He was here because he couldn't stay away. "Is it just a different name? Or do you create a whole backstory and character—"

"Don't fuck this up for me, Robin. If you talk about this, with anyone . . ."

"I won't," Robin said. "I just—"

"Mine's not the only life that'll be in danger," Jules finished. "It's a ten, okay?"

Jesus. Robin had to swallow hard past the fear that was now securely lodged in his throat. "That's pretty intense," he said. "Are you sure you didn't come here as some kind of . . . doomed man's final wish?"

Jules laughed. "Yeah, I don't think so."

But when Robin stood up, he left his cool demeanor, his amusement, his act of calm nonchalance, his entire lifetime-perfected facade behind him on the sofa, and Jules's smile faded.

"You didn't ask me how I was," Robin said quietly. "Sure, you've probably seen me in the tabloids. Now I'm dating Kristen Bell. Now I'm a threat to Sarah Michelle's marriage. Now I'm clubbing with Susie

McCoy. I would've at least expected something like *Gee, Robin, are you still trying to fool yourself into believing that you're relentlessly hetero?*" He answered his own question. "No. No, I'm not."

The look on Jules's face was one that Robin knew he would remember for the rest of his life. Wariness. Hope and defeat. Anger and yearning and weary despair. Hunger.

Hunger. God, yes. Robin knew it was reflected on his own face, in the way he was standing and breathing. It was in his voice as he spoke. "I think I probably said it best when I said, *Jesus, I've missed you.*"

Jules looked over at the door, but he didn't move. He just let Robin come closer. And closer. "I have to go."

"Don't," Robin said. "Stay. We'll both just . . . skip the party."

"I can't." But he wanted to. One thing about Jules, he wasn't afraid to let people know what he was feeling. When he wanted to hide it, he could, but when he didn't . . . There it was. Of course it was still mixed with that despair. Disappointment. Hurt. Mistrust. Doubt.

"Duty calls, huh?" Robin said. All he had to do was keep talking, keep this conversation going. As soon as he got close enough to touch him, they would both just go up in flames.

"Yeah," Jules said. "That one's pretty high on my list of, oh, about five thousand reasons why I can't do this."

"You know, I'm supposed to mingle. Tonight. The festival crew will be introducing me to people. I assume you don't want me to scream and run away if we come face-to-face." Like they were right now.

Face.

To.

Face.

Jules was breathing hard, as if he'd just sprinted up twelve flights of stairs, as if his heart were pounding the way Robin's was.

As if he, too, were remembering the too few times they'd taken their single-minded attraction out for a stroll and kissed.

Only kissed. Because at the time Robin had still been uncertain about his sexuality. Jules had been flatly honest about not wanting to be part of what he called Robin's science experiment.

After two years, the experiments were over. And the results were in.

America's hottest new sex symbol and Hollywood's freshest young action-adventure star, Robin Chadwick, was undeniably gay.

A mere half a dozen people on the entire planet knew this career-flattening fact, Jules being one of them.

Of course, Jules had known the truth before Robin had.

Jules, whom Robin had fallen in love with, almost on first sight, even though, at the time, the idea of falling in love with another man would've made him laugh out loud.

Robin touched him. Just his arm, solid through the soft fabric of his jacket. That was all it took.

Jules met him more than halfway in a full body slam of a kiss that was ferocious. Frantic.

Fantastic.

How could they possibly have spent these past few minutes talking when this was what Robin had wanted—Jules, too—from that first moment he'd opened the door?

It was Jules. *Jules.* Robin wanted to weep—it felt so goddamn good, because it was finally Jules.

The sweetness of his mouth, the softness of his hair, the smoothness of his recently shaved chin, the steel of his arms wrapped tightly around Robin, the solidity of his body—his chest, his thighs—beneath the nuisance of clothing that he knew they both wished could be instantly gone . . .

Robin lost his balance, and they slammed into the wall right next to the door, hard enough to knock the air out of him, hard enough to dislodge a picture, some piece-of-crap artwork that hit the tile floor with a crash.

Jules had to catch his breath. Not Robin, though. He didn't need oxygen to know what he wanted. He didn't want Jules to have time to think, so he spun him around, Jules's back to his chest, Jules's head against his shoulder, his face against Robin's, who reached around him and—

"God," he breathed as he pressed himself against Jules, as he reached with his other hand, fumbling in his haste to unfasten Jules's pants.

Knock, knock, knock!

Someone was knocking on Robin's door.

It was twice as loud, twice as startling, because they were right there next to it, practically leaning against the damn thing.

They both froze, but when the knock came again, Jules made as if to move away from him.

Robin held him tightly, speaking almost silently into his ear. "Shhh. Only person in the entire world that I'm interested in seeing is already here."

Jules closed his eyes. Spoke on a barely audible sigh. "Robin, I don't think . . ."

"Shhh," Robin said again. "It's okay." *Don't think . . .*

Please God, don't let this be only a dream.

"Robin?" Shit, it was Dolphina. "Are you all right in there?" she called through the door.

All they had to do was be quiet for a few more moments, and she would go away—assume he was in the shower.

Except she didn't go away. She rattled the door handle, something beeped and—Jesus! The door opened.

Jules leaped away from him, damn near breaking Robin's wrist before he caught him and pulled him back. The chain was on the door. And where they were standing, Dolphina couldn't see them.

"Robin?" she called through the narrow opening. "Are you okay? Someone heard a loud noise . . ."

"I'm fine," he called back. "I'm still getting dressed. I tripped over something. Where the hell did you get a key to my room?"

"You gave it to me," she answered. "After last night you, well, thought I should have one."

Shit. Ow. Robin let go of Jules. It was hard to hold on to someone when they elbowed you in the ribs. Hard.

"I'll call you when I'm ready to head out to the party," Robin told Dolphina, and she finally shut the door. He turned to Jules, who had his back to him as he fixed his clothes. "Please don't—"

"Don't say anything," Jules cut him off. "It's better if you just . . . don't talk." He headed for the door.

"Will you please just listen." Robin grabbed his arm. "Just wait a sec. Just . . ." He exhaled. Because even though Jules's body language was far from receptive, he'd stopped and *was* listening. "I don't remember giving her my key."

Jules pulled free. "That makes it *so* much less sleazy. You were too drunk to care who you were with, right? So you took advantage of this woman, who probably thinks—"

Robin lost his temper. "Yes," he shot back. "I got drunk. I didn't have the presence of mind to foresee the fucking future and know that the one person I do care about was going to do the one thing he said he'd never do—and walk through my door today."

"Yeah, I gotta go," Jules said.

"You should have *called* me—"

"Oh, so . . . what? It's *my* fault?" Jules stopped himself, visibly trying to curb his emotions. But when he spoke his voice was still clipped. Tight. "Look, it's late, I have to—"

Robin was not going to just roll over and die. "Is there a chance we can have dinner later or tomorrow or—"

"No." Jules didn't hesitate. "No chance. What happened before was a mistake."

"It *was not.*"

"Yeah." Jules got in his face. "It was. This is not what I want. *You* are not what I want."

And there it was. Robin's heart on the floor. Smashed flat. With Jules's shoe print clearly on it.

"Well," he said in the silence that followed that news flash. "Before? When your tongue was in my mouth? You sure could've fooled me."

"Just . . . go back to L.A.," Jules told him, and walked out the door.

CHAPTER
TEN

"Got a sec?" Martell asked, knocking on Ric's office door. "Sorry, I didn't realize you were sleeping."

"No, that's all right." Ric waved him in. "I was just closing my eyes. It's a little hard to sleep with"—he pointed to the ceiling—"elephant woman upstairs."

They'd spent the afternoon moving Annie's things out of her beach house and into his extra bedroom, which was directly above his office. She was up there right now, either moving things around or herding cattle or maybe tap-dancing. Ric wasn't sure which.

"Bro." Martell sat at Ric's desk. "I'm not any kind of relationship expert, but even I know that when there's a woman you want to get with, you don't describe her as elephant-like."

"I meant she was heavy-footed," Ric said. "And I don't want to *get* with her, thanks." Maybe if he said it enough, it would be true.

"Yeah, you really don't want to use *heavy*, either. Not unless you want her living off of cans of Slender and getting so skinny, she'll look like a ten-year-old boy. You'll have to put a paper bag over your *own* head, in order to hit *that* . . ."

Ric sighed. "Can we not talk about Annie, please? Unless you're here to apologize for making a move on her in front of me."

"I was just doing that to piss you off."

"Is that supposed to be an apology?"

"If it makes you feel better, you can call it that. I know it's been a tough day," Martell pointed out. "You've always lived in terror of the girlfriend moving in."

"She's *not* my girlfriend." And it wasn't as if she'd *moved in* moved in. Still, Ric had to admit that lugging Annie's stuff upstairs to his guest bedroom, and making room for her in his single bathroom, freaked him out a little bit more than he'd expected. She was going to be around. Night and day.

Day and night. And night and night and night . . .

"Before we close off that topic of conversation," Martell said, standing up, "I just need to . . ." He came over and slapped Ric upside his head.

"Ow!"

"That's for subscribing to that shit Annie's brother told you," he said. "Far as I can figure, you really must've wanted to believe it. But you did, because it kept her nice and safe, didn't it?"

Ric laughed. "Yeah, from what, me?"

"Nailed it on the head, Dr. Evil. I see you lying there, worrying about how you're going to be able to keep your hands offa her, her living in your less-than-spacious apartment. Lying in your bed every night, knowing that Annie's mere yards away, right down the hall, knowing that she's attracted to you, too. Maybe bumping into her in the bathroom when you get up because you can't sleep, and she's like *Oh, hi, Ric.*" His made his voice breathy and high, sounding more like a transvestite stripper than Annie. "*I can't sleep, either. Maybe if we both go into my room—*"

"Thanks, man," Ric said. Mother of God, he was so screwed. He had one of those bathrooms with two doors—one that led into the hallway, the other that went directly into the master bedroom. *His* bedroom. He was going to have to leave that door permanently locked and get used to using the hall entrance or the chances of them coming face-to-face in there at an inopportune time was a real possibility. "That's really helping."

"Nah, actually," Martell said, "that's not going to happen. Not that easily. You took care of that when you messed around with Crazy McShotmycar. Good job, Enrique. Annie's safe. At least until you convince her you're not a total dick." He stood up. "I gotta go. You gotta get ready for that party. By the way, delivery came. Your tux is hanging out front. Plus there's some box with Annie's name on it."

Ric sat up. "Is it her dress?"

"Like I open boxes that aren't addressed to me?"

Ric went into the outer office, and there it was. A very large box on Annie's desk. "She told Cassidy that she didn't have anything to wear to a formal party, and he asked her dress size and said he'd take care of it."

"I guess that's one of the benefits of working with a gay FBI agent,"

Martell said, slumping into one of the waiting-area chairs. "You end up looking fabulous. Damn, my shit is tired."

"You really think he's gay?" Ric asked.

"I don't know. You're the one who said the word first. I believe I used *brainiac*. You had to bring mirror balls and disco music into the equation."

"Xavier Sanchez, the drummer in my father's band," Ric said. "He's gay." The box for Annie was sealed with tape.

"No shit?" Martell thought about that. "Dude can play."

"Not just drums, but soccer, too." Ric finally found Annie's scissors.

"Sanchez?" Martell's disbelief no doubt came from the fact that the drummer was well over six feet tall and built like a grizzly bear.

"Yep. Someone that big shouldn't be able to move that fast, but he does. He kicks ass." Ric carefully sliced the tape on all four sides of the box lid. He lifted the lid to reveal . . . Lots of tissue paper. "I guess I just wish Cassidy looked more like Sanchez. Or Bruce Willis from *Die Hard*. Instead of Jack from *Will & Grace*."

"Oh, Cassidy's much cuter than Jack." Martell laughed at him. "I'm kidding. Look at you—yeah, *I'm* gay. Bro, if you're worried about him, talk to him. Find out what kind of work he's done, who he's worked with. This case? It's probably not his first. Talk to the other agents. If there's something wrong with him, believe me, they'll tell you."

"Whoa," Ric said as he parted the tissue paper.

Martell stood up to look, too. "Damn." He started to laugh.

So this sucked.

Annie rested on the bed in Ric's guest room, spread-eagled on her back, staring up at a displaced spider walking across the ceiling.

It wasn't the spider that sucked.

It wasn't the room, either, even though it was filled with tired-looking furniture just a step or two up from college-dorm quality. It wasn't Ric's apartment, sunny and bright, with a kitchen that was small but recently renovated, a living room with a flat-screen TV and video-game system that looked identical to the one Bruce had in his basement, and a sundeck—balcony really, since it didn't have any stairs—that overlooked a slightly overgrown but lushly gorgeous tropical garden.

It wasn't even the bed that necessarily sucked, although it did. Ric had told her it was his old one. He'd upgraded to a king when he'd moved into this place. Annie didn't doubt for one second that this mattress was haunted by the ghosts of girlfriends past.

It wasn't the fact that she'd have to carry Pierre, every morning and night, up and down the slightly slippery stairs that led from the first-floor office.

It was Ric, who'd demanded she move in, but clearly hated that she was here. It was the preoccupied grimness with which he had done everything this afternoon. After trying in vain to start a conversation, Annie'd finally given up. They'd worked in silence, packing up her things and bringing them up to this room.

Ric had used the bug sweeper to check all of her earthly possessions for any surveillance devices that Burns's gang might have planted on them while she wasn't home. But then, after clearing space for her in the quirkily tiled bathroom, he'd finally gone downstairs, leaving her to rearrange the furniture because there was no way in hell she was going to be able to sleep with the head of her bed directly on the other side of the wall from the head of *his* bed.

Of course, moving the furniture had revealed a dire need for her to unearth his vacuum cleaner from the hall closet, which was good, because as long as she was moving, working, cleaning, she didn't have to think.

About Ric—with Lillian. About the kind of person who would have sex just for the sake of having sex, with zero emotional connection.

About the kind of person—obviously an idiot—who would still have feelings of attraction to the kind of person who would have sex just for the sake of having sex, regardless of having seen him nearly having sex with another woman.

God help her, even though she'd cleaned and shoved furniture around the room, even though she'd unpacked and showered, Annie kept thinking about the fact that at the party tonight, she and Ric were going to pretend to be together.

And that was *really* going to suck. Especially when he put his arm around her. Or when he smiled at her. Or when his normally heavily lidded eyes did that sexy extra-hooded thing that she had quickly come to recognize as meaning he was going to kiss her . . .

"Hey."

Speak of the devil. Ric was outside of her door, knocking softly, even though it was partly open.

Annie sat up, adjusting the sleep shirt and boxers that she'd thrown on after her shower. "Yeah," she said.

He pushed the door open, saw her and looked away, as if he'd walked in on her in her underwear. "Sorry," he said, holding out a box. "This came for you. It's the dress for tonight."

Annie slid down off the bed. "What color is it?"

"It's, um . . ."

She took the box to the bed, opened it, and . . . It was metallic. Silver and shiny and. . . "Holy crap."

"It's definitely got some *holy crap*, with maybe a little *Jesus* thrown in," Ric said helpfully.

She held it up. This was a dress? It was a sweep of fish-scale-like fabric—and not a whole hell of a lot of it, either—with what seemed like dozens of spaghetti straps. There were shoes, too, at the bottom of the box—silver sandals with a too-high, treacherous-looking heel that could double as a shiv during an unexpected knife fight.

"Am I holding it upside down?" she asked Ric.

He held up a flap of fabric. "No, I think this is the top."

"That's pretty skimpy."

"It looks like some kind of halter," he said. "All these strings probably crisscross in the back. I think you'll have to tie it."

Tie it? How? By looking in a mirror with her hands behind her back? "I don't think I can wear this," Annie said.

"Then don't," Ric told her. "You can stay home."

Not a chance. "You better wait outside," she told him. "I'm going to need help."

This freaking sucked.

Ric stood outside of Annie's bedroom door, wondering how his life had managed to get so totally out of control. Yesterday's problems—convincing Annie to stay on as his receptionist—were laughably small. Damn, what he would give to go back to that place. Yes, there were huge misconceptions that came with it, but it was true—ignorance *was* bliss.

His cell phone rang, and he dug for it in his pocket. Great, it was his mother. No doubt she'd used her maternal superpowers and knew from an anagram of the combined initials of today's guests on *Oprah* that a woman had moved into her only son's apartment.

"Hey, Mom." He braced himself.

"Is your father with you?"

"No," Ric said, relaxing, but just a little. This could be a diversion—make him think he was safe, and then, *bam*, blindside him with *so who's your new girlfriend and why haven't we met her?* "Why, is he AWOL again?"

"He should've been home by now. He went to some meeting . . ."

"There's technology for this," Ric told his mother. "One word: micro-chip. You could probably implant it while's he sleeping on the couch."

"Ha ha," his mother said. "Very funny. He's my husband, not my basset hound."

"He's probably jamming with the band," Ric reassured her. When his father sat down at a piano, time ceased to exist for him. He'd been better lately, though—ever since he'd gotten a new super-slim cell phone. He no longer had to take it out of his pocket when he sat down to play, so when his wife called to tell him dinner was ready, he felt it vibrate. Which didn't mean that he still wouldn't turn it off or even just ignore it if he were in the middle of a particularly good session.

"I know." But his mother didn't sound convinced. "If you see him, will you remind him that we have guests coming for dinner tonight?"

Man, but he hated it when his mother talked in code. Ric looked at his watch. "Mom, if you want me to swing past the studio, see if he's there, just ask me."

"I hate doing that," she said. "I know you're busy . . ."

"I'm working tonight, but it's downtown," he told her. His father's rehearsal space was right on the way to the party at the Bijou.

She sighed. "Will you please stop and see if he's at the studio?" She managed to choke the words out just as Annie pulled open the door. "And kick his butt home if he is?"

"I definitely need your help," Annie said, then realized he was on the phone. "Oops, sorry."

"Will do," Ric told his mother, before she could ask who was the woman whose voice she'd just heard, and was Ric finally going to give her a grandchild. "Gotta go."

And okay. This was interesting. Annie had put on a bathing suit—one of those same racing one-pieces that she'd been wearing since she was twelve years old. With it on, Ric could help her figure out how to tie the dress's strings without any danger of embarrassing them both.

At least not too much.

Clearly Annie was already discomfited. "I should be able to do this."

He saw right away what the problem was. "This needs to go around your neck like . . ." Together they made the adjustment. "Now everything just needs to be tightened, like a giant shoelace."

She stood still, quietly, obediently—possibly for the first time in her entire life—in front of the mirror in her room, just letting him do it. He focused on the string—keeping both sides of it even—rather than on the smooth coolness of her sun-kissed skin beneath his fingers, trying to ignore the way the dress accentuated her curves.

"This tight enough?" he asked, looking over her shoulder at her reflection. She was still holding the top against her breasts, but now she let it go.

"Only if I want to be flashing everyone all night," she replied as he started all over again. "Although maybe that's the idea. I mean, God." She turned slightly, and he realized there was a slit in the side of the skirt that went practically to her hip.

Yeah. God. That was going to be awful for all the people who hated tall, shapely women with gorgeous legs. "We should probably mark the string," Ric told her briskly, businesslike. "So you can put it on again, after you take off the bathing suit."

"I don't need to take off the dress to take off the suit," she told him, laughing at his look of disbelief. "Really. I might need it to be tightened just a little, but I can do it. I once completely changed my clothes— underneath my clothes. It's one of the few female-identified skills that I actually have. That and asking for directions. I'm good at that, too."

Ric tied the string at the small of Annie's back, where many women her age had a tattoo.

Not Annie. Her skin was smooth and soft and naked of all marks.

"So, no cracks about how this substantiates your case?" she asked, frowning at her reflection in the mirror. "My inability to dress myself. You know, reason number four hundred and thirty-three why you believed Bruce?"

"I don't have much of a sense of humor about that," Ric admitted as she began taking off her bathing suit, right out from under the dress, slipping one arm out from the tank suit's shoulder strap and then the other. She had to wiggle it down past her waist and her hips, reaching up under the skirt to pull it off.

And yeah, he probably should've left the room instead of standing there gaping.

"See?" she said, tossing the bathing suit onto the bed.

Yeah, he saw. Without the suit containing her, the dress was even more amazing.

But she wasn't as happy about that. She frowned at her reflection in the mirror—at the way the soft, pale sides of her breasts were exposed. "I'm guessing that throwing a sweatshirt on top of this isn't an option."

"You need me to tighten it again?" he asked.

She shook her head. "It's okay. Just do me a favor and double-knot it."

Ric did, careful not to touch her. "If it's okay with you, I'd like us to leave a little early—I have an errand to run for my mother."

"Of course it's okay," she said.

He nodded. "Thanks. I'll get dressed."

He was halfway down the hall when she said, "Ric."

He turned to see her standing in the doorway, a shimmering vision, like some Annie from an alternate universe.

"Is our friendship over?" she asked. "I mean, the way you're acting . . ."

"I don't know," he answered. "I do know that it'll be really hard to be friends with you if you're dead."

She nodded. "That goes both ways. But . . . wouldn't it also be hard to be friends with me if I cared more for my own safety than the safety of our country?"

"Not everyone belongs on the front lines," he pointed out.

"So . . . I don't, but you do," she said. "But it's more than just because I haven't had police training, isn't it? It's because I'm a woman."

Did she really believe that?

She did. "It is, isn't it?"

Ric tried to explain. "It's more than that. I've got this thing where, I don't know, I can't say it without it sounding like, yeah, I'm sexist, but bottom line, I just want to protect you." It wasn't because she was a woman, it was because she was *Annie*. "And yeah, it has nothing to do with your ability or skill or—"

"You want to *protect* me, but it's not because you're a man and I'm a woman."

His temper sparked at the attitude she was throwing at him. "No, it's not."

"Bullshit." Her own temper didn't just flare, it ignited.

"Are you going to let me attempt to explain or are you—"

She cut him off again. Of course. "Explain what, Ric? How your being sexist isn't really sexist simply because you say it's not?"

He threw up his hands. "Fine. I'm sexist. I believe women belong in the kitchen and in the bedroom, in bed, on their backs. Is that what you want me to say? Are you happy now?"

Fortunately, she wasn't completely listening. She was too busy yelling at him. "I don't want your protection. I don't need it. I'm strong and I'm smart and I'm tough, and I'm not backing down—so you just go ahead and keep being an asshole. Just keep on with the silent treatment—with the pouting—it's *so* attractive."

"Yeah," he hurled back at her. "And you should know. Because there's nothing more attractive than a woman in an evening gown screaming *bullshit.*"

"Says you," she said indignantly. "Because you obviously only like women who are helpless and weak—or pretending to be. Lillian Lavelle—"

Great. They were back to Lillian.

"—outsmarted you," Annie pointed out. "Push come to shove, she probably could've kicked your ass."

"I don't think so—"

"As will I"—she spoke over him—"if you piss me off enough. I didn't haul rocks for six months for nothing."

She actually flexed her right arm, and yeah, she definitely had some nice muscle tone. The sight of her standing there like that, while wearing that dress, should have made Ric laugh. But it didn't. It was possible that he was never going to laugh again. At least not until this was over and he knew she was safe.

Instead, he turned and walked away. "Like I'm going to fight a girl."

"I heard that," Annie shouted. "You are such a—"

Ric closed his bedroom door.

CHAPTER
ELEVEN

J ules hated the Internet.

With cell phone access and the Google, you could jump online dang near anywhere, and find anything your heart desired, in a matter of seconds. In fact, if you weren't careful, you could end up watching the very movie trailer that you'd spent months avoiding.

And there it was, right on the viewscreen of his Trēo, for him to watch as he lurked outside of the Bijou Café, waiting for Ric and Annie to appear.

Play Riptide *trailer again?* his cell phone asked so seemingly innocently, like that snake in the garden of Eden.

Jules naturally clicked on yes. The music started, and on the phone's miniature screen, Robin ran, pounding down a dock, an entire team of police and FBI in pursuit. He didn't break stride as he reached the end, instead diving with beautiful form—thank you, Mr. Stuntman—into the water.

The movie was, according to the reviews included with the trailer, "nonstop action" and "thrill after thrill." Underwater sequences—including a terrifying shark attack, were intercut with plenty of close-ups of Robin's sweaty, dirt-smeared, yet still startlingly handsome face. "Chadwick delivers the year's best acting performance," *Entertainment Weekly* proclaimed—true words of praise for an action movie.

It was stupid to watch the trailer—twice. But Jules was the King of Stupidopia today, no doubt about that.

What had he been thinking, going up to Robin's room like that?

Maybe I'll get some?

And he could've—if he'd stayed. Robin had become quite the aggressive pursuer. No hesitation, no doubt, no question at all of who he was and what he'd wanted. And apparently he no longer needed to be completely blind drunk to get it.

That was an improvement that Jules couldn't deny. And the full fantasy—Robin back in his life, in his arms, and yes, finally in his bed—had been intoxicating. The man was as charismatic as ever, and quite possibly even better-looking than he'd been two years ago. Or maybe self-preservation had dulled Jules's memory, in order to make it possible for him to keep his distance from Robin's shining glory all these months.

God, he really should have continued to keep his distance.

Dear Ben, So I ran into an ex . . . No, Robin didn't even qualify as an ex. Ex what? Ex nothing.

So I ran into this guy to whom I've been insanely attracted for years . . . Ran into? That sounded accidental.

So I intentionally went up to the hotel room of this guy to whom I've been insanely attracted for years and very nearly had sex with him.

Oh, yeah. That was going to go over well.

Although it definitely underscored the nagging question: What was Jules going to say in response to Ben's e-mail?

No doubt about it, Jules had just been handed an additional banquet of things to think about. Because the entire situation played more than one way. Maybe Jules had purposely gone to see Robin because Ben's e-mail had scared the living bejeezus out of him. Self-sabotage had long held a place at the top of Jules's personal bag o'tricks.

Jules pocketed his phone and faded even farther into the shadows as a stretch limo pulled up outside the Bijou. Flashbulbs went off as Robin emerged, as he helped a gorgeous, dark-haired young woman out of the car, as the pair posed for pictures for the paparazzi gathered there.

As Jules watched, Robin leaned close to woman, then laughed at whatever she'd said into his ear, as the pair walked into the party.

And yes, that was definitely jealousy Jules was feeling now—as if he needed evidence beyond the psycho websurfing to prove that he was completely insane.

There was still no sign of Ric and Annie, although Gordon Burns was already inside—Jules had seen him arrive, too. His son had been absent—which made sense. The elder Burns was the Hollywood-phile. According to some nifty information Yashi and Deb had just turned up, Gordie Junior had no use for Hollywood, although he, too, dabbled in movie producing.

Porn.

Why wasn't that a surprise?

Jules stepped forward as Annie and Ric finally pulled up, as they left their car with the valet.

From their body language, it was obvious they hadn't come to any compromise or agreement. Ric was still as pissed at Annie as he'd been when Jules had left their office. And now—bonus!—Annie appeared to be at least as annoyed with Ric, if not more so.

Wasn't this evening going to be just peachy keen?

"Sorry we're a little late," Ric said. "I had to stop at my father's studio. He's AWOL again."

"We're not late," Annie informed him. "We're early. We had enough time to see if he was at the Starbucks."

"No, we didn't."

"Yes, we did."

"Guys," Jules said.

At least they looked good. Ric had the tall, dark, and handsome thing down pat, debonair in his rented but well-fitting tux. The former police detective was very easy on the eyes. And the dress and shoes really worked with Annie's statuesque physique, although she could've gone a bit heavier with her makeup and done something snazzier with her hair.

Still.

"You look amazing," Jules told her. "Good pick with the dress, huh?"

If looks could incinerate, he'd've had to stop, drop, and roll.

"Next time we attend a party, I get to pick what *you* wear, and it's going to be a loincloth," she said as she stalked toward the restaurant door.

Huh?

Ric just shook his head.

Jules chased Annie, caught her arm, and pulled her off to the side, where they wouldn't be overheard.

"It wasn't my intention to make you feel uncomfortable, and I'm sorry if I did," he told her. "I just thought, with your coloring and height . . . You do look incredible, despite the roiling vibe of anger. You're really going to have to lose that before we go inside." He included Ric in his dressing-down. "Both of you. Dial your hostility down a few notches."

Annie looked at Ric, who glanced only briefly at Annie—like, if he maintained eye contact for more than a half a second she might realize just how unbelievably hot he thought she looked in that dress.

God forbid *that* happen.

"Sorry," Ric said, and Annie echoed him. But the apologies were to Jules. They were still both standing there with their arms crossed, rigid in their pointed disregard of one another.

"So I guess the plan is to make Gordon Burns believe you're breaking up," Jules said.

"No," Ric said quickly. "It's not."

They both got the message, glancing at each other again as they awkwardly shifted closer. Ric even gritted his teeth and put his arm around her.

And Jules no longer had any doubt. Before this assignment was over, they were either going to kill each other, or end up in bed. Either way, it was going to be quite the mess.

"Before we go into the party," he told them, "I wanted to update you. We've got some interesting information about your gun-toting client—Lillian Lavelle, which, by the way, is only one of many aliases. She's got a number of different names—stage names, I'd guess you'd call them. She's, um, an adult entertainment artist. Or rather, she was, before she retired."

Annie put it into plain-speak. "A porn star?" She looked at Ric and said with exaggerated enthusiasm, "You almost had sex with a porn star. Dude. Bruce would be so proud."

To anyone unable to listen in, her smile would've looked genuine. It lit her eyes and she sparkled up at him in seeming adoration.

A muscle jumped in Ric's jaw as he finally met and held her gaze. "You heard what Cassidy said. Dial it down."

"Or what?" she countered sweetly, leaning in to kiss him, no doubt purposely right on that twitch. "You'll get me pregnant, steal my shoes, and lock me in the kitchen? You adorable misogynist you?"

"Don't tempt me," he shot back.

"Children," Jules said sharply. "Was this a mistake?"

"Probably," Ric said. "What does Lillian's former career have to do with Gordon Burns?"

"Not so much Gordon as Gordie Junior," Jules told them. "He's been working hard to join the twelve-billion-dollar-a-year porn industry with his company, GBJ Productions. Long story short, he's been having trouble finding funding, since Dad doesn't approve and no one Stateside wants to piss off the old man."

Yashi was focusing on investigating all interest in GBJ from overseas investors. It was probably a dead end, but Jules was determined to check it out. Because what if it wasn't Gordon Burns who was involved in smuggling terrorists into the U. S., but instead his son?

"Apparently someone at GBJ convinced Lillian to come out of retirement. They've got a relatively new title on their list of DVDs—*The Return of Trixie Absolute*. That was her . . . well, her porn name. Not the childhood-pet, street-name thing, but her real one. She was quite the star in the eighties, famous for . . . Well." He cleared his throat. "Just Google her, and . . . Anyway, financially, she had no reason to get back in the business—why she did, for GBJ, is something of a mystery—and possibly the reason behind why she's trying to gun down Gordie Junior. Just to make things worse, her new DVD has been pretty much panned." He paused as he realized what he'd just said. "Which means that there are actually porn critics. Go figure."

"Have you contained her yet?" Ric asked. "Trixie or Lillian or whatever her name is."

"Lillian works," Jules told him. "And no."

Ric was not happy, silently grinding his teeth into stubs.

"This is going to make you even more annoyed," Jules continued, "but she's recently withdrawn a huge chunk of change from her savings account. It's going to be a challenge to find her if she's not using credit cards, which we strongly suspect she won't be. There's been no activity in her accounts for the past five days. Plus, as an actress, she's probably pretty good at altering her appearance."

Ric took the news well, considering. "Does the daughter—Marcy— even exist?" he asked.

Jules nodded. "Past tense. She died just around the time the DVD was released. And Brenda Quinn? She's GBJ's workhorse. The majority of their titles feature her, um, acting skills, under a variety of different names."

"So maybe Lillian has more than one reason to want Junior dead," Annie suggested.

Ric looked at her. "If he's at this party, I want you to stay far away from him."

"Shouldn't that rule apply to you, and Jules, too?" Annie asked. "Unless your penises make you magically bulletproof."

Jules had to work not to laugh, mostly because the word magically made him think of Lucky Charms breakfast cereal and the phrase— magically delicious—that came to mind was particularly inappropriate.

"We'll both be careful, too." Ric's voice was tight, but not because he found any of this even remotely funny.

Okay, then. Jules looked at his watch. "We better go in. Are you ready?"

Were they ready?

Annie was more than ready for a drink, but she ordered a ginger ale from the waiter who'd approached the minute they'd stepped through the door.

The party was in full swing, with a band on an outside patio, music drifting in through the open windows.

Despite that, the AC was blasting. It was cold in there, and she was already starting to freeze despite Ric's hand, warm at her waist.

The place was packed, but even though Annie stood on her toes, she couldn't see any of the celebrities who were supposed to be in attendance. She did, however, spot Gordon Burns over by the bar.

Yeesh. He gave her the creeps. For the first time all evening, she was glad Ric was standing so close.

But then he squeezed her slightly, and she turned to see that he had his phone in his hand. "I've got to take this call," he told her. "I'm going to step outside. Stay close to Jules."

She nodded. "Come right back in." He wasn't the only one who could give orders.

He sighed, because he knew exactly what she was thinking. "I meant to say please."

"I didn't," she told him. "I don't need to." She discreetly flexed the muscles in her right arm. "I don't need no stinkin' polite words to get my way."

Ric actually smiled, and possibly even laughed, although it was more of a heavily exhaled eye roll. Still, it was a potential start in the dial-down-the-hostility plan.

But wow, he'd really pissed her off before—although to be honest, the *you're a woman, you should be protected* thing wasn't exactly news. She'd seen it in action plenty of times back when they were growing up. He was always swooping in to save her. And calling him a misogynist wasn't very accurate. He didn't hate women, he loved them. He just needed to work on respecting them—her—as an equal.

And as long as she was being honest here, part of her pissiness came from her annoyance with her own stupid self. When he'd helped her tighten the lacing of her dress, his hands warm against her shoulders and back, she'd found herself feeling things and wanting things that only a certifiably insane person should have been feeling and wanting.

Like for him to push aside her hair and kiss her on the neck. And then help her *out* of the dress.

As Ric went back out the door, phone to his ear, Annie leaned in closer to Jules, who had just finished a conversation with one of the film festival's organizers. "I'm sorry about before," she told him quietly. "I'll try to remember to act more like a grown-up."

"Don't worry about it. But for the record," Jules said as the waiter delivered her ginger ale and whatever he'd ordered to drink. Annie took Ric's beer, too. "I happen to look great in a loincloth."

"I'll bet you do," a familiar voice said.

And so much for her celebrity search. While she'd been eyeballing the other half of the room, the one and only Robin Chadwick had been standing mere feet away, an extremely pretty woman on his arm.

Jules had his back to the movie star, and for one brief instant, he looked at Annie with an expression on his face that she couldn't quite read. It looked a little like murderous rage mixed with hysterical amusement and a solid dash of sheer panic. And she wasn't quite sure, due to the noise of all the partygoers talking and laughing, but she was pretty certain Jules muttered, "Fuck."

But then there was only *People* magazine's future Sexiest Man in America, holding out his hand to her, as he gave her that trademark Chadwick grin. "Hi, I'm Robin."

Yes, he was. Annie put Ric's beer down on a nearby table, and took Robin's hand.

It was big and warm, and although he wasn't quite as tall as he looked in the movies, he was still taller than she was in her heels.

"I've been trying to get this guy around to the front of the camera for years," he told her, gesturing toward . . . Jules? The FBI agent was now smiling in what could only be described as pleasant desperation. "So what's your gig? Are you a casting director trying to recruit him for a Tarzan picture, or maybe something with cavemen . . . ?"

"Oh," she said, flustered. "No. I'm not . . . You actually know Jules, I mean—" God, the FBI agent was using a different name for this undercover operation, and now she'd gone and blown it.

But Jules saved her, reaching out to shake the hand of the midget supermodel clinging to Robin's arm. "Julian Young," he introduced himself, shooting Annie a reassuring smile. "My friends call me Jules."

"Dolphina Patel," Robin's girlfriend told him.

"Dolphina," Jules repeated, with a look at Robin. "Interesting name."

"My father's a marine biologist," she explained, "and my mother's crazy, so . . ." Her laughter was musical and perfect, just like the rest of her.

"This is Annie," Jules introduced her.

"Annie, would you do me a favor?" Robin asked. "Dolphina was looking for the ladies' room. Would you mind helping her find it?"

And risk Ric's wrath when he came back inside to discover that she'd unglued herself from Jules's side? Not a chance. Still, Annie had spotted the facilities right by the maître d's desk when they'd first come inside. "It's over this way."

She took a couple of steps in that direction, pointing it out to the other woman, who leaned close to ask, "Do I have something in my teeth?" But she didn't wait for Annie to answer. She just scurried off.

"I told you—" Annie heard Jules say to Robin.

"To stay away from you." The movie star finished for him. "Yeah, I thought about that and . . . Sorry, I'm not gonna."

Jules lowered his voice even more. "You *really* don't want to mess with me."

"Yeah, actually, I *really* do, and oops, look, here's Annie, back so soon? Are you from Sarasota, Annie?" Robin asked her, his smile easygoing and relaxed, as if he hadn't been having an intense, cryptic conversation with an undercover FBI agent mere seconds ago. "It's a beautiful area."

"Yeah, I've just moved back," she told him, glancing at Jules, who'd gone absolutely expressionless. Totally blank. "I'm originally from Massachusetts, but we came down here—my mother, my brother and I—when I was eleven." As if he really cared.

"Parents got divorced?" Robin asked, with a wince.

Annie nodded. His charisma was off the charts. He probably got babbled at constantly by people who didn't know what to say to a movie star and he'd learned to deal with it graciously. His full attention—with focused eye contact and active listening—could make everyone else in the entire room fade into nothingness.

Everyone except, of course, Ric, whose unhappiness radiated from him in waves strong enough to penetrate even her deepest fog. Annie spotted him immediately, over Robin's shoulder, as he came back inside.

"That must've sucked," Robin was saying. "Believe me, I can relate. My folks split up before I could walk. Although living near these beaches as a kid? That had to rock."

"Good, here's Ric," Jules said briskly. "Robin, Ric, Ric, Robin. Ric, why don't you and Annie get yourselves something to eat while Robin and I briefly step outside?"

Ric shook Robin's hand without any reaction whatsoever. He didn't even say "Nice to meet you." Instead, he spoke to Jules. "I'm going to need to talk to you, too. As soon as possible."

Whatever that phone call had been about, it hadn't been good.

Annie could see that Jules, too, realized that something was up, but he didn't get a chance to ask before Robin said, "Hey now, here comes somebody I want you all to meet. The host of this party, in fact. Mr. Burns, say hello to my good friends."

And just like that, the game was in play.

"We've had the pleasure. Miss Jones." Gordon Burns took Annie's hand first, smiling up at her. He was shorter than she remembered, but then again, she *was* wearing the Heels of Death tonight. She towered over Jules, too.

She dug deep and found a smile that she hoped was both gracious and warm. "How are you, sir? You remember Ric Alvarado, my . . . significant other." Wow, that really sounded stupid. What was wrong with her, that she couldn't utter the word *boyfriend*?

But Burns didn't seem to care. "Of course I remember Ric. I didn't expect to see either of you here." He shook Ric's hand, too.

"And this is Julian Young." Annie got his name right this time, thank God. "Mr. Young is Ric's business associate. He's also a movie producer— he invited us here tonight to celebrate the release of one of his films."

"Oh, really?" The interest in Burns's voice was genuine. "Which film is yours, Mr. Young?"

"Believe it or not"—Robin spoke for him—"Julian's a financial backer for *Riptide*. He's uncredited—it was really just an investment deal, based on my recommendation." He turned to Jules, and smiled. "Good call, huh? They're predicting the movie's gonna open huge. Hey, you know Gordon's a backer, too. Small world, right? You're business partners, and you didn't even know it."

"It's a pleasure to meet you, sir," Jules lied seemingly effortlessly to Burns, shaking his hand. "*Gefilte Fish out of Water* is mine, too. It's a documentary short about the Jewish community in Dublin, Ireland. And okay, to be honest, it's not *really* mine, it's Westland's—the production company I work with. But it's a fun little film."

"I'll make a point to check it out," Burns said. "Westland Productions, you said?"

"Yes, sir."

The FBI had set up an intricate cover for Jules. Aside from creating a producer's page for Jules on imbd.com, they'd also gotten him included on Westland's massive website. They'd gone so far as to create individual websites for Jules's fictitious direct-to-video movies. They'd even provided links to fabricated reviews. When Burns checked him out—and he would—he'd be convinced of Julian Young's status as an up-and-coming Hollywood player.

"Julian and I go way back," Robin told Burns. "In fact, he's the reason I can't attend your dinner party tomorrow night."

"You were invited to—" Jules cut himself off, giving Robin a disbelieving look that instantly morphed into a smile. "Yes, that's right. We, uh, have plans, don't we?"

"J and I are meeting to discuss future projects," Robin told Burns. "There's one that's really intriguing—there's this FBI agent, and he's gay, right? It's *Brokeback* meets the *Untouchables*. I'm telling you it's got Oscar all over it."

"I've been hearing Oscar talk about *Riptide*," Burns pointed out.

"Fingers crossed," Robin said. He turned to Jules. "You know, you should set up a meeting with Gordon—get him involved." He turned back to Burns. "Why don't you come to our—oh, but you can't. You've got that party. Duh. Brain fade. Sorry. I'm telling you, I'm lucky I know what city I'm in."

"Why don't you just come to my party," Burns suggested. "All of you. It would be my pleasure." He looked at Ric and Annie. "You know how to get to the Point. Tomorrow night, seven sharp."

Robin hesitated. "Well, I *guess* that could work. Maybe if J and I could reschedule our meeting . . ." He looked at Jules. "Maybe for later tonight?"

Burns, too, looked expectantly at Jules, who missed only a half a beat.

"Sure," Jules said. "That's . . . fine."

"I'll see you all tomorrow, then," Burns said. "Right now I need to mingle." He gave Annie one last lizard smile. "You really do look lovely, dear."

"Thank you," she said, and he was gone.

"What just happened here?" Ric asked. He looked at Robin. "You're Robin Chadwick."

He was just realizing this now? He looked almost shell-shocked, Annie realized. "Are you all right?" she asked him, but he didn't respond.

"That *is* what you wanted, isn't it?" Robin's full attention was on Jules.

"Yeah." Jules laughed, shaking his head. "Damn, you're good."

"Yes, I am," Robin said.

As they gazed at each other, Annie felt that same odd intensity she'd intruded upon earlier. But this time it was Robin's date—Dolphina—who interrupted them. She came slinking back from the ladies' room. "I'm sorry, but Robin really needs to circulate."

Ric turned to Annie. "Robin Chadwick got us invited to Burns Point. Tomorrow night," he said as if their entire conversation with Burns had been in Chinese and he needed confirmation.

"Yes," she told him. "What's going on? What was that phone call?"

"My father," he said. "He had a heart attack."

"Oh my God." Jules, of course, overheard, as did Robin and Dolphina. "Is he all right? How bad is it?"

"I don't know," Ric admitted. "I have to get over to Doctors' Hospital. Will you stay with Annie until Martell gets here?"

"I'm going with you," Annie insisted.

"The valet's going crazy—it's going to take forever to get your car." Robin stepped in. "My limo's out front. Take it." He turned to Dolphina.

"Go clear that with Sean." She vanished, and he turned back to Ric. "He's the driver. Just tell him where you need to go and he'll get you there."

"Give me your car keys, and valet tag," Jules ordered Ric. "I'll bring your car over to the hospital for you." He spoke directly to Annie. "Give me a call when you arrive, okay?"

She nodded, and they ran for Robin's limo.

"You all right?" Robin asked.

He and Jules were finally alone. Okay, not *alone* alone. The party was still swirling around them. But Annie, thank God, was gone. She was, no doubt, one of Jules's fellow FBI agents despite the fact that she seemed impossibly young. But she clearly knew Jules, and therefore knew that he was gay. She also now knew a thing or two about Robin—that was obvious from the dawning realization in her wide gray eyes as she'd looked from him to Jules and back again.

Whatever it was that she'd seen, he should've been able to hide it. He was a better actor than that, wasn't he?

Apparently not when it came to Jules.

"I'm fine," Jules said now, but he was obviously lying. Robin knew that Jules's father had died during heart surgery, not long after suffering a massive coronary. This situation had to bring back a lot of unpleasant memories.

"You were fourteen, right?" Robin pulled him over to an empty table in the corner. "When your father died?"

But Jules didn't take a seat. He did a quick scan of the room and lowered his voice. "Why are you doing this? I told you it was dangerous."

Robin snagged a couple of drinks from a passing tray. Jules, of course, declined the one he'd grabbed for him, so Robin put it down on the table. "I thought I made that obvious."

"You want me?" Jules asked, his voice low. "Come on, then. Let's go. Let's do it. I'll go to your room with you right now. *Right* now. God knows I've wanted *you* from the moment you first smiled at me."

Robin couldn't believe what he was hearing. And then he could because Jules wasn't done.

"All you have to do," Jules told him, with that heat in his eyes that promised pure heaven, "is kiss me. Right here. Kiss me and take my hand and I will go anywhere with you."

Robin had to look away. "You know I can't do that."

"No," Jules said. "I know you *won't* do it. Frankly, I'm not sure I would've asked if I'd thought you could. Yeah, I want you. But I also want to have steak and french fries every night. Doughnuts every morning for breakfast. Heart disease runs in my family—I'd be insane to eat that crap."

"My agent's negotiating a new contract," Robin tried to explain. "I'm about to make more money than I ever dreamed—"

"That's one of the ways we're different," Jules told him. "When you dream, you dream about money."

Well, yowch.

"Here comes your girlfriend," Jules said. "I gotta go, see if I can't help Ric."

"We're going to have to talk before tomorrow night," Robin pointed out. "If I'm going to help you . . ."

"Thank you for what you've done," Jules said, all cold FBI professional. "But your help? It ends here. Make up an excuse and go back to L.A., ASAP. I'm serious, Robin. I need you gone."

Jules headed for the door as if their conversation was over, nodding to Dolphina as he went past her.

"I'm not going anywhere," Robin called after him, and Jules stopped and turned.

And in that split second, when their eyes met and the very air seemed to crackle around them, Robin almost did it. Three long strides would bring him to Jules's side. He could picture the disbelief in his eyes—disbelief that would turn to wonder and then heat as Robin drew him into his arms and kissed him as ardently as he'd kissed his co-star, Susie McCoy, at the end of *Riptide*.

But there was no disbelief in Jules's eyes right now—only solid certainty that Robin's feet were glued to the floor.

And sure enough, the moment passed, and Robin realized that his raised voice had caught the attention of a number of the partygoers, who watched him now with unabashed curiosity.

"Except up," he tacked on to his *I'm not going anywhere*, adding a little extra het to the whole exchange with a "Later, dude."

No way could he throw away everything he'd worked so hard to achieve. Still, his stomach hurt as, shaking his head, Jules turned and walked away.

"You need to mingle." Dolphina startled him. She was right at his elbow, and he nearly spilled his drink.

"I know." He tossed it back, finishing it. "Just give me a fucking minute."

He'd spoken much too sharply, but she didn't flinch, or even back away. In fact, she put her arms around him and hugged him. And then surprised him even further. "Was that him?"

Was that . . . what? "Excuse me?"

She pulled her face from the front of his tux jacket and said it again, still quietly, but unmuffled this time. "Was that him?"

Robin looked down into Dolphina's brown eyes. They were pretty—warm and lively—but not even half as captivating as Jules's.

"You don't remember anything you told me last night, do you?" she asked, making a face at him.

Uh-oh. "I remember . . . behaving inappropriately." He chose his words carefully. "And I guess . . . I must've given you my key at *some* point."

"You gave me your key so I could check on you. You spent the night throwing up," Dolphina told him. "And crying."

"Oh, good," he said. "I was afraid I'd simply screwed you and passed out."

"We didn't have sex," she informed him. "You sort of tried, but you were really drunk and it was pretty halfhearted. Not that I would have let you. Smile." She pulled him closer, their faces together, turning toward a news photographer, who snapped a picture for the local paper. "You told me"—she looked around, no doubt to make sure no one was standing close enough to overhear—"that you were in love with this, um, *person* you met a few years ago, and I was just wondering if that was . . . the person."

Robin nodded. Apparently he hadn't bedded Dolphina last night as he'd feared. Instead, he'd come out to her. Great. "What makes you think that?"

"Because I've never seen you look at anyone the way you look at him," she admitted. "I hope someday someone looks at me that way. But . . ." She looked up at him, her eyes apologetic. "You're either going to have to stay away from . . . this person or really tone it down."

"Who exactly do you work for?" Robin asked her. It was stupid that he didn't know, but his entourage was so large, with various assistants working for *Riptide*'s production company and the distribution company and probably even a few sister companies that he didn't even know about.

"You," Dolphina told him. "Well, and Don. I also work for Don."

Don. His agent. Who was working on pounding out a mega-million-dollar three-picture deal. Three pictures. With tight scheduling, Robin could make three pictures in a mere year and a half.

"Tell Don not to worry," Robin told Dolphina. "I'm not going to fuck this up."

CHAPTER
TWELVE

The first thing Ric saw when he burst into the hospital's waiting area was his diminutive mother. The second thing he saw was the makeup-streaked tears on her face.

He was a freaking detective—he didn't need Sherlock Holmes's Guide to Deductive Reasoning to know that the fact that she wasn't in with his father, combined with those tears, was a bad sign.

She stood up when she saw him, and as he went to her and put his arms around her, she cried even harder. Which was why her muffled words didn't make sense.

"He's going to be okay."

Thank God for Annie, who seemed to know that his brain was struggling to process even simple information. "He's going to be okay," she repeated, making sure he understood, her hand solid on his back, warm even through his jacket and shirt.

"It was mild, as far as coronaries go," his mother told him as she dug through her purse for her pack of Kleenex.

He was too dazed to help, but again, Annie was on top of things. She picked up a small box of tissues that was on an end table, and held it out for his mother.

"Thank you." Karen Alvarado was one of maybe four people on the planet who could blow her nose and make it look both graceful and delicate. "They're still running tests, but so far the consensus is that there was no permanent damage."

And again, Annie was there, grounding him, squeezing his hand, even speaking for him. "That's great news."

Ric heard the words, but he couldn't quite believe them. Until his mother turned to Annie, held out her hand, and said, "Hi, I'm Karen. What a lovely dress. Have you known my son for long?"

He could see from the familiar glint in his mother's eyes that she was looking for information that would help her do the math to predict his and Annie's impending wedding date. Length of relationship times extravagance of clothing—Annie's dress was a never-before-seen eleven on a scale from one to ten—divided by her own wishful thinking . . .

If his mother was able to focus on this, his father was definitely going to be okay.

Relief made Ric desperate to sit down, but that would've meant leaving Annie on her own to fend off his mother's ferocious desire to buy a mother-of-the-groom dress. So he stayed on his feet. "Mom, you remember Annie Dugan. Bruce's little sister?"

She looked at Annie more closely, surprise on her face. "The lesbian?"

Oh, good, Mom.

"Ric!" If they'd been alone, Annie probably would've hit him. And with her intensely developed stone-lugging muscles, she no doubt would've made it hurt. As it was, she just laughed her disbelief.

"We support the Human Rights Campaign," his mother reassured Annie. "And Teo just did a fund-raiser concert for PFLAG's Safe Schools program—"

"Not that there's anything wrong with it," Annie interrupted his mother, "but that was just a story my idiot brother told Ric. I'm not gay." She turned back to him. "Is there anyone you *didn't* tell . . . ?" *Asshole.* She didn't call him that in front of his mother, but it was definitely implied.

"Oh, really?" his mother said, turning to look at him, too.

Ric shook his head, totally screwed. He'd only told his mother. But that wasn't the *only* thing he'd told his mother. It was years ago, sure, but this wasn't something she'd be likely to forget. At the time, some girlfriend had just broken up with him—he couldn't even remember who it was—and his mother had called to express her sympathy.

He'd told her he didn't care, that it was just another meaningless relationship that was going nowhere. It didn't matter who he spent his time with. None of it mattered—because he couldn't be with the woman he really wanted.

Annie.

Who was conveniently unattainable.

He'd said it to get his mother off his back, never suspecting that one day it was going to come back and kick him, hard, upside the head.

He sat down, exhausted, and waited for the bomb to drop.

"I thought you were up in Boston." His mother was trying to weasel more information from Annie. "When did you move back?"

"Just a few weeks ago," Annie told her. "I'm working with Ric now."

"Really? He hadn't told me." His mother gave him a look that promised a future ass-whupping. "Is your mother still in the area? I haven't seen her in years."

"No, she's in Savannah," Annie reported. "She remarried, and . . . She's doing well. Her new husband's actually nice. She finally got a good one."

"So where are you staying, then?" Ric's mother asked.

"Well," Annie said, glancing at him for help. "I haven't really, um, found a permanent—"

"She's living with me, Ma," Ric said, jumping with both feet onto the detonator, because hell, as long as his mother now thought his destiny had finally arrived, he might as well let her enjoy the fantasy while it lasted. Particularly since the next few days and weeks were going to be rough for her, with his father in recovery.

Besides, there had been people at tonight's party who were friends of his parents—people he'd seen talking to Gordon Burns. If Ric's name came up, even casually in conversation . . .

His mother took the news remarkably well. No cartwheels or shrieking alleluia. "What do you know?" she said. "A two-miracle day." She turned to Annie, fumbling for another tissue to wipe more tears of joy from her eyes. "We'll have to have lunch."

"I'd like that," Annie lied. She gave Ric a smile that promised a painful death.

Ric got to his feet, intending to head over to the nurses' desk to ask when they would be able to go in to see his father.

"Do you think it's too late to call Martell?" his mother asked, and he turned back to answer her, glancing at his watch. It wasn't even nine-thirty.

"I don't think so," Ric said. "Why do you want to . . . ?"

"We're going to need a lawyer," she told him. "Teo's heart attack? It happened while he was in police custody, in a holding area, awaiting transport to the county jail."

"Slow down," Annie said. "Slow down. Ric. Ric. *Ric.*" She caught his arm, but he still didn't stop until he hip-checked him into the wall of the police station. "How does this help?"

"My father could have died." He was furious.

"How does this help?" she asked again.

"Get out of my way. Go home. Lock the doors. Martell will be there soon."

She stood firm. She'd come here with him from the hospital, in the car that Jules had dropped off.

Before leaving, Jules had tried to talk Annie into letting him escort her home. But she wouldn't leave Ric then, and she sure as hell wasn't going to leave him now, when he was clearly on the verge of losing it—after finally seeing his father, and hearing exactly what had happened to the older man.

"No," Annie told Ric now. "Please. Ric, just take a minute—"

"And what?" Ric asked. "What changes, Annie, if I take your minute? What do you know about what happened to my father tonight?"

Teo Alvarado, world-famous Cuban American jazz pianist, had gone to a political rally, in which a group from the opposite side of the immigration issue had also come, attempting to turn the event into a full-scale brawl. The police had stepped in, taking truckloads of protesters—including Teo—into custody.

When it came time to be processed, Teo discovered that both his wallet and his cell phone had been stolen in the fracas. He had no identification, and the police officers in charge had no sympathy or patience with his heavily accented English, and had ordered him into a holding area for illegals. When he'd tried to stand his ground, he was manhandled and handcuffed—which apparently triggered his heart attack.

And that was when things went from bad to worse—because the police detectives in charge of processing the so-called illegals thought Teo's complaints were merely a ploy designed to get him special treatment. They ignored him—and he collapsed, his hands cuffed painfully behind his back.

It wasn't until another police officer arrived, a uniformed cop named Lora Newsom, that an ambulance was called. She didn't recognize Teo as Ric's famous father, but she did know a heart-attack victim when she saw one, and got him the help he'd needed.

"I know it's wrong—what happened to your father," Annie told Ric.

"Damn straight it's wrong! Since when is this a country where citizens have to carry around papers?" he asked. "Not citizens who look like you, but citizens who look like me, like my father, especially when we speak English with an accent." He picked her up and moved her out of his way.

"Ric—"

There was no stopping him. For someone she thought of as both thoughtful and mostly easygoing, reasoning with him now was like trying to talk sense to a guided missile.

Which didn't mean she wasn't going to try. "Ric." She followed him into some kind of break room, where a coffee machine was set up next to a refrigerator. A folding table was in the center, surrounded by metal chairs.

Two men had been sitting at the table, having coffee and doughnuts, but when Ric came in, they jumped up in alarm and backed away, toward a wall of windows.

"Shit, who let him in here?" the shorter one said.

"Ric," Annie said again.

But Ric had slowed down. He seemed almost calm now as he picked up one of the abandoned coffee mugs, sniffed it, and took a long slug.

"We didn't know it was your father," said the heavier one—the same detective who'd come to Ric's office just that morning. Detective Donofrio.

"It didn't occur to you," Ric asked as he gently set the mug back onto the table, "that even though you didn't know he was *my* father, that he was *someone's* father?"

"You weren't there," Donofrio insisted. "It was a fucking zoo—they were all talking Spanglish. These were people who were throwing rocks at each other—"

"No, these were the people who were having rocks thrown at them!" Ric exploded, grabbing the table and heaving it up and over. It crashed into the far wall, the ceramic mugs shattering on the industrial tile, jelly doughnuts bouncing everywhere.

He spotted her near the doorway, her mouth no doubt hanging open in shock, and he shouted at her. "Get out of here!"

Annie didn't. She stepped farther into the room. "Ric, don't do this. Don't get yourself arrested. We have an important job to do." Her voice shook—she couldn't help it. "Don't make me do it alone."

Finally, she'd said something that gave him pause, but she had no idea what he might've said or done next, because half a dozen police officers burst in through the door behind her, startling her and knocking her off her Heels of Death.

She landed hard, skidding on the filthy floor.

"Don't touch her! Don't you fucking touch her!" she heard Ric shouting as someone grabbed her, their hands rough as they yanked her arms behind her, her cheek against the gritty tile.

"I'm okay," she shouted as she was hauled, still roughly, to her feet, because, God, there were about six police officers working to control him. "Ric, I'm okay—don't make this worse!"

"Annie!" he shouted as she was led from the room, limping, one of her heels snapped clean off. "Annie!"

It was there, in the hall, as she was being led away to get locked up, that she experienced another startling first.

She heard Enrique Alvarado start to cry.

Annie looked hot, in that *I've just survived a plane crash and an attack from a tribe of zombies* bedraggled evening-gown kind of way, killer shoes dangling from one finger, as one of the newbies to the police department brought her out from the women's holding cell.

"Where's Ric?" Annie asked Martell.

First things first. "Sign this," he told her, finishing up the paperwork and holding out a pen for her.

She balked. "I didn't do anything wrong. I'm not going to sign anything that—"

"This just gets you home," he explained. "We'll handle right and wrong tomorrow."

She read through the papers quickly—apparently she had trust issues—but she finally signed her name. "So is Ric in a lot of trouble?"

"Some." Martell pocketed the pen and pushed the papers toward the officer. "But you pretty much stopped him before the little *t* became a capital one. Plus he's still got plenty of friends here. And it's not like he's ever gotten this drunk before, which is also a point in his favor."

Annie had been following him toward the door, but now she stopped short. "Drunk? He wasn't drunk."

"Yeah, he was." He took her arm, trying to pull her outside, but she planted herself. "He smells like a distillery, which is why I won't be able to get him out until the morning. He's an overnight guest in the city drunk tank."

"I was with him all night," Annie insisted. "He ordered a beer at the Bijou, but he didn't drink any of it."

"That you saw."

She was clearly going to argue this one until her face turned blue. She opened her mouth, so Martell spoke over her.

"I'm doing my boy a favor here." He let a whole lot of whine into his tone. "Again. I got court in the morning, early, and you're standing here quarreling with me about scientific evidence? Shut your piehole, beeyotch, and get your badonkadonk into my car."

His name-calling obviously stunned her. She'd been wading hip-deep up shit's creek for quite a few days now on too few hours of sleep, but enough of her brain was working for her to realize that *beeyotch* was not the most important part of the message he'd just delivered.

She snapped her mouth closed and went out the door.

She managed to stay silent until they got into his car, until he ran Ricky's bug sweeper over them both.

It was part of their new daily regimen. Every time they left the house or office, every time someone new came over, and especially every time they came into contact with Burns or one of his friends, including those here at the local police, they were going to check and recheck to make sure they weren't being listened in on.

They were both clear, so Martell said, "Sorry about that. I had to get you to zip it. Beeyotch."

"Badonkadonk was nice, too." Annie laughed, but her amusement didn't last. "Ric *wasn't* drunk."

"I believe you." He just hadn't wanted her shouting that news flash in the police station. "But he definitely wanted someone to think he was."

She stared at him. "You're telling me he *purposely*—"

"When Ric texted me," Martell reported. "Must've been while you were still over at the hospital. He told me two things. *I need you to stay with Annie tonight,* so clearly he anticipated not making it home."

She thought about that as he started the car. "What was the second thing?" she asked.

"Took me a while to figure that one out." Martell laughed as he pulled out of the police-station parking lot. "You'll probably get it right away— WWGBJD, with a question mark at the end."

Annie looked at him, her pretty face angelic in the dashboard light. "What would . . . Gordie Burns Junior do?"

Martell nodded. "That's what I got, too." He had no idea what Ric was up to, but it was clear he was up to something.

Of course maybe he just couldn't bear the temptation of sleeping down the hall from sweet Annie Dugan, so he'd gone and gotten himself locked up.

With Ric, you never knew.

CHAPTER
THIRTEEN

I n Sarasota, news traveled fast.

Which was why, on Friday morning, ten minutes after Ric was released from the Sarasota City Jail, and two minutes after he got off the phone with his mother at the hospital, Gordie Burns Junior took his call.

He had business, Ric told Junior as he drove himself home, that he wanted to discuss in person. That was not a problem—most of Junior's business was the kind that couldn't be discussed over the phone. But Junior wasn't available until Saturday night, late. They made plans to meet at Tammy's, which was Screech's main rival as far as topless dancers went, out west of the highway on Fruitville Road.

Jules Cassidy's rental car was parked in Ric's driveway, no doubt because Martell had needed to leave for court. One thing about the little FBI guy—his word was rock-solid. At least when it came to keeping Annie safe.

Yeah, *Ric* was the one who'd gotten her knocked to the floor of the police-station coffee room last night.

As he let himself into his office, Pierre barked at him from his perch on Annie's lap. She was working at her desk, Cassidy leaning over her shoulder, scratching Pierre's ridiculous ears. They'd both been laughing about something that was on the computer screen, but now they looked over at him in silence, Cassidy straightening up. They both watched as Ric found the hanger for his torn and grimy tux jacket and hung it up.

"Honey, I'm home," he finally said, because someone had to say something, and he knew that expressing his intense jealousy over the fact that Pierre never let *him* scratch his ears would not be well received. Probably because it was wildly irrational. He didn't *want* to scratch the dog's mutant ears. He slipped his bow tie and cummerbund into the tux jacket's pockets, his movements a tad too forceful.

Annie and Jules exchanged a message-laden look, as if they'd become best friends in his absence and could now communicate telepathically.

"I've been in touch with your mother," Annie told him. "Your dad's doing well."

"Thanks," he said. "I know. I spoke to her this morning, too."

She displaced Pierre as she stood up and came toward him—not to embrace him or even punch him in the face, but instead to run the bug sweeper across both him and his jacket. She'd transformed back into a blue-jean-wearing mortal—with a nasty scrape on her right elbow from being tackled to the coffee-room floor.

Ric caught her hand to try to get a closer look, but she jerked it away. "It's not a big deal, so don't turn it into one."

"Not a big deal?" he repeated, sick to his stomach. This was exactly what he didn't want to happen. "Next time I tell you to leave, you leave."

"Maybe next time you should tell me what you're doing," she fired back.

"I didn't have time." He picked up the bug sweeper. "And we didn't have this."

"Then maybe we better get another one and start carrying it in the car"—Annie didn't back down—"because I honestly didn't know what you were trying to do. I still don't know why you wanted to—"

"Bottom line is, when I tell you to leave, you leave."

"You also told me to stick close," she countered. "To never go anywhere without you."

Jules cleared his throat, and Ric turned to see that he'd picked up Pierre and was holding the dog the way only Annie could, which just added to his feelings of annoyance. Like Annie, Jules was dressed down in jeans and a T-shirt. He looked more like a student at the Ringling School of Design than an FBI agent.

"I'd offer to run out and get coffee so you guys can resolve this sans audience," Jules said, "but not only is there already a pot made, but I kinda need to verify that Ric did, in fact, contact Gordie Junior just a few minutes ago via cell phone."

"What?" Annie asked, looking at Ric. "You called Gordie Junior?"

"Yup," Ric said. "I set up a meeting to discuss a potential hit on Bob Donofrio, for nearly killing my father."

"What would Gordie Burns Junior do?" Jules gestured with his head toward Annie. "She told me about your text message."

"When's the meeting?" Annie demanded.

As if she thought she was going with him. "Neither of us said very much." Ric ignored her as he spoke to Jules. "Not over the phone. But I have no doubt that he knows exactly what this meeting's about. It was obvious he'd already heard about my freak-out at the police station last night."

Jules nodded as Annie fumed. "So you think it's the son—smuggling terrorists into the country."

"No," Ric said. "I'm not sure he's smart enough. But one of the things Gordon Senior asked me to do was spend time with Junior. What better way to bond than over a heartwarming plan for a revenge killing?"

Not that it was actually going to happen. No way was Ric going to jeopardize his father's chance to kick Donofrio's ass in court—as well as through the media. Which was why, as much as he'd wanted to, he hadn't put hands on the other detective last night. And he'd never tell Annie this, but having her there, trying to talk him down from the proverbial ledge, had kept him from having to stand there tapping his toes, waiting for the cavalry—what took them so long?—to come and throw his ass into lockup.

"I figured we had our way into Burns Point through your, uh, friend. The movie star." Ric continued to explain himself to the FBI. "I saw a chance to get close to Junior, so I took it." He finally looked directly at Annie. "And it's going to be me going to this meeting. Alone."

"We'll make sure he's got backup," Jules reassured her. He took a deep breath. "About my . . . friendship with Robin Chadwick . . ."

Ric didn't want to hear this. "You don't need to explain. Really."

"A few years ago, I was part of a task force that protected his sister," Jules said. "He was shot and nearly killed, so you'd think he'd want to stay far away from me, but, um . . . He *is* our quickest and easiest way into Burns Point, so we're going to have to use him. On the slim chance that Peggy Ryan's still alive, days—*hours*—could make a difference in keeping her that way." He put Pierre onto the floor and straightened back up. "But Robin's completely inexperienced. He's mercurial and reckless. And an alcoholic. And I *will* die to keep him safe, so . . . I thought you should know that."

Annie was the first to speak after that. "Do you love him?" she asked quietly, as if there were any doubt whatsoever.

Christ. Ric had never really given much thought to what it meant to be gay. At least not in terms of anything but the obvious ick factor. The idea of love being involved . . . Did Jules love Robin? It was both absurd, and yet so obviously an unnecessary question, because it was clear to him that Jules did.

The FBI agent didn't seem put off by the personal nature of Annie's question. He just smiled, albeit ruefully. "Doesn't everybody love Robin Chadwick?"

"I had no idea he was gay," she said. "I mean, until last night."

"Oh, come on," Ric said. "He's an actor. They're all gay. Especially the ones who make a big deal about getting married and having kids."

Annie looked at him in disgust. "For someone who claims they hate stereotyping—"

"Robin Chadwick's not gay," Jules interrupted.

"You mean, he's never publicly admitted it," Ric interpreted, but Jules neither confirmed nor denied it. He just stood there, looking as if he'd rather be doing anything else right now—other than having this conversation.

"He's in the closet," Annie deduced. "Pretty solidly. He's done a really good job—I mean the whole womanizing, heartbreaker reputation . . . Do you think what's-her-name, Sharkette? Does she know?"

"Dolphina." Jules corrected her with a laugh that morphed too quickly into a noise of disgust. "Look, you can speculate all you want. I'm not going to comment on—"

"Why would you want to protect him?" Annie asked, because she still didn't get it.

"Robin's our way into Burns Point tonight," Jules told her, doing the age-old government representative's dodge of not answering the question that was asked, while making it seem as if he was. "After that, he's out of here. He's going back to Hollywood. I'll be making sure of it."

Ric laughed. "Good luck with *that*."

Jules was a very smart man. He surely knew that Robin wasn't going anywhere if he didn't want to. And with Burns all starstruck . . . Chances were greater that Robin would move into Burns Point as a houseguest before he'd willingly fly home to California—if he felt even a fraction of what Jules obviously felt for him.

"Bottom line," Jules said, "I'm not involved with him, and I do not intend to become involved with him—not that it's any of your business." He deftly changed the subject. "We've got a one o'clock spot at a firing range up in Tampa this afternoon." He turned to Ric. "It's not necessary for you to—"

"Oh, I'm going," he said.

"Fine." Jules gathered up his briefcase. "I'll make arrangements for you to meet the rest of my team then. As you requested."

"Good." It was difficult for Ric to meet the FBI agent's gaze, now that his gayness wasn't just rampant speculation.

Jules knew it, too. But he packed up whatever frustration he was feeling, and he took it with him as he headed for the door. Ric knew exactly the kind of self-discipline that required. "I'll be back later. We'll need to leave by noon."

"We'll be ready," Annie said.

Ric bent down and caught Pierre's collar, to keep the little dog from following Jules out into the yard. "Hey, Cassidy."

Jules turned back, careful to keep his impatience from showing on his face.

"Thanks for, uh, staying here with Annie." Ric made himself meet Jules's steady gaze. "I know you got up early to get here before Martell left. I just wanted you to know how much I really appreciate it."

"Not that it was necessary," Annie interjected, and Ric rolled his eyes.

Jules smiled. "It wasn't a problem," he said, and gently closed the door behind him.

"So let's have it," Ric said to Annie as the door closed behind Jules. "You're mad because you don't need a babysitter, you're mad because I didn't tell you what I was up to last night, you're mad because I'm not going to let you go to that meeting with Junior . . . What am I leaving out here? You're mad because . . . now you've got a police record?"

"Yeah, that's not going to stick," Annie told him. She hadn't done anything wrong. "I'm not worried about that."

"Good," Ric said, "because you're right, it's gone. I got it cleared up before I left this morning."

"I *am* worried about your mother," Annie said. "I can't believe you told her that I moved in." How could he have been so cruel? Karen Alvarado was one of the nicest women on the planet. Annie had always liked her. She was smart and sophisticated and creative and funny and unbelievably kind and she did not deserve to be deceived by her own allegedly loving son.

"She was going to find out anyway." Ric shrugged and then threw Annie's own words back at her. "It's not a big deal, so don't turn it into one."

"It's a very big deal for her," Annie pointed out as she scooped up Pierre and went up the stairs to the apartment. "And you know it. He's such an asshole," she told Pierre, who definitely agreed.

The asshole had the audacity to laugh as he followed her.

So she expounded. "Really, Ric. Her feelings are going to be hurt. She's going to feel like she was conned by her own son, who didn't trust her enough to tell her the truth." Annie went into her room and put Pierre on the bed—which was a big win for the little dog. He was too small to jump up on his own, so it was the most coveted napping spot in the entire apartment.

Aside from Ric's bed. But he kept his bedroom door tightly closed to keep Pierre out—and probably Annie, as well.

"So we won't tell her the truth," Ric said. "We'll just pretend we broke up. You'll move out. Everyone's sad but life goes on."

"No digging," Annie warned Pierre, and he settled in with his head on her pillow, apparently fully believing he was a person instead of a dog.

Ric, meanwhile, stood in the doorway, in dire need of both a shower and a shave, the shadow of his beard heavy on his cheeks and chin, his hair charmingly rumpled.

"And yet . . . I still keep working for you?" Annie asked him.

She could read the giant *oops* in his eyes, but it wasn't about the story he was or wasn't going to tell his mother.

"You're going to fire me," she realized. "After this is over. You son of a bitch."

To his credit, he didn't try to lie. "You don't want to be my reception-ist," he reminded her. "And, yeah, I've decided that I don't want you to be anything other than my receptionist, nice and safe here in the office, so . . . I figured you were going to quit anyway."

"What about our deal?" she asked. "I get to do the easy cases—the safe ones."

"The safe ones." His laughter was scornful. "Like Lillian Lavelle's?"

"Not every client who walks through your door is going to be a mur-derous ex–porn star obsessed with avenging her daughter's death," she pointed out. At least she hoped not.

"If that's really what this is about," Ric said.

"I think it is," Annie said, sitting cross-legged on the bed next to Pierre, who gave her his *why aren't you petting me* look. She obliged. "I've been thinking about what Jules told us, the chain of events—the new Trixie Ab-solute DVD. Why would Lillian come out of retirement for this fledgling company that can't even offer her a credible contract? Jules showed me a copy of the deal she signed—it was pathetic. We've seen pictures of Marcy with Brenda, who was described as GBJ's workhorse—God, doesn't that word make your skin crawl?"

"Yeah." Ric looked up from surveying the contents of her dresser top—her bottles of sunblock and other moisturizers, her hairbrush, the pewter-framed photo of Pam holding tightly to a smiling Pierre, a bandanna on her head because her hair was gone from the chemo. "But this entire case makes my skin crawl, so . . ." He picked up the photo to look at it more closely.

"Anyway," Annie continued, dropping a kiss onto Pierre's head because the sight of Ric touching her things with his long, elegant fingers was just too odd, "we know Marcy had contact with Gordie Junior through Brenda. Who's to say he didn't hold Marcy hostage to put pressure on Lillian to make his movie? And you know, it doesn't even have to be that dramatic. He didn't have to lock Marcy in the basement. Maybe he just kept her drugged up. If she was an addict, and he made it possible for her to get high for free . . ."

He put the photo back. "So your theory is that Lillian made the movie for GBJ Productions as part of some kind of deal with Gordie Junior to leave her daughter alone?"

Annie nodded. "But Marcy died anyway. Whether it was Gordie's fault or not, Lillian blames him and wants him to pay."

"She claimed it was Gordon Senior who administered Marcy's overdose," Ric told her, leaning against the dresser. "That he did it intentionally because Marcy was a witness to one of Junior's murders. She told me that her killing Junior was meant to be some kind of eye-for-an-eye thing, with the punishment intended for Burns Senior."

"Hard not to include Junior on that punishment list," Annie pointed out, "since he's the one who'll be dead."

"Yeah, but it didn't seem as if Lillian's goal was to make him suffer," Ric said. "It's Burns Senior she wanted to torment—by making him bury his child, the way she had to bury hers."

"In that way, you're right, it's a definite two-for-one for Lillian," Annie agreed. "It's obvious that Burns cares about his son."

"Although maybe it was bull." Ric sighed. "When Lillian was telling me her sob story, she didn't mention GBJ Productions or *The Return of Trixie Absolute*, so it's possible it was all a lie and—Annie, your arm's bleeding."

She tried to look at her elbow, which was impossible to do, so she scrambled off the bed and over to the mirror, where she could see it. Yup, it was bleeding again. It was just a superficial scrape, but every time it started to scab up, she either straightened or bent her arm, and it opened up again. The good news was each time it happened, it looked less raw and angry. "Did I get it on the bedspread?"

"Like *that's* what I'm worried about." Ric came closer, taking her arm and turning her to the light so he could get a better look.

"How's your leg?" she asked him.

"It's healing," he told her.

"You know the cool thing about me?" she told him. "It's when I get hurt like this? I actually heal, too."

"Yeah, you're funny," he said, still frowning at her elbow. "A real laugh riot." He was standing so close she could smell the coffee that he'd had on his way home. "I hate that I did this to you."

"You didn't," Annie told him. "Any more than Jules did by giving me those shoes to wear. You're going to have to get over yourself, Ick-Ray." Her childhood nickname for him made him smile, but it was far too brief. And he didn't back away as she'd hoped he would. He was still standing much too close. "You're not responsible for me."

"It feels like I am," he admitted. "I feel like . . . I've fucked everything up."

"Well," she said, retreating back to the bed and Pierre. "If that's really what you feel, then you're just going to have to figure out a way to fix it. Although, if you want to know the truth—here we are, assisting the FBI in a high-priority investigation. It feels to *me* as if, despite some of the blunders with Lillian Lavelle, we managed to do something really right."

Tonight Jules would at least have a shot at searching for his missing agent, Peggy Ryan, in the place where she was last known to be—Burns Point. With Burns's electronic security, the wall around his estate, and his army of bodyguards, there was no other way—realistically—that Jules could have gotten in.

"I just want it to be over," Ric admitted. "I want you to be safe and . . ."

She knew what he wanted. He wanted her out of his apartment. Out of his life.

"I better go shower," he told her. "You need the bathroom before I get in there?"

Annie shook her head. "Can I ask you something?"

He stopped. Sighed. Turned to face her. "No, I'm not in love with Robin Chadwick."

"Ooh," she said. "The famous Alvarado sense of humor might just be making a comeback."

"I wasn't trying to be funny, I was trying to be ironic. I couldn't believe that you asked Jules that—first because it was so personal, and second because it was beyond freaking obvious."

It *was* a personal question, but Annie and Jules had just had an extremely personal conversation minutes before Ric had returned. In fact, Jules had asked her the very same question about Ric. Was she in love with him?

She'd told him no. She wasn't *that* crazy.

But she'd admitted to having these foolish feelings of attraction that just wouldn't go away. She knew Ric, and she knew he wasn't going to change. And yet a very significant part of her still wanted to jump him.

There were some people, Jules had told her, obviously choosing his words carefully, that you could never let your guard down when you were around. They were dangerous, not merely because of that intense physical attraction, but because you loved them, even though it was crazy to. It was a shame, really, that you couldn't just decide to love one person, and decide to *not* love someone else. But love didn't know from crazy—it just happened, and the first thing you had to do was be honest about it, at least to yourself.

And then you had to stay far away from that dangerous person, and not fool yourself into thinking you could have any kind of casual, temporary fling with them. It couldn't ever just be about sex—the crazy thing would be in thinking that sex would be enough.

It could never be casual, and it would always end in heartbreak. In a way, it was a gift—the kind of connection that everyone longed to find. But it was far more valuable when the person with whom you had that connection could also bring you joy.

Ric was standing there now, at the foot of her bed, waiting for Annie to stop staring at him and speak up—*Can I ask you something?*—looking like a living advertisement for industrial-strength heartbreak.

Annie had told Jules that she loved Ric as a friend.

Yeah, right. And maybe if she kept repeating that to herself, over and over . . .

"Last night," she asked Ric now. "How did you fool everyone into thinking you were drunk? You didn't touch your beer at the party. You had nothing to drink all night."

Ric nodded. "Not until we got to the police station."

Where he'd picked up that mug and . . .

"Johnny Olson laces his coffee with whiskey," Ric explained. "And at that time of night, it's usually the other way around."

As in, he laced his whiskey with coffee. Check.

"I spilled some down my shirt, too," he told her. "Doesn't take much to make you stink."

Annie nodded. "So . . . how did you know they weren't going to press charges?"

"Because most of the people there are still my friends, and they'd never seen me drunk before. They also know I'm close to my father, so . . ." He shrugged. "Everyone gets at least one free drunken meltdown. It's when it becomes a regular event that you start having real problems."

"And you were certain they'd think you were drunk, not homicidal, or . . . ?" Having some kind of emotional breakdown, the way she'd thought.

"Absolutely." He was definite.

"Because . . . ?"

"Cops—even former cops—don't cry unless they're faced," Ric told her. "It's a law enforcement rule."

"So you pretended to cry so they'd think you were shit-faced." It had sounded hauntingly real to her, the memory keeping her awake long into the night.

He surprised her by saying, "No, I really made myself do it. You've got to get the fluids flowing to be believable—not just tears, but snot and drool."

"Ew," Annie said.

Ric smiled. "It was either that or piss myself, but I didn't think my stank level would rate that."

She couldn't help it—she smiled back at him. "So there's a science to this."

"Totally." His smile faded, and he took a step toward her, but then stopped, his hands on the wooden footboard of her bed. "Can we, um, maybe call a truce here?"

"What kind of truce?" she asked warily. "The kind where I do what you want me to?"

Ric smiled. "Sort of. But . . . I also do what *you* want me to do, which is . . . be safe. Safer. Which is what I'll be if I don't have to worry about you skinning your elbow, or worse."

Annie stood up, rolling her eyes as she crossed to the closet. How many times did they have to rehash this? And what *did* one wear to a firing range anyway? "You better shower, or we won't have time to go see your father before Jules gets back."

"Annie." Ric actually touched her, turning her to face him. "You didn't want me to do this alone. I'm not alone now. I've got Cassidy and the entire FBI backing me up. You, on the other hand, have no experience, and if you want to know the truth, statistics show that if I'm going to die, it's probably going to be because of you."

Annie was silent. What could she say to that?

"I've been thinking," Ric told her, "and what we're going to do is, we're going to go to Burns Point tonight, and we're going to break up. You're going to be far too interested in the movie star—he's going to be sniffing around you, too, so it'll look real. I'm going to get jealous and pissed off and cut you loose. You're going to tell Burns that Chadwick offered you a job—"

"Doing what?"

Ric's patience was not very thick. "I don't know. Building a stone wall around his estate," he said in exasperation. "It doesn't matter *what*, as long as you and Chadwick go skipping off to California, hand in hand. Which, before you protest, is a very important job for you to do because it gets Chadwick out of Cassidy's hair, freeing him up to think clearly."

Annie shook her head. "You're assuming Robin's going to agree—"

"He will."

Because Robin was going to be told that *he* had this big important job to do, which involved making sure *she* was safe. It was, actually, quite a clever plan.

Still it had some major flaws. "You've seen Dolphina," she said. "Who's going to believe Robin would dump her for someone like me?"

"Anyone who meets you," Ric shot back.

So okay, at least he didn't try to bullshit her by telling her she was just as beautiful. And if anyone could pull off the whole dumping-the-beauty-for-the-dumpy-woman-with-the-great-personality thing, Robin Chadwick, soon-to-be Oscar nominee could.

"Your mother's going to think I'm a real jerk," Annie told Ric. "Running off with someone else mere days after moving in with you."

"I'll tell her it was my fault," Ric said. "That I got overwhelmed. Scared. You know, by, um, my terrifying intense feelings for you. I'll tell her I freaked out and cheated on you first."

"Which makes *me* a fool for moving in with you in the first place," she countered.

"Maybe not a fool," he said. "Maybe just foolishly in love."

"Isn't that redundant?" Annie asked. "Foolishly in love?"

"How did you get so cynical?"

"Hello. You and Bruce were my role models. Does the picture of a soccer goal next to Betsy Bouvette's name ring any bells?"

His temper flared again. "For your information, I went out with her for a year and a half."

Annie was stunned. "Are you serious?"

"No, I'm lying."

"How come I never saw her with you?" she asked.

"Because her father didn't like the color of my skin," Ric revealed. "Or the fact that *my* father had an accent."

"What?" Annie couldn't believe it.

"My entire relationship with Betsy was on the down-low," Ric told her. "And Bruce, he gave me endless crap about it, too. He thought I could do better. *Dude, why would you want to limit yourself to just one girl? It's time to move on.* Well, guess what? I was in love with her, Annie. I was willing to sneak around to be with her, but *she* moved on. She dumped me after she went to college, okay?"

He *was* serious. Betsy Bouvette had dumped *him*.

"So Bruce drew the picture of the goal," Ric continued, "and I tried to pretend that my heart wasn't broken. At least I lost my virginity, right? Big whoop."

"Wow," Annie said. She'd had no idea.

"Don't assume you know me," he said. "I am not Bruce."

"I'm sorry. I mean, not that you're not Bruce. I'm actually glad you're not Bruce—"

"Do we have an agreement?"

"Betsy was crazy."

"*Do.* We have an agreement?" Clearly Ric had said all he was willing to say on the subject of Betsy Bouvette.

"Will you call me every day with an update?" Annie asked. "And will you promise that you'll be as careful as you would've been if I were with you?"

"Yes. And?" he said because he knew her well enough to know there'd be more.

"Will you cry when I leave? And I don't mind the drool so much, but could you do me a favor and keep it snot-free?"

Ric laughed. He knew he'd won.

"Thank you," he said, and kissed her.

On the forehead.

The way he'd done when she was thirteen and he was seventeen and in love with Betsy Bouvette, who'd broken his heart.

Jules could tell, as he came out of the urban warfare course, that he'd impressed the crap out of Ric Alvarado. Particularly when he put his name on some paperwork that Yashi conveniently had on a clipboard, ready for him to sign.

"Whoa," Ric said. "You're not a lefty?"

"Nope," Jules said, nodding his thanks to Yash as he headed for the cage where they'd stashed their gear. "That's why I didn't get a perfect score. Still, this isn't bad for my nondominant hand."

That was when Ric surprised him. "You know, you don't have to prove anything to me."

"Oh yeah?" Jules took off his glove and put it in his gym bag. "When did that change?"

"I don't know," Ric admitted, leaning against the chain links. "I guess . . . today. I guess I realized we're . . . more alike than I thought. I'm not gay—that's not what I mean."

Jules laughed as he closed the cage but didn't bother to lock it. "I'm pretty clear on that."

"I just meant—"

"I got it," Jules said. "And I appreciate both your candor and your insight. Too many people focus on differences. It's always nice when someone chooses to join the reality-based world. By the way, I spoke to, um, Robin and I think your plan's going to work. He's willing to help—to get Annie to safety. But he can't leave Sarasota until Sunday night."

And he'd only leave then, if Jules agreed to set aside some time to sit down and talk with him. Just talk, Robin had stressed. They could meet anywhere—even in public, in a restaurant or a bar. It was Jules's call.

He would use the opportunity to try to convince Robin to leave earlier, not that he had much hope of doing that.

"He said Annie could stay in his hotel suite, attend the festival with him," Jules told Ric. "It's not my first choice, but with the festival's security, which is extremely tight, they'll be safe enough."

Ric wasn't happy, but he nodded.

Yashi reappeared. "Annie's getting ready to go in," he reported as he headed up the stairs that led to the spectators' gallery. "She's doubling up with Deb."

"You want to watch?" Jules asked Ric.

"I'm not sure." But Ric took the stairs two at a time, following Yashi.

"She did extremely well on the firing range." Jules followed them, too.

"Yeah, she was excellent."

But this was an entirely different skill set—not only did these targets move, but they fired back. Of course, there were no bullets being used. It was all done with lasers and computers.

Jules took a place with Ric at the window, looking down at the bombed-out buildings and rubble-filled roads of the course. Out of the many targets that popped up, some would be innocent bystanders, and points would be lost for each of those that were "killed."

"Traditionally," Yashi said, "when doubling up, a newbie'll take out his or her more experienced companion within the first five seconds. Most are dead themselves within ten-point-five seconds after that."

As they watched, Annie came onto the course with FBI agent Deb Erlanger behind her. Deb, athletic and trim with lank brown hair that she'd tucked up into a baseball cap, was talking, and Annie was listening and nodding.

Deb was probably telling her to wait for a moment, let her eyes get used to the lower levels of light. Only when she was ready should she give the signal to go.

"So what'd you have to do to get this place completely to ourselves?" Ric asked, his eyes on Annie, who was laughing at something Deb had told her.

"Just one quick phone call," Jules said. "To my boss. You've met him, by the way—Max Bhagat."

Ric looked at him. "Your boss is the head of the FBI's top counterterrorist division?"

"That's him." He could see Ric putting two and two together. If Max was Jules's immediate superior, then Jules wasn't just some boots-on-the-ground, low-level grunt who was going to screw things up and get Annie killed. It was interesting, really. Ric didn't appear to care at all about himself. His single-minded concern was Annie. Jules went on: "Apparently you handled the police investigation when Max's girlfriend's motel room was broken into a few years back. It was out on Siesta Key."

"They stole her prescription meds and underwear," Ric remembered. "Gina. Her last name was something Italian. She was, um . . ."

"She's a pretty good friend of mine," Jules interrupted. "So you might want to hold the descriptive adjective if it's not flattering."

Ric laughed. "No, I wasn't going to . . . Beautiful. She was crazy beautiful, with a little just plain crazy thrown in, too. Like most women I know."

"FYI, Max started a file on you."

Ric looked at Jules now in disbelief. "Because I hit on his girlfriend?"

Had he really? That must've been interesting. "Gina's his wife now," Jules informed him. "But no. It's not that kind of file."

Down on the course, Annie gave the signal and . . .

She and Deb moved together, ducking for cover, and leapfrogging their way to the side of the first mock building.

Seconds ticked by and . . .

Holy shit.

"Beginner's luck," Yashi proclaimed. "Got to be."

Annie's stance was beyond ridiculous, but with twenty seconds down and still counting, she'd managed to keep from getting hit. She'd even tagged her share of tangos, leaving alive the crying toddler pop-up that Ric had accidentally taken out earlier, when he'd done the course.

"*Here's* where Deb buys it," Yashi announced, but the two women cleared the first building without getting hit.

They moved slowly, carefully, which was going to lose them a few points in their final score. But the truth was that they'd win far more for surviving until the buzzer rang. As Jules watched, they headed toward the second building, stopping to eliminate half a dozen targets along the way.

Again, Yashi gave his dire prediction: "Here's where they go down," and again he was proven wrong. Annie was well aware of Deb's position at all times. Whatever crash course Deb had given her before they went in, she'd obviously been paying close attention.

"Holy shit," Jules said again. "Are you sure Annie doesn't have a military background?"

Ric shook his head in wonder as Jules answered the question himself.

"Of course she doesn't, her stance is fugly." She looked like an animated crab with a firearm for a claw. Her aim with the moving targets, however, was astonishing. And Deb—a kick-ass field agent—was paying attention, too. She realized it, revising their strategy right there in the middle of the course. Instead of Annie covering her back, she now covered Annie's—giving her the freedom she needed to take out the targets willy-nilly.

And willy-nilly, take them out she did.

"Look at her," Jules said, as if Ric and Yashi weren't both paying attention raptly. "She's actually listening to Deb's instructions—she's able to multitask while under fire—which is more than I can say about you, Yash."

"Yep, I suck at that," Yashi agreed. His strengths shone when he sat at a computer, inside of a surveillance van. "Firefights freak me out."

"She's always been really good at video games," Ric volunteered. "She used to play with me and Bruce—her brother—all the time."

As they watched, after Annie and Deb cleared the third and then the fourth building, the bell rang and the lights came up. The two women high-fived, and Yashi dashed down the stairs, leaving Ric to ask, "About that file you said Max started. The one with my name on the tab. If it's not . . ."

"It's the kind of file that the recruitment department creates, under the recommendation of someone important, like Max."

Ric laughed his surprise. "You're kidding."

"Nope. Because of Max's recommendation, you're in the process of being seriously considered for recruitment," Jules told him. "It's been years, I know, since he met you, but apparently—despite the hitting-on-the-girlfriend thing?—you made a strong impression. I've seen the file. He's followed your career, and when he found out you left the force, he got the ball rolling regarding clearances and various other standard procedures. I thought you should know that. Just . . . so you know that you don't have to try to impress *me*."

"I can't shoot for shit," Ric said. "Not like you. Not like . . . my freaking untrained receptionist can."

"You're not bad," Jules said, leading the way down the stairs. "You've just got to practice. How often do you practice?"

"These days? Never."

"Well, there you go."

"How often does Annie practice?" Ric countered.

"Some people are naturals," Jules said. "For years I had a partner—agency partner—and she was this world-class sharpshooter. She was amazing. And I was like, *Wow, you must've been practicing since you were three years old,* and she was like, *Nope.* First time she picked up a rifle was after she joined the Navy. It was part of the officers' program, you know, learning to shoot, and she was like, *Hey, look what I can do.* I'm not saying she didn't have to practice a lot—she did. She was extremely disciplined, and practice was the difference between being great and phenomenal. But she started at great. Kind of like Annie."

And there she was. Loaded with adrenaline. Laughing and talking with Deb and Yashi. Sparkling with enthusiasm and glowing with pride.

Jules looked back at Ric, who'd turned, and was making a beeline for the men's locker room.

"Good job," Ric called to Annie before he disappeared.

It was as if he'd taken a bucket of cold water and thrown it into her face. She tried to hide her disappointment, but her smile lost about half of its wattage.

"That was really impressive," Jules told her, told Deb, too.

"It was fun," Annie said. "I bet it's much scarier with real bullets, though."

Deb handed Jules the printout that detailed their score. "She outshot me, almost two to one."

"She outscored everyone but Jules," Yashi observed.

"Because Deb was telling me what to do," Annie pointed out, glancing over at the door through which Ric had vanished. "If I'd been in there alone, I wouldn't have scored so high."

She'd said that—she scored high—as if it were a bad thing. "So what else are you good at?" Jules asked her.

Annie crossed her arms. "You mean like Ping-Pong?" she asked. "Tennis, too, although I don't really like playing. Golf's fun . . . softball, pinball, darts, shuffleboard, pool"—she ticked them off on her fingers—"ultimate Frisbee, volleyball, basketball, skimboarding, waterskiing. I've never actually tried regular surfing, but windsurfing rocked, although I only did it once. I think it was supposed to humble me, but I used to fly kites on the beach when I was a kid, so I really had a feel for working with the wind instead of against it. I had a blast, but my boyfriend got a concussion when he capsized and the board hit him in the head. Two days later he dumped me."

And suddenly it made sense. Annie actually thought Ric had gone off to pout because she'd done so well. Jules wasn't quite sure what to say, since *his* interpretation of the motive behind Ric's vanishing act was far different.

Yashi filled in the silence. "Your boyfriend was an idiot," he said. "Personally, I love women who can kick me to the curb."

"Speaking of the curb, we should hit the road," Deb announced.

"We do need to get going," Jules agreed. They had to be ready to leave for the party at Burns Point in just a few hours, and there was still a lot to do in preparation. "Let's meet in the lobby in fifteen."

Still, he caught Annie's arm, stopping her before she followed Deb toward the women's locker room. "Yo, Annie Oakley." He lowered his voice. "I don't think Ric's problem has anything to do with your skill level."

"It doesn't matter," she obviously lied. "It's not important, either way."

"You should maybe talk to him," Jules said. "I don't think either of you are being honest about—"

"It doesn't matter," she said again. "What matters is that you're going to keep him as safe as possible."

"I will," Jules promised.

"Good," she said. "So what am I wearing tonight? Pasties and a G-string?"

Jules laughed. "This time I gave you a choice."

CHAPTER
FOURTEEN

J ules brought backup to their meeting, in the form of his colleague Ric
Alvarado.

"How's your father?" Robin asked to cover his disappointment as
he closed his hotel-suite door behind them.

"He's doing all right," Ric said. "He's had to cancel some perfor-
mances, and he's not happy about that, but he knows it could've been a lot
worse."

Robin was as aware as hell of Jules, who'd traded in his suit and tie for
a pair of jeans and a snugly fitting T-shirt that said LIFE IS GOOD. It was hard
not to think about the last time Jules was up here in his suite, when they'd
stood *right* over there . . .

Yeah.

Part of what Ric was saying broke through his distraction. "Perfor-
mances?" Robin repeated.

"My father's a jazz pianist," Ric said.

"Teo Alvarado," Jules told him.

"No way." Robin couldn't believe it. "I was just talking to my sister on
the phone, and she told me to try to find him—you know, to hear him
play—while I'm here in Sarasota. She adores his stuff. She went on and on
about him."

Actually, what Jane had really gone on and on about was *Riptide*.
She'd finally gone to see a sneak preview of the movie, and she'd loved it.
Robin's performance as a Navy SEAL nicknamed Crash was her new favorite of all of his roles—including the ones he'd had in the films she herself had written and produced.

It made sense that Jane had liked the character, because Robin had been subtly channeling his brother-in-law as he'd played this part. Like Janey's husband, Cosmo, Crash had a quiet stillness to him, a deep and faithful belief in truth and justice that merged tightly with both honor and integrity. After years of hanging with Cos, Robin had it down pretty accurately.

No doubt about it, this was his new personal favorite role, too. Playing Crash had made him feel strong and clean. Heroic.

A lot like he imagined Jules felt, just living his exemplary life.

Jane hadn't said anything about the fight they'd had before Robin had left to make the rounds of festivals, so he hadn't brought it up, either. Little Billy was doing fine, Cosmo was still overseas with his SEAL team, but he was in a place where he could e-mail her daily, so she was a little less anxious.

She *did* question him about Dolphina—apparently all the tabloids were running photos of the two of them together.

"She's just a friend," Robin had told his sister. "Really. She, um, knows."

That had surprised Jane. That, and the bomb he'd oh-so-casually dropped right after that—telling her that Jules Cassidy was here in town.

Her response had surprised him in return. "Are you self-destructing?" Jane had asked. "Because right now, here in Hollywood? I wasn't going to say anything, because I was afraid it might jinx you, but the buzz—about you, dumb-ass—is incredible. Maybe you should come home, because you need to experience it to really understand what's happening."

"I'm not self-destructing," Robin protested. "I'm being careful." And yeah, okay, maybe that was a lie. But he was going to start being more careful—at least for a little while longer.

"Robbie, people are comparing your acting to Marlon Brando and James Dean," Jane told him. "If you start something with Jules, something that you can't finish because you still want that recognition, that kind of a career . . ." She sighed. "You're going to hurt him more than you already have. And then, when you're finally ready to be honest about what you really want, he's going to be gone. You'll never get him back."

"Yeah, whoops, someone's at the door—I gotta go," Robin had lied, because he'd been too much of a coward to admit that he finally *did* know what he really wanted.

He wanted it all.

And Robin didn't want to tell his sister that. He didn't want to hear a myriad of reasons why he could never make it work, that it was impossible, that no one could ever, really, have everything they wanted. He didn't want to hear that there had to be sacrifice to appease the gods, there had to be sorrow and loss to truly appreciate true joy and happiness . . .

Bullshit, Janey.

He *could* have it all.

Right now Ric was talking about his father's prognosis and progress as he scanned the room with some kind of electronic device. If that was meant to freak Robin out, well, mission accomplished, bro. Jesus, did they really think someone had bugged his room? And, if someone had, they'd gotten an earful this morning when Robin had taken Janey's call.

Jules wandered over to the sliding-glass windows that lined one entire wall of the suite. The last time he was up here, the drapes had been closed. As Jules gazed past the railing of the balcony and out at the breathtaking view of the harbor, hands jammed into the front pockets of his jeans, Robin took it in, too. The water and sky were shades of heavenly brilliance. The green of the palm trees and the white of the sand were equally crisp and clear. It was perfection—as if life here were in high-def. Funny how, with all the hours he'd spent in this suite, he hadn't noticed that before.

Of course, maybe the fact that Jules was part of the picture today had something to do with it.

"The good news is, he's going to be okay," Ric said, shutting off the device. "Room's clear." He looked at Robin and explained: "No listening devices."

"I figured that's what you were doing. It never occurred to me that—"

"I know." Jules turned to face him. His outfit may have been casual, but the expression on his face was all business. "Which is why we need to talk about Gordon Burns and exactly what we're doing here. You better sit down, this could take a while."

Martell knew that Robin Chadwick was part of tonight's big charade. It was, after all, Chadwick who'd gotten Jules, Ric, and Annie the invite out to Burns Point.

But it wasn't until the limo pulled up out front and the movie star walked into Ric's office that the craziness of the situation smacked Martell in the face.

He'd hung with Annie nearly all afternoon, which hadn't been all that much fun since, after a brief and closemouthed trip to the CVS, she'd gone up to her room with her dog-thing and shut the door. Martell had actually finished the Waverly brief on his laptop in Ric's office, despite the fact that sheer boredom made his eyes roll back in his head. He'd fallen asleep at least three times, midsentence, but it was finally done.

But things started heating when Mr. Famous strutted in. He was talking as he entered, Ric right behind him.

"I'm an actor," Hollywood was saying. "You don't have to tell me how to do it."

"Yeah, I do," Ric said. "I don't want you to fuck with her." He looked at Martell. "Where is she?"

She being Annie . . . "She's upstairs."

"You mean, literally?" Robin asked, clearly messing with Ric's head. "Because that would be dramatic. Getting caught in flagrante in some closet, during the party? I like it."

"I mean at all," Ric told him, heavy on the grim.

"Seriously," Cassidy, the little FBI dude, interjected as he closed the door behind them. "It's important that we don't do anything that might offend Gordon Burns. We're going to be guests in his house. Plus there's no guarantee that I'll find what I'm looking for, which means I'll probably have to go back."

"I find that kind of funny—the idea that *we've* got to be careful not to offend someone who's smuggling terrorists into the country," Robin mused. "Like *that's* not offensive. I mean, Jesus." He held out his hand to Martell. "Hi, I'm Robin. I assume you're supposed to be here."

"Martell's a friend," Ric told the movie star. "Former police. He'll be dropping by your hotel suite to check on Annie, frequently, until you leave on Sunday."

Apparently Ric and Jules hadn't managed to convince Mr. Big Stuff to wiedersehen the filmfest any earlier. No wonder Ric was pissed.

But Hollywood's handshake was firm, and his eyes were the same startling blue as his shirt. Martell had always assumed his eye color was digitally enhanced on screen, or at least the result of special contact lenses.

Apparently not.

"Nice to meet you," Chadwick said, and damn if he didn't really mean it, too. The man was the best kind of player—or worst, depending upon one's point of view. His sincerity wasn't just an act. He meant what he said at the moment that he said it.

Martell knew because, as the saying went, game recognized game.

And Ric was putting Annie not just in his care but in his freaking hotel suite for three days and two nights . . . ?

The fool in question ran upstairs to change, stopping briefly to knock on Annie's door. "We're leaving in ten," Martell heard Ric call to her before he went into his room and closed the door with a bang.

"I'll be out in a sec." FBI exited the room, too, taking the garment bag he'd left in the closet earlier, heading into the office bathroom.

Which left Joe Famous wandering around the room, stopping to look at Ric's framed diplomas and various awards, as Martell packed up his computer. "Wow, Ric went to Dartmouth."

"May I, uh, offer you some advice?" Martell asked.

Robin turned toward him. "If it's to tell me to return to California after the party tonight—"

"It's not."

"Then yeah," Robin said. "Offer away."

Okay, so how to say this tactfully? "You're going to be spending a lot of time with Annie," Martell said, "over the next few days."

"That's the plan."

"You may not think so now," Martell told him, "but you're going to find yourself attracted to her. She's, um . . . special, you know? But she's Ric's. She may not know it, and Ric may not even know it, but she is. So, you keep that in mind, aight? And you keep your hands off."

"I will," Robin promised, a picture of somber integrity. Of course, he wasn't just a player, he was also an actor—a professional liar—which made his promises mean absolutely nothing.

"I'm serious," Martell said as Ric came back downstairs, tying his tie. Apparently only potential Oscar nominees could attend a party at Burns Point without a jacket and tie, because FBI came out of the men's suited up, too. But what a suit. It was Armani, clearly from the A-list side of the man's closet. Dude looked *sharp*.

"Serious about what?" Ric asked, but then immediately forgot what he'd been asking about. He apparently even forgot he had a mouth, because he left it dangling open as Annie came downstairs, her dog-thing in her arms.

She looked amazing. She'd gone with the black dress—Martell's recommendation. It was classy, yet the skirt was short enough to show off her shapely legs, its neckline low enough to give just a hint of cleavage.

But it was her hair and makeup that was making Ric look as if he were going to faint from the shock. Apparently that was what she'd been doing all that time, locked away in her room.

Her golden-brown curls were piled on top of her head, the style simple yet, again, pure class.

And the makeup didn't necessarily make her look prettier—she was pretty enough to start with. But with her eyes shadowed, her lashes dark with mascara, her lips outlined, and her cheeks accented with whatever shit that was that women wore on their faces, she'd made herself look so-phisticated. Elegant.

Like the kind of woman even a movie star might try extra hard to get with.

"You look great." Robin, naturally, was the first to find his voice as she crouched to put Pierre onto the floor. The dog had caught a whiff of Jules and needed to rush over to greet him.

"I didn't want to embarrass you," Annie told Robin, glancing at Ric, who, fool that he was, had turned away.

As if he were afraid that if he stared at her for too long, he might go blind.

As the silence stretched on, it became clear that none of the geniuses in the room knew quite how to respond to *I didn't want to embarrass you.*

Jules was kneeling next to the dog-thing, looking up at Robin as if it were his call. But Robin couldn't seem to look away from Jules and Pierre.

So Martell told Annie what they all were thinking. "Damn, beeyotch. You hot dot-com to start with, fo' shizzle. But tonight? You's onion booty, ya know what I'm saying?"

Annie laughed—mission accomplished—as she looked at him. "Actually, no."

"Goodness gracious, madam," he translated in his best Colin Firth. "You are, for certain, always quite attractive. But tonight, your lovely radiance could make a grown man weep."

She sparkled as she laughed. "Well, thank you," she told him, then looked over at Ric again. This time the fool actually met her gaze, managing to manufacture a smile while he was at it. Go, team.

"You don't get to come again," she added, and it took Martell a second to realize she was talking to him. "To the party?" she clarified.

"Oh," he said as Jules gave Pierre one last pat and began pulling what looked like architectural drawings from a cardboard tube. "Yeah, no. Gordon Burns makes me throw up in my mouth, so it's just as good. I'm on backup tonight—you run into any trouble, you give me a call, I'll come save the day." In the meantime, he was heading to the hospital, to visit Teo and figure out who they could sue to get the most media coverage.

Still, he moved closer to get a look at what was definitely the floor plan of Gordon Burns's estate.

"I want everyone to see this," Jules said. "But it's really just for Ric and me." He looked at Ric. "If for some reason I'm unable to slip away—"

Ric nodded. "It'll be up to me. Not Annie. Or Robin. Your job is to distract Burns," he reminded them.

"The party's going to be held here." FBI pointed to the drawing. "There's a courtyard—an outdoor patio, surrounded on three sides by the main living area. The entire area overlooks the harbor—which makes surveillance tricky but not impossible. We've been watching the setup, and from the number of tables, we're estimating there'll be around fifty guests."

That was a good thing. The bigger the crowd, the easier to slip away and not be missed.

"There's a local myth," Jules told them, "that Burns has his entire place wired with cameras and mics, so he can listen in on everyone who comes to Burns Point. That's not true, which is a shame, because if he did, we would've been able to tap into his system. We'll need to be discreet while we're there, but any threat of being overheard or watched will come from the old-fashioned way—Burns's security guards."

"That's good to know," Ric said.

"This is the kitchen, over here." Jules pointed again at the blueprints. "And this is the servants' wing." A hallway led off from the massive kitchen, taking a turn to the right. There were five rooms on either side of the central corridor. Down at the end was a door to a deck, overlooking the back of the garage and a part of the driveway that looked to be a loading area into the kitchen.

"Imagine having five people on staff," Annie mused. She looked up at Robin. "You probably do, huh?"

"Not when I'm at home," he said. "I like my privacy. Although now with *Riptide* doing so well, my manager thinks I need to find a bodyguard. You know, pay someone a christload of money to hang with me when I'm home at night, so I'm never alone. Tag along when I go on location to Thailand or Paris or New Zealand. It'd be a tough job—spending all that time in exotic locations. We've had a lot of applicants, but . . . I'm looking for the right person, someone I really click with."

"Do you mind if we do *this*?" Jules pointed to the map, clearly exasperated.

"I take it that's a no?" Robin countered.

Jules didn't deign to answer him. "Tonight's focus is finding Peggy Ryan." He put her photo next to the blueprints. "We're looking for any sign of her at all."

"Which room is hers?" Annie asked.

"This one." He pointed to the room farthest from the kitchen, closest to that deck. "We know she had a private bath and a single window, facing roughly west. In her last two communications, she'd mentioned being able to see the sunset through that window. She also mentioned how cold it was in her room with the air-conditioning always running. She was definitely trying to tell us something—she repeated that information almost word for word. I suspect we're going to find some kind of message inside the air-conditioning vent nearest to the window."

"I've got a B-and-E kit made of plastic," Ric reported. "It won't get picked up by a metal detector."

Annie looked at him. "B and E?"

"Breaking and entering," he explained. "You know, lock pick, screwdriver to remove the a/c vent cover . . . ?"

How *did* Burns explain the metal detectors to his party guests? Did he just make it part of the festivities, or did he try to disguise it? *Here, walk through this Spanish-moss-covered archway so we can take your photo with Mandy the Manatee.*

And what about the guests who set off the alarm? *Step over here for a cavity search, madam. Joelle will take your drink order while you wait for Mr. Foley to change his latex gloves . . .*

"A plastic screwdriver?" Annie was skeptical.

"Less like a plastic fork," Martell told her, "and more like a plastic gun."

"It will get noticed if you're given a body search," Jules warned. "So be careful."

"Always am," Ric said.

Yeah, right.

Had Martell actually said that aloud? Annie was looking at him as if he had.

But she had more questions for Jules. "Is the plan to go around the side of the house"—she used her finger to point out the route, landing on the servants' deck—"and access the servants' wing through here?"

Jules shook his head. "There're no stairs up or down from that deck."

She looked at the blueprint more closely. "Isn't it ground level?"

"Not that part of the house. It's built on an incline." He pointed. "The garages are beneath the kitchen and servants' wing."

"We're not exactly dressed for climbing," Ric chimed in.

"What, no plastic grappling hook and rope that shoots out of the soles of your shoes?" Annie asked.

Ric shot her a look. "Best plan is to keep it simple," he continued. "Wander down the hall to the kitchen, looking for a men's room."

"I agree," Jules said.

"Where's Burns's office?" Ric asked.

"Second floor." Jules flipped to a second page, and pointed to a room on the opposite side of the house. "Do not go there. He doesn't keep paperwork. There'll be nothing up there — except trouble if you're found poking around." He looked at Robin and Annie, too. "Are we clear on that?"

They all nodded.

"Don't go anywhere alone," Ric reminded Annie.

"You know, I can get us into the kitchen," Robin volunteered. "I always sign autographs for the staff at the end of every party."

"You do?" Jules said.

"Yes. Is that really so hard for you to believe?"

"It's not. It's . . . great," Jules said. "But it's hard to imagine that you'll be allowed down there by yourself. Burns'll go with you, right?"

"Not necessarily," Robin said. "Sometimes the host comes with, sometimes I just go off exploring, with one of my handlers." He gazed at Jules. "Tonight, that can be you."

Chadwick's assistants were actually called handlers? Like he was some kind of dancing bear? Martell glanced at Ric, checking in with his boy to see if he thought that was kind of weird, too, but Ric had on his I-wish-I-were-invisible face, which was doubly odd.

Jules, meanwhile, was clearing his throat. "Right. Or Annie. But . . . if Burns ends up going into the kitchen with us . . . That's not going to work unless we can somehow create enough of a distraction to allow me to slip away while you're signing the staff's autographs."

"You think I can't create a major distraction?" Robin laughed. "You don't have much faith in me. I'm an actor. I've got, like, a degree in creating distractions."

"This isn't a game," Jules said, his voice hard. "You seem to think it is, but it's not. I've got an agent missing and presumed dead. She went into Burns Point and *never came back out*. She's either being held there, still, against her will, or her dead body was taken out in the trunk of a car."

Those weren't the only options. She could have been chopped into pieces and fed to the fishies. Or buried beneath the basement floor. Or . . .

"It's dangerous," Robin said, getting as much in Jules's face as Jules was in his. The party boy was gone, replaced by someone with Teflon cojones, someone who put his head down, revved it into high gear, and just blasted through whatever obstacles were thrown in his path. "I get it. And I'm well aware it's not a game, thanks, since yes, as you're fond of reminding me, last time I was involved in one of your 'games,' I got shot." He turned to Annie. "By the way, Ric wanted me to describe to you what that feels like. It burns like hell—and that's before it really starts to fucking hurt. Apparently he doesn't think very highly of you, because he thinks you're going to hear that and decide to run back to Buttmonkey, New Hampshire, or wherever you're from, like you don't give a damn about what we're doing here."

The look Annie gave Ric was a real shriveler, but Robin was far from done.

He got back in Jules's face. "And by the way, I'm also here because I give a damn—and no, not just about the safety and security of our country, although I care plenty about that—enough, yeah, to volunteer to help when it's obvious that you can actually *use* my help, like tonight. But I also care—very much—about you. You know what I'm afraid of most of all? I'm afraid that you'll disappear from my life again without giving me the chance to say all the things I want to say to you. Jesus, if I've got to knife-fight Gordon Burns just to spend time with you, someone find me a fucking K-Bar and bring him on."

In the silence that followed that outburst, a two-thousand-watt light-bulb went on over Martell's head, and suddenly it all made sense to him. Suddenly, Ric sending Annie to stay with Robin Chadwick in his hotel suite didn't seem like such a stupid idea after all.

But now it was Annie's turn to clear her throat. "Ric and I'll wait in the limo," she said brightly. She caught sight of Martell—no doubt he was standing there with his mouth hanging open. "Time to go."

Martell shouldered his laptop, but managed to linger, waiting for Annie as she hurriedly made sure Pierre had enough food and water to last the evening.

Jules didn't wait for the room to clear before asking Robin, "Are you completely insane?" He'd lowered his voice—not that there was any chance that they wouldn't hear him.

Robin didn't even bother trying not to be overheard. "You won't talk to me in private, fine. I'll have this conversation with you in front of your friends. Seeing you again has . . . Jules, it takes my breath away—how much I just want to be with you."

Martell felt Annie tug on his arm. Damn, this may have been the weirdest conversation between two men that he'd ever heard, but it was oddly compelling. She finally gave up, retreating out to the limo with Ric as Martell dragged his feet, hanging there on the stoop, needing to hear what on earth Jules was going to say in response to that bomb.

"I can't do this," FBI said. "I *won't*. Not twenty minutes before we're due at Burns Point."

"Yeah, sorry about my timing." Hollywood was sincere in his apology. "It sucks, as usual. I didn't mean to make things harder for you. I just . . . - couldn't not say anything, okay? So now you know. Either we talk privately after this party, or we talk in front of everyone. Obviously, I don't give a shit which you pick."

Robin brushed by Martell in his haste to get into the limo, murmuring, "Sorry to disappoint," as he passed.

Jules, too, had a host of apologies for Martell as he closed the office door. "I'm sorry, I don't have a key," was the first.

"I got it," Martell said, fishing in his pocket for his overburdened key ring.

"I'm also sorry for the inappropriate—"

"Like any of that was your fault?" Martell locked the deadbolt. "Actors. Always with the high drama. What are you gonna do?"

Jules managed a smile, but he was still standing there, like he had something more to add. And he did. "Robin's career depends on—"

"I know," Martell again cut him off. "It's okay. Your secret's safe with me, man."

"It's not my secret," Jules said, "but thank you."

"I'm going to have to do this," Ric breathed in Annie's ear as she stood near the outside bar on the patio of Burns Point.

She nodded, understanding. He was going to have to slip away and search for Peggy Ryan's room, because Jules wasn't going to be able to do it.

It was obvious that Gordon Burns considered Jules—producer Julian Young—to be as much of a celebrity as was Robin Chadwick. From the moment they'd walked in, Burns had commandeered both the actor and the undercover FBI agent, taking them around his crowded living room, introducing them to all of his friends and business associates.

"I think you should wait until Robin, you know, hits on me," Annie now told Ric. "Make it look like you're going off somewhere to pout."

Through the open French doors that led into the house, she heard Jules laugh at something Burns had said. It was possible Jules was an even better actor than Robin—in the limo he'd been beyond tense and terse, but now he seemed believably lighthearted and cheerful.

It was almost as if he'd partaken of the very large drinks Robin had mixed right there in the car. But Robin himself had been the only taker—

the movie star's good spirits could, no doubt, be traced to his still rising blood/alcohol levels.

Or maybe, as he'd announced in front of them all back at the office, his happiness came purely from the fact that he was standing beside Jules.

Beside her, Ric nodded. "You smell really good."

Annie turned to look at him. He was scanning both the patio and the living room, no doubt memorizing faces of the attendees for identification purposes later on.

He glanced at her. "What? You do. I'm just saying."

"Do you know how long it took me to put on this fucking makeup?" she asked him.

Her use of the F-word brought wariness to his eyes. He knew he was in trouble. He just didn't know why. "No," he said. "Should I?"

"Over an hour," she declared. "I had to teach myself how to do it—talk about a pain in the butt. Check out my eyes—the liner? Do you know how hard it is to take some little pointy pencil and make a straight line like that? Right near your own eye? Will you at least *look* at it, please?"

He looked. It was a little disconcerting to have him paying her such close attention, but at least now he didn't look as much like a former cop working with the FBI, scoping out a suspect's party.

"Note the mascara," she said, looking up into Ric's eyes, with their naturally thick, dark lashes. Bastard. "It clumps, so I had to use my fingers to unclump it, and then of course, I got it all over my face, so I had to wash it off and start over again. And then the lipstick? God forbid it be easy. No, first you have to use this special outliner crap, and the lip goo itself is applied with this impossible little brush.

"So I do all this, and *you* say . . ." She paused for emphasis. "*You smell good.* What you're smelling is the same hair gel that I use every day," she told him. "But thanks for noticing."

"I said *you smell* really *good,*" Ric corrected her, "which is actually the accepted way of telling your high school best friend's little sister—who spent years being way too young for you—that you think she looks unbelievably hot."

"Nice try." Annie wasn't buying. "Right now, though? I'm looking for *Wow, your eyeliner is really straight. Way to go.*"

"What I really like are your lips," he told her, his gaze on her mouth. "You did an amazing job. You look incredible, and you know it."

"Oh, man," she said, her insides butterflying despite herself. "You were *so* close, but you had to blow it. *You know it?* What is this? Eighth grade? No wonder I'm dumping you for a gay movie star."

He should have smiled, but he didn't. He just kept on staring at her mouth. "You scare me to death," he told her, finally looking into her eyes. "You always have—it started the day we met. Remember?"

Annie nodded. Did he actually think she'd ever forget?

She and her mother and Bruce had just moved to Sarasota. They'd rented a crappy house in a not-very-nice neighborhood—it was the best her mother could do at the time. She'd gotten a job at a store that sold appliances, and eleven-year-old Annie had built a fort in their sandy back-yard with cast-off refrigerator boxes.

It had rained the night before, which wasn't very good for the card-board, and Annie had gotten right to work after school, shoring up the in-sides. It was a task that wasn't particularly easy to do with her arm still in a sling.

"I've been thinking about it," Ric continued, "because of your elbow."

That day, it had been Ric whose elbow was all torn up. Not just his elbow, but his whole lower arm, and his knee, as well. She'd always sus-pected that his full body slide through the gravel in the school yard had given him one hell of a rug burn on his hip, too, right through his jeans. But if it had, he'd never let on.

He was being chased by a gang of older boys. Skinheads.

Their attack on Ric was random. It could have happened to any one of the Hispanic kids attending Sarasota High. For no apparent reason, on that particular day, they'd targeted him.

He should have gone back into the school and called his mother for a ride home. But as he'd told Annie years later, he simply hadn't believed he was in danger. Sure, they were harassing him—calling him names and throwing wads of paper at him.

But he'd never expected them to follow him. Or for those wads of paper to turn into rocks.

By then, it was too late to turn back. He'd run. They'd chased. He'd skidded in the gravel as they cut him off, when he'd tried to get to the ele-mentary school, hoping to find protection in the front office.

He'd gotten away from them, leaving the road then, cutting through backyards.

Until he'd gotten to Annie's and spotted her fort.

He was fast, despite his injuries, and was well ahead of the pack by then, and he'd kept his trail going, out of the yard. He'd circled back, crawling in to hide in the biggest of her boxes.

Which was right where she was using a baseball bat to brace the drooping roof.

They were face-to-face, two total strangers, but he put his finger on his lips, so she swallowed her surprise. It was then that she'd heard it. The sound of all those feet giving chase. All those voices shouting words she'd never heard before coming to Florida. Ese. Spic. Greaser. Cholo.

She'd peered out through one of the windows Bruce had helped her cut in the side of her fortress, holding her breath until they were gone.

"Thanks," Ric had said.

"Do you need to use our phone?" Annie asked, and it was then they came back. They could hear the voices, cajoling now, as if calling a missing cat. *Here ese, ese, ese . . .*

Ric looked out through a peephole. "Go inside your house," he ordered her. "Go. Now. They know I'm in here. *Run.*"

But she hadn't run. She'd climbed out from her fort and stood out there, at the edge of her yard, with her eyes narrowed and her good hand on her hip. "My uncle's home and he's sleeping," she informed them. "You better not wake him up. He's a cop and he gets mad when people wake him up."

The skinhead's leader was not convinced. "You hiding a friend of ours in your boxes, little girl?"

Annie may not have known what *ese* meant, or who these mean-looking kids were. All she knew was the boy with the dark brown eyes was in trouble because these kids were definitely not his friends. She glanced at her fort. "Only thing in there is my dog. His name's Beast. He bites."

"Bullshit." The skinhead called her bluff, stomping toward the boxes, so there was nothing to do but scream.

Loud and long and piercing, it made her brother, Bruce, jump up from his video game and come to the kitchen door to see WTF, as he was fond of saying.

"Hey," he'd shouted in his puberty-lowered voice, which spooked the skinheads into thinking it was her cop uncle coming outside to arrest them.

They turned and ran away, startled, too, by Ric, who'd launched himself at them, brandishing that baseball bat as soon as she'd started to scream. Even back then, he'd been willing to sacrifice his own safety for hers.

"You've always taken crazy risks," Ric told her now.

"I helped save your butt," Annie pointed out.

"More than once," he agreed. "But you don't really think things through. And when I'm with you, sometimes it feels like I start doing the same, like it's contagious."

"So what are you saying?" She struggled to understand. "That some-how it's my fault that you're here right now?" Standing on the patio in the home of a dangerous man who was believed to be responsible for smug-gling terrorists into the United States . . .

"I'm saying that I can't trust myself to make the right decisions when I'm around you," Ric admitted. "Annie, God, it's crazy, the way you make me feel—like the world's going to end, and it's up to me to save it, and I've got to pull either the yellow wire or the blue, only I have no clue what's the right thing to do." He laughed. "And there you are, just reaching for one of the wires, ready to gamble, because doing something's better than doing nothing at all, and when I'm with you, I believe it's true, but when I'm not, I know it's not and, Christ, it's driving me fucking nuts."

"I'm sorry," Annie said, because she didn't know what else to say. "After tonight, you won't have to worry about me."

"Yeah," he said, "like that's going to happen."

"At least I won't be annoying you with my contagious recklessness," she said.

"That came out wrong," he said, but he didn't try to explain what he'd really meant.

She could see Robin through the French doors. He was looking for her, an extra glass of champagne in his hands, ready to do his part to get her to safety—and to keep her from driving Ric fucking nuts. She had about twenty seconds before he spotted her and worked his way over. "Just be careful," she told Ric. "All right?"

He saw Robin coming, too, and was as aware as she that this was prob-ably going to be their last chance to speak face-to-face, until God knew when. "I really liked having you around these past few weeks."

"Apparently not enough to keep me on," she countered.

Ric shook his head. "I want you safe."

"You got it," Annie said, and she kissed him.

It was funny, actually. It was a textbook illustration of her so-called fail-ure to think things through, of her tendency to just act without real regard for the consequences.

It was meant to be a kiss goodbye, a last farewell to the ridiculous at-traction Annie still felt for him, a swift press of her lips against his.

And yeah. Wrapping her arms around his neck and letting him sweep his tongue into her mouth was not the going definition of swift. Of course, this was their second kiss, the first being really quite brief and heart-wrenchingly tender. Her mistake, apparently, lay in not retreating in that moment when she'd gazed into his eyes, as time seemed to hang, a heartbeat stretched on and endlessly on. Instead, she'd moved toward him, or maybe he'd pulled her close. Either way, the outcome was this disaster in which she found herself pressed tightly against him as she tried to inhale him.

If there was any good news at all, it was that he was holding her as tightly as she held him. That he was kissing her back as hungrily, as if he, too, had been dying to kiss her again since that ill-fated night in the Palm Gardens parking lot.

As if he hadn't gone and kissed Lillian Lavelle — the aging porn star — the very same way he'd kissed Annie that very same night.

And that was the end of that. Kiss over. Temporary insanity done and done.

Robin had slowed his steps, clearly uncertain as to whether now was the right time to approach.

"Is that for me?" Annie asked the movie star. Without waiting for his answer, she took one of the glasses from his hand and knocked it back. It was not the way to drink fine champagne, but what the hell.

"Annie," Ric said. He was no doubt about to launch into an apology or some kind of heavy explanation that would make her end up feeling even worse than she already did.

But she could see Jules through the open French doors, still deep in conversation with Gordon Burns, on the far side of the living room. "It's time to go save the world," she told Ric. "Be careful, okay?"

He was just standing there, staring at her, and she finally had to turn away.

"Come on," she told Robin, holding out her empty glass. "Let's go find me a refill."

CHAPTER
FIFTEEN

Once Ric was in the kitchen, no one paid him any attention whatsoever.

It was the getting there that was the giant pain in the balls.

Every time Gordon Burns's goons were distracted enough for Ric to attempt the dive down that hallway, a server with a tray of incredible-smelling food appeared and jauntily informed him that the men's room was in a different direction.

Which had left him with nothing to do but sample the food. And watch Robin Chadwick flirt with Annie. Which was far more unpleasant than he would have believed possible, considering.

The food was delicious, but the hand Robin had on Annie's back had drifted dangerously close to her ass, which pissed Ric off, regardless of the actor's sexual orientation. Fortunately, his response fit with their plan. It was appropriate—his standing there glowering at the two of them as they laughed and talked.

About what? What were they talking about? Annie sure as hell seemed to have forgotten that mere minutes earlier she'd been kissing Ric.

She'd kissed him first. It had totally caught him off guard, but his reflexes were a little too well developed. He'd grabbed her and kissed her back before he even knew what he was doing.

They were a total train wreck ready to happen. He was lucky that she wasn't coming home with him tonight.

At least that was what he kept trying to tell himself.

Right now his luck was holding as one of the white-clad kitchen staff—there were at least two dozen of them, presumably most hired only for this occasion—dropped a huge pan filled with what looked like seafood stew. It had a huge splash radius, and everyone scrambled to get it cleaned up as quickly as possible.

And that allowed Ric to waltz right through the kitchen and down the hall to the servants' wing. All of the doors were closed, and he was prepared for them to be locked, so it was a surprise when he tried the knob of the room that Cassidy had specified as Peggy's, and found that it turned.

It was dark inside, but the light from the hallway revealed that the room was unoccupied.

He went in, closing the door behind him. There weren't any blinds on the window, so he didn't want to turn on the overhead light. He got out his penlight, and as he flashed it around the room, his heart sank.

This room wasn't just unoccupied, it was vacant. It had been stripped bare of furniture and draperies. Even the carpeting had been pulled up and was gone. From the smell, and the rollers, trays, and stepladder still in the room, it was obvious that the walls had been recently painted—the bathroom, too.

It was a classic sanitizing job. Everything cleanable had been scrubbed. Anything that had been stained—carpeting, drapes, mattress, and blinds—had been removed and no doubt destroyed. The fresh paint would cover up any forensic evidence that had remained.

Yeah, the news Ric was going to deliver to Jules wasn't very good. If this was, indeed, Peggy Ryan's room—and Jules had seemed convinced that it was—it seemed highly likely that the woman was dead, most likely murdered right here.

There was only one air-conditioning vent in the entire two rooms, and it was nowhere near the window. It had been removed for the paint job, leaving a rectangular hole, roughly twelve by five, in the wall up near the ceiling.

Ric moved the ladder over and climbed up to get a look inside. His penlight revealed only a paint-speckled standard gray air duct. It was solidly in place, no gap around it in which Peggy might have slipped even a piece of paper. He reached in as far as he could, feeling around in the darkness, but there was nothing taped to the inside, either.

If Peggy had left anything in there, it had already been discovered.

Ric put the ladder back, pocketed his penlight, and opened the door a crack to make sure the hall was still empty. It was, but *shit,* someone was coming.

It would be far worse to be caught inside Peggy's room than out in the hall—that was a no-brainer. He slipped out of the door, closing it silently behind him, heading swiftly toward the door to the servants' deck. With luck, he would make it outside before whoever was coming turned the corner. With luck, whoever was coming would be the gardener, not one of Burns's thugs.

He didn't have time to make it out the door—best he could do was turn so it looked as if he were coming in from the deck, instead of trying to escape.

"What the fuck are you doing down here?" It was Foley, of course— Gordon Burns's right hand—the man who had slapped Annie in the limousine.

No doubt about it, Ric's luck had run out.

Gordie Junior attended his father's party dressed in a suit and tie. His collar didn't succeed in completely covering the tattoos that went up his back and shoulders and onto his neck, and the effect was rather strange.

He'd cornered Robin, whose body language was completely at ease as the two men talked. Still, Jules drifted toward them, and sure enough, Robin waved him closer, introducing the two men. "Julian Young, Gordon Burns Junior."

As Jules shook Junior's hand, he tried not to think about the psychological profile that was part of Gordie Junior's massive file. *Subject is known for sociopathic behavior, including outbursts of intense violence* . . . It was possible that the man whose hand he was shaking was responsible for Peggy Ryan's disappearance. He made himself smile. "It's a pleasure to meet you."

"Junior here says he has a business proposition that he thinks we'll find interesting," Robin told Jules.

"Really?" Jules said. "Where's Annie?" He'd been aware when Ric had left the party, close to ten minutes earlier, but he'd only just noticed that Annie seemed to have vanished as well.

"Ladies' room," Robin told Jules, but his eyes held an absolute *don't know.* "Junior heard about the movie we pitched to his father—"

"The one about the homo FBI agent," Junior interrupted. "It's not my cup of tea, you know what I mean? But I understand there's a viewership for that sort of thing. Plus it's an Oscar role, almost as good as playing a retard." He smacked Robin's arm. "Didn't you get nominated for playing a fag a few years back?"

Nice. Jules could smile through anything, but even without looking, he could feel Robin, beside him, getting tense.

"The accepted term is *gay*," Robin said. "And yes, I did. It was for *American Hero.*"

"Like I said, I don't watch that shit." Junior shrugged. "No offense."

"None taken," Robin lied, his smile tight.

"What I *did* see, however," Junior said, "was all the front-page tabloid stories that popped up after that movie came out. There was enormous speculation that you really were, you know, a gay, which I *know* had to suck. And it still hasn't completely gone away—I saw something just a month ago in the *National Voice.* They're still trying to tie you to what's-his-name, your co-star in that film—turns out *that* guy really was a fag, which must've been creepy as shit, you know, working with him?"

"His name's Adam Wyndham," Robin said. "He's a brilliant actor."

Adam was undeniably a good actor, but he'd also been part of the rift between Robin and Jules all those years ago.

Jules looked at Robin. "I didn't realize you were still friends with him," he said, and immediately kicked himself for saying anything at all, let alone something that sounded even remotely jealous. He'd been working hard all evening to keep everything neutral—everything he said, every look he gave the movie star.

Sure enough, now there was a glimmer of satisfaction in Robin's eyes. "We, um, kind of got back in touch after *American Hero*'s premiere, and . . . Well, it's been a while since I've . . . seen him." Robin admitted. "I kind of ended our . . . friendship. I think he was starting to think I might be a good candidate for, like, a boyfriend or something, and I definitely wasn't into that, so . . ."

And okay. Jules wasn't sure how to feel about the news that Robin had kept seeing—i.e. sleeping with—Adam. Or the news that Adam had wanted a real relationship—as in more than just occasional sex.

It was particularly screwy because part of Jules was jealous not just of Adam, but of Robin, too.

Once upon a time, Jules and Adam had lived together. In fact, it was Jules who'd gotten his ex that audition for *American Hero*, from which Adam had been cast in the biggest role of his career. He'd claimed he wanted to get back together with Jules, but Jules knew better. Of course, at the time, Jules had just met Robin . . .

So naturally, Adam had repaid Jules for his kindness by getting Robin drunk and seducing him.

Yeah, that had been a fun few weeks.

"See, that's just it," Junior pointed out. "You hang with the guy, the tabloids say you're a couple, and what happens? The gay dude starts believing it, too. What'd'ya do, fucking break his face?" he asked Robin.

"Uh, no," Robin said. "I told him we couldn't . . . hang out anymore. I was afraid he might . . . get too attached and end up hurt."

Jules couldn't believe they were having this conversation at all, let alone having it in front of Gordon Burns Junior. Of course, maybe he could believe it. Having a spectator on hand certainly put Robin at an advantage, since Jules couldn't simply come out and say, *What were you doing, having an ongoing sexual relationship with someone you claimed to hate?*

It was also kind of interesting that Robin hadn't just tried to lie to Jules about the whole thing.

"*He* might end up hurt?" Junior was scornful and completely unaware of what this conversation really was about. "What about you? This is a story that will not die. *National Voice* had him visiting your hotel room in London last month. They run that kind of headline, with a movie still of the two of you sucking face from *American Whatever*? That's a problem for you. He couldn't give a rat's ass. Everyone already knows he's a . . . gay."

"I've never been to London," Robin told Jules. "I actually got an e-mail from Adam, about a month ago. He *is* over there, doing an indie. He's doing okay. He says he misses me, but . . . I don't miss him."

"Yeah, I get that," Jules said. "It was . . . good, then, that you ended your . . . friendship."

"Like I said," Robin told him. "I didn't want to hurt him. He's . . . okay. He's kind of screwed up, but . . . Who's not, to some degree?"

"In the *National Voice*," Junior started, but Robin cut him off.

"No offense, but I don't read that shit."

"But someone in your organization does" — Junior was both earnest and intense — "because not a week after that London story, there's an article out about a pregnancy scare with some bitch you're banging. Coincidence? I don't think so."

"It's all just fiction anyway," Robin said. "They're always hooking me up with someone — if it's not Adam, it's some TV starlet. Does anyone really believe any of it? I mean, one of these days they're going to decide that a story about a movie star who's been celibate for six months will sell more papers, and look out. I'll be in that headline, too."

Junior laughed and laughed at Robin's big funny.

Except it wasn't a joke.

Robin was standing there, holding a drink, leaning against a wall. His shirt matched the gorgeous blue of his eyes, and with his movie-star good looks, his hair artfully messed, his long, lean build, and broad shoulders, he looked like hot sex personified.

But he held Jules's gaze and nodded. No, he wasn't kidding.

Jules had to look away.

"Look," Junior persisted, after he'd caught his breath. "Don't you wish you could make it go away once and for all?"

"I probably could," Robin said. "By coming out and living a life of total obscurity with the man of my dreams."

Jules looked up again, right into Robin's eyes, as Junior laughed his ass off all over again.

He didn't dare say it aloud, but as he looked at Robin, he wanted to ask, *As opposed to asking him to give up a career in which he has the ear of the President, to become an overpaid bodyguard, and live in the closet?* He hadn't missed Robin's thinly veiled job offer back at Ric's office.

Speaking of Ric . . . He still hadn't reappeared. As interesting as this conversation was . . . "I'm sorry, you're going to have to excuse me," Jules said.

But Junior caught his arm. "No, wait. Seriously, dude, I got the answer Rob's looking for." He looked from Robin to Jules and back again. "Ready for this?" He paused dramatically. "A sex tape."

Jules looked at Robin, who was clearly as clueless as he was.

"A sex tape," Junior said again as if his meaning was obvious. "It leaks out onto the Internet in little bits and pieces and people are like, *whoa*, and the rumors are over once and for all."

Robin started to laugh.

"I'm serious." Junior was. "*You* know you're not gay, and *I* know you're not gay, but you make a sex tape and the entire world knows it, too. Case in point: Eddie Moss. There was lots of talk about him, right? Until his tape was released. And on top of the obvious answer to the gay thing, it's bitchin' PR—look what it did for Paris Hilton. Here's what I'm thinking: GBJ Productions helps you make it."

Robin had stopped laughing, his amusement mixed with some serious disbelief as he looked at Jules, his hand over his mouth. His pose came off as thoughtful, but Jules recognized it for what it really was—an attempt to stay quiet and even seem respectful in the face of Junior's idiocy.

"It's high quality, it's tasteful, it's well lit, it's a single shot—no cuts, so no body doubles—it's clearly you." Junior continued his pitch. "Of course, this may not be something you necessarily want to do unless God gifted you, if you know what I mean."

"I really don't think," Robin started to say, but Jules cut him off.

"Let's assume there's no issue there," he said. "Go on."

"Go on?" Robin repeated.

From the corner of his eyes, Jules could see him widening his eyes in a very clear *what the hell?* He forced himself to focus on their host's son, taking on—hopefully—an air of interest very similar to Robin's.

"Another issue is the bitch, you know, who's in the film with you," Gordie Junior went on. "You gotta take care of paying her off, although another option is that we can be careful about not showing her face." He laughed. "Her face isn't what's important anyway, you know what I mean?"

It had taken Jules a second to decipher his words—bitch?—but he got it now. Nice.

"The girl you're with tonight," Junior turned to Robin to say. "She'd probably do it for the starfucker factor. I saw the way she was all over you."

Somewhere Annie's ears were ringing.

"So how much are you offering?" Jules said. "I'm assuming that GBJ would keep distribution rights—and you'd stand to make a fortune with a tape like that."

"Well, that's one way to do it," Junior said. "But I was thinking we'd provide the service, so . . . you'd pay us."

"That's not going to happen," Jules said.

Robin was looking at him as if he'd gone mad. Maybe he had, but this was an incredible opportunity both to get information on Junior's fledgling company, and to establish a business relationship with the man.

Not that they were actually going to make a sex tape. No, the negotiations would provide enough of an opportunity.

"Robin'll need a half a million dollars," Jules continued. "Cash. Half on handshake—because this is not a deal that gets anywhere near paper—and half at taping. I'm assuming you'd use digital video?"

"Yeah," Junior said. "That's our format, but—"

"Second half is delivered in cash to the studio on the day of the shoot," Jules said. "It goes home with Robin when he leaves that night."

"That could work," Junior said, "but I'd have to check with my business partners . . ."

"What's to check?" Jules asked. "It's yes or no. A half a million dollars is just a fraction of what you can make with a tape like this, and you know it."

"The company's still in its early stages," Junior explained.

"So you're saying you don't have the capital," Jules interpreted.

"No, I'm not." Junior was offended. And lying.

"Because this deal can't be discussed," Jules said. "Not between you and your partners, or you and your father—"

Junior took umbrage. "My father has nothing to do with this."

That was useful to know. "It's between you and me and Robin," Jules reiterated. "No one else knows. The entire deal is under-the-table. And when GBJ releases the tape, you announce it was sold to you through an anonymous source. You'll have six months to sell the footage through Internet downloads, during which time Robin will file a lawsuit against you. There'll be a settlement that will cost you nothing, but at the end of those six months, you will cease and desist your sale of the tape, so you better have a marketing plan in place right from the word go."

"I'm going to have to think about this," Junior said.

"Think fast," Jules said. "This is a terrific idea, and God knows Robin could use the PR ASAP."

"It's my fucking idea," Junior bristled. "You'll do it with GBJ, or you won't do it at all."

"I'm not saying we'll go elsewhere," Jules soothed him. "I never said that. It would just help to know how long it'll be until you have the money for a project of this magnitude."

Junior was silent.

Jules looked at his watch, not daring to glance at Robin, who still didn't understand exactly what was going on. But he knew Jules well enough to stay quiet.

Come on, Junior. When will GBJ have access to a major chunk of cash?

There was a lot of conjecture here, but if Junior were, say, smuggling a terrorist into the United States, then he would surely be well paid for his treasonous efforts. Finding out when GBJ Productions was expecting a major increase in funds might clue the FBI in to the date of al-Hasan's arrival. Maybe.

If, might, maybe . . .

Jules looked at his watch again.

And Junior cleared his throat. "I might have the cash in a week," he said. "Maybe before that. I got another deal set to happen very soon, problem is the fuckers won't commit to a closing date."

"Another film?" Jules probed.

"It's none of your fucking business, but no."

Jules took out one of the business cards he'd made for Julian Young, and handed it to Junior. "When you know exactly when you'll have the cash," he told him, "you call me, and we'll deal."

As Gordie Junior walked away, Robin murmured, "Sometimes you frighten me."

Jules laughed.

"A sex tape," Robin mused. "With Annie, no less. Ric's going to love that."

What the fuck was Ric doing down here in the servants' wing? was the question that had been asked.

Searching for the men's room was an extremely lame-ass answer, but it was the excuse he'd been carrying around with him, and it popped out of his mouth. Unfortunately it sounded just as lame-ass when he said it aloud, especially since he'd made it look as if he were coming in from outside.

"And then I saw this deck," Ric added, "and it seemed private, so I thought I'd use the opportunity to, you know. Check my meter."

Checking one's meter was street for taking a brief break from a party to indulge in illegal substances. Ric gave a sniff, his thumb against one nostril—a visual aid to make his words ring even more true.

But Foley's expression was as lifeless as it had been the night Ric had saved Gordie Junior's worthless ass. And Ric knew if he didn't somehow sell this thing more convincingly, then he'd really screwed himself, because all Foley had to do to prove Ric was lying was give him a drug test. It would come back clean, and he'd be in deep shit. Or maybe even dead. And it would domino, since he was here with Annie and Jules and even Robin Chadwick.

"I had to get out of there, man," Ric told him. "My girlfriend? She wants to hook up with the movie star, and I'm not okay with that. I mean, would you be? Some guys actually are, but I don't know what they're thinking."

He was just warming up, ready to launch into a story about how he'd told Annie that they had to talk, and that she'd agreed to meet him in the kitchen, but then she didn't show.

But Foley's gaze shifted over Ric's shoulder and the door opened behind him—the same door Ric was still holding. The one that led to the deck.

"Ric, I lost my panties."

Jesus God, it was Annie. She looked from Foley to Ric and smiled sheepishly. "Oops. Busted, huh?"

Somehow she'd gotten onto the deck. She must've come around the side of the house and climbed up. Goddamn it, he'd told her not to go any-where alone, yet she'd slipped away, probably shortly after he had.

She looked disheveled, her shoes in her hands, and he realized what she'd said as she'd come in.

She'd lost her panties.

"Do you have them?" she asked Ric as she slipped her shoes back on. She tucked her bra straps out of sight, adjusting her entire dress, making sure her skirt was straight, as if they'd knocked her clothing askew just min-utes before on the deck. She was making it look—and convincingly, too—as if they'd sneaked away to grab a quickie.

"I don't think so," he managed to say, but she leaned close, reaching into the pocket of his jacket.

"Here they are," she announced. It was classic sleight of hand—she'd had them scrunched up and hidden in her palm as she'd reached in, and now she pulled them out triumphantly, letting them dangle from one fin-ger.

As far as visual aids went, they were extremely effective. They were black and lacy.

Especially when Annie added, "On second thought, maybe you should keep them. Next time you're jealous of Robin Chadwick, just re-member what's in your pocket, hot stuff."

She flicked them at him, as if she were shooting a giant rubber band. He caught them as, still fixing her hair, she breezed past Foley, heading back toward the kitchen, and ultimately the party.

Something actually flickered—amusement or maybe appreciation—in Foley's eyes as he turned to watch her walk away.

Ric watched her, too. It was hard not to, considering her panties were in his hand, which meant, kind of obviously, that she wasn't wearing them. He tucked them back into his pocket, and when Foley turned back to him, he shrugged.

"Busted," Ric echoed Annie.

"Get outta here," Foley ordered him.

He went.

Dinner was one of the most unpleasant meals of Jules's life.

A buffet had been set up in Burns's formal dining room, but Ric planted Annie at a table out on the patio, waited for Jules and Robin to get their dinners, and then went through the line for her.

Something had happened when Ric had gone searching for Peggy's room. Jules had spotted Annie first, slipping out of the hallway that led down to the kitchen, which explained where she'd been all that time.

It also explained Ric's elevated levels of pissed—what was Annie doing down there?—perceptible only to those who knew him, because he covered it with a wide smile when he, too, returned.

"Change of plans" was all he told Jules, after he gave Annie his jacket because suddenly she was cold, despite the eighty-degree heat. "Annie stays with me, at least for tonight. The breakup's off."

The drinks in the limo, plus the champagne, plus whatever was in Robin's glass right now either made it hard for Robin to hear or to understand, because he was already making a beeline for Annie. "Hey, gorgeous, where you been?"

She whispered something in his ear, something that made him laugh—and he pulled her in for an embrace.

Which Ric was having none of. "Take your hands off her," he told Robin, his voice low, his smile gone.

Someone else had come out of that well-traveled hallway to the kitchen—the hired goon that Ric had identified as Foley. Jules saw that he was watching Ric, watching as Robin got the hint and backed off, watching Annie as Ric put his arm possessively around her waist.

Something had definitely happened.

"Just go with it," Jules murmured to Robin. "Continue the interest, but from a distance."

Jules filled his plate from a buffet of the most amazing-smelling food, and with Robin right behind him, he sat down next to Annie at the dinner table. It was then that Ric leaned over and said, "Room's been sanitized."

And that was the end of any appetite Jules might've had.

Robin took the seat next to him, afraid to get too close to Annie, and he'd heard Ric, too. This time, he understood exactly the implications of what Ric had discovered—and that it meant Peggy was surely dead.

"I'm sorry," Robin told Jules softly. "I know you didn't like her, but that makes it even worse, huh?"

Jules had once vented to Robin about Peggy—about how she'd excluded him, time and time again. How she'd avoided him and, when she couldn't, how she'd looked through him.

"You didn't wish this for her," Robin told him now.

"I should have done more." That was what was making him feel sick.

"You followed orders," Robin pointed out.

Jules nodded. "I wouldn't have if it had been Alyssa." *Or you.* He would have launched a full-scale attack the minute he knew something had gone wrong, kicking down the doors at Burns Point.

God help him.

"It's okay to feel what you're feeling," Robin said gently. "It really is."

He was sitting there, quiet for once, no ulterior motive at play. This wasn't about convincing Jules to spend the night or even the next week with him. It was empathy and compassion. It was support, sturdy and wholehearted.

Robin was looking at him the same way Alyssa looked at her husband, Sam. The way Max looked at his beloved Gina. The way Jules had seen Annie looking at Ric.

What was it he'd said to Robin the other night? *You are not what I want.* How could something be true and yet also be the biggest lie Jules had ever told?

He knew he was revealing too much, knew it was right there on his face for Robin to see, but he couldn't look away.

"God," Robin breathed, "you look at me like that, babe, and I'm tempted to do it—just end my career."

Robin with fire in his eyes was easier to turn away from than the Robin who had looked at him with such quiet understanding. "I don't want you to do that," Jules told him.

"Yeah, you do."

"No, I really don't," Jules said, but he couldn't expound because Ric was back, and unlike Robin, he was unwilling to make this a public discussion. It was bad enough whispering while Annie pretended to be preoccupied with getting a splinter out of her hand.

Besides, Ric had more info to share. He murmured it to Jules as he put Annie's plate down in front of her.

"No furniture in the room, no carpet, fresh paint. The single a/c vent was empty. I checked it thoroughly."

Crap.

"I don't know about you guys," Robin said loudly, addressing Ric and Annie, too. "But I've got an early day tomorrow. I'm thinking after dinner we should head back." He turned to Jules. "We still have that . . . business to talk about. I figured we could drop Ric and Annie off—"

"I'm not sure that's such a good idea," Jules said. "You've had a lot to drink."

"I'm fine," Robin said.

"Yeah, well, I'm not," Jules said. Before they left, he was going to have to figure out a way to get into the room Ric had found. He needed to see it for himself. And then he was going to have to report what they'd found, along with his conclusion regarding Peggy Ryan's status—which was now officially presumed dead.

The last thing he wanted to do after that was fight off Robin.

Who, once again, seemed to know exactly what Jules was thinking.

"I really was just talking about talking," he said quietly. "I'm sorry if I come on too strong sometimes." He, too, had no appetite. He just pushed his food around his plate. "I'll get you down to that room—I know you want to go there. When I head into the kitchen to meet the staff, it's going to be extra noisy. I guarantee it. If you came with me, and your cell phone rang . . ."

Jules would have to find someplace quiet to take the call—such as down the hall to the servants' wing.

"How can you guarantee . . . ?"

"I've already talked to a lot of the servers," Robin told him. "It's the caterer's fiftieth birthday. Jenny Milkovich. She's well liked. She's also a fan. They asked me to come to the kitchen to sing 'Happy Birthday,' but I'll definitely make it louder than that. I was planning a diversion, remember?" He pulled a CD jewel case out of his pocket, and looked at the back. "You'll have four minutes and twenty-eight seconds, plus however long they applaud."

"Applaud?" Jules asked.

"Yup," Robin said, adding "Thanks, Giselle" as a woman with a tray brought him just what he needed—another drink. "We're going to give Jenny a birthday to remember."

Robin had been right about the noise level in the kitchen. There was a built-in sound system, with speakers wired into the ceiling, and the music was up extremely loud. But louder still was the reaction of the crowd.

And it was a crowd that was growing larger every second, as Burns's dinner guests came to investigate the noise and stayed for the entertainment.

If a man taking his clothes off to a Billy Preston song from the 1970s could be called entertainment.

Annie seemed to think so. "God, he's hot."

Ric looked at her. She was serious. He leaned in to speak directly into her ear. "He's gay." And ironically Jules, the one person who'd probably truly get off on this, had left the room.

"That doesn't matter," Annie told Ric. "It's the fantasy."

He looked back at Robin, who was taking forever just to get his shirt off, playing it humorously coy as he moved to the music. And okay, from the glimpses of his upper body that he'd given the crowd, it was obvious that the actor was ripped. He put his hands on the button to his pants and dozens of women shrieked their approval.

"So it's a man-as-meat kind of thing," Ric mused.

Annie laughed, genuinely amused, and it was hard as hell not to think about the black lace that was in his pants pocket, damn near burning a hole in his leg. It had been impossible, all evening, for him to look at her and not think about the fact that if her panties were in his pocket—and they certainly were—then she wasn't wearing them. As in not wearing anything. At all.

She was wearing his jacket now, too, still claiming she was cold. And although that meant she was even more covered up, the effect was oddly the opposite. The jacket was almost as long as her skirt, and from behind, she looked as if she were wearing his jacket and nothing else.

Certainly not her panties. Which he knew were in his pocket.

His brilliant plan to get her to safety—as well as safely out of his apartment—had been seriously screwed by her blatant disregard of his instructions: *Don't go anywhere alone.*

Of course her blatant disregard *had* saved his ass.

It had also aroused Foley's suspicions. The man had been watching them ever since. And that was why Ric had nixed their plan to have Annie split up with him in a very public display at the party's end. He didn't think Foley would buy it.

Yeah, *that* was why Ric had nixed the plan. It had nothing to do with the fact that it also meant that Annie would have to come home with him.

"Well, I don't know about the birthday lady," she was telling him now, "but for me, it's more of a fairy-tale fantasy. A hot guy, going to a lot of effort to attract a woman's attention—"

"More like forty women."

"The fantasy," she told him patiently, "is a fantasy. Which means you're allowed to pretend the thirty-nine other women aren't there. It's just you and the hot guy—which is the real fantasy, right? But the odds of ever actually being alone with a hot guy, let alone one who's going to go to this kind of effort to turn you on . . ."

"So it *is* about sex," Ric said, which was a mistake, because talking about sex wasn't going to help him stop thinking about sex, about going back to his apartment with Annie, alone, about locking the door behind them and pulling her close and kissing her the way she'd kissed him just a few short hours ago. Only this time he wouldn't stop. This time he'd just keep kissing her until he'd backed her up against the wall and pushed her skirt up and wrapped her legs around his waist as he pushed himself hard and deep inside of her.

"Hell, yeah," Annie was saying, clearly oblivious to the fact that in his mind he was damn close to making them both come. "Because sex is an important part of any fairy-tale relationship."

Robin Chadwick lowered his zipper another fraction of an inch, and the crowd nearly drowned out the music. Ric forced his gaze away from Annie and down at his watch. Jules had been gone just over three minutes now. It wasn't quite time yet to get squirrelly. But it was getting close.

"But the fairy-tale hot guy isn't just some handsome, princely stud," Annie continued, after heartily applauding Robin's efforts. "He's sensitive and he's funny and he's willing to grocery-shop and do the laundry. And he always says I love you, too, and you live happily ever after." She snorted. "Like I said, pure fantasy."

"So why is that a fantasy?" Ric asked as Annie whooped when Robin revealed he was wearing sky-blue boxers. "I mean, okay, the idea of living happily ever after is simplistically optimistic, but my parents seem to have achieved something pretty close."

"Yeah, well, most people don't even try," Annie told him.

"Ah," he said. "Maybe that's what makes it a fantasy. It comes without any of the hard work."

His own fantasies were along those same lines. He'd spent a great deal of the evening imagining Annie sweet and tight around him, imagining the sounds of pleasure she'd make, the way her eyes would look filled with desire, the rush of his blood through his veins. But not once did he go beyond the immediate gratification to the conversation they'd surely share afterward.

"Remind me sometime to tell you about the first few years that my parents were married," Ric told her, checking his watch again. "Right now, though, I need to . . ."

She nodded, understanding, her full attention on him, not on Robin nor his boxers. "I should go with you."

"No, you shouldn't."

"Yeah," she said. "I should. Just because Foley's not in the room doesn't mean he's not in the room. Check behind me. At one o'clock."

Sure enough, Foley's extra-large co-worker was standing over there. He wasn't watching them right that moment, but he'd surely noted their presence. And he'd therefore note if and when they were gone.

"Pretend that you're jealous," Annie instructed, turning back to watch

Robin. "That I'm a little too into this whole Robin Chadwick stripping thing."

"Like you're not?"

She glanced at him, amused. "So convince me. Make me believe that if we go back to the scene of our previous tryst, you'll entertain me just as thoroughly."

Damn. He didn't want to do this. He didn't want to put her in any more danger than she was already in just by being here. But she was right. If he went down that hallway by himself, he'd be putting them all into jeopardy . . .

Which is what they'd also be in if Jules didn't get his ass back here in the next few minutes.

It was a lose/lose scenario, with both options sucking equally.

And Annie wanted him to convince her . . .

Ric gave up and grabbed her wrist. He pulled her back, into the entry of the hallway to the servants' wing, and pushed her up against the wall a little bit harder than he should have.

"Sorry," he said, because his back was to anyone who might be watching. What they could see was her face, and the placement of his hands. Her skirt was short enough for him to reach just beneath the edge, her thigh cool and deliciously smooth against his fingers.

She drew in her breath sharply, her eyes wide.

"I'm going to kiss you, okay?" Ric told her. "And we're going to move back farther into the shadows. I'm going to need your help though, because every time I kiss you? I get kind of useless and . . . can't seem to do much more than kiss you."

Annie laughed and kissed him, and, God, she was so sweet, her body impossibly soft as she molded herself against him. He concentrated, though, and they moved back—more like staggered, really.

Ric kissed her, harder, more deeply and it seemed as if it took both forever and a fraction of a heartbeat, but they finally rounded the corner. They were in the part of the hallway where they could no longer be seen from the kitchen, and it was time to not kiss her anymore, but God damn if he could make himself stop. They were in danger. He knew they were in ever-growing danger. They had to find Jules. But his hand was now between her legs and he was mere inches from—

"Whoa, hey there, kids, sorry!"

Jesus God, it was Jules and he was practically standing next to them.

Ric and Annie sprang apart. Or rather, he sprang back from Annie— he'd nearly had her nailed to the wall.

"Ow!" she said as he pulled his hand away, which was never a good sound to hear from a lover's lips—even if it was someone who was just pretending to be a lover.

"Are you okay?" Ric asked her. She nodded as she straightened her clothes, her face pink. He turned to Jules. "Are you?"

He nodded, too. He wasn't happy—it was clear just from looking at him that he'd found what he was searching for.

"Sorry I took so long. I got an important phone call, so I came down here to get away from the noise," Jules told them, just in case anyone was listening as they walked back toward the kitchen. The music had ended, but he still had to speak loudly to be heard over the babble of voices and laughter.

"Ric was having some issues with Robin and his blue silk boxers," Annie told him.

"Robin and his . . ." Jules caught sight of the boxers in question and stopped short.

Robin Chadwick stood in the middle of the room, surrounded mostly by women, totally comfortable with the fact that he was shirtless and pants-free. He'd even taken off his socks and shoes. He was smiling and laughing, posing for pictures and signing autographs on cocktail napkins and even on the arms of the bolder of the women.

But then he looked over and caught sight of them.

Them? Try Jules.

In fact, Ric felt so invisible, he used the opportunity to pull Annie aside. "Are you really okay?"

She nodded, but it was clearly not a complete yes. "I got a little scraped up when . . . I'll tell you later," she said. But then she met his gaze. "Maybe after we get home you can, you know, kiss it and make it better."

And no, the room didn't actually tilt. And Annie didn't actually soul-kiss him and drag him back with her onto her bed, opening her legs to him so he could lose himself in her sweetness and heat.

That was just him. They were in the kitchen at Burns Point. The only bed was in his head, in a room labeled WISHFUL THINKING.

"Yeah," Ric said, quickly glancing over at Jules, who'd been waylaid by Gordon Burns himself, who'd pulled the FBI agent over to Robin. Everything seemed to be fine—the three men were laughing. "Wow. Right. About that. I'm . . . not sure if it's the dress or the makeup or what, but I've apparently reached the end of my ability to resist. You. I'm kind of picking up the sense that you're feeling something similar—"

"I'm not," she said with such venom he had to take a step back. Everything warm and welcoming in her eyes had turned to a different kind of heat. "Oh God, I am, but I'm *not*. Shit, I don't want to sleep with an asshole."

What had happened to kiss it and make it better? "You don't want to—"

"You," she said, lowering her voice. "I don't want to sleep with *you*, but at the same time, I really, really do, and if we're alone tonight, we're going to, aren't we?"

She was staring at his mouth, as if, if they were the only ones in the room, she'd be kissing him.

"I'm pretty sure we are," Ric said, because he knew if she kissed him again he'd be toast. "And you're right. It would be a mistake."

Across the room, Robin Chadwick had his pants back on but his shirt hung open. He and Gordon Burns shook hands.

"Ladies," Robin announced, "it has been beyond fun, but it's time now for me to go. Happy birthday, Jen."

Jules caught Ric's eye. *Limo's out front,* he mouthed.

"We need to go," Ric told Annie.

"Call Martell," Annie ordered Ric as she marched past him. "Tell him we need him to babysit. At your place. Immediately."

CHAPTER
SIXTEEN

"A sex tape," Ric repeated as the limo headed south on Tamiami Trail. "With Annie?"

Robin opened up the refrigerator and took inventory of both that and the liquor cabinet, as Annie cracked up. There was Coke and there was . . . plenty of rum. Score.

"Ew," she said. "Am I allowed to say *ew*?" She looked at Robin. "Not that the idea of . . ."

"Don't worry, I'm not offended. I get a heavy whiff of *ew* myself from the idea of getting busy in a studio with Gordie Junior directing." Robin imitated Junior's tough-guy accent, which the thug-wannabe had probably learned from watching *The Sopranos*. "*Fucka harda, Chadwick, fucka harda.*"

Jules spoke for the first time since they'd put up the privacy shield that separated them from the driver, and run Ric's bug sweeper across them, getting the all-clear. "Not everyone in this vehicle is from Hollywood," he said sharply, "so watch your mouth."

Suddenly Jules had a problem with his language? "It was a joke." Robin looked at Annie. "You knew it was a joke, right?"

She nodded, also more than a little mystified.

"It was actually a multilevel, layered kind of joke," Robin continued, "because there's this underlying implication that I think it's okay to make a sex tape, as long as it's not Gordie Junior who's directing."

"Will you please button your shirt?" Jules implored, impatience and annoyance dripping from him.

Robin looked down. His shirt was, indeed, still hanging open. "Why are you mad at *me?*" he asked Jules as he buttoned it. He'd thought the connection they'd shared during dinner was a step toward at least an acknowledgment that this spark between them was something real, something solid.

But now Jules just shook his head, refusing even to look at Robin.

"As freaky as this sex-tape thing is," Ric said, "it's good. It's another connection to Gordie Junior."

"Yeah, and you know, he wasn't married to the idea of it being with Annie," Robin told him. "Any random starfucker would do." He looked at Jules. "Am I allowed to say *starfucker* since I buttoned my shirt?"

"How drunk *are* you?" Jules asked.

"Sadly," Robin said, "too drunk to comprehend your sudden hostility, but not drunk enough to not care." He turned back to Annie and Ric. "Jules gave Junior his card and let him think we were interested." He took a Coke from the fridge and popped open the top. "Anyone want anything?"

All three of them shook their heads. Robin knew that Jules was enormously upset about the evidence they'd discovered—the room that was Peggy's that had been, as Ric had put it, sanitized. But why he was now taking it out on Robin was a total mystery.

"Didn't we accomplish our mission?" Robin asked. He turned to Jules. "Or am I wrong, and you didn't find what you were looking for . . . ?"

"Oh, I found it," Jules said grimly. "Peggy left a message, on the metal window frame. It was hidden until the window was cranked open, and even then I had to really look to see it. She was good. She must've known the room was going to be stripped."

Holy God. That meant Peggy had known she was going to be killed. No wonder Jules was freaking out.

"What did it say?" Annie asked. "Her message?"

Jules shook his head. "It was written in some kind of code. I've already passed the information on to the analysts. I'm waiting for a call back, but it could take a while."

"You're certain she's dead?" Annie asked.

"I'm pretty sure she wrote it in blood."

"Ah, God, babe, I'm so sorry," Robin breathed.

"Yeah, me, too." Jules looked away.

They rode for about a half mile in gloomy silence. But then Robin reached for the plastic cups.

"Okay," he said as he put four into the limo's built-in cup holders, pouring a few fingers of his Coke into each of them. "I didn't know Peggy

Ryan. I never met the woman. I couldn't tell you if I would've liked her, although I suspect I wouldn't've, because word is she was something of a hard-ass, not to mention homophobic."

He tossed the empty can into the recycling, and took the rum from the cabinet. "But regardless of that, she has my respect. She gave her life for our country, for our freedom, for our safety." He opened the bottle and poured a healthy amount of rum into each cup.

"Haven't you had enough to drink?" Jules asked.

Robin stopped pouring. "Are you going back to work after we drop Annie and Ric?"

Jules sighed, a long drawn out exhale of frustration. "Yes," he said. "I probably am."

Which meant that, once again, the conversation that Jules refused to have with him was going to be postponed. "Then, nope, I haven't."

Robin resumed pouring. It was either have another drink or bring the subject up now, in front of Ric and Annie, as he'd threatened earlier. But tonight had clearly been tough enough for Jules. And Robin was just not that cruel.

"Besides, this isn't a drink," Robin added, putting the rum away, and distributing the cups first to Annie, then Ric, and then Jules. "It's a toast." He had to put the cup into Jules's hand, wrapping his fingers around it. "Would it kill you to drink a toast?"

Jules was silent, but he'd finally taken the damn thing, so Robin picked up his own cup, and held it up. "To Peggy Ryan. May her final courageous message be one that saves thousands of lives."

"To Peggy," Ric and Annie unisoned.

Robin looked at Jules.

"To Peggy," he said.

The soda was cold, but the rum warmed Robin. Warmed and fuzzed and made the prospect of going home alone both more and less bearable. Funny how that worked.

Truth was, he was a little disappointed that Annie wasn't coming to the hotel with him. He'd been looking forward to having some company. Someone he didn't have to pretend around. Someone to talk to, someone who knew Jules, too.

Dolphina had taken the night off. She was attending the wedding of a friend in Orlando and wouldn't be back until tomorrow afternoon. So when he went home, he really would be alone.

"So what happened?" Robin asked Ric and Annie now. "You know, the whole change-in-plans thing."

They looked at each other. They were sitting about as far apart as two people could sit on the bench seat, and still be in the same limo.

"Go ahead," Ric told Annie. "I'm interested in hearing what happened, too."

"Okay," Annie said. "Should I start with the part where I saved your life?"

Apparently Jules didn't have the monopoly on being pissed off.

"Or should I start a little earlier?" Annie continued. "I know. I'll start where I saw Ric heading down the hall to the kitchen. So I know he's going for it, right? He's going to find Peggy's room. A few minutes later, I've just come out of the ladies' room, and he's still not back, and I see one of Burns's security guards—a really scary guy named Foley. He's got these zombie eyes—really freaky, like he's already dead. He was obviously scanning the crowd, looking for someone. I noticed that he kept looking at Robin and Jules. I was still lurking over by the bathroom—I know he didn't see me. And I just . . . I somehow knew that he was looking for Ric and maybe even for me. I saw him speak to another guard, who pointed at the hall to the kitchen, where Ric had gone. I was afraid Foley was going to go after him and oh, I don't know, kill him? So I went outside, and ran around the side of the house, and I climbed up onto the servants' deck. Which wasn't as easy to do as it looked on paper."

She pulled back the sleeve of Ric's jacket, which she'd been wearing since dinner, revealing a scrape on her arm that was still oozing blood. So *that* was why she'd claimed to be cold despite the tropical heat.

"Shit, Annie." Ric took her arm and turned on the overhead light to get a better look. The heel of her hand looked raw and sore, too. He looked at her questioningly, in some kind of wordless exchange to which she nodded an almost apologetic response. "Shit," he swore again.

Robin snuck a look at Jules, who was, to his surprise, watching him.

"I'm really sorry," Robin told him silently, even as Annie spoke to Ric.

"I'm okay"—she pulled her arm back—"although I've ruined the lining of your jacket."

"I don't care about that," Ric said as Jules just looked at Robin, as Robin saw a breathtaking echo of everything he himself wanted right there in Jules's dark brown eyes. "Christ, Annie, how many times did I tell you not to go off on your own?"

Annie made an exasperated noise. "I didn't think it applied to a situation in which you were about to disappear, the way Peggy Ryan did."

"You don't know that would've happened."

"You don't know that it wouldn't've," she countered as Robin continued to hold Jules's gaze, his heart in his throat. "Can't you just acknowl-edge that I did something right?"

"You put yourself at incredible risk!"

"It was worth it!" she shouted back at Ric, and Jules finally looked away. "You're here, I'm here, we're all in one piece!"

"Guys," Jules said, once again the peacekeeper.

"What if you'd fallen?" Ric asked. "What if you'd been followed?"

"What if Foley had figured out you were looking for Peggy Ryan"—Annie was not ready to let him win—"and he killed you, and then he killed the rest of us, because we came to this party with you, and then, be-cause you screwed it up and the FBI no longer had access to Gordon Burns and his despicable plans, this terrorist gets into the country and blows up freaking New York City?"

Ric was finally silent.

"It was worth it," Annie said again, more quietly now. "And I'm sorry. I didn't mean it when I said you, you know, screwed it up, because you didn't. It wasn't your fault that Foley went looking for you."

Robin reached for the rum, needing desperately to top off his drink.

"Burns's security team is extremely well trained," Jules pointed out, but Ric didn't seem convinced. "If they weren't so highly skilled, we would've been able to get onto the property long before this. And here, Robin, why don't you just finish mine?"

Jules was holding out his cup, so Robin took it.

"Foley thought we'd had a . . . romantic assignation out on the deck." Annie continued with the story. "So he let us go."

"Annie made it look as if she was, um, appeasing my jealousy," Ric ex-plained. "You know, about her and Chadwick. She was actually very con-vincing. I thought Foley would get suspicious—more suspicious—if she suddenly did a one-eighty and walked out on me an hour later. That was why the change in the plan."

"Good call," Jules said.

"Yeah, right," Ric said, with a glance at Annie.

"Anyone want to know what *I* found out?" Robin asked, and they all turned to look at him in surprise. "What? Just because I'm an actor I'm an idiot? My only contribution was when I took off my clothes? Thanks a lot, team."

"That *was* quite a contribution," Annie said.

"No one thinks you're an idiot," Jules said in a tone that was loaded with subtext that screamed *what an idiot.*

Robin took another sip of his drink, making them wait for it. "So what

I did, was talk to the serving staff, pretty much all night—every chance I got."

No one was impressed. Or maybe they were all just too busy being mad at one another. Although Jules seemed to have forgiven Robin. Except now all he looked was exhausted.

"The staff," Robin repeated. "Including the three women who hold full-time, live-in positions at Burns Point, two of whom worked closely with Peggy Ryan?"

Now he had their attention. In fact, Jules took a small pad and pen from his inside jacket pocket so he could take notes.

"Okay," Robin said. "There's three of 'em, right? Maria, Terese, and Mona. They're all mature—well over forty, which was the first thing I noticed. I thought it was kind of interesting. Burns is richer than God, and he's a widower, why not have a staff of buxom twenty-year-olds?"

"He seems kind of formal—straight-laced—to me," Annie volunteered.

"He's also got a longtime ladyfriend," Robin said. "Ella Whittier, who lives out at Lakewood Ranch." When Ella had introduced herself to him, she'd grabbed his ass. And that was *before* he had his clothes off. "But I don't think she's the reason his staff are all prospective members of the Red Hat Society. One of the temps—the girls who were passing around the hors d'oeuvres and cheer—her name was Giselle. She's done a lot of parties at Burns Point. She told me a few years back she was going to ask about a permanent position, but another of the girls told her not to bother. I asked why not, and she told me that as of six years ago, Burns has only hired older women because, get this—the younger ones had a habit of disappearing. One theory is that Gordie Junior knocked them up, and they were paid off and sent away. The other theory's not as nice, but probably connected to the fact that, also six years ago, one of the staff—a nineteen-year-old girl—drowned in the family pool. Junior was looked at hard, for that one, too."

"I remember that," Ric said. "It was found to be an accident. I wasn't on the case, but I followed it. The girl's family was sure it was foul play— she was an excellent swimmer."

Jules nodded. "I know about her, too. But you're saying there were others?"

"Maybe it's just urban legend," Robin said, "but yeah. At least four. Giselle said she always jumps at the chance to work a party at Burns Point because the money is insane. But she also said that she's careful to steer clear of Gordie Junior. She kind of said his name like she was saying Jack the Ripper."

"I'll have Yashi and Deb look into any other disappearances that happened at that time," Jules said. "I'm not sure where this is going to go but . . . This is good information. Thank you."

"And you thought all I could do was strip," he said. "So, you want the rest of it?"

Jules smiled at that. "There's more." He didn't quite phrase it as a question, but Robin nodded anyway. "Definitely."

"When I was signing autographs," Robin said, "I asked Mona and Terese how long they'd worked at Burns Point. Turns out Terese has been there three years, but Mona's new. She told me she was hired to replace someone who had to leave rather suddenly last week. Which had to be Peggy, right? Apparently the excuse for her hasty departure was that an elderly parent broke a hip. Terese, who worked with Peggy, was a little tongue-tied, so I got her chatting. I asked her what it was like working as a live-in for such a long time, and she told me that she had nothing on Maria, who was a lifer.

"Maria's been there more than ten years—she's married to the head gardener. I got a heavy sense that there was a pecking order—and that Mona and Terese both thought that Maria was stuck-up. I told them that they seemed like good friends even though Mona was new, and it was nice that they had each other. And then I asked Terese if she'd been as close to the woman Mona was replacing—if she wanted me to sign something that she could send to her, you know, to cheer her up as she was taking care of her elderly whoever. Terese thought that was a great idea and had me sign a cocktail napkin for—drumroll, please—her dear friend Peggy. She said she'd have to ask Maria for her address. Maria happens to be nearby, Terese calls her over, explains what's up, and Maria—you met her. She's a nice-looking older lady. Very calm and serene. But now she looks like she can't decide whether to shit or go blind. She takes the autograph that I've just signed and tells us she'll send it to Peggy, and she practically runs away. I think at the very least that she's seen rooms being 'sanitized' before. At best, she knows exactly what happened to Peggy Ryan."

Silence followed. Ric was the first to speak, shifting in his seat. "Well, damn," he said. "That's an amazing amount of useful information."

"People talk to me," Robin said. Of course, there was a great irony there, considering the one person he really wanted to talk to wouldn't. Jules definitely knew what he was thinking, and he glanced up, briefly meeting Robin's gaze.

The limo slowed, and they all peered out the tinted windows—at night it was almost as impossible to see out as in. This thing was built like a fortress. When they'd first climbed in, Ric had been worried about the driver overhearing their conversation. But with the privacy shield up and locked into place, they could set off a small bomb back here, and Sean-the-driver would never know.

There was a reason, after all, why mob bosses did so much of their illegal business in the backs of limousines.

As Robin watched, they took the left turn onto Ric's street.

"Tomorrow night," Ric said. "I've got a meeting with Gordie Junior at eleven P.M." He looked at Annie. "I don't want you anywhere near that."

"You could give her a black eye," Robin suggested. "And after you left for your meeting, she could come running to me, over at my hotel."

Ric gave him such a look of disbelief, Robin laughed. "No violence," he explained. "We do it with makeup."

Annie shook her head. "I don't think I could—"

"I can," Robin said. "I started in indie films, remember? I know how to do FX makeup—the simple stuff, anyway. A black eye's easy."

"How would that work?" Jules asked as the limo pulled to a stop. "Without you coming over here to help her with the makeup?"

Good point. Hmm. "You wear a hoodie," Robin told Annie. "And sunglasses. And you keep your head down and come straight to my room. Women don't advertise domestic abuse—they try to hide it. You can smudge some shadow around your eye in case someone's paying close attention. Once you're in my room, I'll help you. We'll make it look like you've got a bruise that you're trying to cover with makeup. That's a total piece of cake."

Ric glanced at Annie. "Okay," he said. "I guess that's a plan."

It wasn't enough of a plan for Annie, who asked Jules, "You're going to make sure that Ric is safe when he meets Junior tomorrow night, right?"

Jules nodded. "We'll have a surveillance van nearby. I'll be in touch before that," he told Ric.

Ric opened the door and helped Annie out. "Tomorrow, then," he said, and the door closed behind them with a solid-sounding thunk.

Jules glanced at Robin.

Yeah, he'd noticed, too. They were alone.

"So," Robin said. "Where to?"

"Better take me to my hotel," Jules told him. "It's too easy to tail a limo. I'll call for a ride to get me over to HQ." But then he cleared his throat. "I don't really have to go right in anyway. I mean, all I'm doing is waiting for someone to call me back."

Jules's hotel was over near the harbor. Back near Burns Point. Robin pressed the intercom that connected him to the driver. "Take us north again, Sean," he said, "to the Sarasotan Hotel," and the limo pulled away from the curb.

"I'm sorry, I wasn't thinking before," Jules apologized. "You could've dropped me before Ric and Annie."

"It's not a big deal," Robin reassured him. "Besides, you know, this way I get to have a couple of seconds of crazy hope that what you really want is for me to come with you, you know, up to your room and . . ."

Jules was just sitting there, looking at him.

"Holy shit," Robin said. "You're inviting me to your room."

It was funny, actually. Jules could've imagined a dozen different responses from Robin to the news that, yes, Jules *was* actually inviting him back to his hotel room.

It was a mistake, there was no doubt about it. This was going to come back and bite Jules on the ass in more ways than he could imagine—he just knew it. But he was done. He'd had it. He was only human—he could only take so much before he broke.

And tonight, he'd broken.

But while he could've imagined Robin hitting him with another of those full-body-slam kisses that they'd shared just yesterday, Jules never would've thought the man would just sit there, staring back at him in stunned, wide-eyed silence.

Robin finally spoke. "Okay, so now I'm terrified. I'm afraid if I move, or even say anything at all, you're going to change your mind or . . . decide I'm . . . not worth it."

Jules reached for him, which was also kind of funny, because up to this point, Robin had been the pursuer. Jules had imagined giving in, saying yes, and being swept away completely.

Powerless. Helpless. Totally out of control.

Instead, he touched Robin's hair, Robin's face, brushed his thumb across the softness of Robin's lips, felt Robin's breath quicken, and watched his beautiful eyes darken with desire. Instead of being kissed, Jules kissed Robin—gently, slowly.

Thoroughly.

"You taste like rum," Jules said, pulling back to look at him.

"I'm sorry." Robin hadn't been kidding. He was seriously terrified, his vulnerability all over his face. "I know you don't like—"

"Shh. You also taste like you, and that I like." Jules kissed him again.

Harder, deeper, until the softness of Robin's mouth turned demanding, too.

"God, Jules—" This time it was Robin who pulled back. He was breathing hard. They both were. "This doesn't mean we don't have to talk, because we still have to talk, okay?"

Jules laughed. "What do you think? That this is just a fast fuck in the back of a limo?"

"I don't know," Robin admitted, but then realized what Jules said. "Jesus, you're serious—right now? Right . . . ?"

Jules looked at him. God knows *he'd* waited long enough. "Six *months?*" he asked Robin.

Who nodded and moved first, leaping into action, reaching up to turn on the radio that was built into the ceiling, cranking the volume. It was surreal. It must've been tuned to the local oldies station, because "Hooked on a Feeling" pounded as both of their pairs of shoes went flying.

It wasn't the Blue Swede version, thank you, God. It must've been an earlier recording. Jules had never particularly liked the song, but as Robin grabbed him and kissed him again, it rocketed into his top ten.

Damn, as Robin helped him out of his jacket and unfastened his belt, it was his new all-time favorite song.

Robin had his own clothes off in record time, probably from having to do quick costume changes backstage when he did live theater. Socks, pants, shirt. Those blue boxers that were, indeed, silk, and as soft to the touch as they'd looked back in Gordon Burns's kitchen.

"Hooked on a Feeling" segued into the Beatles—"That Boy"—which so wasn't the song Jules would have chosen for this moment with this man who was going to trash his heart. *That boy isn't good for you* . . . Shut up, John, Paul, George, and Ringo. Jules closed his eyes, not needing their warning, as he kissed Robin again.

"I love this song," Robin murmured, in between those long, slow, soft kisses. "It's so romantic, don't you think?" He lifted his head and sang directly to Jules. "*This boy would be happy just to love you . . .*"

Jules had to laugh. "You can sing, too, huh?"

"And play the piano," Robin said. "But not like Teo Alvarado."

"Oh, well," Jules said, "then forget it. Let's call the whole thing off."

"Too late." Robin laughed as he helped him with his pants, which really wasn't very helpful at all, at least as far as taking them off went.

There must've been condoms in a compartment right in the limo's door. Robin covered them both as "That Boy" melted into "Kiss Him

Goodbye"—again not another song that Jules would have picked for this particular occasion's soundtrack.

And then the music didn't matter, because they were finally skin to skin, kissing, touching . . .

Loving.

Sweet God, it felt so good . . .

"I love your smile," Robin breathed, kissing the corner of Jules's mouth.

Jules kissed him back, afraid to speak, afraid of what he might accidentally say.

But it was Robin from whom the truth leaked, his voice a rough whisper in Jules's ear, mere seconds before he found his release. "God, I love you. You know that, right?"

His words took Jules, hard, right over the edge.

Ric and Annie came through the office door fighting.

"I don't understand why you're so mad," Ric told her.

Annie bent down to greet Pierre. "Hello, my good dog. What a good dog. It's so nice to see someone who's not a *total asshole*." She looked up at Ric. "You really can't figure it out, can you?"

"No. I can't," Ric's voice was loaded with frustration. "Hello. That's why I'm asking."

"You said *nothing* to me." Annie lit into him. "Nothing at all, when I kicked ass at the shooting range."

"Yo, guys," Martell said, waving from Annie's desk. "I'm sitting right here."

But Annie kept on going, speaking right over him. "But now, when I put on a dress and makeup, now you want to screw me, is that how it works?" She grabbed Pierre's leash from its hook by the door. "Don't bother answering that—I have to walk my dog."

"He's cool," Martell said. "I took him out when I got here, 'bout ten minutes ago."

"Are you out of your mind?" Ric asked Annie, who put Pierre's leash back. Martell may have been invisible, but apparently he wasn't inaudible. "I have been working my *ass* off to keep my distance from you, right from the second that you walked into my office two weeks ago. And that was despite my thinking that you were still grieving from the loss of your significant other!"

"Oh, good." Annie put her hands on her hips and narrowed her eyes. "Let's bring the fact that you thought I was gay into this, shall we?"

"Jesus God!" Ric grabbed his forehead.

"Guys." Martell stood up. "Are you sure you want to be doing this while I'm here?"

They both turned to him in unison, heavy on the extra fury. "Yes!"

Annie kept going. "Did you believe Bruce because I'm ugly or because I'm fat?"

Oh, no. No, no, no. That was not a question that could be answered, not even with a flat-out denial. Ric would have to say . . .

"God damn it, Annie!"

That worked. Sort of.

"Or maybe it's because I'm smart and strong," Annie said. "Because I'm independent. What kind of society do we live in, that strong, independent women are automatically assumed to be lesbians—that weakness, indecisiveness, flightiness, vanity, and—yes!—stupidity! *Stupidity* is actually *encouraged* among young women and girls, to make themselves more attractive to men!"

"I don't think you're stupid," Ric told her.

"Yeah," Annie said, "but the fact is that you didn't *really* want to have sex with me until I put on some stupid dress and made myself look like—"

"I have wanted to have sex with you," Ric bellowed so loudly that it was likely the folks out on the interstate could hear him, "since you had that stupid birthday party at the bowling alley!"

She stared at him. "When I was . . . twelve?"

"Dude," Martell said with disapproval.

"Not *that* one," Ric said. "The one when all your friends had the flu. Everyone but what's-his-name. Sandy Something. The kid you didn't like. Bruce and I went, too, so you wouldn't have to be alone with him."

"Sandy Beebe," Annie said. "The mouth breather. I was sixteen. You and Bruce made barf jokes all night long."

"That's the one," Ric said.

"It was oddly fun," Annie remembered. "Sandy turned out to be nice, and you . . . You were really sweet."

"Sweet," Ric scoffed. "Right. I wanted to do you, and it totally freaked me out." He turned to Martell. "This was more than ten *years* before she put on the makeup." He turned back to Annie. "You owe me an apology."

She laughed scornfully. "What?"

"You accused me of being extremely shallow. You put on a dress and makeup and suddenly I want to *screw you*—your words," Ric said. "I want you to apologize."

"I'm sorry," Annie said, "that I got it wrong, and that you apparently wanted to screw me back when I was *sixteen*."

"Sixteen's jailbait," Martell said.

Ric looked at him. "No shit." He turned back to Annie. "For the record, I also thought you were outstanding at the shooting range. You totally kicked *my* ass—"

"So . . . what?" She crossed her arms. "You had to run away and pout about it?"

Ric's mad was starting to restructure itself, with a heavy dose of frustration and insanity as its foundation. "No! I had to run away because I've always run away! I ran away when you were sixteen. And I ran away again when Bruce told me I had no chance with you. I'm still running, because now you're back, scaring me out of my mother-loving mind. I couldn't talk to you at the range, okay, because all I wanted to do was kiss the shit out of you. If I got too close, it was all over. Kind of like the way it was when I kissed you tonight."

Martell cleared his throat, breaking the stunned silence. "Should I leave now?" he asked. No one answered.

"Why is that such a bad thing?" Annie asked Ric, her voice just a whisper.

"Because it is!"

"Why?"

"Because for one thing, sex ends friendships, all right? Christ, Annie, it was easier when you were off-limits, because I can live without the sex, but I can't live without you as my friend."

Martell didn't move, waiting for Annie to laugh in Ric's face, and then kick his ass up into the bedroom. She didn't disappoint.

"You can live without the sex?" she asked, with, yes, disbelieving laughter in her voice.

"Yes," Ric lied, heavy on the *s*, as if more sibilance would make him more believable, despite the fact that he was already shaking his head in a very solid no.

"Because I can't," she said. "Just the thought of you walking around all night with my panties in your pocket . . ."

"And it is time for me to go." Martell grabbed Pierre's leash. "Come on, dog-thing. Sleep over at Uncle Marty's."

"You can really live without the sex?" Annie asked Ric again.

This time he answered honestly. "No."

"Then just . . . shut up and kiss me," Annie said as Martell closed and locked the door behind him.

Ric was still angry with her.

Or maybe it wasn't still. Maybe he was angry all over again. Either way, Annie could taste it in his kisses, feel it in the way he held her, touched her, his body taut, his hands slightly rough.

"I thought we agreed this was a mistake," he all but snarled before kissing her again, longer, deeper, harder.

Just like at Burns Point, he had her pressed against the wall. Just like at Burns Point, she clung to him, opening her mouth to him, kissing him back just as forcefully.

She could feel him solid against her, and she opened her body to him, too, wrapping her leg around him, shifting her hips so that he was now pressed exactly where she wanted him.

"Oh God," he breathed, his hands hot and rough against her thighs, pushing her skirt up indecently high, all the way to her waist, but she didn't care. She wanted . . .

"Please," Annie said, but it came out as just a muffled moan, because his tongue was in her mouth again. She could feel him unfastening his pants, heard the jingle of his belt buckle, the sound of something spilling onto the floor.

It was his credit cards, falling out of his wallet. And then it was his wallet, hitting the tile with a slap, tossed aside as he covered himself with a condom that he must've kept in there.

And then he made a sound that may in fact have been her name, but she wasn't sure because she stopped listening, stopped thinking, stopped breathing.

Because there was only Ric—hard and hot and pressed unbelievably deeply inside of her.

She may have cried out, or maybe it was Ric. Again, she wasn't sure. All she knew was that she didn't want this moment ever to stop. She wanted to stay right here, in this particular now, until the end of time.

But then he started to move—slowly, languorously—an excruciatingly delicious sensation. It felt so good she started to laugh, and she discarded that other now for this new one, and the next, and the next, and the next.

"You think . . . this is . . . funny?" Ric's voice came in gasps, and she opened her eyes to find him watching her, his eyes heavy-lidded and filled with heat, but not just from anger, from desire, too. He was feeling the same thing she was. She knew it.

"Is sex always this great?" she asked him, her own voice breathy and oddly high-pitched. "I mean, for you. With you. Because, for me, this is . . . incredible." He pushed himself even more deeply inside of her, and she groaned. "Don't ever stop, okay? I just want to keep doing this forever."

Maybe it was the fact that he was laughing now, too. Or maybe it was the hot satisfaction that flared in his eyes. Maybe it was the fact that she was looking into those eyes, Ric's eyes, losing herself in their rich darkness, surrounding herself with his palpable heat.

Or maybe it was reality giving her a shove. Nothing lasted forever. It was crazy of her even to think the word, let alone utter it aloud.

But she came in a shaking, shuddering rush, and Ric caught her mouth with his and kissed her and kissed her and kissed her until he gasped his own release.

And there they were. Both breathing hard, Ric with his forehead against the very wall where she rested the back of her own head.

His arms and shoulders were still tensed—he was, after all, supporting her full weight. Her feet were off the ground, legs locked around his waist.

This was, without a doubt, one of those times Ric had called her on—where she'd acted on impulse, without much thought as to what would follow.

Someone had to say something. And it was going to have to be her. She started with the obvious. "You should let me down."

He did, lifting his head and opening his eyes, his muscles straining as he made sure her landing was gentle.

And there she was, with her boobs and her ass hanging out. Ric was just as disheveled, his pants down around his ankles, but of course, on him, it all looked unbelievably sexy.

At least it did until he spoke. "Remember how I said that when I'm with you, I usually end up doing something completely insane? This is one of those times."

"Wow, thanks. It was good for me, too." Annie was trying to wrestle her skirt back down, but sweat and spandex were not a good combination. She turned away, embarrassed, glad she was still covered by his jacket.

"I'm talking about the fact that I completely forgot you hurt yourself climbing up to that deck," Ric told her. "You were right—I'm an asshole. Did I hurt you?"

He'd kicked off his shoes and his pants and was standing there wearing only his socks and shirt and tie, with such concern in his eyes, that Annie started to laugh.

"It's not funny," he said.

"Actually," she said, "it kind of is."

He looked down at himself, and almost before she could say, "I'm okay. I'm just scraped up a little—believe me, you didn't hurt me." He'd discarded the condom, peeled off his socks, and tossed away his tie. He took longer with his shirt, holding her gaze as he unbuttoned it. But it, too, soon joined his other clothes on the floor.

"Better?" he asked.

Oh yeah. Some men looked hotter with their clothes securely on— Ric didn't fall into that subcategory. He was all tan skin and well-defined muscles and thick, dark body hair, and . . . She had to clear her throat before she could speak. "Definitely not as funny now," Annie told him.

He held out his hand. "Let's go upstairs and get your scrapes cleaned up."

She didn't move. "You seem . . . okay," she said.

"You mean, as opposed to being in a panic because I just nailed Bruce's little sister to the wall?"

"Will you please forget Bruce?" Annie said in exasperation.

"Okay," Ric said. "Bruce is forgotten. You mean, as opposed to being in a panic because I just nailed a really good friend of mine to the wall?"

"The world didn't end," Annie pointed out. "Look at us. We're still talking. We're still friends."

He laughed. "Friends?"

"Yeah, well, you're now my naked friend, but that really works for me. Look at you—you're my own personal hot-naked-guy fantasy come true."

"Is that really what you think?" Ric was starting to get mad again. "Because there's nothing easy in what we just started. You want a fantasy? Find someone else."

"What we just *started* . . . ?" Annie couldn't believe it. "I'm leaving to-morrow, remember?"

He'd forgotten—she could see it in his eyes, on his face. He'd forgot-ten, and he didn't want her to go.

And oh, the way that made her heart swell with hope—which was a dangerous way to feel. This was Ric Alvarado. What did she think? He was going to *marry* her?

"Maybe the message that Peggy Ryan left," Ric said. "Maybe it'll be enough to end this for good."

And then she could stay for another week or two—a month if she was lucky. It would, however, be one hell of a month.

"Let's go upstairs and get you cleaned up," Ric repeated. But then he kissed her. "And after that I'm going to make you come again. Only it's going to be in my bed this time, with plenty of pillows and candlelight, okay? If we're going to do this, we're going to do this right."

Damn, skippy, when he put it *that* way . . . Annie took his hand and let him lead her upstairs.

CHAPTER
SEVENTEEN

Jules had fallen asleep.

Right there, in Robin's arms, no doubt lulled both by the movement of the limo, and Robin's fingers running gently through the softness of his hair.

Robin had turned down the volume of the radio and gotten on the intercom to the driver, telling him they were having a business meeting back here—instructing him to just drive. Anywhere. Nowhere.

It didn't matter, as long as he could stay right here, right like this, holding Jules for as long as possible.

There was a scar on Jules's side, just above his hip, that he hadn't had the last time Robin had seen him without his shirt. The last time? The only time, before tonight.

Before wonderful, amazing, fantastic tonight.

And okay. There were a couple of blips that marred the total perfection of the evening. The fact that Jules had this new scar from what was obviously a bullet wound.

Was the fact that he'd gotten shot once in the past two years good news or bad? As in, had Jules *only* gotten shot once, as opposed to the average FBI agent, who'd gotten shot twice? Somehow Robin suspected the true average was zero times. And this new scar, combined with all the others Jules permanently wore, created a certain amount of anxiety for him.

And yeah—another blip on his happiness index was the fact that Jules hadn't responded with much more than a "Gah," when Robin had uttered the most important words he'd ever spoken in his entire life.

I love you.

He'd never said it before and meant it. Not this way, with every cell in his body aching with both joy and hope. And terror.

But all Jules had said, after several long minutes spent catching his breath, was "God, that was great. That was . . . stupid, but great." He'd softened his words by kissing Robin before they shifted to a more comfortable position on the bench seat, with Jules, who was shorter, spooned back against Robin, who wrapped him tightly in his arms. "It was significantly better than the fantasy version."

Robin had laughed, playing with Jules's hair. "Yeah, you've spent a lot of time with me in my shower, too, babe."

"Every day," Jules agreed, "since you flirted with me out on your driveway in L.A. I remember seeing you and thinking . . ." He laughed.

"What?" Robin asked, his heart in his throat.

"This one's going to rip my heart to shreds."

Not the words he'd been hoping to hear. "I won't," Robin said. "I promise."

"Sweetie," Jules had told him, his voice already fading. "You already have."

"Tell me about Betsy Bouvette."

Ric lifted his head from the damp tangle of sheets to look at Annie. "Isn't this the part where we sleep?"

She smiled at him, her eyes as warm as the candlelight that flickered across her bare skin.

Annie Dugan was naked and in his bed.

It shouldn't have been that big a surprise, considering what they'd just spent the last hour doing, but the realization was still new enough to send a shock wave of disbelief through him. She was breathtakingly beautiful, but probably not to everyone, Ric knew that—not in this day and age of rail-thin supermodels and anorexic TV actresses. But to him, Annie was the embodiment of everything he loved best about the female form. With her generous curves and smooth skin, she was warm and sweet and unbelievably soft.

As he looked at her now, he felt his body stir, which made him smile. What was he, seventeen? This was crazy, but damn, he couldn't get enough of her.

"She was a year ahead of you in school, right?" Annie asked, reaching out to touch his tattoo, her fingers tickling him as she traced the ocean-wave pattern encircling his upper arm.

"Two," he told her, catching her hand in his and interlacing their fingers. "Why the interest in Betsy?"

"I'm just curious." She propped her head up on her other hand. "Do you think if she hadn't dumped you, you would've married her?"

"Betsy?" Ric laughed. "No. We were kids. I mean, yes, she was special—she was the first girl I ever . . . cared about, but . . ."

"You said you loved her," Annie reminded him.

"Yeah, I did," he admitted. "But that was back when . . . I don't know . . . love was this . . . It was this strange, new thing. It was all mixed up with sex and being fifteen and horny all the time." As if being thirty-five had changed anything. "Betsy was smart and funny—I really liked her. A lot. And she liked sex as much as I did. But did I love her because she wanted to get with me, or did she want to get with me because I loved her? Or maybe she just wanted to piss off her father. I honestly don't know."

"You went out with her for a really long time."

"Year and a half," he agreed. In high school years, that was a lifetime. "Although part of that half year was really just me waiting for her to come home from college for Thanksgiving—which was when she broke up with me."

"Oh, no." Annie made a face. "A turkey drop?"

"Pretty classic," he agreed. "At least we had sex first—before she broke the news."

"You were really . . . monogamous all that time?" she asked.

Ric just looked at her, but she didn't back down. She barely blinked. "Where do you see this going?" he asked her, instead of answering her question. "You and me."

That caught her off guard. And the change in her body language was immediate. She withdrew, taking her hand back, pulling the sheet around herself. Hiding.

"I don't know," she admitted. "I'm pretty confused. About everything except the sex. The sex is . . ."

"Yeah," he said. "For me, too."

She smiled into his eyes, and there it was—that electricity between them that never seemed to stop flowing. Jesus God, just like that, he was hot for her again.

But Annie looked away. "But I guess . . . I didn't realize just how big a mistake this was going to be."

It was stupid. He was stupid. He'd used the word *mistake* himself, but somehow it stung, hearing it from her lips.

"I mean, everything's changed, hasn't it?" she asked.

"Yeah, well, I warned you." His tone was far more snarky than he'd intended.

"I know." She, too, got a little sharp. "But it wasn't just me that got us here. You were a very active participant." She reached down and wrapped her fingers around him. "Look at you—you're ready for more. Or is this another *warning*?"

"Yeah, keep touching me like that." *Was* that a warning or was he begging her not to stop what she was doing? He wasn't sure. Mother of God . . .

"Do you just walk around like this all day?" she asked, her hands not a lot more gentle than her voice. "Just in case a willing woman passes by?"

"You," he told her. "In case *you* walk by. You do this to me."

She let go of him, flopping back on the bed. "God, you're good. I almost believe you."

Almost? He sat up. "Why don't you believe me?"

"Because I don't," she said. "Maybe that's the problem with being friends with, you know, benefits."

Was that really what she thought this was?

"Maybe we just know too much about each other," Annie told him.

"What do you know about me?" Ric lit into her. Friends with *benefits*? "When have you ever asked me what I'm feeling or what I believe in? You're so ready to make assumptions—that I have a problem with you risking your life, that I want to protect you because you're a woman? That's bullshit—that was your word the other night, and it was the right one. But the bullshit was yours—it was you, jumping to conclusions. I don't believe that women are any less capable than men, but *you're* ready to think I do because you think you know me. Ask Lora Newsom what it's like to work with me, Annie, if you don't trust me to tell you the truth."

She sat up, too, more than ready to fight. "Okay, so tell me, Mr. Touchy-Feely, where *you* see this"—she gestured between the two of them—"going. Because you know what I see? I see me leaving tomorrow, and being gone for God knows how long. And if I come back, we'll both have had plenty of time to think, and it will be extremely awkward, because sanity will have returned. Neither one of us will ever be able to look the other in the eye again, and that's it, we'll be done. We'll exchange Christmas cards each year and never see each other again."

"So let's make sure that's not what happens," Ric said. *If* she came back . . . ?

"I don't know how to do that," she said.

"Well, you can start by coming back. Not *if*. Not *maybe*." Ric spoke more sharply than he'd intended.

"Don't yell at me!"

"I'm not!"

"Yes, you are!"

He couldn't take it anymore. He kissed her, and she was fire in his arms, kissing him back as if it had been weeks since they'd last made love, instead of mere minutes. He rolled her over, grabbing protection from a box that he'd already ripped open, pushing between her legs, pushing himself home.

"I can't get enough of you," she gasped, saying aloud what he'd been thinking earlier. "This is crazy!"

"No, it's not, it's great." His eyes were damn near rolling back in his head, it felt so freaking good.

"Right now," Annie agreed, "yeah. But tomorrow's . . . Oh God, it's gonna suck."

Ric couldn't argue with that, since it was more than likely that tomorrow she was going to have to leave. All he could do was hold her as she unraveled in his arms, as his blood roared in his ears and rushed through his veins as she took him with her.

"Come back," he whispered, when he could finally speak again. "After this is over, I want you to come back, okay?"

Annie opened her eyes and looked up at him, about to answer.

But his phone rang. His home line. The one he so rarely used that he set his ancient answering machine to pick up after only one ring.

His cell phone was downstairs, in the pocket of the pants that he'd left on the floor of the office, so maybe it was the FBI, tracking him down. Maybe they were calling to tell him that Peggy's message had revealed all the information they'd needed, and that Yazid al-Rashid al-Hasan and Burns, both Senior and Junior, had been taken into custody, and that Annie wasn't going to have to go anywhere at all.

But the voice on the other end wasn't Jules's or Yashi's or even Deb's. "You're not *sleeping*, are you? Dude, the night is young."

It was Gordie Junior.

"I tried calling your cell, but you didn't pick up. I got a conflict for to-morrow night—I can't meet you then, but I got some free time right now."

Annie had propped herself up on her elbows, worry in her eyes. Ric shook his head, glad he hadn't answered the phone.

But Junior wasn't done.

"The lights are on in your office," he continued, "and your car's in the drive, so I know you're there. Quit banging the double-wide bitch and come downstairs and let me in. I'm pulling up outside."

Jules's phone rang, waking him from the deepest sleep he'd had since he'd gone on vacation in Italy last year.

He wasn't sure at first where he was. It was dark and music was playing softly. And he wasn't alone.

He was in Robin Chadwick's limousine.

It came back to him in a flash, complete with a flare of panic and surge of heat. What had he done? And sweet, sweet Jesus, when could he do it again?

His phone was lighting up, which helped him to find it and flip it open. "Cassidy."

"Where the hell have you been?" It was Max, his boss, and he wasn't happy.

Crap, it was after 1 A.M., and Max and Yashi had both called him three times in the past ten minutes. "I'm sorry, sir. I didn't have my cell on a loud enough ring."

"You all right?"

"Yes, sir. I'm . . . fine." Jules wasn't sure what he was right now—ecstatic or in despair—but either way, *fine* was such an understatement, he almost laughed aloud from the absurdity of what he'd just said.

Warm beside him, Robin was stirring. "Shit," he mumbled, "I gotta pee."

Jules moved across the limo, away from him, trying not to trip over the pile of clothing and shoes. "What's going on?" he asked Max. "Did we crack Peggy's code?"

Robin switched on the running lights, and they both squinted at each other in the dim glow. Hello, naked movie star. Robin smiled, clearly liking what he saw, too, but when Jules put his finger on his lips, he nodded.

"I'm at your hotel," Max told him. "Why don't you just get over here, as soon as possible? I'll meet you in the lobby bar."

"I'm on my way," Jules said, hanging up and reaching for his shorts.

"Where to?" Robin didn't hide his disappointment, but he also didn't complain, his finger already on the intercom button.

"My hotel." Jules sorted his clothes from Robin's as that info was relayed to the driver.

"We're just a few blocks away," Robin reassured Jules as they both hurriedly dressed. "What's up?"

"My boss is in town," Jules said, tying his shoes.

"Max?" Robin asked, and Jules looked up. Robin remembered his boss's name?

"Yeah," Jules said. "He's waiting for me in the hotel bar. He didn't explain why or what's going on."

"Give me your room key," Robin suggested. "I'll go up and wait for you."

"I don't think that's a good idea," Jules said, quickly adding, "not because I don't want you there." He tossed Robin's other shoe to him. "See, with Max, you just never know. He may want to hold a meeting in my room with the entire team. And I don't have a suite like you do, so . . ."

"Then I'll just come in and wait for you—on the other side of the bar. I won't try to crash your meeting, don't worry. I'll behave."

"I'm not worried. I just . . . I don't know how long I'll be." Jules flipped down a mirror and checked to see if he had sex hair. Yes, he definitely did. He tried to smooth it down.

"I don't care."

"Yeah, well, I do," Jules took a bottle of water from the limo's minifridge, and poured some into his hand, using it in an attempt to reactivate his hair gel. Great, now he looked as if he'd just had sex in a swimming pool. "Do you have any idea how tired you look? Go back to your hotel—"

"What are you afraid of?" Robin interrupted. "We've already crossed the point of no return. I want to wake up tomorrow with you in my arms."

God. Jules wanted that, too.

The limo turned in to the hotel driveway and braked to a stop. Unlike at Robin's fancier hotel, there were no bellhops at this hour to throw open the doors.

Which was just as well, because Robin had come across the limo to kiss him, and Jules was unable to do anything but kiss him back.

Except Max was in the hotel, waiting. Jules pulled away. "Go back to your hotel," he told Robin again. "I'll come to you."

It was obvious that Robin hadn't expected him to say that. "Really?"

"It might be late."

"I don't care." Robin dug out his wallet, pulled out his key card, putting it in Jules's jacket pocket.

"Don't wait up for me." Jules smoothed down a piece of Robin's hair that was sticking straight up. He smiled at the protest he could see forming in Robin's eyes. "Don't worry. I'll wake you when I get there."

Robin nodded. And then kissed him again, hard and sweet. He

opened the limo door. And got out. "Don't freak. I'm coming in with you, but only because I have to use the men's. Sean, I'll be right back," he called to the driver.

The hotel's automatic doors slid open, and Jules followed Robin, who was running ahead into the lobby. But then Robin stopped and turned back, waiting for Jules to catch up. He was, without a doubt, the most beautiful man Jules had ever known, especially when he smiled the way he was smiling now.

"You know, I meant what I said before." Robin put his hand over his heart. "I'm yours," he told Jules. And then he turned and ran for the bathroom.

And okay, so maybe that meant it wasn't *the* most romantic moment of Jules's entire life, but it was pretty damn close.

Grinning like an idiot—because there was so much about this that just wasn't going to work—Jules went into the hotel pub. It was dark in there, but he spotted Max right away, sitting at the bar.

"I hope you haven't been waiting for too long, sir," Jules said.

Max turned. "No, the flight just got into Tampa an hour ago."

"Really." What airline had flights landing after midnight? West-coast Florida was a roll-up-the-sidewalks-at-ten-thirty kind of place. "What'd you have, a lot of delays?"

"We hopped a military transport to MacDill." It was only when he heard that familiar Western drawl that Jules realized that the man sitting next to Max was none other than his good friend Sam Starrett.

"Hey, hey, SpongeBob!" Jules laughed as Sam—a former Navy SEAL, hence the marine nickname—slid off the bar stool to give him a hug plus plenty of backslaps to prove that he still wasn't gay. Some things never changed.

"New haircut?" Sam asked. "You're looking good, Squidward."

"Yeah, no . . . Thanks," Jules said. "What is this, a surprise party? It's not my birthday. I thought you and Lys were taking a vacation on Cape Cod after you got back from Europe."

Sam and his wife, Alyssa, worked for one of the nation's top personal security companies, Troubleshooters Incorporated—a civilian organization that was often contracted to task-force with the CIA or the FBI. There was enough work to keep them on the clock 24/7, and for a long time they'd done just that, jumping from one job to another, with no time off in between. Sam recently told Jules that he and Alyssa had made a pact to start taking more downtime.

Of course, maybe *that* was why Sam was in Florida. "Is Alyssa here, too?" Jules asked, looking around the bar. Had he missed seeing her, as well? But she wasn't in sight. Robin was, though. He'd come out of the men's room and was now at the other end of the bar, suspiciously eyeing Sam, who still had his hand on Jules's shoulder. "Doesn't your cousin live in Sarasota? Noah Something . . . Wait for it—it's coming." Jules squeezed his brain. "Gaines, right? Noah Gaines."

Sam shook his head. "Do you remember the names of everyone you've ever met?"

"Only the hot ones." Jules smiled back at him. "Are you here to see Noah?"

"I'm here to see you," Sam told him, his smile fading to grim. "Lys is already in Spain. We got another lead on that missing suitcase nuke—it's pretty high priority, considering Peggy's message. I'm going to catch a flight over in a little while."

A flight leaving after oh-dark-hundred, as SEALs and former SEALs were fond of calling the wee hours of the morning. What plane was Sam going to catch *in a little while*?

But that mystery was going to have to wait. "Peggy's message?" Jules turned to Max expectantly.

"Her code included a date," he told Jules, seeing Sam's grimness, and raising it a million. He had bags under his eyes, and he looked as if he were wearing yesterday's suit, and two years ago's attitude—he was clenching and unclenching his jaw so tightly, his teeth were going to be nothing but shards and nubs if he kept that up. "June thirteenth. She also told us *Atlanta* and *T2* and three letters—*GBJ*."

Gordie Burns Junior. So it wasn't the father. It was the son.

T2 was Tango Two—the code name for al-Hasan.

And June 13 was going to arrive much too quickly. Was it the date of al-Hasan's arrival, or the date he went to Atlanta?

"Sir, we're going to catch this motherfucker, I guarantee it," Jules told Max. "I know that's not going to bring Peggy back, but . . . I really am sorry for your loss."

Max glanced at Sam.

Sam—who had come all the way to Sarasota to see Jules, when he should have been in Spain with his ass-kicking wife . . . ?

It didn't compute. None of it did. A military transport to MacDill Air Force Base up in Tampa? To deliver, in person, information Max just as easily could have given Jules over the phone?

And, come to think of it, Max and Sam weren't exactly buddies. The idea of them traveling anywhere, together, was bizarre.

"Who died?" Jules said, looking from Sam to Max and back.

Oh, Jesus. He was right. He could see it in Sam's eyes. He was going to throw up. "Please tell me it's not Alyssa or Gina or the baby." Although, as soon as he said the words, he knew his friends were okay. Why would Sam and Max come all the way to give *him* news about *their* families?

"They're fine," Sam reassured him, his hand again on Jules's shoulder. "Why don't we go someplace more private?"

"Is it my mother?" Jules asked.

"Your mother's fine, too." Sam tried to move him toward the door.

But Jules shook him off. "Damn it, Starrett, don't make this a guessing game. Just fucking tell me who died!"

"Ben Webster," Max said.

Ben. Oh God . . .

"He was killed outside Baghdad by an IED," Max told him.

Ben, who'd been serving in Iraq, whom Jules really should have thought of first, since he was stationed in one of the most dangerous places in the entire world.

Ben, whom Jules hadn't thought of once today.

"Fuck." Sam was pissed. "We did that so fucking badly."

"Trust me, there's no good way," Max told him.

"Can we help you get upstairs, Jules?" Sam asked, his voice gentler. "Or get you a drink? Tell me what I can do to help you."

"No." Jules shook him off. "I've just . . . got to sit down for a sec."

"Here." There was a table nearby. Sam pulled out a seat, pushed him into it, and sat next to him, a solid, steady presence. "Get him a shot of Uncle Jack," he ordered Max.

"IED?" Jules asked. It didn't make sense. None of this made any sense at all. "He wasn't flying?"

Max put three glasses and a bottle of whiskey on the table in front of them.

"I don't want that," Jules said. "I just want to know why wasn't he flying?"

It was crazy. Dead was dead. Why should it matter so much to Jules that Ben hadn't died while he was doing the one thing he truly loved? The one thing he was ready to give up, because he claimed to love Jules even more . . .

Oh, God. He was going to be sick.

"It was an IED," Max told him as Sam filled the glasses anyway. "A roadside explosion."

"What was he doing out on the road?" Jules asked. Ben had told him in many of his e-mails that he rarely left the Marine camp any way other than in his beloved helicopter.

"He'd just flown a mission," Max tried to explain. "He'd caught enemy fire, and his chopper was damaged, but he brought it down safely, saving the lives of his crew. The problem was, he didn't make it back to the airfield. HQ sent a vehicle to pick them up, get them back to camp. When the bomb went off . . ." Max shook his head. "They must've been right on top of it." Misery was in his eyes. "They were all killed. Ben and all the men and women he'd saved, just hours earlier."

Jules knew a thing or two about explosives. For a bomb to cause that kind of damage to an armored vehicle . . . But then he realized. "The transport wasn't armored, was it?"

Max shook his head. "No."

"What the *fuck*—"

"They were in a safe zone," Sam chimed in, his voice dark. "Supposedly."

God, what a senseless waste.

Sam pushed Jules's glass closer to him.

"I really don't want it," Jules told his friend.

"Maybe it'll help," Sam said, but when Jules just looked at him, he chastised himself. "Yeah, that was stupid. I know nothing's going to help. I'm just so sorry."

"Thank you for coming," Jules said. He looked at Max, too. "And for getting the details for me."

"Lys would've been here, too," Sam said, "if she could've. She was already in Spain—I had to talk her out of swimming the Atlantic to get to you."

"When's the service going to be?" Jules asked Max. "I know this isn't a good time to tend to personal matters, and I understand that I won't be able to go over there to . . ." He had to stop. Clear his throat. "Bring him home. But I would like to attend the service, if I can . . ."

He trailed off, because Sam was staring into his drink, and Max was looking down at the floor.

"You tell him," Sam ordered Max, looking at Jules with an expression that was part heartfelt apology, part homicidal rage. "I'll just fuck it up."

The anger wasn't aimed at Jules—it had to do with the additional bad news he was about to hear.

"Ben died two weeks ago," Max told him quietly. "He's already been interred—"

Two weeks . . .

"—at a military ceremony up in Arlington," Max continued through the roaring in Jules's ears. Ben had already been buried, and no one had called Jules to let him know, to let him attend.

But two *weeks* . . . ?

"When?" Jules asked.

"The ceremony was Thursday," Max said. "The casualty report didn't cross my desk until today. Laronda noticed Ben's name and brought it to my attention." He was as angry about this as Sam was. "I couldn't believe no one had contacted you."

"No," Jules said. "When—what day—was he killed?"

Max had some papers folded up and jammed into his inside jacket pocket. He tried to flatten them on the table as he searched for the information. He found it and read off both the date and the time.

Jules nodded.

"Ah, fuck," Sam breathed, as usual way too perceptive for someone who wore cowboy boots and meant it. "What was it, the same day he sent you that e-mail?"

Yes, it was. And thanks to the Internet, by the time Jules had received that e-mail, Ben was already dead.

He'd never seen Jules's reply—as brief as it had been.

Ben had taken a huge risk—and it was a career risk as well as an emotional one—by putting everything he was feeling into words, by labeling it love, and honoring and prioritizing that love above all of his other hopes and goals and dreams.

And then he'd gone to put in a hard day's work for an organization that wouldn't have wanted him had they known who he really was. And he'd died because the administration thought they could win a war on the cheap.

"What I don't understand"—Sam was putting voice to his fury—"is why his parents didn't get in touch with you."

"He wasn't out to them," Jules said. "They didn't know."

"But he was an officer, he probably had a laptop—"

"He did," Jules confirmed. Ben had told Jules that he'd kept their e-mails—they'd exchanged scores of them. And Ben had said he'd saved them all. If his parents had discovered the truth—and it was hard to imagine that they hadn't—they'd made a choice to keep it hidden, at Jules's expense. "But that's how it goes when you live in the closet, when your entire life's a lie. Some of the people you love—people who love you—don't get to come to your funeral." He stood up. "Excuse me. I have to go throw up now."

He wasn't going to make it up to his room, so he hurried for the men's that was out in the lobby.

"Jules." He was stopped by a hand on his arm by . . .

What was Robin still doing here? He'd never left, Jules realized. He'd stayed in the bar.

"I couldn't help but overhear," he told Jules now.

"Shit," Jules swore, because here came Sam, making sure he wasn't being accosted by some stranger.

"Everything okay?" Sam drawled, his sharp gaze missing nothing, including the hand Robin quickly reclaimed.

"This is my friend, Sam." It was probably beyond absurd to exchange social niceties, considering he was moments from barfing on both of their shoes, but Jules didn't quite know what else to do. Of course, once he'd introduced Sam, he realized he probably shouldn't reveal Robin's name in a hotel lobby, surrounded by curious onlookers, so it was even more awkward and strange.

And then there they were, two of the most important men in his life— the ones still living, that is—gazing at each other with mutual distrust in their ridiculously similar blue eyes.

Sam's squint was particularly narrow. It was clear he recognized Robin, but just couldn't place him. And God knows Robin had heard quite a bit about Sam from Jules.

Under other circumstances, it would've actually been funny—like a big, giant cosmic joke on Jules—because Robin and Sam had almost the exact same coloring and build. Sam was a little taller, but other than that, they could have been brothers.

"I just wanted to say that I'm sorry for your loss," Robin told Jules, his face a mask. "I really am."

He headed for the door out of the hotel, but then turned and came back. One thing about actors—they always made excellent choices in terms of dramatic moments.

"Apparently I don't rate a name." Robin leaned in close to tell Sam, both anger and hurt making his lowered voice shake. "I'm just some random Friday-night fast fuck."

Oh, shit. "Robin," Jules said, but Robin was already running out the door. This time he didn't stop.

"Robin?" Sam repeated, heavy on the incredulity. Over the past few years, he'd heard quite a bit about Robin from Jules, and most of it included the phrase *I'd have to be crazy to get involved with someone as messed up as he is.* "As in *Chadwick?*"

Finding that men's room was still paramount, but now Jules had two other important bullet points on his To-Do list.

Get a verbal ass-kicking from Sam—and Max, now, too, since he'd come out to see where Sam had gone, and had heard everything—and chase after Robin.

Figuring out how to respond to Ben's e-mail was a problem Jules would no longer have to worry about. The stark reality of that—the knowledge that all possibility of a relationship was gone, not by the difficult choice that he'd already made, but because *Ben* was gone, forever . . . Jules had such a sudden, sharp sense of loss, he had to sit down.

But there was nowhere to sit. And his phone was ringing.

He checked the caller ID, hoping it was Robin, calling back to apologize for his knee-jerk reaction to a simple misunderstanding. Despite what Max and Sam thought, despite what *Ben* may have thought, Jules wasn't in a relationship with anyone.

But it wasn't Robin. It was Annie.

She didn't start with an exchange of pleasantries—she just got right into it after he answered.

"We've got a problem." She was speaking quietly, as if not wanting to be overheard. She was also talking very rapidly, and Jules had to put his finger in his other ear to hear her. "Gordie Junior is here. In Ric's office. Ric told me to stay upstairs, and I did. I am. So far. But I looked out the window, because I heard this noise in the garden, and it's Lillian Lavelle. She's dyed her hair brown, but it's definitely her. She must know that Junior's here—she's got her gun. I've been trying to call Ric on his cell, but he won't pick up, but maybe he'll answer if you call. Gotta go."

Click.

"I've got trouble. Do you have a car?" Jules asked Sam and Max as he speed-dialed Ric.

"Out front, in the lot."

"I need help. Are either of you carrying?" Jules asked as headed for the door. He himself was without a weapon.

Max answered. "I'm not, but Starrett is. He's got an entire suitcase, for Spain."

"It's sealed," the cowboy pointed out.

"Break it open," Jules ordered as his call went right to Ric's voice mail. "I've got a situation unraveling."

"What's going on?" Max asked.

Sam sprinted ahead, both leading the way and unlocking the rental car's trunk. He pulled out a metal suitcase, tossing it into the backseat. He threw the car keys to Max. "Don't let vomit boy drive."

"I've got a vengeful ex–porn star," Jules said as he got into the front seat and Max started the engine, "armed with a .44-caliber weapon, bent on murdering our prime suspect. Take a left out the driveway."

"You're fucking kidding me." Sam started laughing from the backseat, as he opened his metal case and started putting together a small arsenal of handguns.

"It's not funny," Jules said sharply. "If we lose our suspect, we'll probably lose Tango Two. Or maybe she'll miss the suspect and kill one of my civilian team members instead. That'll be a laugh riot."

Sam shut up.

"I've already lost my share of friends today," Jules told him.

"Sorry," Sam said as he handed Jules a Sig P226, grip first.

"And, sweetie?" Jules said, double-checking the nicely balanced handgun even as he called Yashi for additional backup. "As far as terms of endearment go, I prefer vomit *man*."

But there was no doubt about it now—getting sick was definitely going to have to wait.

CHAPTER
EIGHTEEN

Climbing down from a second-floor deck was, Annie noted, almost as hard as climbing up to one. Although it was the doing-it-silently part that really made it tough.

The lack of stairs leading from the deck to the ground below seemed beyond stupid, but it was clearly a choice made both for privacy and security.

Ric could sleep with the sliders in his bedroom open wide, the curtains pulled back to let in the fresh night air and the moonlight, and not have to worry about waking up to the electric meter reader looking in at him, with his nose pressed against the screen.

Assuming the meter reader had time in his busy schedule for some random Peeping Tom–age.

Ric's deck was built differently from the one at Burns Point. It just hung off the house, no wooden supports to shimmy down, no latticework to use as rickety finger and toeholds.

There was only the railing—white and wooden, with top and bottom rails, and lots of decorative candlestick-like pickets filling in the space between the two. Annie tested them—none were loose. The entire thing seemed sturdy enough.

But the upshot was that this was a hang-from-the-edge-and-drop-the-last-seven-feet kind of deal. It was pretty much pray and go—the prayer being that she didn't break her ankle and start screaming in pain in the process.

Lillian, meanwhile, was lurking in the oleander, by the window to the office bathroom. Someone had pulled up the blinds, probably to open the casement window a crack, and light spilled out into the yard.

If the bathroom door had been left open, as it usually was, Lillian would be able to see right into the outer office.

Which was where Ric, Gordie Junior, and an unknown number of his posse were discussing the logistics of a potential contract killing of the man who'd nearly let Ric's father die.

Ric was following up his recent performance at the police station by continuing to play the hothead. Annie had heard his voice rise heatedly a number of times since he'd opened his office door and let Junior in.

Although, after spending the past few days with Ric, the most recent hours being intimate ones, Annie was starting to believe that the act was the easygoing guy with the laid-back attitude. The hothead was the real deal—passionate and quick to anger, quick to speak loudly, quicker still to kiss and make up.

He was going to be beyond angry when he found out that she didn't stay upstairs. Annie knew that what she was doing was going to be an ultimate test of his ability to forgive. But how could she just sit by and watch this impending disaster unfold?

Lillian, after all, was as likely to hit Ric as Gordie Junior when she fired her gun.

And Annie had waited for Jules to show up for as long as she could.

She went over, bracing the toes of her sneakers against the sliver of the wooden deck that was on the outside of the railing. Bending her knees, she held the top rail and squatted midair, moving first one hand and then the other to two of the pickets. She walked her hands down them, getting as close as she could get to the bottom rail, until she was in a deep crouch.

Seconds ticked by as she froze there, waiting to make sure that Lillian hadn't heard her furtive movements.

And waiting, too, until the voices from the office rose higher again.

"I don't care that he's a cop!" she heard Ric say, his voice suddenly distinct, and Annie swung her legs down, one at a time, into the terrifying emptiness of the air.

It was a tremendously vulnerable feeling. Her shoulders and arms screamed from holding her full body weight, and her legs were hanging where Lillian might well be able to see them, should she look away from the bathroom window.

Annie was counting on the limitations of human vision to ensure that should Lillian hear her and glance up, she'd only see darkness after gazing for so long into the brightly lit office.

And true, there was an outside shower, with its wooden stall between them, plus a wide variety of ferns and pony palms and other lushly growing tropical plants.

"Where am I—?" Ric again went loud, and Annie did it. She dropped as he said "gonna get," landing on "that kind of money?"

She tried to imitate every cat she'd ever seen in her life, bending to break the impact on her ankles and knees and even her hips, and damned if it didn't work. She not only landed on her feet, but she did it quietly, fading back into the deeper shadows closer to the fence, which gave her a clear view of the entire back of the house.

Lillian, meanwhile, hadn't moved.

Ric was continuing to argue with Gordie Junior, haggling over the price of the hit, but from the sounds of it, Junior had delivered an ultimatum. Take it or leave it. Annie didn't hear the words, but she was pretty certain that that was what was said.

Because Ric replied, not as loudly, but still audible from out here, "I'm going to have to think about it. You're going to have to give me some time, so back off, aight!"

She could see their shadows moving through the blinds. They were in Ric's office now, but they'd have to pass directly in front of that bathroom window—and the barrel of Lillian's gun—when Ric showed Junior the door.

Which was going to be soon.

Lillian knew it, too. She brought her weapon up to the screen, ready to blow away Gordie Junior—as well as anyone who got between him and her gun.

Annie had no choice.

Lillian didn't get the sudden urge to take a bite of the oleander that she was hiding in and drop dead from the plant's toxicity.

Ric didn't say, "Hang on, I gotta answer my cell phone—the FBI's calling me."

Jules didn't show up, creeping through the foliage to save the day.

It was up to the double-wide bitch.

So Annie grabbed a cast-iron chair—it was either that or the tile-topped bistro table. The chair was plenty heavy as she rushed toward Lillian, pulling it back over her shoulder like a golfer gone mad.

Lillian heard her—there was no way she wouldn't have—because

Annie was also shouting, "Ric! Look out! Stay away from the bathroom window!"

Lillian turned, her face startled and pale against her oddly dyed hair, her gun pointing now at the shower stall as Annie swung. She made a sound, "Oof," as the chair connected with her upper back, as the gun went flying, and she went down, hard, into the dirt.

Annie scrambled after the gun, grabbing it, the grip still warm from Lillian's clutches.

Lillian wasn't down for the count—that would have been too easy. She launched herself onto Annie's back, screaming and scratching. The lights went on—big outdoor spots that blazed from the corner of the house—as Annie used the gun as if it were a heavy rock in her hand, smashing it back into Lillian's face.

Lillian was done then. Annie had cleaned her clock, and she lay in the dirt, unconscious, her nose a bloody mess, as Annie caught her breath.

And looked up to find Ric and three of Gordie Junior's heavily armed goons, standing on the deck by the back door.

The level of alert went to magenta as Annie held up the gun she'd taken from Lillian.

"It's your crazy-ass ex-girlfriend," Annie fabricated, looking at Ric, who in turn looked as if he couldn't decide whether to let Junior's men kill her or to do the job himself, "trying to fulfill her promise to shoot your balls off."

"Go upstairs," Ric ordered Annie, holding out his hand for the .44 she'd taken from Lillian.

She refused. Both to hand over the weapon—probably because she knew she was a better shot than he was—or to move from where she was sitting near Lillian's crumpled and unconscious form.

It was a miracle that she hadn't gotten herself killed. Ric fought a wave of icy fear, trying to banish the what-if scenarios. She hadn't broken her neck climbing down from the second-floor balcony. Lillian hadn't shot her.

But the danger wasn't over yet.

Junior had hung back as Ric had opened the back door, but he'd heard Annie's explanation. Crazy-ass ex. It would work—as long as Junior didn't get close enough to recognize Lillian, whom he knew intimately, considering she'd starred in one of his so-called adult movies. Then again, he hadn't recognized her in her Palm Gardens raincoat disguise, either. Maybe he only recognized her when she was naked.

Junior came forward now, and Annie shifted, making sure that Lillian's face was in her shadow. She met Ric's eyes, and he knew without a doubt that they were both on the same page regarding hiding Lillian's identity.

"Get your cuffs," Annie told Ric. "I'll cuff her." She now held out the gun for him, and he took it.

But no way was he leaving her alone out here with Gordie Junior and his men—not even for thirty seconds.

"Dayam, that's some serious hardware." Junior was referring to Lillian's gun. "She was looking to put you six feet under, bro."

Annie meanwhile had flipped Lillian onto her stomach. "Eat dirt, bitch," she said, taking a handful of the mixture of sand and darker mulch and rubbing it into Lillian's face. "Get those cuffs," she told Ric again.

"What do you want with cuffs?" Junior asked. "I had a pain in the ass like this, I'd just pop her now."

Annie looked up from straightening Lillian's legs and pulling her hands so that they were at the small of her back. Ric saw that she had a new scratch on her own arm—the same one with the trashed elbow and variety of other scrapes.

"Can't," Ric said, wondering what other contusions and bruises Annie had collected from tonight's unending fiasco. God damn, but they should've both still been in his bed, right now. "She came by a few days ago, shot out the front window of the office, shot up our cars. The neighbors are skittish. They hear a gunshot, the police'll be on my ass so fast . . ." He shook his head, trying to arrange his face into an expression of regret. Too bad. He couldn't murder an unconscious woman in cold blood. Not tonight.

But Gordie Junior had another idea. "Why'n'cha give her to me? I'll make her disappear." He leaned closer to Ric, as if he were sharing a secret, but he didn't bother to lower his voice. "Snuff films are a growing market. It's good for the current girlfriend to hear that, too, huh? It'll keep her in line." He laughed, nudging Ric. "Look at her face, she thinks I'm serious."

Okay, so that *was* supposed to be a joke. Sociopathic humor. Ric forced a laugh, not daring to meet Annie's eyes.

"Seriously, though," Junior then said. "I can take care of her for you. No charge."

Ric wasn't sure what to say to that offer. *No, thanks?*

Annie stood up, brushing off her hands. She'd done an amazing job concealing Lillian's identity with that dirt. "As much as I never want to see this bitch again," she said, "she's drunk, as usual. If she went to the Harbor Tavern—the way she usually does to get tanked up before she tries to kill you?—there are probably thirty witnesses who heard her say she was coming over here. If she turns up dead—"

"She won't turn up," Junior said.

Annie didn't so much as blink. "If she turns up *missing*," she corrected herself, "Ric could be a suspect in her disappearance. That's the last thing he needs right now."

But Junior was shaking his head. "No body, no case."

That wasn't always the truth, but Ric suspected that arguing with Junior over legal issues wasn't going to help.

"I've got some questions I need to ask her." Ric put some heavy end-of-argument tone into his voice. "There's a not-so-little matter of some missing money."

Annie pushed past them all, heading inside the office. "I'll get the cuffs."

"You change your mind"—Junior holstered his own weapon—"you let me know."

Ric waited for Annie to get back. He waited until she snapped the handcuffs on Lillian's narrow wrists. Only then did he show Gordie Junior and his men out, watching as they went down the path and got into their limo. He waited, again, for the car to pull away, before shutting the door.

He did a quick sweep of the office, the back deck, even Lillian.

Annie was sitting on the middle of the three steps that led up to the first-floor deck, her arms around her knees.

"We're clear," Ric said, shifting Lillian so he could look at the damage that had been done to her nose. It was definitely broken. She whimpered as she stirred. "Are you hurt?"

He looked over at Annie when she didn't answer right away.

"Me?" Annie said, as if she'd thought he was talking to Lillian. "No. Is she all right? I hit her really hard. Twice. It was kind of awful and . . . kind of satisfying—in a really sick way—all at the same time."

Ric sat down next her. "I know what that feels like."

"*Is* she going to be all right?"

He nodded. "Yeah. I need to call Jules. That's what you should've done, by the way, instead of playing Buffy the Porn Star Slayer."

"Screw you." Her voice shook. "I wasn't *playing* anything. She was going to kill Junior, and if that meant she had to kill you, too, well, then she was going to kill you." She stood up. "If you're going to yell at me, just . . . don't. I did the best I could."

"She *did* call me." Ric turned to see Jules stepping into the light.

"And me." Martell stepped forward, too. "Although it would have been a little nicer for me, anyway, if she'd told FBI here that she'd called me, too. We had a small crap-in-the-pants incident back on the other side of your fence—mine being the pants that got crapped in, of course."

"Sorry 'bout that." There were two other men with Jules, but the tall, fair-haired man was not Robin Chadwick, as Ric had first thought. He was older and far more dangerous-looking.

The other man was—oh, good—none other than Max Bhagat, the head of the FBI's top counterterrorist team. He nodded a greeting to Ric as he crossed to Lillian, crouching beside her as he spoke on his cell phone, requesting a discreetly marked vehicle and medical team.

"You did a good job," Jules told Annie. "I saw you stick that landing off the balcony. That was very impressive."

"You got a ten from the judge from Texas," the taller man drawled. "And a solid nine-point-five for the swift dispatch of . . ." He turned to Martell. "What did you call her?"

"Crazy McFuckedup," the Texan and Martell said in unison.

The Texan laughed. "It wasn't perfect." He smiled at Annie. "But it was close."

"I tried calling you," Jules told Annie. "Sam—this is my friend Sam. And Max. My boss."

"Hi," Annie said.

"Sam was in place to grab Lillian," Jules told Annie, "but I didn't want him to do it without giving you warning."

"I left my phone upstairs," she told him. "I was afraid it would fall out of my pocket—"

"It's okay, you did great," Jules reassured her, climbing up the steps to put his arm around her. "Let's get you inside. You're shaking a little, but that's normal after an adrenaline rush. You really did a good job." He shot Ric a look, like, *Are you paying attention and learning something here, asshole?* as he ushered Annie inside.

Annie wasn't the only one who was shaking. Ric had to sit down.

"You okay?" Martell asked him.

"You ever get so scared," Ric asked, "about something that didn't happen, but might've, that it gets a little hard to breathe?"

"Maybe you should come inside, too," Martell suggested. "This has been kind of a crazy night for you, huh?"

Ric just shook his head.

"Alvarado." Max Bhagat, the legendary FBI leader, had closed and pocketed his cell phone, but now he was digging in another pocket for something else. His wallet. He opened it, took something out. "Gina says hi."

Gina. Max's former girlfriend, now his wife. Whom Ric had once hit on. *Mem'ries, may be beautiful and yet . . .*

"How is she, sir?" Ric asked. Back when he'd met Gina, she'd had some serious emotional issues in the wake of a brutal hostage situation aboard a hijacked plane. But that had been years ago. Time, hopefully, had helped along the healing process.

"She's great," Max told him, handing him a photo he'd taken from his wallet.

And yes, there was Gina, still as crazy beautiful as Ric remembered her to be. In the picture, she was holding a very little girl—a baby, really—with dark hair and dark eyes. The baby was smiling and reaching for the camera—or, more likely, the man behind the camera—as Gina kissed her plump cheek.

"Dang, Emma's getting big," the Texan—Sam—said, leaning over Ric's shoulder to look.

"Emma," Ric repeated, handing the photo back to Max. "She's beautiful, too, sir."

"It doesn't get any easier to breathe," Max told him, "but you learn to live with it, because you can't live without it."

Ric stared up into the eyes of this near-total stranger, this man that he'd met only briefly, years before, and suddenly everything made more sense.

Ric stood up. "Excuse me, sir."

He needed to go find Annie.

Martell followed Ric inside.

His boy didn't waste any time. "Excuse me," he said, not even waiting for Jules to take a breath. He just interrupted the FBI agent, who was sitting at the conference table, still talking to Annie.

"I need to tell you what it felt like," Ric said, "to open that door and see you out there, on the ground, with Lillian and her gun."

Jules got to his feet, but Ric apparently didn't give a shit who was listening.

"My whole life flashed before my eyes," he told Annie. "Because I realized what you had done. The idea of you putting yourself into that kind of danger . . . God damn, it makes me crazy.

"And it's not because you're a woman. It's not really even because you haven't had any training. Your instincts are on the mark. You're an asset to the team, I can't deny it. You're clearly cut out for this.

"But I'm not sure I am," Ric told her. "I was trying to get away from this bullshit when I left the force. We haven't talked about that at all—not because you didn't try when you first got here. You did. I just . . . I couldn't. But I have to now. You need to know. So I have to tell you. But can I please tell you in the morning, because right now I am so fucking tired. I just want to go upstairs with you, and go to sleep—without me being mad at you and you being mad at me.

"Can we do that?" Ric asked her. "Please?"

Martell didn't hear Annie's answer, because Jules closed the door.

But he saw through the glass that Annie kissed Ric, which was probably a good sign that whatever she'd said, it had included the word *yes*.

"You, uh, want to talk about it?"

Jules looked over at Sam, who was driving the rental car back to the hotel. Max had gone with Yashi and Deb and the team who'd taken Lillian Lavelle into custody.

"What, did you lose the coin toss?" Jules asked.

Sam glanced at him. "I volunteered. We've been friends a long time, Cassidy. Don't insult me."

"But it's so much fun to insult you," Jules said. Was it really only three A.M.? Would this night ever end?

"I'm being serious here." Sam indeed had on his serious face. "Last time we talked, you told me you could imagine things working out with you and Ben. You said—"

"I know what I said. I was lying." Jules cut him off. "Not to you. Not on purpose. But to myself. Kind of the way you used to lie to yourself about not being in love with Alyssa."

Sam was silent for several long blocks. He was a former SEAL, so he was pretty smart, and it didn't take him long to do the math. "So you're saying you're in love with Robin. Crazy Robin, who won't even admit to being gay."

"He's admitting it," Jules told his friend. "In private." Which was a step, but just not a big enough one.

"So great," Sam said. "Now he's just plain crazy—an actor, too. You said no more actors. Plus he's in the closet, which was the big problem you had with Ben, right? And oh, yeah, Robin's a blackout drunk. Someone hold me back. I just might leave Alyssa and run off with him myself."

Jules shook his head. "Sarcasm always works so well in a heart-to-heart."

"You told me—on more than one occasion," Sam pointed out. "And not just when you got a little emotionally sloppy after too many of those fruity drinks you like—"

"I know what I told you." Jules rolled his eyes. "Thank you very much."

But Sam spoke right over him. "—but also when you were stone sober. You said, *If I ever get the stupid idea to start something with Crazy Robin, knock some sense into me, SpongeBob.*"

"I can't stay away from him," Jules confessed. "I can't do it. Sam, God help me, I've been, I don't know, *obsessed* with him—for years. I've tried, but Jesus, these feelings just won't go away. Every time I see him, my heart just . . . leaps." He'd never felt like this about anyone. Not Adam, not *any*one. "I feel like I could die when I'm with him, but that would be okay. God, but the rest of the time it hurts, because I know he doesn't want me the way I want him. He wants me, but he wants me to hide. And you're right. I wouldn't do it for Ben, but . . ." God help him, he was going to do it for Robin.

He'd been rolling toward that inevitable conclusion ever since he'd knocked on Robin's hotel-room door, just a few short nights ago.

"I've tried keeping my distance," Jules told Sam. "I tried denying it. I tried . . . Ben."

Ben, who'd been dead for the past two weeks. Ben, who'd died thinking he actually had a shot at a future with Jules, who'd never loved him back.

Sam sighed—knowing, as usual, what Jules was thinking. "You can't make yourself love someone," he told Jules quietly. "You just can't. The human heart doesn't work that way."

"Yeah, but I wanted it to," Jules told him. "I really tried. For a while—this was like a year ago—it was after I got back from Italy. I slept with him. Ben. I told myself that I wasn't going to, but . . . I did." He shook his head. "But it didn't feel right. It felt like . . . cheating, so I ended it." He laughed in despair. "Of course, now Robin thinks I was cheating on Ben when I was with him, and . . . Maybe I sort of was, because Ben was clearly in a different place in terms of how he thought about our relationship, and I knew that. I mean, my God, it was obvious from his e-mail. I should have e-mailed him back, right away, and at least told him that I was surprised because I considered us to be just friends."

But that wasn't quite true. Because Jules really hadn't known how he'd felt about Ben—until he'd seen Robin again. It was only then, as Jules had reexperienced the vivid Technicolor of his feelings for Robin, that he'd truly realized he was unwilling to settle for anything less.

"If you'd e-mailed Ben right away," Sam gently pointed out, "he wouldn't have received it. You didn't hurt him, Jules."

"Only because he died," Jules said. "If he hadn't died, he would've been hurt." Instead, the person Jules had managed to hurt was Robin, who still wasn't answering his cell phone. "I've got to go talk to Robin."

Sam had already figured that out. Which was why, instead of pulling up to Jules's hotel, Sam had taken him to Robin's.

"It's not your fault," he said quietly as he stopped at the front doors, "that you didn't love Ben the same way he loved you. I'm just sorry that he's never going to have a chance to try to change your mind."

"I'm sorry, too," Jules said as the doorman opened the car door. "Thanks for coming all this way."

Sam shrugged it off. "You'd've done the same for me, Squidward."

"I love you, too." Jules got out of the car. "Give Alyssa a big wet kiss for me, and be careful out there."

"Always do, always am. You be careful, too."

And with that, Sam was gone.

A hotel security guard was standing just inside the lobby. He nodded as Jules flashed the key card Robin had given him.

He checked the bar first, but it was dark—long past last call.

Which didn't mean that Robin had stopped drinking. His suite was outfitted with a full bar—not just a mini one like most hotel rooms.

The elevator was empty, as was the hall on Robin's floor. But there was loud music playing somewhere, and as Jules approached, he realized it was coming from Robin's room.

He almost didn't go in—he was that afraid of what he was going to find.

But he heard laughter—there was clearly a group of people partying in there—so he knocked. Loudly.

The door was opened by, yes, a scantily clad young woman. She was wearing only bright yellow underwear. It wasn't Dolphina, but instead a blonde whom Jules had never seen before. "We're being too loud," she apologized. "I know. Sorry. We're trying to keep it down."

"Actually," Jules said. "I'm a friend of Robin's."

"Oh, he's . . . not exactly here," the woman said.

"What does *that* mean?" Jules asked, moving his foot so that if she tried to close the door on him, it would literally be *on* him.

"Well, he's here, but not really capable of conversation." She made an oops face. "He passed out about an hour ago."

Enough was enough. Jules pushed his way inside. "Where is he?"

"On the balcony."

On the *balcony*. Because it was so safe to be on a twelfth-floor open-air balcony when one was falling-down and passed-out drunk.

There were two other women and two men—none of whom Jules had ever seen before—lounging in Robin's suite, wearing bathing suits as if they'd come here straight from the hotel pool.

Jules realized that the woman who'd answered the door was actually wearing a yellow bikini. "Tell your friends it's time to go," he told her as he headed for the balcony.

"Not that one," she said. "The one in the master bedroom."

The women all stood up, gathering their beach towels, but the men weren't as willing to follow orders. "Robin Chadwick invited us here," one of them said. "Who the hell are you to tell us to leave?"

Jules stopped. No one moved. Five pairs of eyes were watching him with a mixture of curiosity and resentment.

This was one of those moments that he'd been dreading. *Who the hell are you?* He was going to have to lie about his relationship with Robin.

As far as the actual lie went, there were so many choices.

I'm his cousin—that was a classic.

I'm his brother—although they probably wouldn't buy that one, due to height differences.

I'm his head of security.

I'm his personal manager.

I'm his bodyguard.

I'm his real-estate agent, his yacht designer, his personal shopper, his investment broker.

Anything but *I'm his lover.*

"I'm one of his producers," Jules finally said, because that was his cover on this assignment. "I'm also a good friend. I make sure people don't take advantage of him. Close the door on your way out."

He went through the French doors, into the bedroom. The slider to the balcony was open, and the curtains were blowing in the cool breeze off the Gulf.

And there was Robin, also in his bathing suit, lying facedown in his own vomit. He stirred and moaned as Jules bent down to lift his head, to make sure he hadn't hit it when he'd fallen.

There didn't seem to be any bruises, which of course didn't mean a thing.

"Is he all right?" The woman in yellow stood in the doorway.

"You tell me," Jules answered. "Did he take anything—any drugs I should know about?"

She shook her head no, but then bit her lip. "Well, just . . . the Viagra. He was having a little trouble, you know . . . Sometimes when guys get that drunk, they need—"

"Yeah." Jules cut her off. He got it.

He took off his jacket and tie, tossing them onto a chair and rolling up his sleeves. He was going to have to drag Robin into the bathroom to clean him up, but it would definitely be better to wipe his face off before he tried to move him. He turned on the bathroom light and looked into the room. It was spacious, and there was a separate shower stall—a large one—which was good. It would be easier to get Robin in there, rather than over the side of the tub.

Jules grabbed a towel and took it with him back across the bedroom to the balcony.

"I left my phone number," the woman in the yellow bikini told him. Was she still here? "It's on the table, by the sofa? In case Robin wants to, like, finish what we started."

"You didn't finish . . ." The words were out of his mouth before he could stop himself. Because really, what difference did it make? Robin wouldn't remember any of it in the morning anyway.

"We didn't really start, because he kind of passed out," she explained. "Oops, it looks like I put his bathing suit on him backwards."

Indeed, she had.

"I didn't think it was very dignified for him to be, you know, just lying there naked, especially after taking the Viagra," she continued.

Certainly not as dignified as going up to someone's room to have sex with them merely because they were a movie star and too drunk to care whom they were with.

"Do you want me to fix it?" she asked as Jules moved Robin back and gently wiped off his face. "I mean, you probably don't want to, and I don't mind." She laughed. "It's not like I haven't seen what's under there."

"Please go," Jules said.

Yet still she lingered. "Will you . . . tell him I—"

"I'll tell him," Jules said. "Believe me, I'll tell him. Now get the fuck out of here before I call security."

She ran, inspired by both his words and tone, but he followed her to the door, making sure she was gone, locking the chain behind her.

He made a quick circuit of the entire suite, checking behind the furniture and under the beds to make sure there were no other surprises.

He'd had all he could handle tonight.

He managed to pull Robin into the bathroom, where he stirred.

"Dolph?" Robin's speech was slurred, but it was clear he thought Jules was his assistant. "I'm okay, babe. You don't need to . . . I just gotta . . ."

There was no way he could lift himself off the floor, even to reach something as low as the toilet, so Jules dragged him into the shower, and let him empty his stomach over the drain in the tile floor.

It was dawn before Robin stopped throwing up, and seven-thirty before the dry heaves finally ended. By eight, Jules had him cleaned up and tucked into bed, rolled carefully onto his stomach just in case he got sick again.

He smoothed Robin's hair back from his face, and just sat for a while, watching him as he slept.

He looked peaceful. Angelic and deceptively innocent.

He *was*, undoubtedly, the most beautiful man Jules had ever known. He was smart, too. And funny. And sweet, and kind, and sexy and . . .

He was perfect in so many ways.

Some of the time.

"I can't do this," he told Robin, who, even if he could hear him, wouldn't remember what he'd said.

Heart in his throat, Jules kissed Robin on the forehead. And leaving his key card on the table next to the slip of paper with Yellow Bikini's phone number, he locked the door behind him.

CHAPTER
NINETEEN

Ric woke up in a rush, sitting up in bed. "Lillian Lavelle," he said. "Holy Christ."

"Wow." Annie was already awake. Clearly, she'd been lying there, just watching him sleep. "Way to guarantee a sex-free morning. Wake up shouting the name of the ex–porn star you nearly drilled." She pushed herself out of bed, walking naked across his room to his door to the bathroom, heavy on the attitude.

She was kidding, but not entirely.

"Wait," Ric said, but she'd already closed the door behind her. So he shouted through it. "You've got to check out what my brain came up with while we were sleeping."

"Ignoring you!" Annie shouted back through the door.

"I am definitely getting some. You're going to be all over me when you hear this."

His cell phone was on his bedside table. He'd brought it upstairs with him the second time he and Annie had gone to bed. It was done charging, and he unplugged it and speed-dialed Jules.

Who answered with a croak that might've been his name. "Cassidy."

Ric had clearly woken up the FBI agent.

"Damn," Ric said. "What time is it?"

Jules sighed. "That better not be why you called me, Alvarado."

"It's not."

"Good. It's . . ." Jules laughed. "Ten. The scary thing is that I actually feel rested after my fifteen minutes of sleep. What's going on?"

"Last night," Ric said, "Gordie Junior volunteered to get rid of Lillian's body. Well, he didn't know it was Lillian, of course, he thought it was some crazy ex-girlfriend of mine."

"Yes," Jules said as Annie opened the bathroom door, wearing his robe, toothbrush in her mouth, so she could hear Ric better. Ric put his phone on speaker. "I *was* there."

"So today, you have to call Junior," Ric said. "On my phone. I'm in a panic, so you're the one who calls him—because, ready for this? I've killed her. You follow? You tell him I got a little too rough when I was asking her about the money she stole—remember, I told him—"

"Oh, yeah," Jules said. He was sounding far more awake now. "I know where you're going with this, and it's brilliant."

Ric looked at Annie. See? But she didn't get it.

"We're calling for Junior's help," Ric continued, mostly to explain to Annie, "to get rid of the body. You tell him if he does this for us, you'll lower the price for the Chadwick sex tape to four hundred thousand. He won't say no, we'll all bond, and he'll have something on us to make us keep our end of the deal—"

"And we'll put a series of tracking devices inside the body," Jules finished for him, "and find out where he dumps his victims—maybe stand a shot to recover Peggy Ryan."

Across the room, Annie was still frowning. "Where are you going to get a body?"

"Can you get us one?" Ric asked Jules. "It's got to be female and relatively young."

"I'll see what I can do," Jules said. "Stay put, all right? I'll call you back, but be patient. This could take a while."

"Will do." Ric hung up his phone and went into the bathroom, where Annie was finishing brushing her teeth.

"What if he chops them into little pieces," she asked as she dried her face on his towel. "Junior seemed so convinced that a body would never be found."

"I think Jules was taking that into consideration," Ric told her, "when he said he'd put a *series* of tracking devices into the body." He flushed the toilet.

"God, that's grim."

"Yeah." Ric washed his hands and splashed water onto his face. Annie handed him his towel. "Thanks. It may not work, but if we had hard evidence that Gordie Junior was involved in the murder of a federal agent . . . Even just some DNA—bone fragments—I don't know exactly how much they'd need. But if we could get it, Junior'd be looking at the death penalty, and he might be willing to make a deal—give up information that would help the FBI apprehend al-Hasan in exchange for a life sentence." He grabbed the belt of the robe she was wearing and pulled her in for a kiss. "I thought it would be worth a shot."

"It is brilliant," she agreed.

Ric kissed her again. "Mmm."

Annie pulled back, unable to hide her smile.

Damn, but he loved the color of her eyes, and the light and life that danced there. He loved the shape of her face, the curve of her smile, the smattering of freckles across the bridge of her nose.

"You owe me one heavy conversation," she pointed out. "If you think you can trick me into forgetting—"

"Can't we have sex or breakfast first?" He kissed her, more deeply this time. "Or sex while we're having breakfast . . ." He got the robe open, and he slid his hands inside against the softness of her body and the smoothness of her skin. "You . . . *and* waffles. Sweet."

Annie laughed as she kissed him back, but it was clear from her urgency that she was as aroused as he was. As usual, it didn't take much to get them both revved up. Even last night, as tired as he'd been when they'd finally gone back to bed, he hadn't been able to resist sliding into her sweet heat, and rocking her until they'd both exploded.

Still kissing her, Ric now lifted her onto the bathroom counter, pushing between her legs, pushing himself all the way inside of her. All the way.

It felt unbelievably great, deliriously, staggeringly, astoundingly incredible, and as he moved inside of her he knew he was going to come right away, which was okay, because he'd be ready to go again in minutes, she turned him on that much and . . .

He wasn't wearing a condom.

Ric realized it at the exact moment Annie did. She opened her eyes and looked up at him, as he froze, pushed deeply inside of her.

"Ric?" she said. "We need to get—"

"I know," he said, but he didn't move. He couldn't move.

She looked at him, expectantly.

He closed his eyes. "I'm afraid if I try to pull out, I'm going to come."

"Oh God," she said.

"Don't move," he warned her.

"I'm not." But she started to laugh.

"Don't laugh!"

"Picture me pregnant," she told him. "Picture me—"

"Don't," he cut her off. "That's turning me on."

"Really?"

"Oh, yeah."

And there they were, staring at each other.

"Marry me," Ric said. He just opened his mouth and the words came out.

Annie laughed—just once. "You just want to come inside of me."

"Shit, yeah," he said. "For the next fifty years."

She laughed again, but her smile faded as she looked into his eyes. "You don't really mean it, do you?"

"I do," he whispered. "I love you, Annie."

She kissed him.

And she came, too.

Robin woke up with a headache that rated a solid ten on the hangover scale of agony.

His room was dark, and the air conditioner was running, and he was actually in the bed instead of on the floor, lying in his own puke and filth.

That was new. A ten on the agony scale was usually accompanied by disgust and utter humiliation.

But he was clean, the sheets on the bed were clean, and he had no idea how he'd gotten here.

There was a bottle of water on his bedside table, as if someone had placed it there just for him, and he opened it and took a cautious sip. When it didn't come right back up, he drank some more, swishing it around the cotton of his mouth.

Through a fog of disjointed pictures and sounds—a laughing man in a bathing suit; a stern-faced security guard, *Time to move it upstairs, folks;* a spilled bottle of Jack Daniel's; a woman's voice, *We can fix that*—Robin remembered Jules.

In his limousine.

It was distant, like a memory from years ago, or a dream.

A really good dream.

Jules. Kissing him. *Go back to your hotel. I'll come to you.*

What the fuck had happened between then and now?

Robin swung his legs out of bed—no easy feat, considering his head was on the verge of imploding. The message light was blinking on his room phone, so he picked it up. Pushed the voice-mail button.

"You have one hundred and seven new messages."

Jesus.

Robin hung up, dropping the phone back into its cradle.

Someone had plugged in his cell phone, which was still set on silent, and he checked to find that it, too, had over a hundred new voicemails. Forty new text messages. Two hundred and fifty missed calls.

He scrolled through the list—most of them were from his sister, Jane; his agent, Don; and Dolphina—the most recent being two minutes ago.

His manager had also called, along with a number of people from *Riptide*'s production and distribution companies.

He'd even missed a few from his brother-in-law, who'd called him from overseas.

Robin kept scrolling down—the bulk of the calls started at around ten o'clock this morning, his time. It was only when he got beyond that, that he found five missed calls in a row from Jules—starting shortly after one A.M., each spaced about thirty minutes apart.

What had happened? Why did everyone have their panties in such a twist, trying so hard to reach him?

Everyone but Jules, who'd dropped off the map.

Who died? Jules's voice echoed in his head and Robin's memory shifted, but not enough for him to remember . . . what?

Jules stumbling sightlessly for a seat, anguish and grief glazing his eyes.

Someone had died.

Fear filled Robin's throat, throbbing in time with the pounding in his head.

And when his cell phone lit up—its ring still silenced—and his caller ID told him it was his sister on the other end, he answered. "Jane?"

"Robin, oh my God. Are you all right?"

"I don't know." He lowered the volume with one hand and grabbed his head with the other, to keep it from splitting in half. "Am I?"

"Okay," she said. "Where are you? Are you at least safe?"

"I'm in my hotel room," he told her. "Janey—"

"Are you hurt?" she asked.

"Who died?" he asked.

"Who what?"

"Someone died," he told her. "I want to know who it is."

"I don't know what you're talking about." She'd started this conversation upset, and it was escalating. Her voice shook. "Is someone dead?"

"That's what I'm asking you."

"Okay," she said. "Okay. Let's try it this way. Are you alone?"

He walked—carefully—into the empty living room. Where a spilled bottle of Jack Daniel's stained the hotel carpeting. The other bedroom was empty, too. "Yes."

"So there's no one in your room with you—"

"That's what I just told you," he snapped, the act of which nearly sent him whimpering to the floor, to curl into a fetal position.

"—either alive or dead?" Jane asked.

"No," he said. "Jesus! There are hundreds of messages on both my phones, you've been trying to reach me for hours while I was sleeping off a slightly exuberant night—"

"A *slightly exuberant* night?" she repeated, her voice going up an octave and making his eyes tear. He held the phone away from his ear. "Do you have any idea what you did last night? Does a balance-beam routine on the rail of your *twelfth-floor balcony* ring any bells at all?"

Robin looked out the sliders to the balcony. "Oh, shit," he said as somewhere, way back, a shred of memory flashed. *I'm the king of the world!*

"Someone uploaded digital video to YouTube," his sister told him. "There are two different cell phone movies that hit the Web last night. One of them has you stripping to 'Will It Go Round in Circles' in some kind of, I don't know, restaurant kitchen? The other has you stripping, too—except this time it's full-frontal nudity. You can be thankful it's low quality, but the audio track makes it clear what's happening—or rather what's not. Congratulations—one and a half million people and counting have now watched you not get it up. I'm so proud."

Robin sank onto the sofa. "Oh, shit. Who was I with?"

"Some blonde," Jane told him. "It was a woman, so congratulations again—your career's not completely over. The rest of *that* one is seven minutes of the most terrifying footage I've ever seen. You're partying, and I don't know who all you're with, but they are *not* your friends. You're doing this crazy stuff—cartwheels into this pile of beach chairs, walking that railing, and . . . and . . . chugging a bottle of whiskey when you're already too drunk to stand—and they're *cheering* you *on*." On the other end of the phone, Jane was apeshit. "I was sure you were dead, if not from a twelve-story fall, then from alcohol poisoning."

On the table next to the sofa was a note with a phone number. *Call me if you want to hook up again. (Again?)* It was signed *Ashley.*

Next to it was Robin's key card.

The one he'd given to Jules. Right before Jules had walked into his hotel bar and found out from his boss and another friend that his significant other—Ben, the Marine—had been killed in Iraq.

Who died?

"Oh, shit," Robin said again, past the misery that caught in his throat. "Oh, Janey, oh my God, I've really screwed everything up."

Annie stood in the shower, trying not to cry, letting the water drum down upon her head.

"You okay in there?" Ric called.

Oh, God. "Yeah," Annie called back, making her voice sound cheerful. "Sorry, am I taking too long?"

"No," he said as she shut off the shower and squeegeed the water out of her hair. "I just . . . I know I surprised you. I kind of surprised myself."

She so didn't want to talk about this. She reached out from the curtain for her towel. "Did Jules call back?"

He helped her get it. "Not yet."

"The two men who were with him last night," Annie said. "The shorter one was his boss, right?"

"Max," Ric said. "Dark hair, vaguely Indian American. India Indian."

"What's he doing here?" Annie asked, wrapping the towel around her and pulling back the shower curtain.

Ric was leaning in the open door—the one that led to his bedroom. He'd pulled on a pair of shorts, but that was it. It was a fashion statement that worked well with his six-pack. "I don't know. The other guy wasn't FBI. Sam. He works for some California-based private investigators— something called Troubleshooters Incorporated. Apparently it's a big company, with lots of work—so much they can't handle it all. He was trying to recruit us. You, actually."

Annie turned from brushing out her hair to look at him. His smile was rueful.

"It definitely had more to do with you," Ric admitted, "since all he'd seen me do was stand around with my thumb up my butt. I guess he figured if he could get you, he'd make do with me. I told him you had virtually no training, he said they'd take care of that. He left his card."

"Are you serious? That could be so great—"

"I was afraid you were going to say that. I told him I'd tell you, so I had to tell you, but . . ." Ric shrugged. "I'm not interested."

She stood there, just looking at him, her hairbrush in her hand.

"And now I've disappointed you," he concluded.

"No," she said. "I didn't say that."

"You didn't have to."

"Since when can you read my mind?" she asked.

"Since you were eleven?"

Annie had to smile at that. Ric *had* had an uncanny ability to show up at the least likely times, usually right when she was on the verge of doing something incredibly stupid.

Such as the time, shortly after they'd met, that she decided to go live with her grandparents in New York. Of course, she didn't have much money—certainly not enough for a train or bus. So she'd made herself a sign on a piece of cardboard—similar to the signs she'd seen desperate-looking men holding on street corners: WILL WORK FOR FOOD, theirs had said. Hers read: WILL WORK FOR A RIDE.

In retrospect, the danger of what she'd almost done—an eleven-year-old hitchhiking hundreds of miles—took her breath away. She'd been a tough little kid, having survived all those fights between her parents—the last ones terrifyingly physical. But in so many ways she had been impossibly innocent.

Ric had not only figured out that she was leaving, but that she was planning to leave in the middle of the night—*that* night. He showed up, tapping on the back door at two in the morning—just as she was filling her backpack with food.

He'd come all that way because Annie's mother had turned the ringer off on their phone. Annie's father had managed to get their new number, and after last call, when the bars shut down in Boston, he often indulged in some heavy-duty drunk dialing.

At the time, Annie had believed that since her father found their phone number, it was only a matter of time before he showed up at their house in Sarasota. She'd tried to talk her mother into moving again, but her mother just told her they were fine—without giving her any details. It was only later that Annie had discovered that her uncle Ian, who was a Boston cop, was keeping track of her father. If he disappeared, Ian would call Annie's mother right away.

Unaware of this, Annie figured if she went to Grandma's, her mother and Bruce would soon follow—and they'd all be safe there.

That night, Ric not only talked Annie out of leaving, but he figured out her motive, and he got her to talk—for the first time since it happened—about what it had been like to see her father hitting her mother—and then to have him turn that rage on her.

It had started the healing process—and had taught her to ask questions instead of making assumptions when she got scared.

Ric had also used his mind-reading abilities through the years to mysteriously appear when Annie had accepted a dare to climb out to the end of a rocky breakwater as the tide was coming in, and when she tried to rescue a friend who was being targeted by a middle school bully.

But he'd missed quite a few, too. Like her decision, in tenth grade, to go to that party at Skipper Gleason's—the one where his parents were out of town, and there were four kegs of beer and about four hundred high school students hell-bent on getting drunk. Or her genius choice, senior year, to go all the way with Mike Mattson, the big loser.

Although Ric *had* asked her about Mike, when he found out they were dating. "You sure this guy's good enough for you?"

At the time, Annie had been offended. "You don't know him," she'd defended Mike. "He's nice. You just think all guys are like you and Bruce."

Ric had backed down and kept his distance—and Mike, the loser, decided it would be better to just be friends after taking Annie's virginity in the backseat of his father's Town Car.

"You only read my mind correctly half the time," she told Ric now.

"Five hundred is an excellent batting average," he pointed out. "I know you, Annie. I know what you're thinking. You don't understand why I wouldn't be interested in a job with a real salary, but . . ." He laughed, obviously embarrassed. "You're going to think I'm crazy when I tell you this . . ."

"I already think you're crazy, Alvarado, so don't worry about it." She kissed him as she went past him, going out the door into the hallway, toward her room, with her closet and her clothes.

He followed her in, and made himself comfortable on her bed. Apparently he was going to watch her dress.

She tried not to feel self-conscious as she took clean underwear from the dresser, and shorts and a T-shirt from the shelf in the closet.

But then he said, "You know I left the police force because I killed this kid, right?"

And Annie forgot about getting dressed. She wrapped her towel more tightly around her and sat down on the other end of the bed to give him her full attention. "No," she said. "The story I heard is that he almost killed *you.*"

"*Almost* is one of those words that doesn't mean a whole hell of a lot in this business. You're dead or you're not. I wasn't. He was." Ric looked down at the spread on her bed. "He was the tenth for the precinct, for that year." He looked back up at her with eyes that were haunted. "Tenth kill."

Annie reached out and touched him—her hand on his. "I didn't know."

"I quit," he said quietly as he laced their fingers together. "But I guess I didn't really think it through. I thought I did. I thought if I worked for myself, then I could take the jobs I wanted, maybe do something worthwhile that didn't include a body count. Instead I'm breaking up marriages—getting evidence for divorces. It really sucks. My one most lucrative job was retrieving what's-his-name."

"John Beasley." Annie would never forget him—or the fact that his brother Frank had kicked Ric in the side so hard that he'd peed blood. Over the past few days, between the two of them, they'd acquired an impressive collection of fresh scrapes, nicks, and bandages. But she could still see a faint trace of the bruise that Frank Beasley had given Ric two weeks ago.

Ric smiled at the vitriol in her voice. "I didn't enjoy that job very much, either. And yeah, he's a scumbag who kicked the crap out of his girlfriend, so I can try to pretend that putting him in jail was a good thing, but . . . Turns out she deals drugs to high school students but they don't have the evidence to bring her in, so who am I saving here, you know?" His smile faded. "Gunning down some kid who accidentally killed his own cousin . . . I wasn't helping anyone, Annie. I was a youth officer for a while, until budget cuts took away the position."

The muscle jumped in his jaw. "I think that was why I was so eager to take Lillian's case. I actually thought I could help her. You know, find closure for her, for her daughter's death." Ric laughed his disdain. "Instead, it's more bullshit. Instead, I'm the big freaking hero by saving Gordie Burns Junior—and I end up putting your life in danger. Christ, it's like I'm this force of nature, destroying everything in my path."

Annie squeezed his hand. "No, you're not."

"That's what it feels like," he told her. "I come from this world where everyone—*everyone*—is creative."

She knew that he'd spent a lot of time as a child in his father's recording studio, and when he wasn't there, he was home, where his mother was painting.

"The musical-talent gene obviously skipped a generation," he continued. "I love listening, but . . . And you've seen me draw."

She couldn't hide her smile. Yes, she had. Playing Pictionary with Ric had always been hilarious. "There are other ways to be creative."

He nodded. "That's what I always thought, but . . ."

He was silent then, and Annie just waited, because she knew he wasn't done.

"I just . . . This isn't what I want to do," he admitted. "The private investigations thing. It's just not. I've been thinking about it a lot and . . . I'm going to shut down the business. Or at least really revamp it." He looked up at her. "No more divorces. No more destruction."

Annie nodded. "Ric, I've done your books. Without the divorce cases . . . You earned approximately three hundred dollars last year finding lost dogs."

"No more lost dogs, either," he told her. "Unless it's Pierre."

"Then . . . ?" She had no idea where he was going with this.

He smiled. "This is the crazy part."

Annie waited.

"I really like the idea of helping to keep someone safe," Ric told her. "It wasn't until Robin said that he was looking for a head of security that I realized . . . I mean, I know he's just a movie star. It wouldn't be like protecting a head of state or . . . But I like him. I like his work and I like him as a person. He's in a vulnerable position because of his sexual orientation and it shouldn't be that way. He's going to need to find someone that he trusts to handle his security—someone who already knows his secrets. Someone who'll help keep him safe as well as protect his right to privacy."

Annie didn't know what to say. Ric wanted to work for Robin? It had been so obvious that Robin wanted *Jules* to work for him. But she didn't want to start listing the reasons why Ric's idea wouldn't and couldn't work.

She didn't have to. Ric was right there, with her. "I know when he brought it up, he was talking to Cassidy, but that's not going to happen. Jules isn't leaving the Bureau." He leaned toward her. "But I'm perfect for the job. I appreciate creative people. Most people think they're nuts, but I understand them. And I'm good at what I do. So if it's okay with you, I'm going to approach Robin. See if he'll settle for me. Us. If . . . you want there to be an us."

"Ric," she said, her heart in her throat, uncertain how she was going to say this.

But he stopped her. "You should think about it," he said. "Along with everything else. I mean, you never gave me an answer to, um, my proposal. Which is okay," he quickly added. "I guess I hoped you wouldn't have to think about it, but . . ." He laughed—a rueful burst. "Of course maybe the answer's already a given. If you're pregnant . . ."

Annie had to look away, because now he was looking at her as if he wanted to give getting her pregnant another go.

"Most guys don't find that a turn-on," she pointed out.

"I never did before," he admitted. "But now . . ." His hand was warm as he slipped it beneath her towel, his palm pressed against her belly. "The thought of you walking around with something of mine, growing inside of you . . ." He kissed her, and his hand slipped lower.

Oh, God. "Ric." Annie caught his wrist. "Remember how you said when you're with me you always end up doing something crazy? Well, this really *is* one of those times."

He shook his head. "No, it's not."

"I'm not talking about the job with Robin thing," she told him. "Although you should probably think about that a little more, too. It's . . . your other idea that's, well, insane."

"All right," Ric said. "I get where you're coming from, and okay, after some of the things I've said and done, particularly lately, sending out all these mixed signals . . . I understand how you could think that I'm, you know, less than sincere—"

"I don't doubt your sincerity," Annie interrupted him. "I think *you* think that you meant what you said, especially when you said it. And maybe you'll be able to convince yourself that it's true for a while. Maybe even for a few months, because, yes, the sex is incredible. But come *on* . . ."

Her blunt honesty hurt him. She could see it on his face, in his eyes. But he was trying hard not to get angry. "I'm sorry you feel that way," he said. "Because you're wrong."

"You don't have to marry me for us to have sex like that," she tried to reassure him. "I'll come back after this is over—I'm going to come back."

"Good," he said. "Because if you don't, I'm going to come find you and, wow, *that* sounded creepy. I didn't mean it to sound like a threat."

"I know," Annie told him. "Look, after I come back, we can both get tested, and as long as we're both healthy, I can start taking the pill. Although, if you cheat on me, and put me at risk, I'll never forgive you. And I do mean *that* as a very real threat."

"I would never put you at risk," Ric said. But then he looked away. "Except I did, just this morning, didn't I?"

"I was there, too," she pointed out.

"Yeah, but I'm the man." He smiled. "I said that just to piss you off. How'm I doing?"

Annie rolled her eyes. "Extremely well."

"Annie, do you love me?"

It was a question she'd never in a million years expected him to ask her, not point-blank like that. And now he was watching her, like a police detective scrutinizing a suspect during questioning.

"I don't know." It was stupid to lie, but she was flustered. She looked away. "I really don't."

Ric nodded, taking it as truth—or at least choosing not to challenge her. He was silent for a long time. When he finally spoke, it was just one word. "No."

Annie didn't understand. "No?"

He shook his head. "Nope."

She still didn't get it.

"I was going to say okay to the whole *let's get tested and have lots of sex* plan," he explained. "I was going to ask you how long, you know, it would take before you believed me. Six months? A year, maybe two?" He was watching her closely. "Two would do it, huh?"

Annie laughed her disbelief, because, yes, two years with Ric probably would convince her of his sincerity. God, the idea that he might have actually meant what he said, that he actually loved her . . . It was almost too much to bear. "What did I do, twitch?"

"No," Ric said. "I just know you."

"Oh, you know me, but I don't know you?"

"I think if you stopped and really thought about it," Ric said, "you would trust me. I've never lied to you. I've never tried to bullshit you— well, not for the things that mattered. This isn't about me at all—this is about you being scared. You don't want to love me. I know you've convinced yourself that I'm not capable of a real relationship, and I know the thing with Lillian kind of sealed it for you, but damn it, Annie, look at me, and trust me when I tell you that I'm not that man."

"Oh," Annie said, grabbing onto the obvious, because getting mad was something she could handle. "Oh, good. Bring up Lillian. Unbelievable."

"I kissed her," Ric said, "because I was scared, too. I was scared of everything I was feeling for you—"

"That is such a load of crap—"

He was getting pissed now, too. "Did you hear anything I just said?"

"No," she said. "Because I'm too *scared.*"

"Great," Ric said. "Very mature." He stood up. "My answer's no. If you don't want all of me, you're not getting any."

Annie laughed. "So . . . what does that mean? You're going to withhold sex . . . ?"

"Yup. I'm not going to be your toy. You either love me or you don't, and if you love me, you're going to have to trust me. It's that simple."

"Does the phrase *cutting off your nose to spite your face* mean anything to you?" she asked.

But Ric didn't answer her. He just gently closed her door behind him.

CHAPTER
TWENTY

"We found a body to play the part of your dead ex-girlfriend," Jules reported to Ric via cell phone. Jules shut his hotel-room door behind him, taking off his jacket and tie. Lordy, he was tired. The maid hadn't been in yet to do up his room, but that was fine—he was going back to bed. "It's in transit. ETA two o'clock. I don't want to call Gordie Junior until we actually deliver it to you." God forbid Junior offer to come by and clean things up right away. "We're going to need a couple hours to implant the tracking devices—we're using a high-tech system that won't be discernible to any bug sweepers that are currently on the market. We've also got to get her dressed in the same clothes Lillian was wearing."

"It's going to take that long, huh?" On the other end of the phone, Ric didn't sound very happy.

"Yeah, you know, getting this done involved just a *little* more work than a phone call to Bodies 'R' Us." Jules couldn't keep the testiness out of his own voice as he kicked off his shoes and stepped out of his pants.

"Sorry," they both said at the same time.

"No," Jules said, flopping back on his bed. "I apologize. I'm just . . . really tired. I'm going to use this time to get some sleep."

"Before you go," Ric said. "Have you been in touch with Robin? Because Annie's going to go over to his hotel, do the black-eye thing. I thought we could tie it into last night's brawl. You know, have Annie leave because she's mad about my ex showing up?"

"I haven't spoken to him this morning," Jules said, closing his eyes. "No."

"Um," Ric said after a few moments of silence. "Will you call him? Or . . . I wasn't sure if you wanted to give out his phone number . . ."

Crap. Jules really needed to give Ric a heads-up about the whole Robin situation.

"I'll give it to you," he said, staring now at the ceiling, "but before you talk to him, and definitely before you send Annie over there, you need to go online. YouTube dot-com. Do a search for Robin Chadwick. Our friend was pretty busy last night. You may not want Annie anywhere near the media circus that's going to be following him around over the next few days." He laughed. "On the other hand, maybe that's the safest place in the world she could be, with an army of paparazzi protecting her. It's your call, of course."

He gave Robin's cell phone number to Ric and shut his phone and his eyes.

Please God, don't let his phone ring again. Please God, don't let him think about Robin or Ben. Please God, just let him fall into a state of total unconsciousness. Please God, help him get this stupid song out of his head . . .

I can't stop this feeling deep inside of me . . .

Jules turned over, pulling the covers up practically over his head. Think about the time he went to that spa in Provincetown and had a hot-stone massage. Think about the beautiful hills and scenery of Italy, where he'd actually taken a vacation last year. Think about how, back when he was a kid, his mother would sit beside him at bedtime to talk about his day. She'd pretend that his stuffed hippo was trying to sneak up on him, to jump on his head. The attack hippo, they'd called it. The hippo would always get him when he least expected it, and they'd laugh and laugh . . .

I . . . I'm hooked on a feeling, I'm high on believing that you're in love with me . . .

Yeah, right.

He finally got up and took a shower, hoping the warm water would relax him — or at least wash away the scent of Robin that still clung to his skin. It was only then, with the water pounding down on him, that he finally let himself cry. For Ben, for Robin, for himself.

Even for Peggy Ryan.

Finally, both emotionally and physically exhausted, with his hair still damp, he crawled back into bed, and sleep finally approached, washing over him in waves of . . .

Tap, tap, tap.

Jules opened his eyes.

Tap, tap, tap, tap.

Had he put the "Do Not Disturb" sign on his door? He couldn't re-member.

Knock, knock, knock.

Crap. He rolled out of bed and staggered over to the door, not even bothering to pull on more than his boxer shorts. "Just give me some fresh towels and—"

"Hey," Robin said. He was wearing sunglasses, no doubt to hide his bloodshot eyes, but he took them off now. "Mind if I come in?"

"Yes," Jules said, and shut the door in his face. He crawled back into bed.

Knock, knock, knock.

Please God, please make him just go away.

Knock, knock, knock, knock, knock, knock, knock, knock, knock, knock, knock, knock, knock, knock, knock, knock, knock . . .

"Jesus!" Jules flung open the door. "If you really want to get your ass kicked, then by all means, come on in."

He searched for his pants and savagely yanked them on, then crossed to the windows and opened the drapes. The room was flooded with bril-liant sunlight, and Jules got a perverse sense of satisfaction as Robin winced and put his sunglasses back on.

Of course, the bright light meant that his own red eyes were right there for Robin to see, too. He also obviously noticed Jules's unmade bed, as well as the fact that he was only half dressed.

"You were sleeping," Robin deduced.

"Not yet," Jules snapped. "Not since—" He cut himself off. Not since he'd fallen asleep in Robin's limousine, in Robin's arms—not exactly something he wanted to discuss. "I had a busy night—I spent most of it cleaning your bathroom."

"That was you?" Robin asked.

"Who'd you think it was?" Jules retorted. "Elves?"

Robin shook his head. "I wasn't sure if it was you or, um . . ."

"Ashley," Jules said. "At least that was the way she signed her note to you. And yeah, I guess if you're drunk enough, you can't tell us apart. Al-though here's a hint. I'm the one you claim to love."

Okay, it was time to shut up and just let Robin say what he'd come here to say, so that he could leave as quickly as possible and Jules could get to sleep.

"I'm so sorry." Robin looked and sounded as if he meant it.

It was actually pretty impressive that he was up and about. And the fact that he'd dared to come here at all was at least noteworthy.

And yes. That was definitely his dick talking, not his brain. Jules was so freaking attracted to this son of a bitch, he could watch that YouTube footage three times—not the PG-rated but still astonishingly sexy stripping-in-the-kitchen video, although he'd watched that more than once, too—and *still* try to find excuses for why Robin should be forgiven.

"There's a lot I need to say," Robin continued. "To apologize for. Including interrupting your nap. But I'm going to take Annie back to California—as soon as I can get us a flight—and I really wanted to see you before I left. May I sit down?"

Jules gestured to the pair of chairs over by the window.

Robin lowered himself gingerly into one of them.

"Were you hurt when you fell?" Jules asked, despite his resolve to keep his mouth shut.

Robin looked at him over the top of his sunglasses. "Did I fall?" he asked. "I don't . . . remember very much of it. I remember coming back to my hotel after you got the news about Ben—that was when I really started drinking."

"That was when you *started* drinking?" Jules repeated. As if the copious amounts of alcohol that Robin had consumed in the limo and at Burns's party were insignificant.

"I guess I went a little overboard," Robin said.

He *guessed.* "Haven't you watched the clip on YouTube?" Jules asked.

Robin carefully shook his head. "No."

"You should," Jules said. "And yeah, you fell. Fortunately not off the twelfth-story balcony." He was going to turn away, even close his eyes so that Robin wouldn't see the hurt, the fear, the agony he'd felt while watching that nightmare unfold on digital video. Instead he looked straight at him. "You motherfucker."

"I'm so sorry," Robin said.

"You already said that," Jules pointed out. "It wasn't good enough the first time, either."

"I know." Robin looked down at the floor, contrite, ashamed. Or at least that was how he was playing it. The man was, after all, on the verge of receiving an Academy Award nomination.

His silence stretched on a little too long. "Tick tock," Jules said, and Robin looked up, tears in his eyes.

Which was not a big surprise—not as big as what he said when he finally spoke. "I'm really sorry about Ben. I can't imagine what you're going through. I wanted to, um, see if you wanted to go up there," Robin said. "To Arlington—the National Cemetery. That's where he was buried, right? I mean, maybe you don't want *me* with you, but . . . I just didn't want you to . . . You shouldn't have to go alone and . . . I'll go with you, if you want."

It was a generous offer—one that Jules was not sure he himself would have been able to make had their roles been reversed.

"That's what I should have said to you last night," Robin told him. "I should've grabbed you, and held you and . . . helped you. Instead . . ." He shook his head, roughly wiping his eyes with the heel of his hand so that Jules wouldn't see him cry. "Who am I to judge you? Who am I to judge anyone?"

"It would have been nice," Jules said carefully, in danger now of tearing up himself, "if you'd given me a chance to explain."

But Robin shook his head. "You shouldn't've had to explain anything. I let you walk out of my life years ago. I did everything but put a fucking bow on you and hand you to Ben—God, I wish I'd met him, Jules. He must've been . . . really special."

"He was," Jules said. "But Sam and Max got it wrong. Ben and I were just friends. I tried to love him, but . . . I didn't. I couldn't."

Robin froze, silent. It was possible he'd even stopped breathing.

"I hoped it would happen," Jules continued, "that one day I'd wake up and, I don't know, maybe just . . . magically be in love with him. He was . . . He wasn't perfect—he was in the closet, even to his parents, and that sucked. But he was funny and smart and sweet and faithful. He deserved better than me, because if I'd been man enough to let myself admit it, I would have realized that I was just using him—as a friend who I knew thought of *me* as more than a friend. Maybe someday I'd love him—I dangled that possibility out there in front of us both, but in truth I was just using him to mark time while I waited for the impossible."

He looked at Robin, who was sitting in that chair on the other side of his hotel room as if every cell in his body hurt. His skin was pale, his hands were shaking, his chin was unshaved, his eyes were rimmed in red. It was crazy, but Jules still found him almost unbearably attractive.

"I was waiting for you," Jules told him softly. "I'm still waiting. For something that's . . . now even more impossible than it ever was."

Robin sat forward. "No," he said, coming even closer then, actually on his knees on the floor in front of Jules. "It's not. Babe, listen, okay? Just please listen, because I've figured it out. I know you hate that I hide who I am, and I know how hard it'll be for you to be in a relationship with me while I'm still not out, but if you give me three pictures—just three, that's the deal my agent's putting together right now—then I promise I will give you the entire rest of my life."

"Except for the parts that you can't remember." That kind of grand, sweeping promise would've gone over a little better if Jules hadn't been able to smell the whiskey on Robin's breath. And it wasn't last night's whiskey, either.

"I've stopped drinking," Robin told him, his blue eyes filled with steadfast resolve. Kneeling there like that, he was a picture of sincerity.

Jules laughed in his face. "As of when?" he asked. "Ten minutes ago? What'd you do, stop in the bar downstairs before you came up here?"

"Hair of the dog?" Robin tried to make it a joke—both the fact that he'd had a drink and lied to Jules about it.

Jules stood up. "Get out of my room."

But Robin didn't move. "I'm sorry," he said. "And you're right—it *was* only a few minutes ago that I made that decision. But I swear that I mean it. If I have to quit drinking to keep you, then—"

"Jesus Christ, Robin," Jules practically shouted. "You have to quit drinking to keep from *dying.*"

But Robin didn't believe him. Jules could see it in his eyes.

"What do you want?" Jules asked him. "You want to sleep with me again? Is that what this is? You want it so bad you'll say and do anything? Yeah, *babe*, I'll quit drinking . . . Just a three-picture deal . . . I'm yours . . ." His voice broke. Yeah, Robin was his—as long as Jules didn't mind that he sometimes got blind drunk and had sex with total strangers.

"I am," Robin whispered, reaching for him, and Jules knew that he was doomed.

"Yeah, well, I'm not yours," he said, but he closed his eyes when Robin kissed him. And he knew he was as much of a liar as Robin, as he gave in to the soft pleasure that was Robin's mouth, as he sank back with him into the warm sunlight that played across his bed.

Annie came downstairs with a suitcase packed and a hooded sweatshirt on.

"How does this look?" she asked Ric, pulling the hood over her hair and putting on sunglasses.

The hood, with its slight point at the top, made her look like a little kid, bundled up for a cold day. And the sunglasses . . . They were slightly cat-eye-shaped and reminiscent of a 1950s-era schoolmarm, which, combined with Annie's sun-kissed cheeks and full, soft mouth, he found . . .

Hot. He turned away. "Ridiculous."

She took off both the hood and the sunglasses. "Excuse me. You're not allowed to be mad at *me* because *you* decide never to have sex with me ever again."

"I never said never," Ric corrected her.

"Yeah," she shot back. "You did. You implied it."

Before he could argue, the doorbell rang.

Annie went to the window. "There's a truck out front. Is this . . . ?"

"Yeah." Ric opened the door. It was the FBI. The agent nicknamed Yashi was standing there in a pair of coveralls, holding a computerized clipboard.

"Good morning, sir," he said in his trademark deadpan. "We're here to install your new weatherproof flooring."

And sure enough, over Yashi's shoulder, two other overall-clad agents were carrying a roll of cheap carpeting up the driveway. The body of his allegedly murderous ex-girlfriend had to be inside, in a body bag. Ric stepped back to let them in.

"Don't worry." Yashi patted his arm, no doubt because the look on his face warranted it. "Jason and Apolonia are forensics experts. They'll set up the crime scene. Just tell us where you want the victim, and they'll make it look real."

"In my office." Ric pointed the way as he closed the door behind the agents with the carpeting.

"Hey, Annie," Yashi greeted her. She'd sat down at her desk, and was looking a little pale. "You squeamish, too?"

"Maybe a little," she said. "I'm kind of freaked about . . . I mean, who was she?"

"We weren't given her name," Yashi said. "She's former CIA counterterrorism, though, we do know that. She had an inoperable brain tumor that metastasized—making her useless as an organ donor. She died of a self-inflicted gunshot wound, day after her doctor gave her four months to live."

"Oh, God." Annie went another shade more pale.

"Her family was adamant that she would've wanted to continue to help fight terror," Yashi continued. "They signed off on all releases—they don't expect to get her body back."

Annie looked up as Ric touched her shoulder. "Let's get out of their way," he suggested, "and let them work."

Amazingly, she didn't argue. She let him take her hand and pull her out of her seat—and all the way up the stairs, back into his apartment.

She still looked as if she needed air, so he led her through the living room and out the doors to the screened-in porch.

"Maybe I should just go," she said as she leaned on the railing overlooking his garden. "I can drive myself to Robin's hotel."

Ric looked at his watch. "Martell will be here soon."

She nodded. "Once I'm in California, you're not going to be able to micromanage my every move."

"Are you sure you want to go to California?" Ric asked, and she looked up at him. "I mean, instead of Boston, or I don't know. Savannah. You could visit your mother. Or Bruce."

He'd watched that digital video of Robin on his computer, with Annie looking over his shoulder. Neither of them had said much at the time, but Annie had touched him, her hand warm on his back. "This kind of blows, huh?" was her sole comment.

It did—not just for Jules, who clearly had feelings for the movie star, but also for Ric. So much for his stupid plan. He wanted to provide security, not be a babysitter. It was obvious that Chadwick needed both—and that one would be the other.

"I thought I'd take advantage of the flight to California," Annie said now, "and check out that company that Jules's friend Sam works for— Troubleshooters Incorporated. I went to their website and found out that they're not private investigators, although they do provide that service. Their big thing is personal security—which is exactly what you want to do. It seems like a really good organization, Ric. And if they'll provide training . . ."

She loved him. She was standing there, planning for their future. But instead of calling her on it, Ric nodded. "Just . . . keep me in the loop, okay?"

"Okay." She forced a smile. She looked tired and was still pale, her usual sparkle subdued.

He tucked a stray piece of her hair behind her ear. "I'm sorry Yashi was so insensitive."

"He didn't know. How could he?"

"Yeah, but . . ." Ric sighed. "This was the last thing you needed, huh?"

"I'm okay. I'm pretty tough, you know."

Now she was gazing up at him, her gray eyes wide, looking anything but tough. Her mouth was tight with determination, but Ric knew how soft she really was.

Which was probably why he leaned over and kissed her.

He didn't mean to. He'd tried not to, but damn. He could taste her surprise, and he made himself pull back. "Sorry," he said.

She was as rattled as he was—but she managed a shrug. "It's your stupid rule," she told him. "If it were up to me, I'd be squeezing in one last quickie, right there on that lounge chair."

Ric turned to look at the lounge chair in question. He couldn't help himself, and she laughed.

"You want to." It wasn't quite a question, but it also wasn't not. Annie moved closer, her hands on his belt. "It might be a long time before we see each other again . . ."

He caught her wrists. "You just don't want to talk about Pam."

"What's to say?" But she couldn't hold his gaze.

"I called Bruce, and he told me that she asked you to help her die." Ric pulled Annie close, and she seemed to surrender, her head against his shoulder. "What did she ask you to do?" he asked her quietly. "Leave her painkillers where she could reach them?"

Annie sighed. "If you already know, why ask me?"

"Because you need to talk about it. If the mere mention of someone else with terminal cancer—"

"Whoever that is downstairs," Annie said hotly, "she was a fool. She had four *months* to spend with her family—probably even more—and she threw it away. Pam was only given three, and she lived more than twice that."

"And yet, in the end, she chose to stop fighting," Ric said quietly. "That must've been so hard for you. To know she'd given up all hope . . . ?"

Annie was silent, and he knew he'd gotten it right. He'd struck a chord.

"I couldn't do it," Annie finally admitted. "Ric, she was in so much pain, and she begged me, but I couldn't do it. God—and I'm still so angry with her."

Ric nodded. "Anger *and* guilt. That's got to suck."

"Yeah," she agreed.

"Give yourself a break," Ric told her. "You did the best you could."

"Did I?" She looked up at him with such sadness. "I don't know. Because I wouldn't help her, she somehow got out of bed. She must've just rolled herself out. She crawled into the kitchen, where we kept her prescriptions." Her eyes filled with tears. "She was just having a bad day. We had this mantra—tomorrow'll be better. And sometimes it was."

"But sometimes it probably wasn't," Ric said.

"She told me she hated seeing us—her parents and me—in so much pain. She did it for us—and all we wanted was to have her around for another day."

"Annie, she was ready to go," Ric said quietly. "And think of it this way. You'll never have any doubt that she loved you."

"Yeah," Annie said. "And I loved her so much that she died, all alone, on her kitchen floor. I was the one who found her later that night, curled up around Pierre."

Ric smoothed her hair back from her face. "If she was with Pierre," he told her, "then she didn't die alone."

She was going to kiss him. Ric saw it in her eyes, saw it coming, and he didn't stop her. It was, after all, just a kiss.

And he was a freaking idiot, because there was no such thing as just a kiss when it came to him kissing Annie, and Annie kissing him.

She was going for that lounge chair, and damn it, he was, too, because, man, she was right—neither of them knew how long it was going to be before they could do this again.

Except this wasn't what he wanted.

"Stop," he said. "Stop!" as he finally disconnected his mouth from hers, which was flat-out ludicrous, since he was the one who had her up against the side of the house. He was the one pressed hard between her legs.

She laughed at the absurdity of the situation, which was his downfall, because he could never force himself to back away from her when she was laughing, even when her eyes were filled with tears. Which meant he was standing there, stupidly staring at her—an easy target—when she kissed him again.

Jesus God. "I'm not doing this," Ric insisted.

"Okay," Annie said, reaching down into his pants and—Gahd— wrapping her fingers around him.

"I'm serious," he told her, closing his eyes as she touched him.

"I can see that." She kissed him again. "Let's go inside."

"No," he said, but he followed her. It was definitely the moment of truth. Once they got into his bedroom, she'd take off her clothes, and that would be that.

But Martell saved him. "Yo, Annie, you ready to go?" From the sound of it, he was taking the stairs up from the office, two at a time.

Annie managed to get her hand back before Martell came in, but just barely. Ric sat down fast. Of course, now that he'd been saved, he wished desperately that he hadn't been.

"Everything okay?" Martell said, looking from Annie to Ric.

Annie had turned toward the window, pretending she wasn't wiping tears from her eyes.

"You, uh, need a few more minutes?" Martell asked. "It's pretty hot out, I should go get Pierre out of the car, if you're gonna—"

"No," Annie said, taking a deep breath and turning back around. "I'm ready to go, and Ric should get back downstairs. Did you see what's going on in his office?"

"No," Martell said. "What's his name, Yashi, told me you were up here."

"Don't look," Annie said. "It's going to be awful."

"Okay, now you made me curious." Martell started down the stairs.

"I'm not kidding," Annie called after him. She turned to Ric. "Be careful."

He nodded. "You, too." *I love you.* He didn't say it, because it would have made her more upset, which was crazy.

"Thanks for . . . trying to make me feel better about Pam," she said, and followed Martell down the stairs.

"Damn!" Ric heard Martell shout. "Why did you let me look?"

"*Let* you look? I warned you," Annie's voice drifted up the stairs, and then was gone, as she and Martell left the building.

Ric sat there, with the silence bearing down on him. It was heavy on his chest, making it hard to breathe.

He launched himself off the sofa and thundered down the stairs. "Annie!"

The craziness was hers. She was just going to have to get used to hearing him say it.

He threw open the door, but she was already in Martell's car as he backed down the drive, transmission whining. She didn't even see Ric—she didn't look back—she was preoccupied with greeting Pierre, laughing as the little dog licked her face.

Ric watched as Martell's car disappeared down the street.

"Jules just called," Yashi reported as he went back inside. "He's running a little late, but he should be here any minute."

Robin sat at the desk in Jules's hotel room, in front of Jules's computer, sick to his stomach.

Jules was in the bathroom, getting ready for his meeting with Ric Alvarado and Gordie Burns Junior. It was a jeans–and–T-shirt meeting, but Jules had also pulled a loose-fitting, lightweight jacket out of his closet and tossed it onto the bed. The jacket was to cover the gun he'd taken from a locked case—the gun that he'd tucked into the shoulder holster he'd matter-of-factly strapped on. His donning of that holster and his quick, professional check of that gun screamed of routine and everyday, ordinary habit in a way that was both sexy as hell and terrifying.

Robin could hear him now, brushing his teeth, the bathroom door ajar.

On the computer screen, the digital video footage that had been up-loaded to YouTube ended with Robin's evil twin chugging a bottle of whiskey and tripping over the ottoman in his hotel suite—landing hard on his back, all while laughing hysterically.

He hadn't dropped the bottle, though. As he brought it to his mouth, the footage froze into a still shot—a close-up that was undeniably of Robin's own face. His eyes were open, and he was laughing.

It could have been worse. The amateur filmmaker—a budding direc-torial genius with the YouTube handle of CelebrityHunter—could have chosen to end with a still of that extremely nonflattering but thankfully al-most completely nonrecognizable, two-second-long close-up of Robin's nonresponsive private area. Of course, that didn't mean that any of the two and a quarter million viewers hadn't thought to hit pause at that particular moment in the download.

A little work with Photoshop to sharpen the image and, voilà. There he'd be, the perfect desktop background for millions of personal comput-ers. Robin put his head in his hands.

"Watch it again."

He looked up to see that Jules had come out of the bathroom.

"No," Robin said. "I've . . . seen enough. It's . . . like the ultimate out-of-body experience. He looks like me and he sounds like me—"

"He? It's *you*, Robin." Jules put on his jacket, zipping it closed at the very bottom. "You did all those things last night."

"Yeah," Robin said quietly. "I know." Which was why he didn't want to watch it again. When he watched it, he couldn't imagine Jules ever forgiv-ing him.

"I've got to go," Jules told him just as quietly. "You do, too. You're sup-posed to be meeting Annie."

"I left her a key card at the front desk of my hotel," Robin said. "I called and told her I was going to do that, so . . . If it's okay with you, I thought I'd shower here before I, uh, go meet her."

Jules nodded. "Just don't be here when I get back."

Ouch. Robin forced a laugh. "I guess you know me pretty well. I thought if I just never left, you'd come back and, well . . . You seem to like me better when we're in bed, so I thought . . . Maybe you'd either forgive me or forget why you were angry, if we just made love for, like, two weeks, nonstop—"

"Sex," Jules corrected him sharply. "This was sex, what we just did. Don't get it confused with something that it's not."

Wow. That one really stung.

"Shut down my computer when you're done watching that again, and make sure the door locks behind you." Jules turned to leave.

Robin stood up. "So this is what, then? Goodbye? Thanks for the sex—see you around in a year or two?"

Jules stopped but he didn't turn back. "I don't know what this is," he said, his voice low. "I don't know anything anymore."

"I do." Robin's voice shook with conviction. "I know that if you want me to watch this fucking awful video again, I'll watch it again. I know I'll do whatever I can to make this up to you. I'll stop drinking. I've already stopped—"

Jules laughed as he turned to face him. "Are you kidding? You better watch that video another fifty times if you think you're just going to be able to announce that you quit and—"

"I am. I did."

"Forty-eight hours." Jules's anger was palpable. "I give you forty-eight hours, tops, before you take another drink—although it's probably going to be more like four."

Jesus. "Your unmitigated support overwhelms me."

"You want me to take this seriously." Jules got in his face. "You check yourself in somewhere. You do a lockdown rehab—twenty-eight days, minimum—"

"I can't do that, and you know it." Robin stood his ground. "I got a movie about to premiere. I don't need that anyway. That's bullshit. I'm not an alcoholic—"

Jules headed for the door.

"I'm *not*." Robin followed him. His own mother had been an alcoholic who'd lived and died—literally—for her next drink. If she didn't have her gin and tonic, her hands would shake and she would become physically ill, like a drug addict needing a fix. She'd died when Robin was eleven, when she drove her car into a tree during a late-night booze run—Jules knew that. "I should know the difference between an alcoholic and someone who sometimes parties a little too hard—"

"Yeah," Jules agreed. "You should." He closed the door firmly behind him.

"I *do* know!" Robin shouted, because the alternative was to chase him down the hotel corridor dressed only in his boxers.

Instead, there he stood. Alone in Jules's hotel room, with the silence bearing down on him. *Just don't be here when I get back.*

At least Jules hadn't said goodbye.

When Robin finally sat down at Jules's computer, there was an e-mail alert flashing in the lower-right-hand corner of the screen.

He clicked on it. He knew he shouldn't have. This was Jules's personal e-mail account.

But Jules knew he was using it. He knew Robin was sitting in front of his laptop computer right now, and maybe he'd sent an e-mail from his phone, saying that he'd reconsidered, and maybe it *would* be a good idea for Robin to wait there for him to get back from this meeting, which he'd just found out was going to take only a few minutes anyway . . .

But the e-mail wasn't from Jules. It was *to* Jules. It was from someone with an e-mail address of SpongeBob at some freemail account. And the subject line read *RE: RC WTFO?????*

He was RC—Robin Chadwick. And WTFO was Navy radio-speak for "What the fuck, over?" After playing a SEAL in *Riptide*, he spoke their language well enough to know that.

Robin clicked to open the e-mail, and a picture—a photo—appeared in the upper left corner of the screen. It was the same tall, drop-dead gorgeous man—Sam—who'd come into town to give Jules the bad news about Ben's untimely death. In the picture, he was standing next to a strikingly beautiful black woman in a wedding dress. Jules, also tuxedo clad, was on the woman's other side, and all three of them were laughing.

These were Jules's best friends—Sam and Alyssa. A few years ago, Robin had spent a very pleasant evening with Jules and several pitchers of sangria, in a Mexican restaurant in West Hollywood, listening to stories about Jules's former FBI partner Alyssa Locke. At the time, he'd wondered if—despite Jules's claim of being gay—there wasn't a little unrequited sexual attraction in Jules's longtime relationship with Alyssa-the-Amazing. But now, looking at that photo, he could see only happiness on Jules's face.

Happiness, and unconditional love.

And that was when he should have clicked to close that e-mail, and gone back to YouTube to do as Jules had demanded, and watch him nearly kill himself all over again.

Instead, Robin read the words on the computer screen.

Hey, it's Alyssa, borrowing Sam's email addy. I just thought I'd give you my 2 cents, sweetiepie.

1) I'm so sorry about Ben.
2) the tadpole is definitely gay, single, and interested in meeting you—and, yes, really cute. Really.
3) you spent years trying to talk me into dating people you thought were really cute, but I was in love with Sam, so . . .
4) the perfect career isn't perfect if you're not happy
5) I love you—you'll always have a private sector job waiting for you, working with me
6) if you really love the fuck-up (Sam's word, but it does seem to fit) that much, GO FOR IT!!!!

Directly beneath that was a copy of an e-mail that Jules had apparently sent this afternoon, probably while he was setting up his computer for Robin to watch the YouTube disaster. Robin had still been in Jules's bed, hoping that Jules would climb back in.

He hadn't, much to Robin's disappointment. *SpongeBob,* Jules had written.

I'm not offended. I hear you. Thank you for being such a good friend. I'm probably going to do something really stupid, but God help me, I love him.

Robin's heart was pounding. Jules loved him. Jules *loved* him.

Even today, when I'm so angry with him—when I'm so hurt by what he's done that I'm practically bleeding from the ears, I still love him with every breath I take. I know exactly who he is and what he is, and God damn him, I love him anyway. He's an alcoholic and a liar—he lies to himself most of all—and I don't know if he really loves me enough to try to make this work—or if he's just going to bulldoze over me and break my heart. Again.

"I'm not an alcoholic," Robin said, but of course there was no one in the room to argue with him. *I don't know what I'm going to do,* Jules had written, and now Robin's heart was pounding for an entirely different reason—fear.

I suspect I'm better off without him. And yes, I know what I'll be giving up if I don't make myself walk away. I do hear you, and I've obviously got a lot to think about. I love you guys. Stay safe. More later.

Beneath that was, presumably, a copy of the e-mail Sam had first sent to Jules, several hours earlier.

I'm assuming you've seen this, but in case you haven't . . .

There was a live link to the YouTube.com footage, of course.

I heard what you said in the car, but holy fuck, Squidward, you sure know how to pick 'em. I'm probably going to offend you, but I gotta say it—you sure you're not confusing love with lust? Maybe I'm wrong about this, but I'm pretty sure you've gone a long time without getting any on a regular basis, and that can do funny things to the human brain—particularly the male one.

Again, I'm probably gonna offend you big time here, but I think I know what you're looking for (Alyssa with a penis?) (only half kidding), and I do understand that Ben wasn't it. I thank God for that, considering the current circumstances. But I can't believe it's crazy-ass RC, either.

Right now Lys is shouting at me not to do it, but I got to tell you that my old team's in the neighborhood doing drills, and one of the tadpoles has set my highly honed gaydar aflame. I'm not going to give you his name in an email, but after your vacation's over, I highly recommend you drop in at Coronado. I think he might be your type—tall and blue-eyed. (Holy fuck, did I really just type that?) Lys says he's even cuter than RC.

Jules had told Robin that Sam—and it was definitely Sam writing this e-mail—was now in Spain, working with Alyssa to track down a rumored suitcase nuke. No doubt SEAL Team Sixteen—which was Sam's "old team"—wasn't just in the neighborhood to do drills, but rather to provide any backup that might be necessary should the civilian team need assistance.

As for the tadpole that Sam had mentioned . . . A tadpole was a young, new member of a SEAL team. Apparently Sam was trying to set Jules up with a gay SEAL. One who was, according to Alyssa, who'd confirmed it in her message at the very top of the e-mail, cuter than Robin.

"Like hell he is," Robin muttered.

But that wasn't all Sam had to say.

I know you hate the whole "don't ask, don't tell" bullshit that this tadpole brings with him to the table, but think about what you'll get with RC. You've got to know that your career won't survive a relationship with that crazy fuck-up. Even if he goes into rehab and dries himself up, this YouTube shit's not gonna go away. It's going to haunt him forever—any time he so much as farts in public. And that's not even taking into consideration the scandal that'll hit when he's finally outed—and he WILL be outed sooner or later, count on it. Idiot like that's gonna fuck it up royally, too.

You could risk it—keep your relationship with him on the down low, but that's some fucking irony, huh? I know you want to be in an open relationship, but even if RC came out tomorrow, you'd STILL have to keep your affair with him jammed in the closet. You know this—don't fool yourself into thinking there's a way this will work. No way are you going to be picked to replace MB if you're in a public relationship with RC. You WILL be passed over. You know it.

MB — Max Bhagat. Holy shit, was Jules really up for that kind of a promotion? He hadn't mentioned it to Robin at all.

I'm not saying that you can't be in an open gay relationship and win this position—you can. As long as it's with some nice, quiet, anonymous civilian. Or even some military hero who eventually resigns his commission and comes out when he joins the civilian world. (And this kid I'm talking about already has a job waiting for him with me and Lys—that's a guarantee. He's a solid operator.)

I just want to make sure you think about what you'll be giving up. It's a huge deal, Squidward. You're gay and you're out—and you will be in charge of THE most important counterterrorist unit in the U.S.

Or you can be tabloid fodder.

Is the fuck-up really worth it?

Sam signed off with *Stay safe. Love, SpongeBob.*

Robin closed the e-mail and went back to YouTube, where he clicked on the link to replay the footage that CelebrityHunter had posted there just this morning. Since he'd viewed it last, there had been another additional quarter of a million hits to the site.

And as he watched himself knocking over a pile of deck chairs by the hotel pool, as he watched himself teetering on the rail of his balcony, twelve stories above the ground, shouting "I'm the king of the world!" all he could think was *no.*

No, the fuck-up featured in all his drunken glory on this digital video wasn't worth shit.

CHAPTER
TWENTY-ONE

Robin looked like hell—probably at least partly on purpose, to avoid the scores of reporters down in the hotel lobby—as he let himself into his hotel suite. "It's just me," he said, chaining the door behind him.

"Dolphina called," Annie told him from the sofa, quieting Pierre, who'd stood up but thankfully didn't bark. "I wasn't sure whether to answer the phone, but it just kept ringing. She was pretty upset that you weren't here. She wanted you to call her back on her cell as soon as you got in."

When she'd first picked up the phone, Annie had been afraid that the woman's distress was from jealousy and hurt. But it soon became apparent that Dolphina not only knew that Robin was gay, but that she also knew about his relationship with Jules. Or nonrelationship, as Jules had claimed.

Dolphina had been worried both that Robin was embarking on day two of a record drinking binge, and/or that he would find himself mobbed by paparazzi and end up saying something on the record that couldn't be unsaid.

"She said to tell you to stay here," Annie told Robin, who was already heading for the bar. To her relief, he only opened the minifridge and pulled out a Dr Pepper. "She doesn't want you to talk to anyone about the YouTube nightmare until you speak to her. Apparently, she's bringing in some major PR guru who's going to spin this whole thing to your advantage." If that was even possible.

Robin turned to look at her as he popped open his can of soda. "Did you watch it?"

Annie nodded. "Was that really from last night?" she asked.

"Apparently so." He was embarrassed, taking a long slug straight from the can, glancing at the bottles of liquor lined up against the mirrored wall behind the bar.

"You didn't seem that drunk in the limo."

"I wasn't," he said.

There had been so much sexual tension between Jules and Robin last night. Annie had been certain that there was going to be a major change in their relationship status as soon as they found themselves alone. She would have bet a year's salary that mere moments after she and Ric had left the limo, Robin had been unable to bear it a second longer, and had grabbed Jules and kissed him.

Of course, maybe he had. And maybe Jules had pushed him away.

"What happened?" Annie asked softly. "I mean, I'm not trying to pry, I just . . . If you want to talk about it . . ."

"I don't remember very much," he admitted. "At least not after I got back to my hotel."

He'd made room to pour something with a kick—probably rum— directly into his can of Dr Pepper. That was his MO, Annie realized. He could walk around, seemingly drinking an innocuous can of pop, but in truth working to get his swerve on in a major way.

And sure enough, he set his soda down on the bar and grabbed for one of the bottles, opening its twist top.

But then he surprised her by pouring it down the sink. "Help me do this," he said. "I've got to get this shit out of here, like five minutes ago."

Annie stood up, uncertain. There were so many bottles, some of them almost full. "Shouldn't we just call room service and have them—"

"I need it gone," he told her, his voice tight. "Now."

He was serious—and seriously sweating, as if doing this was neither a whim nor an easy task.

There was so much of it. Annie grabbed the nearest bottle and dumped, vodka mixing with the whiskey already gurgling down the drain. They worked in silence, emptying bottle after bottle. Robin finally turned on the water to help disperse the strong smell of alcohol that was wafting up from the sink.

"So," Annie finally said. "This is . . . something of a surprise."

"I promised Jules I'd quit drinking." Robin was gritting his teeth as he watched the last of a twelve-year-old scotch disappear.

"Was that where you went before?" she asked. "To see him?"

Robin nodded.

"So you're just . . . quitting," she said. "Just . . . white knuckle, that's it, no more . . . ?" She couldn't hide her dubiousness. "That's not just stupid—it's dangerous. Alcohol withdrawal needs to be done in a hospital. Alcoholics have serious side effects when they—"

"But I'm not an alcoholic." He was instantly defensive. "What is it with people who don't drink? They think everyone who likes to party has some kind of problem."

"I drink," Annie said. "But not the way you do."

"I'm not an alcoholic," he said again.

Apparently he didn't realize that insisting that he wasn't one was a sure sign that he was.

"My father was," she told him. "You know, he never remembered what he did when he was drunk, either. He was great when he was sober. A lot like you, actually. Funny and handsome and . . . really charismatic, but—"

Robin didn't want to hear this. "I'm sure you think you know—"

She spoke loudly, right over him. "When I was eleven, he hit me and broke my collarbone and my arm. He got a rib, too, and it punctured my lung."

That shut him up.

"I don't think he ever really believed he was the one who put me in the hospital," Annie told him. "He even passed a lie detector test. He was so convincing that the DA didn't think we could win the case, especially since my mother wouldn't let me testify, so . . . We moved to Florida to get away from him. He was too much of a loser to follow us all the way from Boston. But he wrote to me, for years, trying to convince me that it must've been someone else who hit me."

She would never forget, though, the way his face had been twisted with rage. He'd been screaming at her mother, and Annie had tried to make him stop.

Ric had once pointed out, years ago when they'd first tentatively talked about it, that Annie *had* made him stop. Her mother, apparently, had been either able or willing to accept her father's violence and abuse—but only if *she* were the punching bag. As soon as it was Annie, though, it was over. His theory was that somehow Annie, although only a child, had subconsciously realized that would be the case.

"I'm sorry," Robin said. "Jesus, I can't imagine a grown man hitting an eleven-year-old girl."

"He couldn't imagine it, either," she told him. "Too bad we didn't have YouTube back then, huh?"

Robin emptied the last of the bottles. "It's nice to know I have your support."

"You do," she said. "I think it's great, Robin, really."

She didn't have to say the *but*. He said it for her. "Jules doesn't think I can do it, either." He went into the master bedroom—and came back out with four more bottles—two of them empty, the others only a quarter full. "You know, just quit. But I can. I've done it before. It's not that big a deal. I'm nothing like my mother."

If it wasn't that big of a deal, then why was he so intent upon removing every last drop of liquor from his suite? Annie kept that question to herself.

"Your mother . . . drinks?" she asked instead.

"Drank," he put it into past tense. "She died—DUI—when I was just a kid."

"You do know the disease—alcoholism—can be hereditary," Annie said.

"Yeah, well, lucky me—I got my father's genes," he retorted as he finished up his task. And then he changed the subject. "I'm trying to get us a flight to California. Leaving tonight. Best I've found so far is a charter that won't leave until tomorrow noon."

So soon? Annie swallowed past the sudden lump in her throat. "I hate the idea of leaving. I mean, I know Ric and Jules both are good at taking care of themselves, but . . ."

"Yeah," Robin agreed. "But it's what Jules wants, so . . ." He looked at the bottles as if he wished he hadn't emptied all of them. "Did you know he's up for this huge promotion? It's the kind of position where he'd actually have a shot at being the head of the entire FBI someday."

"He didn't mention it to me," Annie said.

"He wouldn't." Robin smiled. He was still looking at those bottles, but his gaze had softened, as if he were no longer seeing them. "I once had . . . well, it wasn't really a date with him, but . . . it really was. I was just too stupid to know." He met her eyes, his own filled with regret. "God, if I could only just go back in time . . ." He shook his head. "Anyway, we talked for hours and . . . I remember he suddenly got embarrassed and he said something like, *Wow, all I've been doing is talking about myself,* except here's the kicker—he wasn't. He was talking about how great his friends were. His friends, his boss, his mother . . . I had to really work to get him to say anything about himself. He doesn't see himself as special and . . . He's the most amazing person I've ever met." He picked up the hotel phone. "This is suite 1270. As soon as possible, I need a maid to come up and pick up some trash. A lot of trash—she'll need a cart. Yeah, thanks."

He hung up the phone, but his cell rang immediately. "Chadwick." He took it over to the sofa and flopped down, his legs outstretched and his head back. Pierre moved away, eyeing him mistrustfully, his butt pressed against the far arm.

"Yeah," Robin said into his phone. "If that's the best you can . . ." He listened again. "Okay. Let me know if it changes. We can get to the airport in twenty minutes and . . . Yeah, okay, I . . . Yeah. Thank you for trying." He snapped his phone shut. "No luck with that earlier flight. We're stuck here until noon tomorrow. But at least we'll be on a charter—you can take Pierre right into the cabin."

Annie brought him his Dr Pepper. "Noon tomorrow's fine with me." Maybe Jules and Ric would get the evidence against Gordie Junior that they needed before then, and she and Robin wouldn't have to go anywhere.

Robin held his arm out, offering Pierre his hand to sniff as he looked up at Annie. "So how'd it go with you and Ric last night? Great sex or really great sex?"

Annie had to laugh at his directness. "Those are my only two choices? How about *no sex*?"

Robin gave her a look. "Annie. I saw the way he kissed you. You're really going to stand there and try to lie to me?"

The scratch that Annie had gotten while climbing up to the deck on the servants' wing of Burns Point was mostly superficial—barely a welt marking the pale inside of her thigh.

The ouch factor came from a splinter that was in a place from which it would have been difficult for her to remove without Ric's assistance.

Last night, during that brief reprieve after Martell left and before Junior and crew came a-calling, after Ric had made love to Annie for the first time down in his office, she'd sat on the closed cover of his toilet seat as he'd knelt on the bathroom floor before her, with a sterilized pair of tweezers and a needle and . . .

"What's so funny?" Jules asked, startling Ric out of his reverie.

He'd been sitting at Annie's desk in his outer office, leaning back in the chair with his feet up, and now he nearly went over backward. "Nothing," he said, catching himself on the desk. "Just . . . thinking about something Annie said to me last night."

Jules poured Ric a mug of coffee and brought it to his desk.

"Thanks," Ric acknowledged. They'd been waiting for Gordie Junior to call them back for hours now. They'd left a message on the man's cell, as well as his office line. It was nearly sunset, and still no word.

The FBI surveillance teams reported that he'd gone into Burns Point last night. He was either still inside his father's house, or he'd gone out via a hidden route. Which was not impossible. After two years of investigation, the FBI had determined that there was an unknown way both into and out of Burns Point. They just hadn't been able to find it.

"I could use a good joke right about now," Jules said, taking a sip from his own mug. "Annie's pretty funny."

Ric shook his head. "This was . . . You wouldn't get it. Private joke." Extremely private.

Ric had finally gotten Annie's splinter out, much to his intense relief. The idea that he was hurting her had made him sweat. She hadn't said a word, not a single *ouch*, but he knew from her tension that it had been no picnic.

Of course, the fact that she'd been sitting there with her legs spread, with her panties still in the pocket of the pants that were down on his office floor—that had made him sweat, too, for an entirely different reason.

Damn, but she smelled so good.

He'd made her leg bleed just a little—the splinter had been in deep—and as he reached up for the cloth to wash her off, pressing its coolness against her, he tried to hide the fact that he'd gotten completely aroused again.

Annie, being Annie, was not deceived. In fact, as he met her gaze, he was nearly knocked over by the heat and desire in her eyes.

"Thanks," she'd whispered. Heat, desire—and amusement—mixed with her own obvious embarassment. But she smiled at him—and it was quite the smile, filled with all kinds of promises.

He'd actually gotten flustered, too, mumbling something hopefully appropriate in response, and sat back to let her up. But she didn't move.

"I promised you we'd never speak of . . . certain sexual acts ever again," she'd said, "so communicating is going to be a little tricky . . ."

He knew exactly that to which she was referring, and he had to laugh. "I take it back," he said.

"Nope," she said. "I promised you. The words will never cross my lips. But maybe if I use telepathy . . ."

She never did say those words—she didn't have to. Her telepathy worked just fine. She wanted exactly what he wanted, and he'd kissed her, right there in the bathroom, until she came. And then she took his hand and led him into his bedroom and returned the favor, her mouth so wet and soft and . . .

"Are you hungry?" Jules asked, startling him again. "Maybe we should send out for something to eat."

Ric looked at him, and then looked at him again. The FBI agent was clearly exhausted, strain showing on his face. The coffee was only making things worse.

"Are *you* hungry?" Ric asked. There was a fairly decent pizza place nearby that would deliver. Or they could get Chinese . . .

But Jules shook his head. "No." He pointed to Ric's office door, which was tightly closed, and he rolled his eyes. "The forensics lesson pretty much killed my appetite for the next two weeks."

Before Yashi and his team had left, they'd brought Jules and Ric into the "crime scene," and told them exactly where Ric would have had to be standing to inflict the fatal gunshot wound to the dead woman who was now lying on Ric's rug.

She'd been shot, point-blank, in the face.

The story they were going to give Gordie Junior—if he ever called back—was that Ric had been threatening his ex-girlfriend, his gun right up against her nose. He wasn't intending to kill her, but the gun had accidentally fired.

Oops. Big, dead oops.

"I was just . . . thinking about things I don't want to be thinking about," Jules continued, sitting on the edge of the sofa across from Annie's desk. "I got news last night that a friend of mine . . . He was a Marine, and, um, he was killed in Iraq."

Ric sat up. "Shit, I'm sorry, man."

"Yeah," Jules said. "Me, too. His name was Ben. He wanted us to be . . . more than friends, but . . ." He met Ric's gaze. "TMI, huh? Did I just freak you out?"

"No," Ric said, and to his surprise, he wasn't lying. "Damn, *that* on top of the Robin Chadwick thing . . ." He shook his head. No wonder Jules looked as if he hadn't slept in days. He probably hadn't.

But now Jules was looking at him oddly. "The Robin Chadwick thing?"

"On YouTube?" Ric specified.

"Oh," Jules said. "Yeah. Right."

What, was there *another* Robin Chadwick thing that Ric didn't know about?

Jules had put down his coffee mug and was now intently focused on retying the laces of his sneakers.

Mother of God.

It was beyond obvious that at some point between the time Jules had announced that he was not and would never become involved with Robin Chadwick and, oh, say, *right now*, he *had* become involved with the movie star. As in, sexual hookup involved.

And *that* wasn't really that big of a surprise, either. Ric hadn't missed the way they'd been looking at each other, particularly during last night's limo ride home.

Holy Christ.

Ric's stomach hurt, but not because he was freaked at the idea of two guys he knew and liked having sex. No, he was freaked because it was beyond obvious that Jules loved Robin—and that Robin loved Jules.

If they *had* hooked up, and then Robin had gone and done his YouTube performance . . .

How could things between them have gone so completely, utterly wrong?

Jules finished with his shoelaces and glanced up at Ric. He sighed, no doubt because Ric was unable to hide his major shell shock.

"I did something really stupid last night," Jules admitted. "You're not just smart, you're a good detective, so I know you've already figured it out. I don't think it's going to get in the way of this investigation, but it might, because, well . . . I went to his room last night. Robin's. I know you probably don't want to hear any of this, but you really . . . need to know. There was a party going on in his suite when I got there, a little after three A.M. The people there must've been the ones who took that footage of him.

"Robin was already unconscious when I arrived. I kicked everyone out, and I stayed with him until he stopped throwing up, which was a long time. Someone—one of Burns's men—might've made note of that. If we were being followed—I don't know that we were, but . . . If we were, someone also may have noticed that, earlier in the evening, Robin and I stayed in his limo for quite a few hours after we dropped you and Annie off."

Jules and Robin, in the limo . . . ? Ric so didn't want to picture that.

But then again, there were quite a few heterosexual people that he absolutely never wanted to picture having sex. His parents. Yeesh. Bruce and his too-skinny trophy wife, Val. Brrrr. The UPS guy. The lady with the neck hair who worked at the post office. Bobby Donofrio and his sainted wife, Arlene. Martell and any one of his numerous one-night stands.

The truth of the matter was, there were very few people on the planet that Ric wanted to picture having sex. Kate Winslet had long been one of them, but right now he could barely remember what she looked like. All he could think about was Annie sighing her pleasure, their fingers interlaced as he held her gaze and rocked her world.

Annie, who'd thought he was bullshitting both her and himself when the truth had shot out of him like some verbal premature ejaculation.

He wanted to spend his life with her.

The idea terrified him, yet at the same time he knew that this was what he wanted. *She* was what he wanted.

That conversation he'd had with his mother, all those years ago? He'd been telling her the truth. For him, it was Annie or no one. It had always been Annie.

Sure, she made him want to take crazy risks. But so what? She made him feel alive.

Ric glanced up at Jules, uncertain of what to say to alleviate both the man's embarrassment and his obvious pain. But Jules wasn't done.

"Robin also came to my hotel this afternoon," he quietly said. It was clear that he wasn't telling Ric this because he wanted to, but rather because he felt it was information he needed to disclose. "Where once again, he stayed for . . ." He cleared his throat. "Quite some time."

"This afternoon," Ric couldn't stop himself from repeating. As in *after* Jules had seen that YouTube video?

"Yeah, I'm an idiot," Jules admitted.

"Love'll do that to a guy," Ric said quietly.

Jules looked up at him, obviously surprised.

"I don't get it," Ric admitted. "The whole gay thing. But I also can't understand why the entire rest of the world isn't crazy in love with Annie. On the other hand, I'm really glad that they're not because if they were, I wouldn't stand a chance with her."

Jules was quiet for a moment, but then he asked, "When did you decide to be in love with Annie?"

Ric laughed. "Decide? Man, I didn't decide. I just *was*."

"Yeah, I know," Jules said. "That's how it was with me and Robin. How about being straight? How old were you when you decided to be straight? You know, attracted to women?"

Ric stared at him. "You're kidding."

"Your answer's the same, right?" Jules told him. "You didn't decide. You just were. It was the exactly the same with me, except I've always been attracted to men. It wasn't a choice. It just was. I am who I am. And I like who I am—I wouldn't choose to be anyone else."

"You really wouldn't choose to be straight?" Ric couldn't keep himself from asking. "I mean, if you could just snap your fingers and . . . ?"

"I really wouldn't," Jules said. "Like I said, I like me. Why would I want to mess with the way God made me?" He smiled, but it was rueful. "Although, if I could, I'd probably choose not to love Robin as much as I do."

That one was a no-brainer. If it were Annie on that YouTube video . . . Ric wasn't sure what he'd do.

Jules correctly guessed what Ric was thinking. "There are circumstances about last night you probably don't understand," he tried to explain. "The news of Ben's death came at a really bad time and . . . Robin got drunk—more drunk—because he thought . . ." But then he shook his head. "It shouldn't matter what he thought. The fact is, he got so drunk he nearly died. This is not the first time he's done this, either. He's an alcoholic—I know that. He says he'll stop drinking, but I know that he won't be able to, and it's going to kill me. Because I'm going to have to walk away from him, and I don't want to. God help me, I don't, but I will. And then I'll go into therapy and try to figure out why the hell I'm always attracted to men who end up hurting me."

They sat there in silence for quite some time, probably both praying that the phone would ring, because yes, *that* had been too much information. They both sat there hoping that Gordie Junior would call so that this nightmare could be on its way toward ending.

"I really am sorry," Jules finally said quietly. "For what it's worth, I've never gotten my personal life mixed up in a case before. Well, that's not completely true, since I met Robin while on an assignment, except *that* time I managed to stay away from him. Mostly."

"It's not as if Robin's the suspect," Ric pointed out. "And so what if you were watched and Junior gets the word that you and Robin are . . . involved? That doesn't change anything in terms of our business deal with him. In fact, it makes it more believable that we'd want to make a sex tape—something that'll keep Robin safely in the closet."

Jules attempted a smile. "Well, I appreciate your positive thinking. I just can't shake the feeling though, that somehow something I've done has messed everything up. I mean, why hasn't Junior called?"

"Because he's got other evil to do," Ric reassured him. "He'll call."

Jules nodded, but it was clear he was still beating himself up.

"You know, if you want to go take a nap," Ric suggested, "I'll man the phones."

"No." Jules shook his head. But he did finally let his head rest against the back of the sofa. "Thanks, but no."

Ric got up to refill his mug with coffee. It was weird. If someone had told him yesterday that he'd be sharing secrets with some gay guy that he'd just met, he would have laughed his ass off. But he trusted Jules, he realized, and it somehow seemed fair to not let him be the only one baring his soul.

So he said, "I did something really stupid last night, too. Well, it was this morning, actually." He put the pot back in the warmer and took his mug back to the desk. "I asked Annie to marry me. That wasn't the stupid thing," he said as Jules opened his mouth to respond. "The stupid thing was, when she wigged, which she did, I gave her this ultimatum. Kind of an all-or-nothing thing, you know—and *that* was stupid. I know that she loves me, but I just . . . I let my pride get in the way, you know? For some reason, I got all wrapped up in what I thought she should do. She should trust me. If she doesn't trust me then . . . what? I'm going to go back to my miserable, boring life without her? I mean, okay, that's one option. Or I could say, yeah, I'd like for her to trust me, right now, today, but who says it has to be that way? I said it. It was my rule—and it's a totally arbitrary one. I mean, come on. I know if I give her enough time, she'll eventually know I'm for real."

Because if he gave her enough time, Annie would learn to trust him.

And Ric also knew, compared to what Jules was going through with Robin, that loving Annie was laughably easy.

Jules toasted him with his mug of what was probably now cold coffee. "Here's to breaking stupid, arbitrary personal rules, which for me is summed up with one word—Robin."

Ric lifted his own mug. "To Robin," he said.

"And Annie," added Jules.

And the phone finally rang.

Ric put the call on his speakerphone. "Alvarado," he said.

"Yo." It was Gordie Junior. Thank you, baby Jesus. "I got a 911 call from your bud Julian Young. What's going down?"

Jules looked at Ric, who nodded, letting him take control.

"I'm here, too." Jules spoke up. "You're on the speaker. Ric's a little upset, so I'm going to do the talking, okay?" He didn't let Junior respond. "There was an . . . accident, and he called me. He told me you were here last night, and that you made him an offer to, um, help with the cleanup if necessary and . . . It's necessary."

"I made the offer"—Junior didn't sound very friendly—"before I saw that bullshit video on YouTube. I thought we had an understanding—"

"I had nothing to do with that video," Jules interrupted him. "That was just Chadwick being Chadwick. He's a fucking idiot." It wasn't hard to put conviction in his voice.

"So, what, it was just a coincidence?" Junior didn't buy it. "The very night we discuss a tape, one appears?"

"Dude," Jules said. "That was not a sex tape. In fact, it was the Antichrist of a sex tape. You really think we purposely put out a video in which Chadwick needed Viagra to get it up? Jesus, now more than ever, we're looking to do business with GBJ Productions. Enough so that we're willing to drop our price a full fifth. Provided you help us out with our little . . . hygiene problem."

On the other end of the phone, Junior sniffed and hacked a loogie, no doubt while he scratched his balls. "Aight," he said. "Hang tight. My boys'll take care of you, but not until tomorrow. Figure sometime around midmorning. Maybe ten."

"Ten?" Ric said, his voice up an octave. "Junior, what the hell?"

"I got other obligations," Junior told them.

"Does this mean you'll have the money to make the tape soon?" Jules asked.

"Are you always so fucking nosy?" Junior retorted.

"Just in a hurry," Jules countered, "after this YouTube thing. Chadwick's movie opens wide next Friday. If we can get it done before then . . ."

Junior was silent for several long moments. "I'll have the money on Tuesday night. Is that soon enough?"

Yes. "Then let's plan to shoot on Wednesday morning," Jules said. "I'll call Chadwick."

"What I want to know," Ric interjected, "is how you're going to clean up my . . . mess in broad daylight."

On the other end of the phone, Junior laughed. "I do it all the time. If you want, you can come along and watch." He hung up before Ric or Jules could respond, the dial tone buzzing through the speaker.

As Ric disconnected the office phone line, Jules was already dialing Yashi. Someone was going to have to call Robin, too. "You mind calling Annie?" he asked Ric. "Filling her and Robin in?"

Ric was more than happy to have an excuse to call.

"Find out if they managed to get an earlier flight out," Jules ordered as Yashi picked up.

"Hey, boss," Yashi greeted him. "We intercepted Junior's call—we got it all on tape. And get this—Junior's been spotted. He's still at Burns Point. Apparently there's some kind of party going on. Birthday for some grandson of Burns Senior's main squeeze. Junior's sitting out by the pool right now."

Good. "Keep me updated," Jules said.

"Now might be the right time to get some sleep," Yashi suggested. "No offense, but you looked pretty wiped when I was over there."

"Keep me updated," Jules said again, and shut his phone with a snap.

Ric had taken his own cell phone into the conference room—no doubt to talk to Annie privately.

And wasn't Jules the idiot? He'd given away an excuse to call Robin. Although, what good would it do him? He didn't have a potential happy ending lurking in his future, the way Ric did with Annie.

He was willing to do it—to do like Ric and explode his arbitrary personal rules—especially the one that made him insist that he would not have a relationship with a man who was not out and open about who he was. He'd already come to the realization that, at least where Robin was concerned, he was willing to sacrifice that which he'd always considered his prime relationship directive—the ability to walk in the sunlight.

But how about this one: *I will not give up my career for you.* Was he willing to toss out that rule, too?

Or: *My partner will be faithful to me at all times, under all circumstances.*

Except when blind drunk and completely out of control?

How many YouTube videos would Jules need to watch, before he couldn't take anymore? That number was somewhat less arbitrary.

But the answer, obviously, was more than one.

Robin put the pay-per-view movie—a real charmer with Rupert Everett and Kathy Bates—on pause when Annie's cell phone rang.

"Hey," she said as she answered it, glancing at Robin, who clearly knew it was Ric on the other end.

"Hey," Ric said back. "I'm just calling to check in. We won't get any action from Junior until morning. Apparently, he's tied up until around ten."

"Junior's busy until ten A.M.," Annie reported to Robin. The frustration on his face surely mirrored her own. But then he checked his own phone, as if hoping he'd somehow missed Jules's call. And she knew that, as far as frustration levels went, if this were a contest, Robin would win.

"Our flight leaves at noon," she told Ric. "We weren't able to get any-thing earlier."

Robin stood up and headed into the hotel suite's master bedroom, to give her privacy, as Ric said, "Make sure Robin knows that we've set a shoot date—this Wednesday morning—for the tape with GBJ Produc-tions."

"You mean, the sex tape?" she said, and Robin turned back to look at her questioningly.

"It's been scheduled for Wednesday morning," she told him, and she could see that he knew, instantly, what she was just realizing. Gordie Ju-nior had given Jules and Ric a date by which GBJ Productions would have a major chunk of money—which they both hoped and feared was his pay-ment for smuggling that nasty-ass terrorist into the country. It also meant that things were probably going to get hairy for the good guys, really fast. She could read Robin's worry for Jules in his eyes.

"Jesus, I need a drink," he said.

"No, you don't," Annie said. She spoke into the phone. "Will you please ask Jules to—"

"No, don't," Robin said. "He needs to focus. I don't want to make it harder for him."

Ric no doubt could hear Robin's voice through her phone, because he said, "Genius should have thought of that last night."

"Just . . . tell Jules we're thinking about him," Annie said with an "Is that all right?" face at Robin.

He sighed and shook his head—it was hard to tell if it was a yes-shake or a no—as he went into his bedroom. She heard him close his bathroom door behind him.

"It wouldn't hurt if Jules could call him," she told Ric, sotto voce.

"Jules asked me to convey this info," Ric responded. "I've got to as-sume it was because he didn't want to talk to Robin."

Okay. And here she'd been thinking that Ric had called because he wanted to talk to her.

"Your mother called me," she reported.

"Ah, great," he said. "I'm sorry."

"Yeah, that was so much fun," Annie said. "She wanted us to have lunch next Friday. It was easier to just say yes." She'd figured she'd just let Ric call his mom. Let him deal with the fallout after Annie was in Califor-nia.

"I'm sorry," he said again. "I'll call her and cancel."

"And explain?" she asked.

"Yeah," he said. "I'll tell her . . . everything."

"Your dad seems to be doing well."

"He is," Ric agreed. "Look, will you tell Robin that we're going to be buying a plane ticket for him to get back to Sarasota on Tuesday night," he informed her. "Under no circumstances should he use it, but . . . We've got to assume Junior has connections to someone in the travel industry. If he's at all suspicious over these next few days . . ."

"Why would he be suspicious?" Annie asked.

"We're just dotting all our *I*'s," Ric said. "Jules is pretty thorough."

"Then maybe you better buy a second ticket for me," she countered. "Aren't I supposed to be Robin's co-star in this video?"

"Yeah, right. Over my dead body," Ric said.

"Since I'm not going to be having sex with you," Annie pointed out, "I might as well have sex with *some*one."

He didn't laugh, as she'd hoped. But he did say, "That was the other thing I wanted to talk to you about. The us-not-having-sex thing."

"Hah," she said, her heart in her throat. "I knew you'd regret not going for that quickie."

This time he did laugh. "Yeah, well, you got that right. Although, really, it wouldn't've made much of a difference. I'd still have wanted you again, a few minutes later."

"So what are you saying?" Annie asked. "I'm like the Chinese food of sexual partners?"

Another laugh. This one low, sexy. "That's not how I'd put it, but there are definitely some similarities. I love eating Chinese food, too."

"Oh," Annie said at his insinuation. She hadn't meant to say anything, but the sound just kind of came out of her.

"Yeah," Ric said. "So now you know what I've been thinking about for most of the day." He laughed, the sound a soft rumble in her ear. "That— and the fact that I'm an idiot. You want a year or two? You want an entire decade? Okay. You got it. I'm not going anywhere, and sooner or later, you'll have to believe me when I tell you that I love you."

Oh, God.

But Ric wasn't done. "You want to pretend we're friends with benefits until then, well, that's fine, too—as long as I'm the only friend you're . . . benefiting."

He paused then, as if he wanted her to say something, but her mouth was dry and she couldn't speak.

"Are we clear on that?" he asked, in his take-no-shit voice.

"Yes," she managed. But the argumentative side of her couldn't keep from blurting, "But it has to go both ways."

Ric laughed again. "What part of *Will you marry me?* makes you believe that I have even the *slightest* interest in fooling around with anyone else—except of course you *don't* believe me, so, yeah, okay. You have my word. You'll be my only fuck buddy, too."

"Oh, *that's* nice," she said. "God, Ric—"

"I'm just calling it what it is," he countered, his temper obviously flaring. "If you don't like the name for it, maybe you shouldn't be—" He cut himself off and exhaled hard. "Look, for the record?" He lowered his voice. "When I'm inside of you, when I'm moving the way I know you love for me to move? I'm *making love* to you. That's what *I* call it. So why don't you pack *that* in your bag and think about it while you're in California? Of course, if that concept's too intense for you, maybe you should just focus on all the ways I'm going to make you come, next time we're alone together."

She was silent for such a long time that he asked, "You still there?"

"Oh, yeah."

"Good," he said. "I'm going to call Martell, have him drop by to check on you in the morning, okay?"

"Yeah," Annie said again.

"I love you, Annie," Ric said. "I'll talk to you tomorrow."

She took a deep breath. "Ric—"

But with a click, he was gone.

Great. Now *she* needed a drink.

She and Robin were quite the pair.

Martell stopped by Ric's on his way home from work.

The forensics nightmare was still set up in Ric's office, but Ric and Jules were nowhere in sight.

He followed the sound of the TV upstairs to the living room—where they were sitting side by side on the sofa, playing Grand Theft Auto.

"No," Jules was saying, shifting to keep Ric from taking the joystick out of his hands. "No, no, no—I play this game differently from you. Check this out. Look, okay, okay . . . *here* we go . . ."

On Ric's flat-screen TV, the perp that Jules controlled with his joystick got out of the sports car and ran toward the fire truck that had skidded to a stop. The driver's-side door opened, and the computer-image person who'd been driving the truck was tossed to the ground. Jules's perp climbed behind the wheel.

"Yeah, baby!" he said as the fire truck rumbled away.

"What the fuck are you doing in the fire truck?" Martell asked from the doorway. "You can't get up any real speed in that thing."

Both men glanced at him.

"Nice to know your security system works," Jules said to Ric.

"He has a key." Ric's attention was back on the TV, where Jules was running over both people and cars in the ultraviolent computer game, gaining more and more speed.

Boom! He just plowed through a police road block set up to stop him.

"Okay," Martell said. "Maybe that's what you're doing in the fire truck. Ric, you want to update me—"

"No, no," Jules said. "Full attention on the TV, gentlemen . . . Wait for it, wait for it . . ."

He was moving at a pace that Martell wouldn't have dared, not even in one of the smaller cars, sliding the fire truck onto the ramp up to the highway, but whoa! Instead of driving on the road, he was on the grass between the on- and off-ramps, dodging trees with a lightness of hand that was fucking amazing.

The grass turned to a concrete ramp and the truck went up it, still gaining speed and—

"Yeah!" Ric shouted as the concrete ended abruptly and the fire truck launched into midair.

"Dude!" Martell shouted. The hang time was amazing. The giant motherfucker just soared. Jules added glitter to the visual by spraying water out of the fire truck's hose. It was beautiful.

But what went up must come down . . .

Except Jules managed to land the truck with amazing grace on the parking area of a nearby roof, again working that joystick like a pro to keep it from flipping on its side and plowing through the flimsy guardrail.

"Insane stunt bonus," Jules announced, even as his words flashed on the screen. His score skyrocketed.

"Dude!" Martell said again.

Jules took the fire truck down the parking-lot ramp, all the way to the street below.

"And that," he announced as he handed the joystick to Ric, "is the *only* way to play Grand Theft Auto."

"Shit!" Ric immediately crashed the fire truck as Martell high-fived Jules.

"You awe and inspire me, my gay brother," Martell told him.

"My personal life may be turning to shit, but I am," Jules agreed, "the king of the insane stunt bonus."

"So what's going on?" Martell asked, sitting beside them.

"There's Chinese takeout in the kitchen if you're hungry," Ric told him, turning off the TV.

"I'm assuming that's not the reason I got three missed calls from you on my cell," Martell said.

"I was hoping you'd have time to check in on Robin and Annie in the morning," Ric said. "Their flight out doesn't leave until noon."

Martell had to be in court first thing in the morning, arguing a case against an assistant DA named Bob Andersen. They were appearing in front of a grim-faced man he and Ric had nicknamed Judge Doom, back when they were on the police force. Doom had a propensity for bringing in guilty verdicts.

Martell knew exactly—almost word for word—what his morning would be like. Bob would greet him by saying, *Mr. Griffin. Back for more punishment today, are we?*

Judge Doom would bang his gavel and Martell would argue the case, using Damien Johnson's lame-ass excuse that he'd held up the Circle K while under the influence of sleeping pills that he'd taken by mistake, thinking they were aspirin. He was sleepwalking.

Right.

The Doomster wouldn't buy that shit any more than Martell had. The jury wouldn't, either, and Johnson would not pass "Go" before going directly to jail.

And Bob would smirk. *Mr. Griffin. Have I started showing up in your nightmares?*

Like it had been some great contest of skill that Martell had failed, instead of an exercise in necessary futility, since a trial by jury was a constitutional right of all citizens—including each and every lame-ass who insisted he or she was innocent.

And Martell wouldn't say, *Actually, Bob, I run when I see you coming because you bore me to tears.*

But he'd want to.

"Sure, I can stop in, but it'll be early," he told Ric now.

"Thanks," Ric said.

Jules stood up. "I'm going to bed."

Was he serious? "The king can't go to bed at eight-thirty," Martell protested.

"The king is tired," Jules said. He looked at Ric. "Wake me if Junior calls to say he's coming any earlier than ten."

"Yeah," Ric said. "Hey."

Jules stopped in the doorway.

"You know, Annie was thinking you might want to call Robin," Ric said, adding, "Or not. She's just . . . you know . . . being Annie, so . . ."

Jules just nodded, but Martell could see the intense exhaustion in the man's eyes along with a little something extra. He'd seen that look before—in the eyes of people who were grieving a loss. He didn't respond, except to say a quiet "good night."

They sat there then, in silence, as his footsteps receded down the hallway, as he gently closed the door to Annie's room behind him.

"He okay?" Martell asked.

"Yeah," Ric said. "He'll be fine."

"So that's what gay guys do, huh? Sit around racking up insane stunt bonuses on Grand Theft Auto," Martell mused. "Who knew? I expected to find him redecorating your kitchen."

"I got Colt 45s in the fridge," Ric said. "Want one?"

Martell laughed. "Zing."

"He's a lot like us," Ric said. "He just . . . has sex with . . . men."

Martell turned his head to look at him.

"I know," Ric said. "It's kind of weird, but then again . . . *You* had sex with the lieutenant."

God Almighty, Enrique was never going to let Martell live that one down. Their former boss had been temporarily separated from her husband, and Martell had just left the force to start law school. They'd both been drinking and . . . Crazy shit happened. So to speak.

"I'd have sex with Robin Chadwick," Ric continued, "before getting naked with the lieutenant. And since the probability of my having sex with Chadwick is somewhere between negative two billion and never . . ."

It had been a one-time-only thing—thank you, Jesus—the true blessing being that the lieutenant reconciled with her husband mere days later. But it had been far from the awfulness that Ric no doubt imagined. Still, it was a night Martell chose to remember only selectively, squinting to dull the clarity of his memories.

"You know," Ric said pensively, "I think I'd have sex with Pierre, before—"

"Shut up," Martell said, laughing. "You're such a prick. You ask me to do you a favor and then you dis my woman?"

"Your woman?" Ric repeated in disbelief.

"She was fucking hot," Martell said, just to make the prick squirm. Also because it was not a lie. He threw one in for good measure. "She wore leather and made me call her ma'am."

"Man, I so don't want to know that," Ric said. "Please tell me you're shitting me."

"I'm shitting you." He stood up. "I gotta go."

Ric stood, too. "Call me after you check in on Annie. Leave me a message if I don't pick up."

He was seriously concerned about her safety, so Martell didn't make a joke about either comforting her or alleviating her loneliness. Instead he just nodded. "Will do."

Ric followed him into the kitchen, where Martell helped himself to some Szechwan chicken that was still out and open on the table. "You sure you don't want this?" he asked, even as he took a plastic fork from Ric's drawer and started eating right out of the white cardboard container. It was cold, but damn good. He was hungrier than he'd thought.

"I'm sure," Ric said.

There was a smaller container of steamed rice, and Martell unglued some of it, combining it with his chicken. "Because you know what they say about Chinese food. It tastes great, but you're hungry again thirty minutes later."

For some reason, Ric found that really funny.

"Bro," Martell told him as he went down the stairs to the front door, Ric following to lock up behind him. "You're losing it. Get some sleep while you can."

"Thank you again for helping," Ric said. "When you see her, tell Annie that I love her."

Martell turned to look at him in surprise, but he'd already shut the door.

Smiling, he stabbed another piece of chicken with his fork as he walked to his car. Considering Ric was one of the best detectives Martell had ever known, it had taken him much too long.

But apparently he'd finally gotten a clue.

CHAPTER
TWENTY-TWO

R obin was coming down with the flu.
Had to be.
His head was pounding, he was sweating as if he had a fever, he couldn't sleep, and his nausea level was off the charts.

Which, of course, made Dolphina's 5 A.M. phone call all that much more fun.

"I really don't want to do this right now," he mumbled into his cell as he staggered into the bathroom to take a leak.

"Are you drunk again?" she asked sharply.

"No." He leaned against the wall above the toilet, too ill to stand without support. "I'm very much undrunk. I was sleeping." He'd finally managed to nod off when his phone rang, jolting him awake.

Dolphina, finally back from her cousin's wedding in Orlando, had told him earlier that she'd call when the PR genius that HeartBeat Studios hired had come up with a plan of attack regarding the YouTube debacle. But this was ridiculous.

"Can't we discuss this in the morning?" he asked, flushing the toilet.

"By morning the story will have broken," she said. "Robin. Listen carefully. I just got a call from a reporter from TMZ dot-com. He wants a comment—from you—regarding the man who came into your hotel room last night."

Robin made his way back to his bed, where the bottle of water on his bedside table was empty. "There were no men in my hotel room last night."

"Last night," she repeated. "Not tonight."

He put his head in his hands. "You mean . . ."

"I'm talking about the night from the YouTube video," she clarified.

"There were two men," he told her, "in that video. I've never seen either one of them before."

There was silence on the other end of the phone, but then Dolphina said, "Robin, did your . . . special friend come to your room that night, too? Because this reporter says he's seen new footage of a man who came into your room and kicked everyone out. It's just gone up online, and he's giving us a chance to comment for the story he's writing—a story that's going to break in just a few hours. A story that outs you."

Ric came out of a really good dream with a hand on his shoulder and a voice in his ear. "Ric. Alvarado, come on. Wake up."

It wasn't Annie's voice, which was disappointing—doubly so when he opened his eyes to see Jules standing over him.

"Sorry," the FBI agent apologized. "I knocked on your door, but you were out cold."

"What's up?" Ric sat up, pushing his hair out of his face, aware of both his lack of shirt and his raging hard-on.

In his dream, he'd been sitting on the lounge chair out on the screened porch and Annie had appeared, the way Annie often did in his very best dreams. She'd whispered his name as she'd straddled him, pushing him hard and deep inside of her.

Yeah. Good dream. Really good dream.

He bunched his blanket in his lap.

But Jules had already moved back across the room to the doorway, respectful of Ric's privacy. "Junior called on my cell," he reported. "He said he's running late, but that he should be here by noon."

Ric looked at the clock on his nightstand. It was slightly after 5 A.M., and the first faded pink hint of the coming sunrise was lighting the sky.

"He used the words *our little field trip to Myakka*," Jules said.

"Myakka," Ric repeated. Myakka was a state park, filled with alligators and long desolate stretches of swampy river. It was the perfect dumping ground for murder victims. As a cop, he'd helped drag the river many times.

Jules nodded. "I've spoken to Yashi. He's got three different teams already on their way out there. They'll be in place by the time we leave. By the time *I* leave with Junior. I've been thinking about it, and there's no reason for you to go, too. Which is why I woke you. I don't want you here when Junior arrives."

He was serious.

"And Junior's not going to think that's weird?" Ric asked. "That I'm not along for the ride?"

"Not when I tell him that your father had another heart attack, and that you went to the hospital," Jules replied.

That was a good cover, but . . . "You'll be alone," Ric pointed out.

"My entire team will be in place."

"And what if this Myakka thing is disinformation?" Ric countered. "Your team will be in Myakka and you'll be God knows where."

"Then I really don't want you with me," Jules told him.

"You think something's going to go wrong." Ric's jeans were on the floor next to his bed, and he grabbed them and pulled them on, yanking up his zipper so they could have this conversation face-to-face.

Jules didn't try to deny it. He was standing there, in the doorway, in jeans and a T-shirt, with his feet bare and his hair sticking straight up in places like a frat boy with chronic bedhead. "I hate to go all Han Solo on you, but yeah. I got a bad feeling about this. So take a shower, get dressed, and go over to the hospital."

"Jules, come on . . ."

His face got hard and the frat boy vanished. "That wasn't a request. That was an order. This isn't a democracy, Alvarado. You work for me. So get your ass to the hospital."

"Okay," Ric said, holding out both hands as if he were trying to reassure Pierre when Annie had been gone for too long. "Whoa. Wait. Let's not go into panic mode just yet. We've got plenty of time to, I don't know, think up a counterplan."

Jules laughed. "You don't think I've got a counterplan? I've got teams coming out here within the hour. They'll be in place to provide backup, long before Junior arrives. They'll follow, wherever Junior takes me. Plus, the body'll be trackable. Go to the hospital, Alvarado. Don't make me break your arm to send you there."

Those were fighting words, meant to piss him off, but Ric wasn't going to argue that one. "Look, man, I know you can probably beat the hell out of me if you want to. And yeah, maybe you're going to have to, because I'm not going anywhere. You had to know that my leaving you alone with Junior and his men just wasn't going to fly. I can see that something's got you spooked. I've been there. You get a feeling, you don't know why, but you're usually always right. So okay. Let's work this through—"

"I've worked it through," Jules said again, "and you're going to the hospital."

"I realize that you're afraid for me," Ric said, "and I appreciate that, but . . . it goes both ways. I'm afraid for you, too."

Jules didn't move. Ric didn't know how he did it, but one second he was standing there, the hard-ass FBI team leader, and the next, he'd completely changed. It was as if he'd flipped a switch and morphed into someone else.

"I had no idea you cared," Jules said so softly, Ric almost couldn't hear him. And his eyes, which had been so hard, were now filled with heat. He gave Ric a long, slow once-over, looking at him in a way that Ric had never been looked at by another man before. It was extremely disconcerting.

But Ric knew exactly what Jules was doing. Or rather, *trying* to do. It wasn't going to work. He didn't scare that easily. He wasn't going to run away.

Instead, he called Jules's bluff. "Come on," Ric said. "Let's take a walk on the wild side, *babe*." He purposely used Robin's term of endearment for Jules. "We've got a couple hours to kill . . ."

Ric went as far as to step toward Jules—who took a big step back, away from him. Just as Ric had known he would.

"What," Ric pushed. "Isn't that what you want?"

"Don't be an asshole," Jules said. The heat was gone from his eyes— in fact, he was finding it difficult now to meet Ric's gaze.

"Oh, *I'm* the asshole?" Ric asked. "I thought we were friends. I thought that you respected me. But if you were really thinking you could scare me into some kind of, I don't know, homophobic panic . . . ? Fuck you, for thinking so little of me. And fuck you, too, for apparently assuming I wasn't paying attention when you were talking about Robin. Christ, if anyone out there is a one-man . . . man . . ." Damn, but that was weird to say. "It's you. Asshole."

"I'm sorry," Jules said, his eyes now contrite. "And you're right. I'm an idiot. But you're still going to the hospital, where you'll be safe."

Ric didn't get a chance even to open his mouth to begin to argue.

Because his doorbell rang.

This was not good.

This was very, very not good.

Annie hit play, and Robin's laptop computer ran the latest digital video, this one posted on a popular celebrity news website. In it, Jules was here, in this very hotel suite.

"Tell your friends it's time to go." That was definitely Jules's voice, even though it took the camera several moments to find him. And then there Jules was, wearing the same suit he'd worn to Gordon Burns's party, sans tie.

Whoever was filming him must've been using their cell phone, the quality was so poor.

But they got a good close-up of him as he turned away from the sliders to the living-room balcony, as someone nearer to the phone's mic said, "Robin Chadwick invited us here. Who the hell are you to tell us to leave?"

It was then that Jules just stopped. He not only stopped moving, but he practically stopped breathing.

Robin was sitting next to Annie, reading a printout of the impending accompanying TMZ article. "Look at how much he wants to just say it," he breathed. "*I'm his lover . . .*"

Annie glanced over to see that he'd looked up from the article and was transfixed by the image on the screen. By Jules.

Tears gleamed in Robin's eyes. "God, I wish he had," Robin whispered.

But Jules finally spoke. "I'm one of his producers," he said. "I'm also a good friend. I make sure people don't take advantage of him. Close the door on your way out."

The camera followed him as he headed toward the French doors that led into Robin's bedroom. He disappeared through them.

There was a cut, and the film jumped to an even grittier, lower-light shot of Jules, crouched next to Robin, who was facedown on the tile of the bedroom balcony.

It must've been a woman holding the cell phone camera now. Her voice was clear as she spoke to Jules.

He asked her about any drugs that Robin might've taken.

She brought up Viagra, and the expression on Jules's face was not that of a mere friend. The filmmaker knew it, and froze on it, zooming in as tightly as possible.

Annie risked another glance at Robin, who'd started to cry. He didn't cry the way he did in his movies, with one tear and then another sliding down his perfect face. Instead, he tried to hide it from her, wiping his eyes, trying to blink back all of his emotion.

"I can't believe I did that to him." Robin's voice shook. "What the fuck is wrong with me?"

That was the end of the video, but the website included links to photos, as well as another video link—no doubt to the now infamous Robin

Chadwick YouTube footage. Annie clicked on the first of the photos. It was a still of Robin and Jules. They looked to be standing on a soundstage, and Robin was wearing some kind of old-fashioned military uniform.

"That's from when we were filming *American Hero*," he told her. "It was taken two years ago."

Jules looked the same, but Robin was obviously younger. He was much skinnier back then, his face more boyish and slender.

In the photo, the two men were smiling at each other, as if sharing a joke. A private joke. Their gazes were locked, and their attraction was palpable.

The second link led to a photo that must've been taken just seconds later. They were still standing in the same spot, but in this picture Jules had looked away while Robin still gazed at him. Neither man was smiling now, and the look of sheer longing on Robin's face was heartbreaking.

"I was in character," Robin said. "I was playing Hal Lord, who was gay, and I was still in character." He paused. "That's what we'll say."

Annie looked at him. "Or . . . you could tell the truth."

"I can't." Robin stood up, taking the article with him to the sofa. Annie had already read it, and it was all conjecture, but pretty damn accurate.

She swiveled in her chair to face him. "Sure, you can."

"No"—Robin raised his voice—"I can't." He pressed his hand to his forehead. "God, I have a headache. I think I'm coming down with something." He flipped open his cell phone and speed-dialed a number. "Yeah, Dolph," he said into it, "it's me. Here's what we're going to do. You call the reporter back, you identify Jules—his full name is Julian Young." He spelled it for her. "You tell the reporter that he's a friend of mine, that he's a producer, that I've known him for several years."

Annie turned back to the computer as Robin continued speaking to Dolphina. She clicked the back button and clicked on the link to the second video.

There was a pause while the computer downloaded it into Media Player and then . . .

Oh, shit.

This was not the video she'd expected.

"Robin," Annie said, "you better come look at this—right now!"

"My cell service is down," Ric reported.

Jules's Trēo, too, was completely useless. "The signal's being jammed," he realized.

Ric swore. "The landline's dead."

It was, of course, Gordie Junior and three members of his goon squad, standing on Ric's front stoop, ringing the doorbell again. The fact that they were here at dawn when Junior had just called to say they'd be delayed until noon was ominous. Disinformation, anyone?

"Here's what we're going to do," Jules decided. "You're going out the back—"

"Two more men on the back porch," Ric informed him. "And e-mail's not an option. They must've taken my cable out, too."

"You'll have to hide," Jules told him.

"You think they won't search for me?" Ric countered. "I say we play it like we don't know they've taken out our phones. We've got the tracking device in the body . . ."

That was assuming Junior was going to take the body with them. Of course, if they played it as Ric suggested, maybe he would.

"Okay," Jules said. "Get the door. I'm going to leave a message up here, for Yashi."

Ric nodded and headed downstairs.

Jules stood in Ric's bedroom, trying to think.

Really, the only piece of information that Yashi wouldn't have was the time of day that Junior had shown up. But how to tell him that without leaving something as obvious as a note—something Junior's men might find if they searched the place.

Over on Ric's nightstand, his alarm clock's LED display switched from 5:22 to 5:23.

As Jules heard Ric opening the door and greeting Junior—"Man, it is so good to see you"—he went across the room and set Ric's alarm for 5:22 A.M. There was a notepad on the table, right next to the clock, and a pen that Jules used to write with.

He made a short To-Do list. *Get milk. Clean bathroom. Set alarm. Go to Post Office.*

"I broke away much earlier than I expected." Junior's voice carried up from the office. "Where's Julian?"

"Right here." Jules came down the stairs. "Hey, I thought you had a situation that was going to keep you until noon."

"It got itself handled," Junior told him. "I figured since we just spoke on the phone, you'd be up. I tried calling you back but the fucking cell service is down. Some dipshit must've hit a tower."

Or some dipshit—like Junior himself—had access to a signal jammer. Jules's hair was standing up on the back of his neck, but he made himself smile. He had no doubt now that Junior had somehow found out that Ric and Jules were a threat. There was something about the man's eyes, the way he was standing, the tone of his voice . . . Junior knew. But he was playing it like he didn't, so Jules played along. "Well, thanks for coming," he said.

"No problem." The men who were with Junior were all young—younger than the men in the security team Jules had seen at the Burns Point party. They were dressed for the beach, or maybe a fishing trip out on Myakka River—Hawaiian shirts hanging open over barely concealed shoulder holsters and weapons aplenty. "So where the body?" Junior asked.

"In my office," Ric answered, pointing toward the closed door.

"Get it ready to travel," Junior ordered, and two of his men went to do just that, closing the door behind them.

"Ric was asking her about some missing money, and the gun went off." Jules volunteered the information, but Junior wasn't interested.

"Whatever." He smiled at Jules and Ric. "My boy Donny here's gonna pat you down and check you for wires. It's something I learned from Daddy. I check out my own boys every time we meet up. It's just my thing, so no offense."

"None taken," Jules said, watching Donny run his hands down Ric's jeans-clad legs—he'd come downstairs bare-chested.

"You want me to run upstairs and get you a shirt, bro?" Jules asked Ric.

Maybe if they stalled in a major way, the teams assigned to watch and follow would arrive in time to do their jobs.

"Yeah," Ric said. "Thanks," but Junior thwarted that plan.

"Go upstairs and grab him something to wear," he told the goon in the purple shirt, who immediately thundered up the stairs.

It was more than obvious, from the amount of time he was gone, that he was making sure there was no one else up there, and that they'd left no notes or messages behind.

Meanwhile, Donny tossed Ric's cell phone onto Annie's desk.

"I kind of need that," Ric said. "I know it's not working right now, but—"

"No technology," Junior said. "I like you guys, you know I do, but with people using phones these days to take picture and movies . . . ? You can live without your phones for a couple hours."

Jules took his own phone and handed it to Donny, then spread his legs and put his hands on Annie's desk. He'd always hated getting patted down, but Donny, though thorough, was quick. He ran a bug sweeper over them both, then . . .

"Check out the body," Junior ordered him, adding, "No offense."

"It's clear you've got a system down," Jules said, praying that the hot new technology that the FBI had used so they could track the body was as hot and new as promised.

And sure enough, Donny was back in a flash. "It's all good," he told Junior, holding the door for the other two men, who'd rolled the dead woman in Ric's area rug. Junior held the outside door, and they trotted out to the van that was in the driveway, just behind a shiny new Lexus.

Purple Shirt came downstairs, carrying . . . Jules's windbreaker?

"That's mine," Jules said. "It's not going to fit him." Stall. Stall.

But Purple held it up. It was loose on Jules and it looked as if it would fit Ric just fine.

"It's just until we get on the boat," Junior said. "While we're out on the water, you're going to wanna work on your tan, anyway. I got a bit of a time crunch, so we're going to have to get moving. So let's do it."

He led the way, and with Donny behind them, there was nothing left to do but walk out the door, sans weapons, sans phones.

Ric gave stalling one more try as he pulled on Jules's jacket. "Guys, I just woke up. I really gotta take a leak before we drive all the way to Myakka."

Junior turned to Donny in exasperation. "Go with him."

He put himself between Jules and Annie's desk—where their phones had been left—as Donny followed Ric into the office bathroom. They kept the door open, and it was clear Ric hadn't been lying about needing to go, at least.

Still, when he came back out, the look he shot Jules was unhappy.

"How far is it to Myakka?" Jules asked as they got into the Lexus with Junior and Donny. One of the other men, a skinhead, squeezed into the backseat with Jules and Ric. "I've never been."

"Yeah," Junior said as Donny, behind the wheel, pulled out of the drive, following the van. "Change of plans. Myakka's too crowded this time of year. We're going to do a little deep-sea fishing instead."

Swell. But not unexpected.

Junior turned to face them from the front passenger seat, two cups of coffee in his hands. "You boys want Starbucks? We picked up a couple extra on our way over."

As if they were going to drink anything that Junior offered them. "No. Thanks, though." Jules kept his voice light.

"I'm good," Ric said. "I had a little too much caffeine yesterday."

Junior laughed. "No such thing, in my book." He took a sip from one of the cups.

So much for the poison-in-the-Starbucks theory.

Still, despite the friendly show Junior was putting on for them, Jules knew—he *knew*—that their cover had been blown. And unless someone was constantly monitoring the movement of their dead body, it was possible that Ric and Jules were going to disappear as completely as Peggy Ryan had.

He should have broken Ric's arm instead of spending all that time arguing with him about whether he should or shouldn't've gone to the safety of the hospital.

He should have made Junior break down the door, instead of opening it for him.

He should have met the bastard with a hail of bullets.

He should have knocked on Robin's door a year ago—why the hell had he waited so long to see him again, anyway? Stupid arbitrary rule—it shouldn't have mattered that Robin was in the closet. What mattered was that Robin *loved* him.

He should have called Robin last night and told him that he loved him, too.

Because now it was looking more and more likely that that was something Robin would never get the chance to hear.

Robin's hands were shaking so badly, he almost dropped his cell phone. But he sat down next to Annie, which helped him gain his equilibrium, as he hung up on Dolphina and dialed Jules's cell.

Annie was using her own phone to try to reach Ric.

Because there, under someone's amateurish cell phone video footage of Jules running *toward* a house from which people were firing rifles at a crowd of police and FBI, was the identifying caption *Federal Agent Jules Cassidy—Heroics Under Fire.*

Jules's voicemail picked up. "Cassidy. Leave a message and I'll get right back to you."

"Jules! Jesus, your cover's been blown," Robin said. "Call me—please, God, call me right back!"

As he hung up, Annie was leaving a similar message for Ric. "I'm trying Martell," she told him when she was done.

"Do you have what's-his-name's number?" Robin asked. "Yashi."

Annie shook her head. "No, I've always called Jules directly. Ric had Yashi's . . . Damn it, Martell's not picking up either. Martell, it's Annie. Call me."

"Should I call 911?" Robin dialed Jules again, as on the computer screen the video footage showed Jules skidding to a stop next to an injured man who was wearing some kind of police uniform. He grabbed the enormous man beneath the arms and hauled him to safety. God, he had balls . . .

"That might make it worse." Annie's voice was shaking, too. If Junior saw this video . . . "Ric was certain someone on the police force was on Burns's payroll."

Robin was again bumped to Jules's voicemail. He cut the connection and dialed information. "I need to speak to an operator," he told the computer system when it asked him which city and state.

Annie, meanwhile, was digging in her handbag for something.

His phone's call waiting beeped, and his heart leaped, but it was only Dolphina. Robin stayed on his call, ignoring her. He was rewarded as, miraculously, a real, living person spoke into his ear. "May I help you?"

"Please," he said. "I need the number for the FBI headquarters in Washington, D.C. I'm trying to reach an FBI official named Max Bhagat." He spelled Max's last name for her since it was tricky with that extra *h*.

But of course, Jules's boss wasn't on any phone list available to the public. "I'm sorry," the operator told him. "I don't have . . ."

"Can you just give me some kind of main number for the FBI," he implored. "It's an emergency, so please hurry."

Annie had found what she was searching for—a business card. She was dialing a number off the card, and when she was done, she saw that Robin was watching, so she showed it to him.

Sam Starrett, he read, *Troubleshooters Incorporated*. It included the company's California address and phone number.

"It's the middle of the night in San Diego," he told Annie as his call waiting beeped again. Again, it was only Dolphina and again he ignored her call.

"I know," Annie said. "I'm getting sent to some kind of voicemail system. Shhh, there's a message—maybe there's an emergency number . . ."

Robin stayed silent, praying as he waited for the operator to give him the FBI's main phone number, but Annie too quickly shook her head no. "No luck," she said, but then left a message. "Hi, my name is Annie Dugan, I'm a civilian working in Florida on an important case with FBI agent Jules Cassidy. I can't reach him and I've just discovered that his cover has been blown in a huge way. He's in terrible danger. If you get this message, please contact anyone you can think of who might be able to help him . . ."

"Shall I connect you directly?" the operator asked.

"Yes," Robin said, "but give me the number, too." He wrote it down on the TMZ article as she rattled it off.

Whatever number she'd connected him to rang. And rang and rang. He looked at his phone—it was barely 5:30 in the morning. "Come on," he said. "Someone be there . . ."

There was a knock on his door—it was, no doubt, Dolphina, pissed that he'd not only hung up on her, but was ignoring her repeated calls.

Good, he could enlist her help. "I need you to call the White House," he said as he unlocked the chain and opened the door. "I want to talk to the—"

President, he was going to say, but it wasn't Dolphina standing there. It was a man, with another man behind him. Both were large, and they were holding guns.

Robin dropped his phone and tried to close the door, but they forced it open, forced their way inside, pushing him back—hard enough to hit the dining table with a crash. As he scrambled to keep from falling, he knocked over two of the chairs.

Annie was on her feet. "Robin!"

"We're not armed, don't shoot," Robin said, trying to get to Annie before they did.

But they weren't moving quickly—not after they got inside and closed and locked the door behind them.

"Drop the phone," the larger man—the one built rather like a refrigerator—said as the other stepped on Robin's cell with the heel of his boot.

Annie looked at Robin, and he tried to tell her with his eyes to go for it—dial 911. They didn't have a whole hell of a lot to lose, considering Robin recognized both men from that party at Burns Point.

They worked for Gordon Burns—or for Gordie Junior.

"I said, drop it—right now or I'll blow his fucking head off," the refrigerator demanded, his gun aimed unerringly at Robin.

Dial it anyway, he tried to tell her, but she didn't.

She dropped it.

"Kick it over here."

She did, and the skinnier man did his boot thing on her phone, too.

Fridge, meanwhile, had taken out his own cell, dialing and holding it to his ear. "We've got 'em both," he told whoever was on the other end.

"He just opened the fucking door for us, and we just walked in." He laughed. "Fucking idiot."

Yep, that pretty much described Robin.

"I'm sorry," he told Annie.

"Are you all right? Your nose . . ."

Sure enough, it was bleeding. He'd gotten smacked in the face with the door. He didn't think it was broken—it hurt, but not that much more than the hellish headache that had been plaguing him all night.

"We're not out of the hotel yet, so it's probably best not to call him until . . . Yeah," Fridge continued. "I'll let you know as soon as we're clear."

As the man pocketed his phone, Robin told them both, "We're not leaving the hotel." It was only a matter of time before Dolphina came knocking. Since he'd reclaimed his key card, she wouldn't be able to get in. Knowing her, though, she'd call hotel security.

All they had to do was stall.

And pray that Jules and Ric were somewhere safe.

Junior's yacht was a ship. Though Ric had lived for most of his life near the ocean, he wasn't a boat person, but even he recognized the distinction. He didn't know exactly what he'd been expecting, but it wasn't this luxurious monstrosity. It was huge.

There were two full levels belowdeck.

Ric knew that Jules had been tense in the car, too, but once they'd arrived at the moored boat and seen that roll of rug from Ric's office already waiting on the ship's gleaming deck, they'd both taken something of a deep breath.

As long as that body was with them, the FBI could and would track them. Jules's team was probably already being called back in from Myakka. Other agents were probably gearing up, enlisting the aid of Coast Guard ships, preparing to follow them.

Or at least monitor their location.

As they headed for the open water of the Gulf, Ric tried to get a head count. One man—the driver, Donny—had gone immediately to the wheelhouse or bridge or whatever the control room was called on a yacht this size. Ric could see him up there, in a windowed area. As far as he could tell, Donny was alone.

At this point, he was clearly driving this thing. But once they left the harbor, he could probably put on the cruise control or autopilot—or maybe even just shut the engines down and let the ship drift.

Two men—wearing suits—had picked up their rug-wrapped body, and, in a brisk, businesslike fashion, they'd carried it below.

Another two—the skinhead and the fool in the ugly purple shirt—hung close as Junior gave Ric and Jules a tour of Daddy's yacht—as if this really were just a pleasure cruise. As if they really were just a bunch of buddies hanging out, drinking beer and fishing.

Ric knew that Jules was counting heads, too. The FBI agent had put his hand on Ric's shoulder, feigning a need to steady himself when they went down the full flight of steep stairs leading to the staterooms. While his hand was there, he tapped Ric six times.

That was the number Ric had come up with, too. There were six armed men aboard this ship—including Gordie Junior.

There was more than one flight of stairs leading down from the main deck area, Junior told them in his best tour-guide imitation. The other went directly to the galley or kitchen. This one led to this set of staterooms—individual luxury suites that were elegantly decorated with nautical themes and gleaming with brass. He only opened one door though. It was likely the other rooms had been trashed by Junior's less-than-elegant friends.

The starboard and port hallways connected at the front of the ship in a spacious home theater, with rows of comfortable-looking, leather-covered seats.

"She sleeps twenty," Junior told them. "Not including crew and staff. Of course, today I gave most of the crew the day off."

Of course.

"We'll have to wait until we're out of sight of land before we can get down to business," Junior told them. "But I'm sure you'll be interested in seeing this . . ."

A door opened to reveal a companionway to the lower level, these stairs even steeper than the first set.

"This level's used mostly for storing shit." Junior led the way down into an area that was basement-like. "Although the crew's berths are down here, too."

Not only did the lower level give a sense of being unfinished—with pipes and venting systems unhidden—but it was also badly lit and damp. Ric had never thought of himself as claustrophobic before, but he could not wait to get back to the deck and the fresh air.

The movement of the ship beneath his feet sure as hell wasn't helping.

"Food's kept directly beneath the kitchen," Junior continued as he led them through a door that was more like a hatch than the ones on the upper levels. It was open and locked into place. "There's actually a ladder going up into the galley, as well as a dumbwaiter and . . ."

Holy Christ. Junior kept talking, but Ric didn't hear more than the murmur of his voice as he stopped short just inside that hatch. He felt one of Junior's thugs bump into him from behind, finally pushing him aside when he failed to make room for the two of them.

He and Jules had followed Junior into some sort of area that was no doubt intended for fish cleaning. The room was designed to be hosed down completely—it had a big drain in the floor. Stainless-steel tables flipped down from the slanting, porthole-less walls—of course, they were beneath the water level down here.

The rug from Ric's office was on the floor—the body'd been put on one of the tables, and was being worked on by Junior's men.

They'd put it into a freaking bizarre version of a sweatsuit—the fabric was covered with explosives, all wired together.

". . . used to use a meat grinder," Junior was saying, "just flush all the evidence down this drain as fish food, but the skull and teeth were always problematic. I got this idea years ago when I heard about those suicide bombers. It always amazed me, though, that there'd be, like, an arm or a hand left intact, found in the rubble. So we're careful to cross the arms beneath the main explosives on the chest. We also use mittens to wrap the hands in C4, since, you know . . . Hands and heads being the body parts you most don't want washing up on shore. Hence the hood."

They'd put a Spider-Man-like, tight-fitting head-and-face covering on the body. With the explosives attached, it made her look like some bizarre beauty-salon participant with freakish curlers not only in her hair but across her concealed face as well.

Her . . . ? Wait a minute . . . Ric looked closer and . . .

"We'll set off a fuckload of firecrackers," Junior continued, "right before this is set to blow. We dump the body and back away—don't want to get hit by *that* spray, you know what I'm saying? We use a special underwater fuse, cut long enough to give us a time delay. Remote-control detonation's too expensive." He laughed. "Dude, you look green."

He was talking to Ric.

"He's always been prone to seasickness." Jules took him by the arm and steered him toward the hatch. "He just needs some air."

Jules pushed Ric up the stairs and back into the theater area. He hustled him through what looked to be some kind of wood-paneled den or game room, and then up a half flight of stairs into the ship's galley. It was much bigger than the kitchen in Ric's apartment, and far more lavishly appointed.

A half flight of stairs led up to an indoor dining area. Another made the galley easily accessible to the main deck. There was also a window in the galley that looked as if it could be opened to create a pass-through directly to that open part of the yacht.

Ric was already feeling much better, but when they hit the fresh air on deck, Donny was there to greet them.

"He's gonna hurl," Jules announced.

"I'm actually," Ric said, but Jules elbowed him hard, so he changed his *feeling better* to "prone to projectile vomiting."

Jules started to muscle him to the railing, but Donny intercepted. He'd conjured up a bucket from somewhere. "It's hard to clean that off the side," he told them, and then backed away.

Apparently nobody liked the idea of projectile vomiting.

Junior and the other two men finally caught up to them. "Just breathe and keep your eyes on the horizon," Junior instructed Ric. "You don't need the fucking bucket—"

But Ric did. It was the only way he was going to be able to talk to Jules without being overheard. He clasped the damn thing as he turned away and stuck his finger down his throat.

It wasn't as if he really needed that much help to empty his stomach. He added some nasty sound effects and . . .

Junior and his men all took several giant steps back.

"That body wasn't a woman," Ric told Jules between gags. Whoever was on that table was significantly bigger than their tracking-device-implanted Jane Doe.

"I noticed," Jules whispered grimly. "I also saw more of those explosive suits."

What? Ric hadn't seen that. He looked up at Jules.

"Four more," Jules said.

He didn't need to say the words for Ric to know what he was thinking. Two for them, and two more—for Robin and Annie.

Ric didn't need any help throwing up a second time.

"Can someone toss me a towel?" Jules called to Junior and his goons. One of them must've complied, because Ric felt him turn to catch something. "Thanks."

"I'm going to kill him," Ric breathed. "If he so much as touches Annie . . ."

"Yeah," Jules agreed. "He's dead. There's a problem, though. We're unarmed and outnumbered."

"Screw that," Ric said. "Let's just take them. If one of them gets close enough, we grab his weapon."

"Getting ourselves killed isn't going to help Annie and Robin. If we were closer to the edge, I'd say we go over the side," Jules said. "Split up and swim for shore. One of us would make it."

Getting free and getting to a place where they could contact the rest of the FBI, to make sure Annie and Robin didn't leave their hotel room, not even to go to the airport, was a damn good plan.

"Let's do it," Ric said, then pretended to heave. "Right now."

"We wouldn't even get to the rail," Jules told him. "The one named Donny has his weapon drawn. He's pretending to clean it, but . . . I'm betting he's their best shot. Let's just be ready. Try to work our way to the side. If one of us can go . . ." He helped Ric wipe his mouth, helped him to his feet, and then he swore.

As Ric stood up, he realized that while they were taking Junior's tour, they'd moved completely out of sight of land. According to the ship's wake, they'd been cruising in a big, slow circle for quite a few minutes now.

Even if they could get over the side and into the water, they'd have no idea which way to swim to reach land.

CHAPTER
TWENTY-THREE

The "you've got voicemail" ring on Martell's cell phone was among *the* most obnoxious in the world. It was a series of notes running up and down the scale.

He usually silenced his phone at night, but with Ric worried about Annie, he'd purposely left all the ringers functioning.

The sun was barely up as Martell reached for the little fucker. How he could have gotten a message without getting called was . . .

Okay. There was not one, but two missed calls from not Ric but Annie. Apparently Martell had finally learned to sleep through his regular, less obnoxious ring tone.

He dialed in his password to listen to her message and . . .

It was brief. *Call me.*

Martell did just that, but he went right to *her* voicemail.

"This is Annie Dugan. Leave a message."

"Yeah, it's Martell, returning your call." He hung up, then dialed Robin's cell. Same thing. Immediate voicemail.

So he called Robin's hotel. "Room 1270," he requested. But again, his only option was to leave a message.

He called Ric and then Jules—no answer from either of them.

Shit.

Martell swung his legs out of bed, and jammed them into his jeans, his feet into his sneakers.

Just what he needed—a 5:30 A.M. trip to the hotel.

For shits and giggles, he cowboyed up, covering his holster and sidearm with a loose overshirt.

Grabbing his car keys, he took out his phone and dialed Ric's number again as he went out the door. This time he left a message. "All I can say, home slice, is I better be best man."

Pierre started barking from his perch on Annie's bed. She'd left him sleeping there when Robin had first woken her up.

But now the loud voices in the hotel suite had roused the little dog, who couldn't get down by himself.

"Shut that thing up," ordered the larger of the two gunmen—the one who'd been in the limo when she and Ric had first encountered Gordie Junior.

Annie headed for the bedroom, praying they wouldn't follow her. There was a phone by the bed. If she could just lift the receiver and dial 8-911 . . .

But the skinnier man was right behind her, which made Pierre get even louder.

"Lock him in the bathroom," the gunman commanded. "Tell him to shut the fuck up or I'll break his neck."

Annie scooped the dog off the bed. "It's okay," she told him, and luckily, he quieted. "I'm going to put his bowls of water and food in with him so he stays quiet," she told the gunman.

He seemed okay with that, so after she put Pierre on the bathroom floor, telling him again to hush, after she closed the door on his bewildered little face, she picked up her jeans from where she'd dropped them on the floor last night. She pulled them on, right over the boxers she wore as pajamas.

She picked up her bra, too, putting it around her waist to fasten the clasp, pulling it up beneath her nightshirt, pulling her arms inside her sleeves and then back out after she'd gotten her underwear into place.

"Put on your sneakers while you're at it," the gunman said.

"Fuck you," Annie told him. Of course, before he'd suggested it, socks and sneakers were next on her list. But now she walked barefoot back into the suite's living room.

Where Robin was sitting at the desk, by the computer, holding a . . . crack pipe?

"What are you doing?" she asked, her voice sharp. She'd never seen one up close and personal, but that was definitely what that thing was.

"Get your prints on the vial, too," the heavier gunman was saying.

Robin wasn't using it—he was just touching it. Getting his finger-prints all over it.

He looked up at her, and the misery in his eyes made her heart stop. "Junior has Jules and Ric," he told her. "If we don't do exactly what we're told, he's going to kill them."

Oh, God.

"Believe me," the big gunman added, "he's just looking for a reason to pull the trigger."

The skinnier man dropped Annie's sneakers at her feet. "Put them on," he ordered.

She sat down. Right on the floor. Slipping her sneakers on, she tied the laces with fingers that were suddenly clumsy and cold.

They had to get out of there before Dolphina showed up.

Robin was finding it hard to think clearly, but that was a no-brainer. If Dolphina brought a security team to his door, Robin and Annie wouldn't be able to do as they were told, and Junior would kill Ric and Jules.

Of course, that was assuming that he hadn't already killed them.

Heart in his throat, Robin went into his bedroom and quickly got dressed. Jeans, T-shirt . . . He had to dig for his sneakers in his closet—which made Frigidaire antsy. He could practically feel the barrel of that gun, aimed at the base of his skull. He normally wore boat shoes or loafers—slip-ons with bare feet, but today was a sneaker day.

God willing, he, Annie, Ric, and Jules would all be given a chance to do some serious running.

As Robin put his sneakers on, he was unable to think of anything but the fact that he was responsible for all of this. If he hadn't gotten drunk, there would have been no YouTube footage of Jules—at least not that video linking him to Robin.

His hands were shaking as he pulled on a baseball cap. He grabbed his sunglasses and the refrigerator followed him back into the living room.

Skinny Dude was at the door, checking the hall. "Good to go," he said.

Annie took Robin's hand as they left his suite. She squeezed his fingers and he shook his head in warning. He knew she was thinking that their best chance in getting away was going to be in the elevator. She was prob-ably right. But his life was worth dick without Jules, and he wasn't about to risk Junior's wrath.

She squeezed his hand again, harder.

"We're compliant," he told Fridge, even though he was really talking to Annie. "Call Junior and tell him."

"As soon as we're out of the hotel," the man said.

He led them past the elevator banks, and though a door marked STAIRS.

Which kind of took Annie's revolt-in-the-elevator plan off the table. Thank God.

Twelve flights of stairs took forever to walk down, but when they kept going, Robin realized they were heading down to the parking garage. Of course. Rather than trooping through the hotel lobby . . .

"There might be paparazzi waiting for me in the garage," he warned their captors.

Annie was looking at him as if he had the fastest-occurring case of Stockholm syndrome in history.

He looked back at her with equal disbelief.

How could she be so willing to risk Ric's life? Except she wasn't, he realized. What she wanted was to go Buffy on their asses—to kick down doors until she found and rescued Ric.

Apparently, she did not live in a reality-based world—a world where they were all going to die because of Robin's idiocy. A world where Dolphina would get the security guards to unlock the door to his suite—where drug paraphernalia with his fingerprints all over it would be right there for them to find.

A world where his death would be just another drug-related tragedy. He was just another star who burned too bright, too fast.

And Jules's name would go right beneath Peggy Ryan's on that too-long list of agents lost in the line of duty.

Robin wanted to throw up.

Instead, he followed Fridge on legs that were unsteady, out of the steel door marked GARAGE LEVEL ONE. Their footsteps echoed in the emptiness as the burly man pulled him closer, his gun pressed into Robin's side.

"Oh, no," Annie breathed, and he realized that that sound he'd heard was the sound of a car being locked. And, yes, that *was* Martell heading straight toward them, with a "Hey!"

Robin tried to bluff—"Fucking paparazzi," he said loudly enough for Martell to hear. "Leave me the hell alone!"

But it was already too late. Skinny somehow realized that Martell knew them. Or maybe he saw that Martell was reaching for a weapon.

Skinny fired, and the sound of the gunshot reverberated brain-shakingly loudly through the enclosed garage.

Annie was screaming as Martell was pushed back from the force of the bullet, a bloom of red sprouting on the front of his T-shirt, his handgun falling and skittering across the concrete.

"No!" Robin heard himself shouting, too. He didn't realize he'd pulled away from the refrigerator until the man hit him, hard, upside his head. A second blow was aimed unerringly at his balls, and the pain blinded him. He hit the ground and retched.

"How about you? You want to go a round, too?" Robin heard the man's voice as if from a distance. He was talking to Annie, threatening her.

Robin pushed himself up onto his hands and knees. "Annie, don't—"

But the gunman hit her, too, and as she went down, Robin crawled to her, to try to cover her, to try to keep her from being hit again.

"I got his gun, his phone, and his wallet," Skinny reported, talking about Martell. "It'll look like a mugging."

"Go get the car," the bigger man ordered.

"We can't just leave him here!" Annie was down but not out. "He'll die!"

There was a screech of tires—the car hadn't been far. Robin felt himself picked up and thrown into the dank-smelling trunk of a Cadillac. Annie soon joined him.

The last thing he saw before the trunk lid closed on them was Fridge's face. "He's already dead." He smiled. "And you are, too."

As Ric watched, Junior's men dropped the body over the side. As it hit the water with a splash, he met Jules's eyes. Now was probably not the time to dive over the railing—next to enough C4 to put a huge hole in the side of this yacht.

Not that either one of them thought for a moment that they had a chance to make it safely into the water without getting shot. It was a long way down from this deck to the water. And even then, at this range, the water wouldn't slow the bullets enough to keep them from being killed.

It didn't even matter that Donny was back in the bridge. Junior's other men were standing close enough so that shooting them wouldn't have required much skill.

As the yacht swiftly moved to a safe distance from the explosives, Junior started setting off an array of firecrackers. Ric knew he was doing it just in case anyone was in earshot. That C4 blast was going to make one hell of a noise. A resounding boom on its own might send the Coast Guard to investigate. But if it was just part of some jerk-off having a party or trying to impress his girlfriend—well, they'd wait to check it out until they got the call saying the jerk had blown his hand off.

"Ten more seconds," the skinhead announced.

It was surreal. The sun was fully up and the sky was a brilliant shade of blue. It was a beautiful Florida day, filled with promise and an ocean breeze. It was the kind of day that usually made Ric feel glad to be alive.

The C4 exploded with a roar, sending a column of water shooting up into the air. Junior cheered as Ric found himself praying. Mother of God, if he died before he could save Annie, if Junior found her and brought her out here . . .

The water settled quickly back into its usual chop, the wake from the explosion rolling out and gently rocking the yacht. It might've been Ric's imagination, but it seemed as if there was a pink tinge on the surface.

If there was, it faded quickly, even as Donny turned the yacht and took them straight through it.

Jesus help him, but Ric found himself praying that Annie would already be dead before Junior strapped her into that C4 suit.

Fridge and the skinny dude were getting a verbal ass-kicking by the thug called Foley—a fact that made Robin glad, despite his ongoing urge to throw up. Jesus, he was sick. His hands were shaking and he'd already yuked twice in the trunk of the car—which couldn't have been much fun for Annie.

"Fucking A, I'm pissed," he could hear Foley say to his underlings. "Go back to the hotel and clean it up."

Robin and Annie had finally been dragged out of the car trunk and tossed belowdeck on a deep-sea fishing boat that was docked along what looked like a deserted stretch of one of Sarasota's many canals.

Shouting for help was an option that was unlikely to do much more than get them both soundly smacked around again. Besides, since Foley himself wasn't bothering to keep his voice down, Robin was certain there was no one around to hear them.

"Make sure he's dead," Foley reprimanded the two men who'd taken Robin and Annie from the hotel. They were, no doubt, discussing Martell.

"He was definitely dead," Refrigerator insisted.

"A shot to the chest is not a double pop to the head," Foley countered.

And wasn't that a macabre rule to live by, along with *An apple a day keeps the doctor away*. "Go back and make sure."

Skinny mumbled something too quiet for Robin to hear as Annie gently touched Robin's shoulder. "Here," she said, handing him a damp cloth.

"Thanks." He wiped his face as, up on the dock, Foley told Skinny and Fridge that he'd take care of them—them being Annie and Robin.

"Call me when it's handled," Foley ordered. "Junior'll want to know."

After tossing them down the companionway and kicking them into this stateroom, Foley had locked the door behind them. It wasn't one of those flimsy airplane bathroom doors that Robin had seen on some boats. This one was solid, with a substantial lock.

The good news was that they had the run of the room. Annie had already begun to explore while Robin had decided to keep from barfing again by going into a fetal position where he'd landed. "I'm sorry," he told her. Of all the lousy times to get the flu.

"Are you okay?" she asked, concern in her eyes.

"I'm pretty sick," he admitted.

Outside, on the dock, Foley was speaking again. "It's me." He was, no doubt, making a phone call. "I got the cargo—both of 'em."

Foley paused, and then laughed as Robin looked around. The cabin they were in was big enough to store a stack of suitcases and several large coolers, and still have enough space—several times over—for him to lie on the floor. There were narrow beds and cushion-covered benches around the sides of the room. They were built in, along with an array of cabinets and cupboards that made efficient use of the rest of the wall space.

"There's a bathroom over here, if you need it," Annie told Robin.

"Yeah," Foley said into his phone. "It's going to take me about forty minutes to reach the rendezvous point. Best go ahead and take care of the cargo you already have. I'll take care of mine."

He was talking to Junior—Robin knew this with a cold sense of dread that was reflected in Annie's horrified eyes. Dear God, if they were right, and Foley *was* talking to Junior, then the cargo to which he was referring had to be Jules and Ric.

"No!" Robin shouted. "You tell him to keep them safe!" but Foley surely didn't hear him over the roar of the boat's motor as it started.

Martell was dead.

Except he'd always believed that death would not hurt, that death would bring him to a beautiful, peaceful place, where gorgeous naked angels would sing him all of his favorite Motown hits.

Wherever he was now, no one was singing him shit and the beauty factor was about a negative billion. It was cold and damp and dark and hard and dirty, and every breath he took hurt like hell.

But since he didn't believe in hell, there could only be one solution to this puzzle.

He wasn't dead yet.

He reached for his phone, but of course it wasn't in his pocket. If *he'd* gone over to the dark side of the force and decided to shoot someone and leave them to die, he wouldn't let them keep their cell phone, either, just in case they roused before they kicked.

So Martell bent his legs, pulling his feet up to his butt, and he pushed himself, sliding on his back along the concrete, through the puddle of blood he'd already lost. Damn, there was a lot of it, and damn, just moving a little hurt enough to make him scream.

Maybe he'd been wrong all those years, and hell really did exist.

Still, he pulled his legs back up, weeping from the effort and the pain, and he did it again, following the arrow that hung from the concrete ceiling, beneath the words that meant even more to him right now than *life everlasting in heaven.*

ELEVATOR TO HOTEL MAIN LOBBY.

Annie didn't know what else to do, except keep going.

She'd heard the same words Robin had, and she knew that when Foley used the phrase *take care of them,* he didn't mean pulling an ottoman up to the sofa for their feet, and feeding them chocolates.

He was going to kill them both.

She knew, too, that if Junior really was with Ric and Jules, there was a good chance that they already were as dead as Martell—whom they'd left lying in a pool of blood.

But sitting here, defeated and broken, trying to figure out how she would survive in a world without Ric's quicksilver smile . . .

It was just not her style.

And wouldn't *she* feel stupid if Foley unlocked the door, ready to drag them up onto the deck to kill them—without having discovered if one of the cabinets in the room or one of those suitcases in the corner held a cache of automatic rifles and ammo?

Or a cell phone. A cell phone would be really nice.

"Help me," she told Robin as she opened the cabinets and found a fully outfitted wet bar, a stash of orange life preservers and foul-weather clothes, a collection of bikinis of all shapes and sizes—mostly tiny—and various types of fishing gear.

He saw what she was doing, and dragged himself over to the suitcases. Apparently they were unlocked, and he pulled the top one onto the floor and unzipped it. "What the hell . . . ?"

Annie came over to look.

"This is C4." Robin looked up at her. "There's enough here to . . ." He shook his head, his eyes rimmed with red. "Shit, I don't know. Blow up Florida? I've never seen this much before."

"C4, the explosive?" she asked. It looked like blocks of whitish-gray putty, like huge chunks of that sticky stuff she'd used to put posters up on the wall of her college dorm room. "Are you sure?"

"Very," he said. "I played a Navy SEAL in *Riptide* and there's a scene where I build a bomb. Most of it ended up cut out of the movie because it read as a little too 'how-to manual.' When we filmed the sequence, I used actual C4. Just like this."

"Are you serious?" They had him working with real explosives?

"It's stable," Robin told her. "Believe me, the studio wouldn't have let me touch it if it was dangerous. The blow-a-thumb-off part is the blasting cap, which . . . wow . . . Careful—that's what you've got in there."

Annie had unzipped another of the suitcases to reveal sets of metal boxes—the blasting caps, eek—and coils of gray-green wire.

"That's something called time fuse." Robin pointed to the coils. "Holy shit, we've got everything we need to blow this boat to hell."

Provided they knew how to hook it all together. Most people wouldn't have a clue—which was why Foley had so casually locked them in here with all this stuff. But most people hadn't played a Navy SEAL in their latest movie.

Still . . . A movie wasn't the same as real life.

"You really could do it?" Annie asked Robin now. "Make a bomb? One that works?"

"I don't think you can call it a bomb if it doesn't work," he pointed out. "But yeah. I mean, I've never used real blasting caps, but . . . Yeah. I could do it."

So, great. They could kill Foley by blowing up the boat. Of course, being locked belowdeck meant they'd die, too. It was not quite the plan Annie had hoped to come up with.

"I'll need a knife to cut the time fuse," Robin continued. "And we'll need matches." He laughed derisively. "*And* massive doses of Tylenol to bring this fever down. My hands are shaking. This is going to be hard to do."

He honestly believed he had the flu.

"Blowing ourselves up seems like it should go, oh, say, last on our list of options," Annie told him. She was still hoping to find an AK-47. She opened one of the coolers and . . . Dear God. "Um, Robin, did your character in *Riptide* by any chance know a *lot* about bombs?"

The thing at the bottom of this cooler looked an awful lot like a makeshift bomb on some kind of a timer. It hadn't been turned on—the LEDs were unlit and weren't counting down, thank God—but it still managed to look dangerous with all the wires and jerry-rigged parts.

"Who would put a bomb in a cooler?" Robin asked as he came to look at it. "You don't think . . . ?" He looked up at her.

Annie knew what he was thinking—she'd already gotten there herself. "A *cooler* nuke?" It sounded so unlikely that it just might be possible. But this thing looked as if it had been made by someone's insane uncle Bob in the basement of his soon-to-be foreclosed-upon house. "Aren't most small nukes made with parts stolen from the former USSR?"

Except there it was, down toward the bottom of the thing, beneath the snarl of wires: a metal piece that had Cyrillic writing.

"It looks . . . awfully amateur for a nuke," Robin said. "But my experience comes purely from watching James Bond movies. I probably wouldn't be able to recognize a real assassin with a blade-edged bowler hat, either."

Annie laughed, despite the knot in her stomach, despite Martell's brutal murder, despite her fear for Ric's safety, despite her fear of her own potentially impending and surely painful death.

Robin was smiling, too, but his smile was not one of humor. It was tight and grim and it matched the almost unholy spark of light in his eyes.

"Whatever it is, let's not let these motherfuckers use it," Robin said. "Help me rig this C4 to blow. Find me some matches. We don't need a knife. We'll just use the shortest coil of cord." He unwound one of the coils of what he'd called time fuse. "This'll do it. It's shorter than I thought. We'll light it when we hear Foley coming below. It'll give us lots of time—around ten minutes for a piece this long—figure between thirty and forty seconds a foot. We let him drag us up on deck, where we bash his head in, grab a life preserver, jump overboard, and swim like hell. You can swim, can't you?"

Annie nodded.

"Good," Robin said. "We better work fast. The boat's moving slowly, which means we're probably still either in the canal or the harbor. As soon as we reach open water, Foley's going to put the pedal to the metal. And when we're out of sight of land, he's going to come below, and *take care* of us." His eyes were grim. "Let's be ready for him."

When Junior's cell phone rang, Ric glanced at Jules, who was on the same page.

This was not good. He, too, had picked up all the signals that Junior was killing time, waiting for something to happen—like a phone call telling him that Robin and Annie had been contained.

"Here we go," Ric murmured as Junior, clearly pleased about something, hung up his phone.

"Fallback's the galley," Jules told him, his voice low. They couldn't have been in a better position for that. They were standing a few long strides from the half flight of stairs down. Junior and his men were all closer to the back of the boat—the stern.

And sure enough, "Okay, boys," Junior said, and his men all drew their weapons. "Surprise," he told Jules and Ric as five gun barrels were pointed at them.

"Yeah," Jules said, intentionally sounding bored. "Not really."

If they could get their hands on even just one of those handguns, they could hold Junior and his men off indefinitely, from the safety of that galley.

"How's this for a surprise, then?" Junior said. "You remember Foley, don't you, Ric? He's got your Amazon of a girlfriend." He looked at Jules. "And your . . . dick-loving faggot of a boyfriend."

"Accurate," Jules said, putting his hand on Ric's arm to keep him from going off, "but not quite politically correct." His own heart was in his throat. It was all he could do to keep talking, but he knew if he didn't, he and Ric were going to be very dead very soon. And then there'd be no helping Robin and Annie.

"You make me sick," Junior said. "Pretending to want to make a sex tape and—"

"You know all about pretending, don't you, Gordie?" Jules interrupted. "Robin told me you tried to get him to give you head in the bathroom during your father's party. You are going to *love* prison, bro."

Ric was looking at Jules as if he'd lost his mind. But sometimes jumping on homophobic buttons worked. Especially if the homophobe was a psychopath.

Jules's goal here was to get Junior angry, and sure enough, the man was frothing now with outrage. So he pushed him even harder, this time in a different direction. "If you expect us to believe you've got Robin and Annie just because you say so, then you're even dumber than I thought. If you want to negotiate, I'm going to need proof of life, so you better get back on that phone to your bitch, Foley, and tell him to keep Robin and Annie alive."

"Negotiate?" Junior was beyond pissed. "You're in no fucking position to make demands. You have some giant balls."

Jules shook his head. "There you go again. You know, for a so-called straight guy, you're much too interested in what's in my pants."

"All right. That's it." Junior had had enough. "You know what, asshole? I was going to kill you fast, but now I'm not."

As Robin would say, *score*.

Junior kept ranting. "I'm going to make you watch your friends die, starting with the faggot, and then the double-wide, and then the spic. And then it'll just be you, you disgusting piece of shit, in the water, praying you drown faster—knowing you're about to be blown apart." He turned to the skinhead. "Tie them up."

The skinhead approached. "Get on the deck, hands on your head."

Jules looked at Ric, who was looking back at him. It was go time. As soon as he got close enough . . . And they couldn't ask for a better setup. Skinhead was between them and the rest of the gunmen. If any of the others tried to shoot Jules or Ric, they'd risk hitting their friend.

But the way the skinhead was waving his weapon around was a bullet wound waiting to happen. It was unlikely Jules and Ric were going to be able to do this without one of them getting shot.

Ric was proving himself to be the best partner Jules had had since Alyssa Locke left the FBI, because once again, he was following Jules's exact line of thought.

"It'll be me," he told Jules, meaning he should be the one to put himself in front of that gun barrel. "You're a better shot. We need you in one piece."

"Shut the fuck up and get on the deck!" Skinhead got louder.

And closer.

"Now!" Ric shouted, leading the charge, and Jules heard the skinhead's handgun go off.

"I totally get why Jules loves you," Annie told Robin as she went to the cabinets she'd rifled through earlier, no doubt to search for matches. "You're not only funny—you're also smart."

"Cute, too," Robin said as he tried to will his hands to stop shaking. So far, no go. "Don't forget cute. And hot. The *L.A. Times* called me a contender for *People* magazine's Sexiest Man of the Year." He looked up because it sounded as if she were pouring liquid into a glass.

It sounded like that, because she was. She was holding a bottle of Johnny Walker and a glass, which she now offered to him.

"What the fuck?" Robin couldn't believe her.

"You don't have the flu," Annie told him quietly. "You're sick because you're detoxing."

"Get that away from me!"

But she didn't. She came closer. "You're going through alcohol withdrawal, and you know it. If you want steady hands, if you want to be able to swim to shore, you're going to need a drink first."

"It is, too, the flu," he insisted, but his heart was sinking and he knew she was right. How many times had his mother promised to stop drinking, only to lie ill and shaking on the couch? Her mysterious illness had always vanished, though, as soon as she'd given in and poured herself a tall one.

And Jesus, he wanted that drink Annie was offering him almost as much as he wanted to keep breathing. "I promised Jules," he said.

Annie nodded. "I know," she told him, sympathy in her eyes. "I also know he'll understand. Robin, if we get through this . . ." She stopped and corrected herself. "*When* we get through this, you're going to need to detox someplace where you'll have medical supervision. Until then . . . If you don't drink this . . . One out of four people have seizures during alcohol withdrawal. If you have a seizure when we're in the water . . . I'm sorry, but I'm not a strong enough swimmer to keep us both afloat."

"How do you know that?" Robin asked. "One of out four?" She'd said something like that before, back at the hotel, but it still sounded like total bullshit. She had to be making it up.

"It's true." Annie sat down next to him. "When I was in college, I had this plan to save my father. I did all this research and . . . See, he was ready to admit that he might have a problem, but he kept saying he wanted to handle it himself. I tried to talk him into going into a program—because of those health risks. Of course, I shouldn't have worried—he never actually quit. But I'll always remember that. It *is* one in four, Robin. Do you really want to gamble with those odds?"

His lips were dry and he moistened them with his tongue. "If I drink this," he said, "and I'm still sick . . ."

"Then you *have* got the flu." It was obvious that Annie didn't believe that for a half a second.

Robin held out his hand for the glass. God damn, but it felt as if he were betraying Jules. His hand was shaking so much, Annie had to help him bring the damn thing to his lips. And then the scotch burned and then warmed and Jesus, it tasted so simultaneously awful and good . . . He drained the glass, then held it out to her. "More."

Annie hesitated.

"I need more," he told her.

"That's probably not a good idea. If you're drunk you're not going to be able to swim to shore, either."

"I don't give a damn." He took the bottle from her, and drank straight from it, using both hands to steady it.

"Robin." She was getting pissed. "Stop."

"I don't want to live without him." Robin was crying now, tears just streaming down his face, because he could feel the scotch in his fingers, in his feet, in his blood. And it was true. He was a fucking alcoholic.

But it didn't matter, because here in this vague place between brain-scramblingly, detoxingly sober and completely skunked, he knew that Jules—his beautiful, amazing Jules—was probably already dead. "*That* should be our plan," he said. "We'll light the fuse and go on deck and I'll grab Foley while you go overboard and get to shore. I can't swim sick and I sure as hell can't swim drunk—you're right about that . . ."

"Stop," Annie said again. "We're both going. We're sticking together." She was crying now, too. Great, he was emotionally contagious. "I refuse to accept the fact that Ric is dead. I *will* not accept that possibility. He's alive, and Jules is alive, too. We are going to see them again. We need to believe that."

Robin let her take the bottle from him. "Even though it's a lie?" he asked.

"Yeah." She nodded, wiping her tears from her eyes. There wasn't room there for both her grief and her determination. "Lie to me, Robin. Lie *for* me if you won't do it for yourself. You're an actor. I need you to act."

She was quite possibly the most magnificent woman Robin had ever met—brave and strong and smart and beautiful. In a lot of ways, she reminded him of his sister, Jane, whom he'd always adored. Martell had been right. If Robin were straight, he would've fallen for her, hard.

Maybe it was that second helping of scotch finally kicking in, numbing him to the point of acceptance. Whatever it was, Robin couldn't bear to disappoint her. So he nodded. "All right."

And he got to work with fingers that could have threaded a needle on the very first try.

CHAPTER
TWENTY-FOUR

He was hit.

It shouldn't have been a surprise. Ric had been expecting it, but it still knocked him down and took him into another dimension, where everything moved in fits and starts.

It didn't hurt. He wasn't sure where he'd been hit, but he saw the blood. It was on his jeans and his jacket—it was everywhere, and he knew from experience that the lack of pain was only temporary. In a matter of seconds, he was going to be screaming.

He hit the deck as he wrenched the skinhead's weapon from his hand, as he turned it on the man and fired. Once. Twice.

Skinhead fell on top of him, solid and unmoving. Ric felt Jules grab him and drag him, but as they moved he still felt that deadweight, bumping against him, and he realized, Christ, Jules was using the skinhead's body as a shield.

It was Junior's shaved-headed friend that Ric had just killed—that kid who'd been in the limo with Junior on the night that Ric had saved his life.

Ric had saved Junior's life.

And now, because of that, Annie was going to die.

Fueled by fury, he finally snapped back to here and now—just in time to realize that Jules had pulled him to safety. They were already in the galley, hunkered down. Jules had possession of both that gun and a switchblade knife, and he was pulling extra clips of ammunition and everything else he could find from the dead kid's pockets. A cigarette lighter and a pack of smokes. A roll of twenty-dollar bills. Two vials of crack cocaine.

"Cell phone?" Ric asked.

Jules shook his head. "No luck. How bad is it?" He sat on the floor beside Ric, their shoulders against the restaurant-size oven. Wedged there between the refrigerator and bank of below-counter cabinets that included a heavy-duty dishwasher, they had a clear shot—literally—at all entrances and exits from the room—including the door that led down to the lower-level pantry.

"I don't know," Ric admitted. "I don't even know where I'm hit."

"Right leg," Jules told him without even looking. His full attention was given to watching for another attack, listening for sounds that would let him know from which direction it was coming.

Ric could hear Junior screaming at his men, from wherever they'd run to safety.

"We get any of the others?" Ric asked.

Jules's response was terse. "No."

"Sorry."

"You're kidding, right?" Jules asked. "You did great."

In Ric's opinion, great would've been Junior and all five of his henchmen lined up on the deck, ready for body bags.

As it was, they were trapped here, indefinitely.

One thing was in their favor, though. Someone had closed the door leading from the galley to the game room, as well as the door leading up to the deck-level dining room.

Someone? No doubt it had been Jules—while Ric was off in la-la land.

"Now what?" Ric asked.

"We stall," Jules told him. "You need me to help you stop the bleeding?"

"No," Ric said. "I'm, uh, just . . . you know . . ." Moving a little slowly on account of having been shot.

And oh yeah, he'd definitely been hit in his upper thigh. The wound wasn't that bad as far as entry and exit went. The bullet seemed to have missed both the major arteries and the bone, which was good.

But oh. Christ. *Now* it hurt.

Jules took off his T-shirt so that Ric could use it to stanch the flow of blood.

"Proof of life, Junior," Jules shouted as Ric pressed the shirt to the top of his leg. He was going to need something else for the exit wound. He started opening drawers, hoping for a stack of rags or . . . Dish towels. He grabbed two.

"I want proof that Robin and Annie are still alive," Jules continued. "You get me proof of life—only then will we negotiate. Do you hear me?"

Negotiation was a classic stall tactic.

"Fuck you!" Junior shouted back. "I'm calling Foley and telling him to kill them."

Ric was ripping Jules's T-shirt into a longer strip of fabric to tie the towels in place, but now he froze. Was this going to backfire? He looked at Jules.

"We don't know that Foley really has them," Jules reminded him, then shouted back to Junior: "You do that, and we will sit right here until my team discovers I'm missing. You got mere hours, *dude*. They *will* come looking and they *will* find me. You want to kill me? You're going to have to do it soon. You want me to surrender? Give me proof that Robin and Annie are alive and that you're going to keep them safe."

Annie couldn't find any matches.

She'd checked everywhere and then she'd checked again.

She'd searched the pockets of all of the raincoats and slickers hanging in the stateroom's cabinets. She'd emptied everything out of every bench compartment. She'd searched the bar and the bathroom more than twice.

To no avail.

Robin had worked his magic on the suitcase filled with C4, adding a blasting cap and that long length of time fuse.

"This stuff works underwater," he told her as he worked. "They call it underwater demolition. It's pretty amazing—but what's *really* amazing is how into it some of the SEALs are. Not so much Cosmo"—Robin's brother-in-law was a SEAL—"but the others . . . There's a SEAL named Izzy. I swear, he likes blowing things up better than sex."

Robin was talkative to start with, but the Johnny Walker had loosened his tongue even more than usual.

As he piled the suitcases back into a stack, leaving the det cord dangling out from the one with the largest amount of explosives, he talked about Jules.

"It's more than just sex," Robin told Annie, "although the sex is . . . We could have sex 24/7 and it still wouldn't be enough."

That sounded pretty familiar.

"And yet . . . at the same time, just being in the same room with him is enough." He tucked the length of fuse around the edge of the room. "You're not supposed to coil it on top of itself," he explained, then went right back to Jules. "You know what I love? I love just sitting next to him. Just talking to him. When our eyes meet, and I know we're both thinking the same thing or, I don't know, laughing at the same stupid joke, or even just enjoying the same instant of time . . . It's . . . unlike anything I've ever felt before."

He poured himself another drink.

"You sure you want that?" Annie asked.

"Oh, yeah," he said. "I'm sure. You know, I can picture Jules smiling at me like that, the same way, when we're both, like, eighty years old."

He swayed and it wasn't just the movement of the boat beneath his feet making him unsteady. Annie took the glass away from his mouth and poured the rest of it down the bathroom sink. "Help me look for matches, okay?"

"He was the love of my life, you know," Robin confessed as he obediently started searching through the bench storage area, even though she'd already been through it. Maybe he'd find something she'd missed. "And it was mutual. I know that he loved me. I read this e-mail that he wrote to one of his friends, and . . . I probably shouldn't have read it, but . . . I'm glad I did now, because I know. It really helps to know."

In a way, Annie could completely relate. Ric had told her he'd loved her, so she, too, knew.

But she'd been too much of a coward to admit that she'd loved him — and what was she doing, thinking in the past tense? She *was* going to see Ric again, and when she did, she was going to tell him that she was in love with him, too. Present tense. Simple as that.

"At first, I was all freaked out," Robin continued, "because I found out in this e-mail that Jules was in line for a promotion. And I started thinking I should walk away, you know, for his sake? But I've been thinking more about it and, if we get through this . . ." He looked over at her. "*When* we get through this. I'm going to grab hold of him and I am never going to let go. And I'm going to do it for *his* sake. Because finding someone who loves you as much as you love them? It's a gift. It's a . . . a . . . motherfucking miracle, Annie."

"Yeah," she said. "I do know." Although she probably would have used a different adjective.

"Most of the time it's one-sided," Robin told her earnestly. "Like it was with Jules and Ben." Last night, Robin had told her about Ben, Jules's Marine friend who'd died in Iraq. "And with Jules and Adam. And with me and Adam."

"Who's Adam?" Annie asked.

"We kind of share an ex," Robin told her. "Not at the same time," he quickly added. "That's not . . . Just . . . Don't ask. It's . . . a long, ugly story.

In a nutshell, I screwed up because I was too much of a coward to realize what I'd found. With Jules, I mean."

"This was back when those pictures were taken?" Annie asked. "The ones on the Internet?"

Robin nodded. "My point," he said, "is that finding someone who loves you, too, the same way you love them? It's a one-in-a-million thing. But I've seen it happen—it's real. My sister, Janey, and her husband, Cosmo . . . They are so connected, so solid . . . I'm telling you, it's not something you can just throw away, especially not just because you're a little scared."

"What if you're a lot scared?" Annie asked.

"Tough shit," Robin said. "Even if you're a lot scared, you just have to . . . grow a pair. You have to take the risk and to tell yourself that you're willing to do whatever it takes both to make it work and to make it last. Because it's worth it. I mean, sure, okay, it might *not* work out. Life has no guarantees. You might try your best and still crash and burn, but what if it *does* work? Then you get a lifetime with someone who loves you as much as you love them . . ." He stopped himself, listening. "What's that?"

It was more like, *what* wasn't *that?* "Foley killed the engine," Annie realized.

Sure enough, he was coming downstairs.

"Matches?" Annie asked.

Robin shook his head, as empty-handed as she was.

And Foley unlocked the door.

Pulling himself up to push the elevator call button took everything out of him.

It was all Martell could do, when the door finally opened, to stick a foot in to keep it from closing and disappearing again.

It was harder to push himself forward than back, but he got down to work, inching his way into the elevator.

He was leaving a trail of blood, so that if someone came looking for him, they'd find him in about four seconds. But even that thought wasn't enough to make him move any faster. Apparently, he was already going at his top speed.

When the door tried to close on his shoulder, the pain was so intense, he nearly blacked out. Maybe he did. God knows how long he lay there, with the elevator buzzing angrily at him for holding the damn door too damn long.

Getting angry was good. It was sheer anger that took him those last few inches, so the door could finally close.

Martell didn't have the strength to push any buttons, but the elevator moved, going up, thank you, Lord Jesus.

The door opened with a ding and Martell found himself looking up into the stunned faces of a woman and a little boy. They both started to scream.

It was nice that they did it for him, because he had nothing left.

Still, he knew he couldn't quit. Not yet. He had to tell them—tell someone—that Robin and Annie had been taken. ·

But he couldn't remember the FBI agent's name. He couldn't remember and . . .

Martell fought the darkness, but it was too much.

He had nothing left. Nothing.

And the darkness won.

Foley was on the phone.

As the door opened and Robin moved to stand in front of Annie, he heard Foley say, "You're lucky. The water's been choppy, so I stayed up on deck." He paused. "Yeah, I get fucking seasick, but you're a fucking idiot. And now *they* want proof of life. Just waste 'em. How hard could it be to just plug the sons of bitches?"

Another pause, during which time Robin looked at Annie.

Hope made her almost glow. "They're alive," she told him.

He nodded. "Yeah." How hard could it be to plug Jules and Ric? Pretty hard, apparently. He should have had faith. He shouldn't have had that last drink. Could he swim like this? He honestly didn't know.

"Jesus Christ," Foley said in exasperation. "All right. Just . . . give me a few minutes." He hung up his cell phone and drew his gun. "Up on deck," he ordered them.

They hadn't lit the fuse. With no matches in the stateroom, that part of the plan had to be aborted.

But apparently Annie wasn't ready to give up on anything, because as Robin followed her out of the stateroom and through the tiny galley to the companionway stairs, he saw her reach out and take a cigarette lighter from the countertop.

She palmed it as she pretended to lose her balance, as she used the counter to steady herself.

Robin could feel Foley right behind him, and he braced himself for the man's retaliation. But it never came. He hadn't seen her theft.

"Move it faster," Foley said as Annie slipped the lighter into the front pocket of her jeans.

Part two of their plan was to grab something and knock him over the head. It was ridiculous—the idea of their getting the jump on someone like Foley, even though it was two to one.

But Foley was seasick—fucking seasick was how he'd described it.

Maybe they actually had a chance.

Junior was stalling.

Jules had good ears, and a few minutes ago he'd heard what sounded like Junior, sotto voce, ordering one of his men to call Foley. *Make sure he keeps Robin and Annie alive.*

Of course, it was possible that Junior had intended for Jules to over-hear him. It was possible that Foley didn't have Robin and Annie—that they were still safely back at the hotel.

Junior's voice was plaintive as he shouted to Jules now. "How the fuck am I going to give you proof of life?"

Jules shouted back to Junior: "Call Foley, have him put Robin and Annie on the line, then toss your phone in here so we can talk to them."

"I'm not going to give you my phone," Junior said. "What? Do you think I'm a moron?"

Ric glanced at Jules. "Nice try."

Ric was in serious pain, and he'd lost quite a bit of blood, but he looked less shocky and more with it to Jules, as every moment passed. No doubt about it, he was using sheer will to keep himself alert and focused.

"No one's coming to help you," Junior shouted. "I know you think they are, but they're not. They're all heading for the Everglades, following a UPS truck. We found your tracking device and mailed Alvarado's alleged ex to Belle Glade—same-day delivery."

Okay, so that wasn't the best news, but again, it was no surprise. Jules made a mental note to make sure tech support knew that their untrackable tracking device had already been compromised by a two-bit Florida criminal.

"You may have found *that* one," Jules called back, "but you didn't find the long-range wire I'm wearing. This conversation that we're having? It's being monitored, right now, by the FBI. It's just a matter of time before a wall of helicopters comes over that horizon."

Junior laughed. "You're full of shit. If you were wearing a wire, they'd be here by now. No one's coming," he said again. "And we can sit here for as long as you can."

But it was possible, because he'd given the order for that call to Foley, that Junior was bluffing, too.

Just jumping overboard wasn't an option.

Unless Annie could somehow stun Foley before they went over the side, she and Robin didn't stand a chance against him in the water.

Foley had a gun, and like his co-workers who'd shot Martell, he wasn't afraid to use it.

Annie had never been seasick, but her sister-in-law had. Bruce had booked his bride a surprise cruise for their honeymoon, and Val had spent most of the trip in bed, and not in the good way. It had been years, but Val still talked about it as being *the* most awful week of her life. She was so self-absorbed, she never noticed how quiet Bruce got whenever she brought it up.

And okay, yeah, so Bruce and Val weren't exactly role models in terms of the allegedly perfect relationship Robin had been talking about just before Foley came to the door. In fact, Annie had had exactly zero role models when it came to good relationships.

But it was definitely time to stop thinking about that, to focus on the here and now.

Her heart was pounding so hard, it seemed strange that Robin and Foley didn't comment on the noise. Please God, let this work . . .

The only thing on deck to grab and swing was a pole with a hook on the end that looked as if it might've been used to pull the boat in to a dock, or maybe help with the deep-sea fishing in some mysterious way.

There were no other obvious choices—a seat cushion, a life ring—so Annie again pretended to lose her balance, going down on her knees with a thud, right onto the deck. As she waited for Robin and then Foley to climb up the stairs, her fingers closed around the cool metal of the pole.

And then Robin was past her, and Foley grabbed her by the arm to pull her up, and it was time to fight back.

She swung the pole with all of her strength, bringing it up, as hard as she could, between Foley's legs.

The pole was ridiculously light—it must've been aluminum—and it bent from the force of the blow.

Still, her aim was true, and Foley went down, shouting in pain. He dropped his gun, and although it slid across the deck, it slid away from both Annie and Robin.

Seasick or not, even with crushed testicles, Foley was a formidable opponent. He used one leg to kick Annie, hard, into the bulkhead next to the stairs, even as he grabbed Robin, who'd immediately jumped into the fray.

Robin was no lightweight, and in that moment, as Annie struggled to pull air back into her lungs so she could go to his aid, as she saw Robin's knee connect again with Foley's groin, Foley picked him up and threw him in the opposite direction from which his gun had gone.

"Annie!" Robin cried, but then his head hit the edge of the boat with a sickening crunch, and the weight of his body took him over the side.

"Robin!" She launched herself after him, but Foley was there, blocking her. She bumped him and he pushed her back.

He laughed as he saw her gaze flicker over to his gun, still lying there on the deck. Too far away to go for. Damn it. *Damn* it.

"Whatcha gonna hit me with now?" Foley asked.

"Robin!" she called again, her eyes never leaving Foley's.

But Robin didn't answer.

He didn't so much as splash.

"What's taking so long?" Ric couldn't stay silent another moment. They had to do something, instead of just sitting in the galley, waiting, in siege mode. It was driving him mad.

It was hot as hell in here, too, which wasn't helping. Junior had turned off the air-conditioning, presumably to make them as uncomfortable as possible.

"The longer it takes," Jules said, "the more I'm convinced that Robin and Annie are safe." He took a sip from one of the bottles of water he'd found in the refrigerator. It had been sealed, so it was safe to drink. "It'll be hard for Junior to give us proof of life if Foley doesn't really have them."

Jules was as calm and controlled as he would've been had they been sitting on a park bench, taking a break from a Sunday-afternoon stroll.

"Or if Foley's already killed them," Ric offered.

Jules shook his head. "It doesn't help to think that way. I know you want to take Junior down. I know you want to go on the offensive, but . . ." He shook his head. "Let's wait a bit longer before we get ourselves killed, okay? I've got a lot to live for."

"I thought you were going to walk away from Robin," Ric said.

"Yeah," Jules agreed, "but I've got about three months' worth of hope that he really will stop drinking. That's ninety days, and call me selfish, but I want every one of them."

Ric glanced at him. "You're even optimistic when you're pessimistic."

They sat in silence for a moment, then Jules said, "I'm sorry for . . . what I did."

"For being optimistic?"

"For disrespecting you. This morning," Jules explained. "I hate that I did that, and I wish I could take a do-over and . . . do it differently."

"Sometimes," Ric told the other man, "I speak Spanish just to piss people off. So don't sweat it, man. It's one of your weapons—you worked it with Junior. We all just . . . use what we've got."

"I know," Jules said, "but I shouldn't have used it against you."

"So now that you know me a little better," Ric said with a shrug, "you won't make that mistake again."

This time he broke the silence they fell into. "It doesn't bother you?" Ric continued. "The way Junior was talking to you before? Calling you and Robin . . . those names?"

Jules shrugged this time. "I've got a pretty thick skin." But then he sighed. "Robin doesn't, though. If he ever does come out, that's going to be one of the hardest things for him—the name-calling." He glanced at Ric. "There's no way to protect him from that. I have entire arguments with myself about whether or not he should just stay in the closet for the rest of his life. And you know, I can win, taking either side, so . . . I don't know the right answer."

"Maybe you should let Robin decide what he wants to do," Ric said. He had to smile at his sage advice. All he'd ever wanted to do was protect Annie. And all he'd done was make mistake after mistake—by staying away from her, by making decisions for her, by making choices that he thought would be best for her.

It made him crazy—sitting here, thinking that she was in trouble. And yet her willingness to take risks, to put herself into danger, was one of the things that had made him fall in love with her.

"You know, when I first met Annie," Ric told Jules, "she was eleven years old, and she had her arm in a sling. Her father was a violent drunk, and she put herself between him and her mother."

Jules laughed. "Why doesn't that surprise me?"

"Robin hit his head," Annie told Foley. "We have to pull him back in, or he'll drown."

"It's up to you," Foley said. "You gonna cooperate?"

"I'm cooperating." Annie was frantic. How long could Robin go without breathing, before brain damage set in? Plus, she had no idea what the currents were like out here. If they didn't hurry, he might float away from the side of the boat.

"Lie down," Foley ordered. "On your stomach, hands on your head, face turned away."

As Annie obeyed, she heard him crossing the deck. It was all she could do to follow his instructions, to keep her head turned as he surely picked up his gun.

She then heard his feet as he went back across, and then, "Fuck," she heard Foley swear. *"Fuck."*

Oh God, please, no . . .

Annie got to her feet. She put her hands back on her head as she, too, went to look over the side.

Robin was gone.

But the water was choppy. It would be hard to see anyone floating out there, let alone someone unconscious.

"Get back down on the deck," Foley ordered her.

"Please," she begged him. "Let me go in after him. Maybe he's just below the surface."

"No way am I losing both of you," he said.

"Please," she said again.

"Move back," he ordered, shouting when she didn't move. "I said, move back and *sit down!*"

He pulled his gun, and it was only then that Annie finally did as she'd been told.

"She's always been able to talk me into doing the craziest shit," Ric admitted. "Like, this one time, she was convinced that this guy her mother was dating was married. He lived, I don't know, it was north and east of Orlando—about a three-hour trip from Sarasota. And there I am, driving her across the state to do surveillance on the son of a bitch. Of course, she was right. Her mother had the lousiest taste in men. It's no wonder she's jaded when it comes to relationships."

"Give her time," Jules said.

"Yeah," Ric said. He turned to look at Jules. "I don't know how much longer I can sit here like this."

Jules knew.

"If Junior can prove Foley's got Annie," Ric admitted, "I don't know what I'm going to do. I know you'd rather wait, but it's occurred to me that we might want to put a plan in place. I mean, I'm not sure I'm even going to be able to *think*, let alone — "

From out on the deck came the sound of Junior's cell phone ringing. Once. Twice.

And all of Jules's calm just dissolved. "Pick it up, Junior." He kept himself from shouting it, clenching his teeth around the words. It was important not to let Junior know just how rattled he was by the idea of Robin and Annie in Foley's hands.

Junior's phone rang a third time, and Jules turned to Ric. "How about we fucking kill them and take control of this ship?" he asked. "How's that for a plan? Unless you have something else in mind?"

"*Fucking kill them* works for me," Ric told him. "But I have an idea with, you know, a few more details. I don't know if you're going to like it, though."

"Try me," Jules said.

"It won't be the first time a movie star's body washes up on a beach," Foley said into his cell phone, "and it sure as hell won't be the last. It's not a problem we can't take care of."

He'd restarted the engine and the fishing boat was moving forward — away from the spot where Robin had gone overboard.

Annie sat on the deck and let herself cry. She didn't try to hide it, she just wept.

Let him think she was defeated. Let him think her fight was gone.

What was she going to hit him with now?

She was working on it.

Foley turned to look at her. "We still got the girl for that proof-of-life shit. A few words into the phone . . . Put it on the intercom, it'll go throughout the yacht. They'll hear it, wherever they're holed up."

Annie tried to hide her reaction to that news. Jules and Ric were holed up somewhere on Junior's yacht. They were safe. Alive . . .

"You think he might be dead?" Foley asked. "Okay, so that's not so good. The one you've been talking to isn't the . . . ?" He was not happy. "So we have the wrong leverage. That's just fucking great."

She was the wrong leverage. *You think he might be dead?* It wasn't hard for Annie to imagine what that meant. If she were the wrong leverage, Ric was the one that Junior thought might be dead.

Oh, God. If Ric were dead . . .

Foley turned away and lowered his voice, but Annie strained to hear him. "Okay, look. Your father's going to kill me because he loves that yacht, but here's what we're going to do. Get Geo and Pete to use the C4 you've got on board to, you know, do what C4 is supposed to do. I should be in sight of you within a few minutes. When we connect, you and the boys just . . . walk away. Just light the fuse and come onto the fishing boat with me."

Foley was talking about blowing up the yacht, where Ric and Jules were holed up . . .

"Jesus H. . . ." Foley was exasperated. "You really think it's worth a try? Like they're just going to surrender when they hear her voice? We don't even know if the boyfriend's alive." He sighed, clearly put out. "All right, all *right*. Let's just fucking do this."

Foley came over to her. Spoke to her. "When I hold out my phone, you will speak loudly and clearly so it picks you up . . ."

Some sort of intercom system switched on, and Ric stopped arguing with Jules about his plan—about who should be the one to go belowdeck to get the explosives.

It was stupid to argue, anyway. It was going to have to be the one of them who didn't have a T-shirt tied tightly around a bullet wound in his leg.

And that wasn't Ric.

It had freaked him out a little to see Jules's cool slip. It was now obvious that the man's careful control was just an act. He was as much on the verge of losing it as Ric was.

If Junior had Robin or Annie, if he so much as breathed on them wrong, Jules was going to be right beside Ric as he made the bastard bleed.

"Yeah, that's the right button," a voice that had to be Donny's echoed through the ship. "Push this one when you're done."

"Thanks." Junior was louder—he probably spoke more directly into the microphone. "Here comes your proof of life, assholes," he said.

There was feedback, then another male voice that could well have been Foley's. "You say your name, you say you're with me on a fishing boat, you say you're all right. You say anything else at all, and I will beat you within an inch of your life. Are we clear?"

Ric held his breath, listening harder. But there was nothing discernible in response, just the sound of someone crying. Whoever it was, it couldn't be Annie. He'd never heard her make that kind of pathetic, defeated noise in his entire life.

"Jesus H. Christ." Foley's voice came through the speakers. "Speak the fuck up."

Still there was nothing—until there was something loud, something that sounded like Foley shouting. "Hey!" It was cut off, though, midword.

Ric looked at Jules. What was that?

Junior's voice, over the intercom, broke the sudden silence. He was equally perplexed. "What the hell . . . ?"

Annie threw herself down the companionway, Foley's phone in her hand.

Ric had been right. Tears, along with various other fluids, really worked when it came to putting people off their guard.

As she'd hoped, Foley had assumed her spirit was crushed. When she'd cowered from his threatening words and mewed a pitiful, barely audible version of his request, he'd leaned over, putting himself off balance as he held his phone closer to her mouth.

Whereupon she'd snatched it from his hand and scrambled away.

But God, he was right behind her now. She dialed 911 as she threw herself into the stateroom where she and Robin had been held, but she didn't hear more than the phone ringing on the other end before Foley slapped it out of her hands. He grabbed her and threw her toward the cabinets that lined the wall.

She hit with her shoulder and back, turning to try to protect her head, then landing on the floor with a bone-jarring crash.

Foley'd gone after his phone, slamming it shut. He came toward her, now, and the look in his eyes was murderous.

"We lost the connection," Donny's voice said over the intercom.

"Get it back." Junior, too, still echoed through the ship.

"Let's do this now," Jules decided. "While they're distracted." He held out the sidearm that he'd taken from the skinhead, and Ric reluctantly took it.

"I can't shoot like you," Ric told him.

"I'm just looking for covering fire." Chances were that they weren't even going to need that. Jules moved the ammo closer to Ric and opened the switchblade knife, testing it with his finger. Yeah, ouch, it was plenty sharp. He snapped it shut.

Junior was probably up on the bridge with Donny. That left three men unaccounted for.

At least one was watching the stairs from the galley to the main deck. No, make that two—they were having a conversation out there. Jules couldn't make out their words, but he definitely heard the buzz of two different voices. Thanks for that intel, guys.

It meant there was only one man watching one of the three other ways out of the galley.

Although it was possible, from the amount of blood Ric had left on the deck, that Junior was going to assume he and Jules weren't going to budge from their cozy and protected position there. So maybe he wasn't watching any of the other exits at all.

Up on the bridge, Donny and Junior had finally realized their words were being broadcast throughout the yacht. It was like a bad comedy routine, ending only as they finally turned off the intercom.

Jules cracked open the door that led to the ladder access down to the food storage area below and listened.

Nothing. No movement. No breathing.

He looked at Ric and nodded. He was going.

He opened the door wider and stuck his head into the passageway—just a quick dip down and back. There was no one in the immediate area, so he swung himself down, feetfirst this time. He dropped as silently as humanly possible onto the metal of the deck below.

It was slightly cooler down there, thank you God.

The entire lower level was badly lit, but it was brighter out in the hall. Jules crept toward that light and . . . Shit.

One of Junior's men was down here. Jules could hear him moving about in that nasty little bomb-making room where those extra suits of explosives were stored.

Which was exactly where Jules wanted to go.

He froze, as a sudden noise echoed, but it was just the intercom clicking back on. And then Foley's voice came through a tinny-sounding speaker.

"We're going to try that again." The man's words were slightly distorted but comprehensible. "I'm here with the girl, and she's going to say her name into the phone, or she's going to get hit and then you'll know she's here because you'll hear her scream."

Annie shook her head at Foley.

She wasn't going to do it.

Even if he hit her, she wasn't going to make so much as a sound.

He was just going to kill her anyway. She knew that. As soon as she did as he asked, she was dead.

And she was damned if she was going to help Junior force Jules and Ric to surrender. She put her hand in her pocket, her fingers closing around the cigarette lighter she'd taken from the galley.

"Okay then." Foley set his phone down on top of one of the bench cushions. "I guess we're going to do this the hard way."

As Annie backed away from Foley, she tried to inch closer and closer to the end of the fuse that Robin had run, hidden, along the edge of the room.

"You gonna say it now?" Foley's voice was muffled as it came over the intercom.

It could've all been just a giant head game—Foley, alone in a room somewhere, kicking things over, making crashing noises to make it sound as if he were beating someone up.

He had the girl, he'd said. He'd made no mention at all of Robin—Jules tried not to think about that as he continued to move down the dimly lit passageway on the lower level of Junior's yacht.

"Is that enough?" Foley asked, but apparently it wasn't, because there were more thuds and crashes.

The door to the explosives workroom was still locked open. That was lucky. There was definitely someone in there—Jules could see his shadow moving.

The noises coming from the intercom masked any sounds that Jules might've made as he peeked around the edge of the open doorway.

Yes, one of Junior's so-called boys was there in the room, his back to Jules. It looked—sweet Jesus!—as if he were working to connect all of the suits of explosives together. And wasn't *that* the nifty plan. Blow the entire yacht. There was enough C4 here at least to put a huge hole in the hull.

But explosions were tricky things. It would be a risk for Junior, who liked having a guarantee there'd be no random DNA evidence floating around for investigators to find. And unless they brought the C4 up and tossed it into the galley . . . which, of course, was what they were probably going to do, as soon as they had another ride home.

Great.

So much for Jules's *we can sit here all day* threat.

"What?" Foley asked over the intercom. "Do I have break your arm to make you scream?"

Annie cried. Silently.

One of her eyes was swelling and her mouth was bleeding, cut from her own teeth. She was battered and bruised, but at least so far no ribs had been broken, thank God.

It had been years since she'd gone into the hospital with a rib-punctured lung, but she still remembered what that had felt like. She would do nearly anything to prevent a replay of that desperate, gasping, lack-of-air sensation.

Anything but risk Ric and Jules's lives.

Foley's last punch had made her head spin. She almost wished he'd hit her harder—and knocked her out. But her biggest regret was that Foley's last punch had taken her farther away from the end of that time fuse.

Annie now looked at Foley and shook her head.

"Look," he said. "I respect what you're trying to do, but . . ."

She just kept shaking her head.

"Last chance." He waited, just a few more seconds, then grabbed her left arm and twisted and . . .

Annie felt her wrist give, felt the bones snap, felt the scream ripped from her very throat.

"There," Foley said, his voice rough as he released her, as she fell back, cradling her arm against her chest, sobbing. "There's your fucking proof of life."

No. No, she was not going to let him win. She was not going to let Ric die. Not a chance.

So she shouted. As loudly as she could so the phone would pick her up, even from way across the stateroom. "Ric, I love you—don't let them kill us both. Robin's already dead, Foley killed him, and I'm dead, too. I'm bleeding to death," she lied. "I'm not going to make it—save yourselves!"

Anger and fear.

Ric's reaction to the sound of Annie's voice was sheer, blinding anger and soul-shredding fear.

She was alive, but Foley had hurt her. The echo of that piercing scream resounded inside his head, making his hands shake.

He nearly dropped the gun, but he forced himself to breathe. Keep breathing. Annie wasn't dead yet.

"She's lying." Foley's voice reverberated in the galley. "I roughed her up and broke her wrist—but she's not bleeding. And, uh, the, uh, movie star's in the other room, too drunk to speak coherently."

"I love you, Ric," Annie sobbed, and Ric felt his heart break. He'd wanted her to say it, but Christ, not like this. Her voice continued over what sounded like Donny and Junior shouting. He didn't pay attention to them, he focused only on her words. "I'm so sorry I didn't tell you before. Please—save yourself. Foley's the liar. I'm dead. Just like Robin. Foley threw him overboard and he drowned. Jules, I'm so sorry, but I couldn't save him and he's gone—"

Someone cut the connection—it was the intercom being switched off.

"Hey," Ric bellowed. "Bring her back! Put her back on! I want to hear her talking!"

But no one answered him and the intercom wasn't turned back on.

"Hey!" he shouted again, totally bullshit. As long as Annie was talking, he knew she was alive. "Put her back on, and I'll come out!"

He meant it. He'd somehow pushed himself to his feet and was on the verge of dragging himself over to the stairs to the main deck when he heard a sound. Someone was coming.

He turned, trying to hold the gun steady with hands that were numb. God only knew what Foley was doing to Annie right that moment . . .

"What the hell are you doing?" It was Jules. He was back, pushing the ladder door open. "Get down!"

Ric realized he was standing right in front of that window. He turned to look out at the deck—there was no one out there. "Junior!" he shouted again. "Put Annie back on, you son of a bitch!"

Jules flung what looked like a vest of explosives onto the floor ahead of himself, then climbed out. "Get down," he said again.

Christ, the FBI agent was covered with blood. It was mostly on his hands and his arms, but it was also streaked across his chest and face like gruesome war paint.

He was holding a gun, but he'd gone below armed only with a knife and . . . Jesus God, apparently, he'd used it.

Jules grabbed him and dragged him down to the deck. Ric's leg was on fire, and even more pain jolted through him at the rough treatment. But it provided a greatly needed reality check. He wasn't going to help Annie by charging out onto the deck half-cocked.

No, he had to wait until he was fully locked and loaded. He knew that and he made himself breathe. "Are you hurt?" he asked Jules.

"It's not my blood." Jules's eyes were as hard and cold as Ric had ever seen them. "One of the business-suits was down there. I took him out."

Permanently, apparently.

"Two down, four to go," Jules continued, reporting the information matter-of-factly, as if he were commenting on the day's lack of rain. "Purple Shirt, Business-Suit Number Two, Donny, and Junior."

"And Foley," Ric said. Who had Annie. Who'd already killed Robin. By drowning him. Except, there was something wrong with that picture, something that made Ric find that concept hard to believe.

"Yeah," Jules said. "Let's not forget Foley." He tucked the handgun into the back of his jeans, then stayed low as he rinsed his hands and arms in the kitchen sink. "I'm going to need my jacket back."

"No, you're not," Ric said. He raised his voice. "Junior! Hey!" Where the hell was the bastard?

"Yeah, I am." Jules started to pull on the explosives. It was one of Junior's sweatshirt creations, but the sleeves had been cut off—which made it less unwieldy.

"*I'm* the one going out there," Ric told the FBI agent.

"No." Jules didn't stop what he was doing. "Annie's still alive."

"I'm sorry about Robin," Ric said as he pulled himself closer to Jules. "You know I am, but it has to be me out there, man. It's got to be. You're the better shot."

Jules knew that was the truth. Yet still he hesitated.

Ric all but felt a vein pop in his head—Junior's silence was killing him. "Junior! Where the fuck are you? I want to hear Annie's voice again!"

But Junior didn't answer. It was possible he'd discovered the man that Jules had sliced and diced while he was down below, and had decided to stay somewhere protected—like that bridge. Which would totally screw up Ric and Jules's plan.

"Junior!" he shouted again.

Meanwhile, Jules was determined to self-destruct, wrapping some kind of grayish cord—the fuse—around his waist.

"You disconnected that, right?" Ric asked.

Jules looked up at him. "Yeah." For the first time since they'd met, Ric couldn't get an accurate read on whether or not Jules was telling him the truth.

"Come on, man," Ric pushed, his voice lowered. "Think about it.

This plan only works with you as the shooter. If you go out there in that"—he gestured with his chin toward the sweatshirt vest of explosives as he took off his jacket—"leaving me back here, we don't stand a chance at saving Annie, and you know it."

Jules looked back at him with those empty eyes, in a face that had turned to stone. He may have checked his heart and soul at the door when he'd heard about Robin, but his brain was still online, thank God. He finally nodded, and yanked off that vest.

"I am sorry," Ric said as Jules helped him pull the explosives over his head. Damn, but it was heavy—there was a lot of C4 on this thing. "You're sure you pulled out the right wires?"

"I'm sure," Jules told him, and then dropped a different bomb. "Junior's got to stay alive."

Ric looked at him. He was serious. "Robin's dead, Annie's dying, and you're worried about *Junior*?" Ric couldn't believe this.

"I'm worried about Atlanta." Jules's hands were rough as he helped Ric back into the jacket, zipping it up so that it hid the explosives—all but a piece of that gray cord that stuck out the bottom. Jules handed him the skinhead's lighter. "Junior's our link to al-Hasan. He stays alive."

"If he kills Annie—"

"He stays alive," Jules repeated, his voice as flat as his eyes.

"Robin's dead and you—"

"Yeah," Jules said, with a sudden sharp flare of emotion. "Keep saying that—it's really helping me."

"I'm sorry," Ric said again. God damn, but those were two of the lamest words in the English language. He turned away from Jules, shouting up to Junior, wherever he was. "Junior, I want to make a deal!"

"I gave you your proof of life," Junior finally shouted back. "You come out on the main deck with your hands on your heads!"

Ric did a quick scan out the window—Junior wasn't on the main deck. No one was.

"I want Robin's death to mean something," Jules told him quietly. "So let's do this right. Let's save Annie and let's save Atlanta." His voice was rough as he helped Ric over toward the galley stairs. "You ready?"

Ric nodded. "You call Foley," he shouted to Junior, "and you get Annie back. I want her voice on that intercom—now!"

"If I don't make it," he lowered his voice to tell Jules. He had to say it. "Tell Annie how much it meant to . . . hear her say she loved me, too."

Jules made a sound that was little more than an exhale, but it was filled with pain. "You can tell her that yourself."

Unlike Jules, who would never be able to tell Robin how much he'd loved him. Christ, that was so unfair. Unfair and wrong . . .

"Fuck you!" Junior shouted back from his hiding place. "It's my turn to make the demands. You get your asses out here, now, or I'm going to call him and *tell* him to kill her."

"No!" Ric shouted.

"Where the fuck do you think you're going?" Jules shouted, full volume, even though Ric hadn't moved.

"Get away from me!" Ric shouted back, even as he reached out and roughly, impulsively, gave Jules a hard, quick hug.

"I'm not going up there with you," Jules shouted, and as Ric stepped back, he saw the truth in Jules's eyes—he didn't expect Ric to survive this.

"Oh yes, you are," Ric shouted back.

"You're crazy!" Jules shouted. "What, you really think she's alive? She's dead—she's as dead as Robin!" His voice broke realistically.

"I have to talk to her," Ric made himself sob. "Just one more time."

"What are you doing?" Jules put panic in his own voice. "What, are you going to *shoot* me?"

It was then, right before Ric dragged himself out onto the main deck, that he realized exactly what it was that had been bothering him—what was wrong with that picture of Robin Chadwick falling overboard and drowning.

"You saw the movie trailer for *Riptide*, right?" he quietly asked Jules, then shouted, "I wanna talk to Annie! I've got to . . ."

The FBI agent just stared at him, uncomprehendingly, the flat nothingness back in his eyes.

"Robin's a kick-ass swimmer," Ric told him, his voice low. "He told me he did his own underwater stunts. A guy like that just doesn't drown."

Jules didn't believe him. There was no change on his face. No flicker of hope. Still . . . "Thanks," he said.

"Don't make me do it!" Ric shouted, then lifted his weapon and fired two shots into the wooden deck.

It was showtime.

CHAPTER
TWENTY-FIVE

Dripping wet and shaking with exhaustion, anger, and fear—his head still throbbing from where he'd damn near cracked it open—Robin crouched on the foredeck of Foley's fishing boat, regaining his equilibrium.

Climbing up the slick side of the boat was much harder to do in real life than it was when filming *Riptide*. For one thing, the boat he'd infiltrated on the movie set had been moored. They'd used special effects to make it look as if he were boarding a speeding vessel. This one, however, had been moving forward at a steady clip.

Plus he'd been freaking dizzy from smacking his head when Foley had pitched him overboard. And yeah, he'd also had quite a bit to drink, which hadn't helped.

His first thought had been to swim to the distant shore, but the idea of leaving Annie alone with Foley was too awful.

So Robin had clung, at first, to the anchor, way up at the bow of the boat, afraid if he slipped or was shaken free he'd be swept away. Or worse—swept underneath and into the churning propellers.

The side was too slippery to climb without the aid of the props department and their ropes and netting, handily placed for him to grab. He'd finally managed it by creating a rope of sorts with his jeans and his shirt. He'd used the sodden clothing, tossing it up onto the boat until he knocked one of the hawsers free.

But the rope had dangled there—just out of his reach. Again, he'd tried using his clothes to pull it closer, but it soon became clear that he'd just have to let go of the anchor and leap toward the damn thing, catching it as the boat moved past.

Robin was athletic—as long as he wasn't detoxing or shit-faced. This was the kind of stunt he would have enjoyed doing on a movie set.

Problem was, real life allowed for only one take.

He went for it, though, when he heard Annie scream. Jesus, what was Foley doing to her? She'd started shouting then, so he knew he hadn't killed her, thank God. Robin could still hear her now, crying, from down in the stateroom.

He wrung out his boxers as best he could and moved as silently as possible toward the stern of the boat, and those stairs leading below.

"You are so fucked," Foley told Annie as he got off the phone. "It could have been quick. But no. Junior wants you alive. He's going to take a knife to you on the deck of that yacht, with your boyfriend watching. Congratulations, you stupid, stupid bitch."

He went out the stateroom door, closing and locking it behind him.

It was the dead last thing Annie'd expected him to do. She was so completely stunned, she just lay there for several long seconds, her wrist clutched to her chest.

But it wasn't some kind of cruel joke Foley was playing on her. He didn't jump back into the room shouting "Kidding!" before he shot her in the head.

Annie heard him stomp his way back up to the galley, and she roused herself, dragging her damaged body over to the end of the fuse to Robin's bomb. The lighter was in her front-left jeans pocket—she had to use her unbroken right hand to get it out, which wasn't either easy or quick.

It gave her ample time to consider exactly what she was about to do.

She, who never quite forgave Pam for taking her own life, was about to do the very same.

She had to admit that she liked the irony of Foley dying as a result of Robin's bomb. He may have killed Robin, but with Annie's help, Robin was going to even the score.

And over in the not-quite-as-bloodthirsty column of reasons to light the fuse was the fact that together, she and Robin would eliminate Junior's option of blowing up the yacht and killing Ric and Jules. This way, they'd have a chance. Maybe the massive explosion would help them in some way. Maybe it would draw the Coast Guard.

Yes, if Robin were here, he'd definitely be urging her on.

She finally got the lighter free.

And lit the fuse.

Jules silently moved into position, watching as Ric stumbled and limped up the companionway and onto the deck.

This man, whom he'd come to respect and even love as a friend, was marching unswervingly to his all-but-certain death.

Annie was never going to forgive Jules for letting Ric do this. And yet Ric had been right. There was no other way.

"Don't shoot," Ric called to Junior.

From where Jules lay atop the galley counter, slightly back from that window, he had a clear view of Ric.

He held his hands up, his gun loosely in his right, in a position of surrender. He limped with each step he took—farther out onto the deck, but not too far from this window where Jules was waiting. "I'm here. Jules is no longer a threat and I . . . I surrender. Don't let Foley hurt her . . ." He dropped to his knees, which had to have hurt his wounded leg. "Please . . . Don't let him hurt her . . . I'll do whatever you want."

The day was beautiful. The ocean air was clear and fresh, and the sky was a remarkable shade of blue.

It wasn't quite as beautiful a blue, though, as Robin's eyes.

Jules steadied the hand that held his weapon, forcing all thoughts of the past and future out of his mind. There was only now. There was only his heart beating, his eye on Ric, his steady finger on the trigger as he waited.

And waited.

Junior would eventually send his men out to disarm Ric. Although one of them would probably shoot him first.

"She loves me," Ric sobbed, the picture of a broken, desperate man. "She said she loves me—I gotta talk to her, please, just one last time . . ."

Robin found a flare gun and a bottle of gin in the storage bin beneath the bench seats on the deck of the fishing boat.

The flares were wrapped in plastic—he almost couldn't unwrap them, but he did, and he got one loaded into the gun with hands that were once again shaking.

Which was why he took a healthy slug of the gin.

But nope, his hands didn't stop shaking. He *wasn't* starting to detox again—he was just scared shitless by what he was about to do.

He put the bottle down and was in the process of taking a series of deep, calming breaths—an exercise an acting teacher had taught him years ago—when Foley came out of the stateroom and started crashing around in the galley.

Robin quickly pulled himself back along the side of the above-deck cabin.

After what seemed like hours, the microwave finally beeped. Then came the unmistakable smell of coffee, and the sound of a spoon against the side of a ceramic mug.

And then Foley stomped up the stairs and onto the deck. He took out his phone and dialed, coffee mug in his other hand. "Yeah," he said. "I got a visual—I see you—I should be alongside you in five, maybe ten minutes."

It was now or never. And while he would have preferred never, as Foley shut his phone, Robin stepped out onto the deck, flare gun held in his best double-handed Navy SEAL grip.

"Hands where I can see them!" Robin said.

Foley laughed at him. "You're fucking kidding me," he said. Dropping the mug, he reached for his gun.

So Robin leaped forward and shot the flare, point-blank, into Foley's ugly face.

The flare sent Foley staggering back, and his gun clattered on the deck as he screamed, his hair on fire.

Jesus. But Robin didn't stand and stare. He scrambled after the real gun as Foley fell to his knees, batting at his head. But then, still smoldering, he was up again, and he roared as he came after Robin, like some horrific version of the Energizer Bunny.

The tears always worked.

People always underestimated a grown man who broke down and cried, the way Ric was crying now—on his knees on the main deck of the yacht.

And as for Junior, well, here he came. More than ready to put his bootprint on the back of a man who was shattered. "Put the gun down and push it away from you," Junior commanded, his voice coming from slightly above and behind Ric—from the deck atop the galley.

That was good. Junior was close enough to get a full visual.

There were a variety of potential ways to play this. Ric's original plan was to go out onto the deck without a gun, hands empty and outstretched. When Junior approached, Ric's intention was to open his jacket and reveal the explosives and the fuse that he'd already lit.

He could feel the heat from the time fuse as it burned, slowly making its way around and around his waist.

When Junior saw what he was wearing, he'd panic, calling for his men to help him throw Ric overboard. Well, Ric's body. Because before he hit full panic, he'd surely shoot Ric in the head.

But the handgun that Jules had taken from the man he'd killed on the lower level brought a few other options to the table.

One or two of which had an outcome that included the possibility of Ric's living through these next few minutes.

"I lit the fuse," he said, loudly enough for Junior to hear him as he unzipped the jacket. And then the time for talking was over. Ric pointed the gun at himself.

And he pulled the trigger.

Annie sat on the floor of the stateroom as the fuse burned, drinking from a bottle of vodka and trying to imagine the life she would have shared with Ric had things worked out differently.

Trouble was, she couldn't get past the sex.

When she tried to picture them having dinner together, even though she started the fantasy with herself perched on one of his kitchen stools, just watching him cook, it soon led to hijinks atop the dining-room table.

She could imagine them taking a flight out to California, to talk to Sam Starrett about working for Troubleshooters Incorporated—and being unable to survive the trip without slipping into the tiny airplane bathroom together.

It didn't matter where they were or what they were doing, all Ric would've had to do was look at her, and she would've looked back at him and . . .

She wished she could have left a note. She wished she could be sure that Ric had heard her say she loved him.

She wished—

Boom! Something that sounded a lot like a gunshot made her smack her head on the wall behind her.

Oh, God. Had she lit the fuse too late? Had they already reached Junior's yacht?

She could hear Foley talking—he was on the phone again as he un-locked the stateroom door.

She braced herself, gripping the neck of the bottle with her right hand, ready to use it as a weapon. She was not leaving here without a fight. She had no idea how many minutes it had been since she'd lit the fuse—maybe all she had to do was stall a little bit longer.

Foley was having trouble with the lock, which was good, but he finally got it, and with a crash, he pushed it open wide.

Except it wasn't Foley, it was . . . Robin?

"Oh my God, you're alive," Annie said.

He had a red welt on his forehead, but he was definitely breathing. He'd stripped down to his boxers, and he was holding both Foley's hand-gun and his phone.

"I'm on a boat in the middle of the Gulf, off Sarasota," he said into that phone. "Coordinates? I have no clue. We're out of sight of land, there's a lot of water—it's blue. There's another boat out here—a big one, a yacht, where FBI agent Jules Cassidy is being held by Gordon Burns Ju-nior. He needs backup and he needs it *now.*"

"Oh my God," Annie realized. "Robin! Shit! I lit the fuse!"

As Jules watched from his position in the galley, Ric shot himself.

The force pushed him onto his back, where he lay motionless and silent in the aftermath of the deafening gunshot, his jacket flapped open.

Junior was as surprised as Jules.

"Holy fuck," he heard Junior say as he, too, saw the blood seeping onto the deck. And then he saw the explosives Ric was wearing.

"Holy fuck," Junior said again. "He said he lit the fuse! Jesus Christ, help me throw him overboard!"

And here they came, thundering down from the deck that was directly over Jules's head. Donny, Purple Shirt, and Suit Number Two. Even Ju-nior came down, although he hung back as his men rushed toward Ric—as they rushed toward the window to the galley, where Jules was waiting.

Where he finally stopped waiting, and opened fire.

Ric rolled as Jules proved himself to be as good a shot in the field as he was at the firing range.

The FBI agent took out Junior's men, shooting to kill.

Meanwhile, Ric headed for Junior. But Jules fired again, shooting Junior's weapon out of his hand, making the son of a bitch scream with pain, clutching bloody fingers to his chest.

Ric heard Jules kicking out the now-broken galley window, trying to get to Junior—to keep him from leaping over the side of the yacht.

But Ric reached him first. He grabbed the bastard's legs, knocking him down to the deck and making him scream, again, like a little girl.

But it wasn't because his hand was hurting him. No, it was the explosives Ric was still wearing that made him frantic to get away. Apparently he thought Ric was still going to explode in a fiery ball—taking Junior with him.

The length of cord—time fuse—was still burning, although it had to be almost done. Sure enough, a little flash of fire jumped out of the unconnected end.

"Bang," Ric told Junior. He looked up at Jules, who pulled Junior away from him, grabbing the bastard's cell phone out of his pocket before shoving him down onto the deck.

"Hands on your head," Jules ordered. He glanced at Ric. "You shot yourself."

"Yes, I did," Ric said as he surveyed the damage he'd done to the fleshy part of his side. He was bleeding and it hurt like hell. But he'd figured if *he* hadn't done it, Junior would've. And in shooting him, Junior wouldn't have aimed for the exact spot where Ric had been shot just last year. The ER doctor who'd stitched him up had told him that he couldn't have been hit by a bullet in a less invasive place if he'd tried. "How about it? Do I get the insane stunt bonus?"

Jules actually laughed. "Yeah." But then he stopped laughing, his face back to grim.

Ric looked up to see what Jules had spotted, off to the ship's starboard side.

Foley's fishing boat. Had to be. It was still some distance away, but the gap was closing fast.

Annie had lit the fuse.

Okay—*that* was one scenario Robin hadn't considered.

Jesus, she was badly hurt. She tried to push herself to her feet, but she didn't get far.

"How long ago did you light it?" he asked.

"I don't know," she said. "Can we cut it? Or just . . . pull the fuse out?"

She reached for it, but he stopped her. "Don't. I don't know. I just . . . don't know." He'd never defused a bomb before—he didn't know enough about it. He *did* know that dousing the fuse with water in an attempt to put it out wouldn't work. It was called *underwater* time fuse for a reason.

Could he just pull it out? And if he could, why, in the movies, did people defuse bombs carefully, with sweat dripping down their faces? Why didn't they just grab and yank?

No, Robin knew of only one way to be absolutely certain they would survive this—and that was to get off this boat and swim like hell.

He swung Annie up and over his shoulder and ran for the deck.

Jules handed Junior's cell phone to Ric and began tying up Junior.

"Call Foley," he said. "Tell him I'm dead, but that you've got Junior. Tell him you'll make a trade. Junior for Annie."

Ric was already accessing Junior's phone book. Foley was right there, in the *F*s. He pressed the talk button and . . .

"It's ringing," he reported to Jules, who was now collecting weapons and ammunition from the men he'd killed.

"No one else has a phone," Jules complained. "As soon as you're done, I need to call Yashi for backup."

"I'm getting bumped to Foley's voicemail." Ric was trying not to freak. He turned to Junior and asked, "How many men did Foley have aboard?"

"Fuck you," Junior said, but Ric couldn't hear him. He saw Junior's mouth move, but the sound of his words were obliterated by the roar of an explosion.

He turned to see Jules staring out over the deck railing, horror on his face.

Jules's mouth moved, too. *No . . .*

Ric spun to see what he was looking at, and realized that Foley's fishing boat had exploded in a fireball.

Water shot up into the sky, and debris rained down into the Gulf.

The silence that fell was broken only by Junior. The son of a bitch was laughing.

Ric drew his sidearm.

"Don't," Jules said quietly.

"I don't give a fuck"—Ric's voice broke—"about finding al-Hasan."

"Robin and Annie did," Jules reminded him, and knocked Junior on the side of his head with the butt of his handgun. It looked almost gentle, the way that he did it, but Junior stopped laughing and immediately slumped unconscious.

Ric sat down on the deck.

Jules sat, too, holding out his hand for the phone.

"I thought we were going to do it," Ric said as Jules dialed. "I thought . . . Robin was still alive, and . . . I thought . . ." He shook his head.

"I thought we had a chance, too," Jules agreed. There were tears in his eyes. "I'm so sorry. Yeah, Yash," he said into the phone. "It's me. I'm here with Ric. I'm somewhere off Sarasota on . . ." He paused. "You *what?*"

The change in his voice made Ric look up.

"He called *when?*" Jules pushed himself to his feet. "Backup's already on its way," he told Ric, repeating information he was getting from Yashi. "There are ten helicopters—six of them military—heading in our direction, ETA twenty minutes. They were called in about four minutes ago by *Robin.* You were right, he didn't drown—holy shit. Yeah, yeah, Yash . . ." He held out a hand to help Ric up, then led the way to the bridge, speaking again to Ric. "He wants us to try to send out a radio signal—an SOS— from the bridge, so they can get an exact . . . Yash, listen. Tell the pilots there's a big column of smoke. A fishing boat just exploded and . . . We're right there. They can't miss us."

Ric followed him up the stairs to the yacht's control room. There was a huge steering wheel, right in front of floor to ceiling windows. He went over to it.

"Steer toward the wreckage," Jules ordered him.

It didn't budge. "The wheel's locked," Ric reported.

"Yashi," Jules said into Junior's phone. "I need info on how to get this thing out of autopilot and how to slow it down. ASAP." He looked at Ric, hope back in his eyes. "They were alive four minutes ago."

"Four minutes ago," Ric pointed out, "was before that blast."

"Shit," Robin said. "They're heading toward us."

Robin had told Annie that Junior's yacht seemed to be on a course that would pass the wreckage. But now, apparently, they'd turned.

The salt water had finally stopped stinging Annie's multitude of cuts and scrapes as she and Robin clung to a floating bench cushion he'd grabbed on his way off the boat. Well, Robin clung—both to the cushion and to Annie. Her ability to cling to anything was limited by her injured wrist.

"Leave me here," Annie told Robin.

"What?" he said. "No way."

"Please," she said. "You're a strong enough swimmer—you can make it to shore."

"I'm not leaving you," he said. "You're hurt."

"You have to," she said. "If Junior finds us, Ric and Jules will die. I don't want them to die."

"Help is coming," Robin promised her. "We just have to hang on a little bit longer."

Yashi was the man.

He'd helped Jules and Ric gain control of the yacht's steering system, and shut down the engines.

Of course a ship didn't have brakes, so they still moved forward. But they were slowing rapidly as they circled the wreckage.

Jules stood at the railing next to Ric. They were using binoculars to search the water for survivors. It was so damn choppy, and there were bits of things floating all over the surface of the water and . . .

Wait a sec . . .

"One o'clock," Jules told Ric. "That's definitely someone out there, isn't it?"

Ric shook his head. "I can't tell."

Whatever it was, they were moving closer to it and . . .

"I'm going in," Jules decided. He kicked off his sneakers and went over the rail with a splash. He swam underwater as far as he could, telling himself not to hope too hard.

But it was too late—hope had kicked in. Mere minutes ago, Robin had called for help. God couldn't be so cruel to have let him survive these past few hellish hours only to kill him four ridiculous minutes before Jules and Ric kicked Junior's ass.

But then Jules got close enough to see that the thing he'd spotted *was* a body—but it had been torn almost in half by the blast. It was floating facedown and . . .

God!

It was Foley. And not only had someone done some serious damage to his right eye, but he also had a bullet hole in the center of his forehead. Jules treaded water for a moment, trying to catch his breath and calm his pounding heart.

Was finding Foley like this a good thing or a bad? He didn't know. But God, he wanted Robin and Annie to be alive. Please God, *please* . . .

Jules quickly swam back to the yacht, to the rope that Ric had tied to the railing for him.

He'd only climbed halfway up the side, when Ric said, "Whoa. Whoa, wait. I see something."

"Where?" Jules asked, turning to look, sweeping his hair back from his face.

"See that red thing?" Ric asked, pointing to a big piece of something red bobbing on the waves. "Right behind that, like they're trying to hide."

Jules dove back into the water.

"Shit," Robin said again. Annie had been right. Junior was sending his men into the water to look for them. The sun was too bright for him to see Junior at the railing. It created a glare off the white hull of the huge ship, blinding him. Still, he'd caught a double flash that could only have come from binoculars.

And then he saw a splash as someone went into the water.

"Go," Annie said. "Please, Robin, they don't know you're alive."

"I'm not leaving you," he said for, like, the four thousandth time. But he *did* pull Foley's gun from where he'd tucked it in the back pocket of Annie's jeans.

"What are you doing?" she said just as someone surfaced about three feet away from them.

Robin had no idea if this type of gun could fire after being immersed in water, but he held it as if it did. "Back off!" he shouted, about to pull the trigger to see what would happen when . . .

"Jules?" Annie said.

Jules.

"Oh my God," Jules said as he treaded water. "*That* would've really sucked."

Robin let his hand drop into the water with a splash. Holy, holy shit, he'd almost shot *Jules.*

"I can't believe you're both all right. *Are* you all right?" Jules asked. The expression on his face as he looked into Robin's eyes was one Robin would remember for the rest of his life. It was as if Jules had been granted a reprieve from an eternity in hell. Robin could relate, because he was feeling the exact same thing.

He nodded. He *was* all right. Because Jules was *alive* . . .

Jules took immediate charge, gently prying the gun from Robin's fingers even as he turned, his full attention on Annie, who looked as though she'd been hit by a truck.

"How badly are you hurt?" he asked her, holding on to their float as he stashed the weapon at the small of his back.

"Where's Ric?" was her urgent response.

"Ric's fine," Jules told her.

"Then where is he?" she asked.

"Broken wrist seems to be the worst of it, although she may have some internal injuries," Robin answered for her.

Jules met his eyes and nodded before turning back to Annie. "Ric's fine," he repeated, trying to reassure her.

"Are you . . . Did you . . . escape . . . ?" Robin asked.

"We have control of the yacht," Jules told him as he moved closer to Robin now, looking at the welt he knew he had on his forehead. "Ric and me. Junior's in custody. Are you sure you're not hurt?" He touched Robin, just a hand on the side of his head, as if he needed solid proof that he was really there, and really in one piece.

Robin was holding on to Annie, but if he could have, he would've put both arms around Jules. And never let go, ever again.

Instead, he just grabbed Jules's arm and squeezed. "I'm fine. Now," he added. "Now that you're here, I'm . . ." There were no words. Fine didn't even begin to cut it.

"Me, too." Jules's response was heartfelt. "When we saw the fishing boat blow . . ."

"That was my fault," Annie admitted.

"Yeah," Robin said. He mimicked that old TV commercial, saying in a heavy Southern accent, "But ah helped."

It made Jules laugh. But he was in FBI mode, so he didn't hold Robin's gaze for more than a few short seconds. "Help me get Annie to the yacht."

But Annie had another agenda. "Jules, I'm sorry to be such a pain in the ass, but will you please define *fine*? I mean, if Ric's so fine, where is he?"

Jules chose his words carefully as together he and Robin kicked to move the float—this time toward the yacht instead of away from it. "Someone had to stay with the ship, and, well . . . We just thought . . . Okay, this is going to sound bad, or at least worse than it is, but we both thought he should stay out of the water out of . . . well, fear that he might, um, attract . . . sharks?"

Sharks. Robin hadn't even thought about sharks. They didn't need Ric in the water to attract them—old dead Foley could do that well enough on his own. He kicked harder, moving them faster.

Meanwhile, Annie's eyes had narrowed. "So he's fine, but he's . . . bleeding?"

"Um, a little?" Jules normally wasn't such a terrible liar, but wow, that was pathetic, and he knew it, too. "He was shot," he finally admitted.

"Shot," Annie repeated.

But Jules was saved from having to give details because they'd reached the side of the ship. Ric had dangled a number of ropes over the side, but it was still going to be tricky getting Annie all the way up there, to that deck.

"Ric?" she shouted, looking up at the hulking side of the vessel.

"Annie!" he shouted back.

"Stay up there, Alvarado." Jules joined the shouting. "We'll bring her to you."

"She's hurt worse than she's letting on," Robin told Jules quietly as Annie shouted, "Are you all right?" to Ric.

"I know," Jules said. "Junior played it over the ship's intercom. They were trying to give us proof of life, and she wouldn't do it. She finally screamed and . . ."

"I'm fine," Ric shouted back to Annie. "Are *you* all right?"

"See?" Jules told her as they looped the rope under her arms. "Told you he's fine."

"I am now," she called to Ric, echoing Robin's words. Just moving her arm had to hurt like a bitch on fire, but she didn't complain. She did look at Jules, though. "I thought Robin was dead," she said. "Did you hear me say that, too?"

"Oh yes," Jules said.

Jesus. Robin looked at him. "So you thought . . ."

"Yeah." Jules touched him again, his hand warm and solid on the back of Robin's neck. "I was having a really bad day for a while there." He turned to Annie. "Sweetie, try to hold your wrist securely against yourself," he told her, "to keep from jarring it as we pull you up."

"It's going to hurt," Annie said. "I know. That's okay, let's just do it. I'm ready."

She was. And Robin knew she would've endured anything. She would have walked through fire to get up onto that deck where Ric was waiting—Ric, who'd been shot. He could still see Annie's worry for Ric in her eyes, despite all of Jules's reassurances.

Yeah, she was ready for anything.

Jules was giving her a nod and his best *you're in good hands* smile. "Okay." He looked at Robin. "Get upon deck and help Ric with the ropes. I'll help Annie."

"For the record," Robin told him, "I'm ready, too."

Jules didn't know what he was talking about. Or maybe he did, and he just didn't believe it. "Just . . . go help Ric," he said.

So Robin climbed the rope.

"Choppers ETA five minutes," Ric reported as he tried to untie the rope that was beneath Annie's arms. He had to delegate the task to Jules, because Annie was far too interested in checking out Ric's injuries. "We've got paramedics coming."

"You said he was shot," she accused Jules, "not that he was shot *twice*."

"Shot's also the plural," Jules defended himself.

"I'm okay," Ric tried to reassure her. She, however, was in serious pain. "Oh, Annie," he said. She was going to have one hell of a black eye. And her lip . . .

But she ignored it completely and kissed him.

And that was it for him. Game over. Ric just sat there on the deck with Annie in his arms.

Robin came out from the galley with some ice wrapped in a dish towel. But he put it down within Ric's reach, and as Jules had done, he silently and quickly faded away.

It was funny, really.

Ric would've thought a couple of gay guys wouldn't be so freaked out by the sight of a grown man crying like a baby.

"I'm so sorry," Annie whispered through her own tears, "that I screamed. I knew you were listening and I tried not to—"

"I'm sorry," Ric said, "that I couldn't keep Foley from hurting you."

"It's okay now," she murmured. "Everything's okay." But then she lifted her head, misery in her eyes. "Oh, God, everything's not okay. Ric, Martell was . . . They killed him."

"No," Ric told her. "He's all right."

She didn't believe him.

"He's in the hospital," he said, wiping his face in the crook of his arm. "He's already out of surgery. Yashi told me. He made quite a scene in the ER, but . . . He's going to be fine."

"Oh, thank God," she said, relief in her eyes.

"Yeah," he agreed. "I'm doing a lot of that right now. Thanking God." He touched her poor, bruised face, and yeah, there came the waterworks again.

"Jules told me . . . Did you really shoot yourself?"

Ric nodded, laughing now, too.

She was looking at him as if he'd gone mad. "You're always telling me *that's not funny*, but that's *really* not funny."

"Yeah," he said. "It kind of was. See, I wanted Junior to think I'd killed myself, so there had to be blood. But I didn't want to hit anything vital and . . . I also had to fall back and not move and . . . dead people generally don't scream *shit, shit, shit*, because it hurts, you know? But, Christ, it really hurt."

Now she was laughing, too, but more with horror than with humor. "God, Ric . . ."

He kissed her again. Gently. Careful of her battered mouth. "I wanted to live," he told her. "It was an imperative."

And that got *her* tears going again. Between the pair of them, they were just never going to stop. "God, I love you," she told him. "I should have told you—"

"It's okay." He cut her off. "I know. I knew. I love hearing you say it, but . . . Annie, I knew."

She kissed him.

And he knew that *she* knew that he loved her, too.

"That's when Annie lit the fuse," Robin told Jules as they stood on the deck of Junior's yacht, waiting for the fleet of helicopters to arrive. "She was ready to die to save Ric. You, too, but really . . . Ric."

Robin was leaning both elbows on the railing. Dressed only in his boxers, he was quite the sight, with all that smooth, tan skin and his tousled blond hair. Jules just stood there, next to him, drinking him in.

Jules still couldn't believe that his cover had been blown thanks to cell phone video footage taken of him both in Robin's room and last year, during that hostage goatfuck. Next time he went undercover, he'd have to change his hair and eye color—maybe even grow a beard.

"She loves him," Robin continued. "And she's lucky, because he loves her, too. Most people don't find that. You know. That kind of . . . equal adoration."

No kidding. Jules stood there, lost for a moment in Robin's eyes. But then Robin looked away.

Something was definitely up. Robin was acting oddly. "I, um, saw Foley's body," Jules said. "Are you . . . okay?"

Robin nodded vigorously. "Yes, I am. My big regret is that I can't kill him again and make it hurt even more this time." He turned to look at Jules. "Are *you* okay?"

"Yeah," Jules said, even though he couldn't keep himself from shaking his head no. He was both the most okay and the furthest from okay that he'd ever been in his life. "I'm just . . . still really . . ." God help him, he needed . . . Robin. He needed to hold on to him for about a week, just to convince himself that this wasn't some dream that he would wake up from, to find he really was dead and forever gone.

But Robin had turned away again, staring down into the water.

Enough was enough. "What aren't you telling me?" Jules asked. "Did Foley . . . hurt you, or—"

"No," Robin said. "Jesus, no."

"Then, are you, like, breaking up with me?" Jules asked.

That got him eye contact, at least. And some of the despair was displaced by a glimmer of hope. "Are we together?"

"Damn straight," Jules said. "Well, you know what I mean."

And that got him a smile, although it faded much too fast.

Jules touched him, his shoulder, his arm. "Talk to me."

Robin closed his eyes. "God, I want to kiss you."

Jules looked at his watch. "In about three minutes, we're going to be surrounded by helicopters, so, since I really want to kiss you, too—"

"See, here's the thing," Robin said. "If I kiss you, you'll know that I had a drink—" He stopped himself. "Yeah, right. A drink? Try a bottle. I was starting to detox, Jules, and God, I was sick." He was so upset, he was on the verge of tears. "I was pretending it was the flu, but Annie . . . She, like, wiped my face in the truth. She told me I was going through withdrawal. She said I need to detox in the hospital or I could die—because I'm . . ." He choked the words out. ". . . an alcoholic."

Robin looked so miserable. He was so distressed, so ashamed.

Yet all Jules could think was . . . Alleluia.

"I'm so sorry," Robin said. "I broke my promise to you."

"Sweetie, God, come here." Jules reached for him, and this time, instead of turning away, Robin grabbed hold of Jules so tightly, it took his breath away.

Dear Lord, what Robin and Annie must've gone through. Jules suspected the story that Robin had told him was the Cliff's Notes version.

And then I went overboard, and after Foley thought I was dead, I just . . . climbed back aboard the boat. It was obvious now that none of it had been quite as easy as Robin had made it sound.

"I'm just like my mother." Robin's voice was choked.

"No, you're not," Jules told him, his heart in his throat. "You're nothing like her. She never admitted she had a problem. She never asked anyone for help."

"I need help," Robin said. "Will you help me?"

"Yes," Jules said. "I'm here. I'm with you—whatever it takes." He used Robin's own words. "I'm yours."

Robin smiled, but there was still massive unhappiness in his eyes. "Look, I totally suck. I violated your privacy. I read that e-mail you got from Sam. The one where he said a relationship with me would hurt your career . . . ?"

"Robin." Jules shook his head.

"I'm sorry. I know I'm a bad person . . ."

Jules laughed. "No, you're not. It's just . . . you should know better. Or at least know enough to realize that if you're going to read someone's e-mail, don't just read half of it—read it all."

"I did," Robin said.

"You read what I wrote back to him?" Jules asked. He'd used the word *love* in that e-mail, way more than once.

Robin nodded. "And also what Alyssa wrote back to you."

"Alyssa e-mailed me?" Jules asked. "From Spain?"

Robin nodded again.

"What did she say?"

As Jules watched him, he knew Robin was considering pretending that he didn't remember. But he clearly didn't want to lie to Jules, so he finally told him. "She said, *go for it.*"

Jules nodded. It was exactly what he'd expected Alyssa to say. "You know, I often take her advice."

"So your whole career," Robin clarified. "You're just going to throw it away. For me."

"Maybe," Jules told him. "Maybe not. Maybe I can have it all."

"What if you can't?" Robin asked.

"Then I'll be happy with what I've got," he said quietly, "because I'll have the most important part." Jules touched his face. "I spent a large part of today believing you were dead," he said, "and none of that other stuff mattered. All I knew was that I was never going to smile again. I was never going to be able to look into your eyes and . . . You always know what I'm thinking and what I'm feeling and . . . You know me. And you love me anyway. I thought I'd lost that forever. I thought I'd lost you."

Robin had tears in his eyes again. "That's what you wrote in that e-mail. That's the way you told Sam that you love me."

Jules stepped back from him. "Yeah," he said. "That's the way I love you. And that's the way you love me, too. You know, not everyone finds that. Not everyone's that lucky."

Robin reached for him again.

But Jules shook his head as he took another step away. "Robin, the helicopters are here."

Robin looked up into the sky as if he were surprised. Had he really not heard them coming? Apparently not. Most of the helos were equipped to land on the water, but one was smaller, and just circled endlessly overhead. A logo for Channel 7 was on its belly.

Jules followed Robin's gaze up to it. "Yeah," he said. "Smile for the camera. Yashi told me a news copter caught a whiff of the activity and followed everyone out here." He smiled at Robin. "I'll kiss you later. Count on it."

But Robin caught him around the waist anyway, tugging him closer.

"Robin." Jules resisted. "I can wait for three movies. For you to come out. I'm okay with that. I really am." He was willing to wait forever if he had to.

But Robin kept pulling him. Closer and closer, into an embrace.

Jules was hypnotized by the feel of Robin's body against his, by Robin's mouth so tantalizingly close, by the love in Robin's eyes. But even as he wrapped his arms around this man he wanted to spend the rest of his life with, he insisted, "I can wait."

Robin just smiled. "Yeah, but I can't," he said, and he kissed him.

Right in front of the whole, wide world.

CHAPTER
TWENTY-SIX

"So he comes to, in ICU," Annie told Robin, talking into the phone that sat next to Martell's hospital bed. "He's post-op, right? He's hooked up to every machine in the world, but he tries to get out of bed. He's, like, ripping the IV out of his hand—"

"For the record," Martell shouted over her, "I don't remember *any* of that."

"—and insisting that they call Yashi, at the FBI," Annie told Robin.

Martell was looking much better today—as was she. The swelling around her eye had finally gone down. Now it just featured the colors of the rainbow. Her mouth wasn't quite so sore, either.

Still, she looked pretty battered, and with her wrist in a cast, people had looked at Ric askance the few times they'd left his condo. But then they saw that he, too, was bruised and limping, and they relaxed, probably imagining a car accident.

They had no idea.

"Can you put Martell on?" Robin asked her now. He had, after all, called Martell's hospital room from the pay phone in the rehab center, where he'd been for nearly a week now. Jules had helped him find a facility in the D.C. area, near where he lived and worked. They'd probably hoped that having Robin in a program outside of Hollywood would reduce the paparazzi factor, but they were wrong.

Robin had stopped and given an impromptu interview to a crowd of reporters on his way to checking himself in. Even after all this time, his statement was still getting a lot of airplay. Annie had seen it at least half a dozen times on various TV news programs.

"I'm an alcoholic," Robin had said right into the camera, putting his cards out on the table. "I learned to drink because it numbed what I was feeling—it took the edge off the fear. Fear of who I was, fear that someone would find out. Alcoholism has always been a huge problem in the gay community. It's easier to drink than to be honest about who we really are—honest to others *and* to ourselves. But this weekend, I made the decision both to stop hiding and to stop drinking. To stop being afraid." He turned away, but then turned back. "Oh, and for those of you—like my former agent—who think that a gay man can't play an action hero in a movie? You really need to meet my partner. This past weekend, he helped save the world. Again."

"I'll put Martell on in a sec," Annie told Robin now. "I just . . . wanted to tell you—"

"Please don't," he said. He sounded tired, but good. Apparently he was done with the detox part of the program, and was on to the learning-to-live-sober, one-day-at-a-time part.

"You and Jules left so soon, and I didn't get to—"

"Yeah, yeah." He brushed it all off. "I saved your life. Get over it."

"I don't *think* so." Annie looked up to find Ric watching her from his seat over by the windows. He did that a lot these days. Just sat and watched her, as if, if he weren't vigilant, she might vanish. "You're a hero. You can pretend you're not, that it was all Jules and Ric. But I wouldn't be here right now if it weren't for you. And when we were in the water? When you wouldn't leave me . . . ? I just wanted to say . . . ditto. You need me? Just call."

Robin was silent for a moment. "You shouldn't feel indebted," he said.

"I don't," she countered. "That's not—"

"Because really what happened out there is that *you* saved *my* life," Robin told her quietly.

"I just told you the truth," Annie said. "The way any friend would. You're the one who chose to listen."

"I'm glad I have friends like you," Robin said, "and okay, pass the phone to Martell now. If this Hallmark Moment goes on much longer, I'm going to start sobbing, and since I'm out here in the common room—"

"I'm really proud of you, Robin," she told him.

"Thanks," he said. "Some friend. God *damn* it . . ."

"He wants to talk to you." Laughing, Annie gave the handset to Martell.

"Dude!" Martell said into the phone. "All I do in here is watch TV, and all I see on the entertainment news is your incredibly gay face. Congrats on *Riptide* opening huge. Your agent come crawling back yet?"

Annie went to sit next to Ric. "You've got to stop doing that," she told him quietly.

"Doing what?" He honestly didn't know.

"Staring at me." She lowered her voice even more. "Without thinking about sex."

Ric laughed as he glanced over to make sure Martell was focused on his phone call. "How do you know—"

"I can tell," she said. "This is different from your *I wonder if she would be into trying the Kama Sutra Flying Squirrel position* look."

He took her hand. Kissed her palm. "Oh, really?"

"Very different."

"Maybe it's because I'm currently getting some whenever I want it." He lifted his eyebrow at her, that familiar heat now simmering in his eyes.

"You're thinking about sex now," she said. "See how I can tell?"

"Flying squirrel," he said. "I'm intrigued."

"You have to stop worrying about me," Annie said.

He shook his head. "I don't want to drive you crazy, but . . . You're going to have to give me time."

The big irony here was that Annie had been kept in the hospital for observation for several extra days. One of the doctors' concerns was that she'd been peeing blood. Foley had kicked her in the kidneys, and there'd been a little damage. But it was nothing that couldn't heal itself over time. Kind of the way Ric's kidneys had.

Her head injury had been superficial, too. Slight bruising, nothing more.

"I guess," Annie said, "I'm a little worried that you're going to start wrapping me in gauze."

"Only if the gauze is part of the flying squirrel thing." Ric stood up. "In which case, I think we have to go now."

Laughing, she tugged him back down. "I'm being serious."

"So am I." But he sat. "So I talked to my mother this morning."

Typical Ric. Changing the subject. She sighed and went with him. "How's your dad?"

"He hates his new diet," Ric told her as he played with her fingers. "That's not a big surprise. Anyway, Mom's willing to take Pierre."

Annie stared at him. "Why do we want to give my dog to your mother?"

"While we're in California. We can't take Pierre to a job interview." He snapped his fingers. "Come on. Keep up."

"You seriously want to . . ." They hadn't spoken about Sam Starrett's attempt to recruit them for Troubleshooters Incorporated since . . . Before Foley.

"I had a chance to speak to Jules about the Troubleshooters," Ric told her. "He thinks we'd like working for Sam—and for Tom Paoletti. He's the commanding officer—most of them are former military, which'll be weird, but interesting."

"And you honestly want to go talk to them?" Annie asked.

"I do," Ric said. He smiled. "See? No gauze."

She would have kissed him, but he looked up—a woman was knocking on the open door.

"Whoa," Ric said.

"I must be in the right place," the woman said. "How are you, Alvarado?"

She was wearing a police badge and her hair was up in a tight bun atop her head. She was pretty in a scary kind of way. Clearly she wasn't here to arrest anyone because she was carrying a stack of paperbacks.

Over in his hospital bed, Martell quickly ended his phone conversation. "Yeah, Rob, look, I gotta go, too. Right. Okay. Later, man." Annie got up to help him hang up the phone as he greeted the woman. "Hey. Lieutenant. This is a . . . surprise."

"I was in the neighborhood," the woman said. She, too, was ill at ease. "I thought you might want something to read."

"Thanks," Martell said.

"I can't stay." The lieutenant handed the books to Annie, as if afraid to get too close. "I just wanted to . . . see how you were doing."

"Better," Martell told her.

"Good. Okay, then . . ." She vanished as quickly as she appeared, leaving Ric and Martell looking at each other, exchanging an entire encyclopedia of information with nary a spoken word.

"Hello," Annie interrupted them. "Introductions much?"

"That was the lieutenant," Ric said, shooting Martell another cryptic look.

"Yeah, I got that," Annie said. She turned to Martell. "Is she your . . . special lieutenant?"

She was ready to go into full tease mode, but Martell shut her down.

"She's married."

Oops. "Sorry," Annie said. "I didn't mean to . . ."

"Don't worry about it." He cleared his throat. "So, rumor has it Junior cut a deal. What's up with that?"

"It's good news," Ric said, apparently as eager as Martell to change the subject. "Burns Senior got a deal, too. Junior gave up the info the FBI needed to apprehend Yazid al-Hasan in exchange for life sentences for both Burnses. In regular maximum-security prison—not Gitmo—lucky for them. Junior claimed he didn't know al-Hasan was al Qaeda. He thought he was helping to smuggle in a drug runner. Or so he says."

Annie didn't believe that for a second. Due to his father's unwillingness to fund his porn schemes, Junior had been forced to look outside of the United States for potential investors. He'd found the money he'd needed through a pair of Saudi businessmen—provided he help them handle an "immigration" issue.

Yeah, Junior didn't know. Right.

"Burns Senior being charged as an accessory?" Martell asked.

"In the death of Peggy Ryan," Ric confirmed. "Jules got a warrant, and went into Burns Point. He's got the yacht in dry dock, too, looking for more DNA evidence, although the message in blood on the window frame in Peggy's former room was pretty damning."

Annie had spoken to Jules about that, too. He desperately wanted to provide closure for Peggy's family. He'd told Annie that if Junior had made a habit of steering the yacht through the water where he'd just made his victims vanish, there could be DNA in the propeller system or God knows where. If it was there, they'd find it.

Jules was amazing. On the day of the explosion, he'd gone with them to the hospital, had a cursory check, and then he'd gone back to work.

Over the course of the next forty-eight hours, Jules and his team successfully apprehended al-Hasan, and verified that the bomb Robin and Annie had seen on the fishing boat was *not* any kind of nuclear device but rather conventional explosives.

What really cheesed Annie off was the lack of attention given to al-Hasan's capture. Sure, *The New York Times* and *USA Today* had run front-page stories, but only for a single day.

Unlike the ongoing feeding frenzy surrounding the outing of a certain movie star . . .

Ric broke the silence they'd all fallen into. "You look tired, man."

"No," Martell said. "I'm okay."

But Ric was giving Annie a look that was . . .

"Well, *I* could use a nap," she said, and Ric stood up.

"Let's get you home, then," he told her, trying to give her his concerned look. It wasn't a bad effort, but flying squirrels were definitely leaking out around the edges.

"We'll be back tonight," Annie told their friend.

"With real food?" Martell asked hopefully.

"Take-out from Mediterraneo." Annie kissed him goodbye. "We'll call in a few hours to get your order."

"You better," Martell said. His voice followed them into the hall. "And if you guys think for one second that I don't know you're heading home to get your freak on, you're completely deluded."

Robin stood respectfully, about twenty feet back, as Jules approached Ben's grave.

His marker was standard issue—white with a rounded top. Inscribed upon it were Ben's name and rank. His birth date and the date he'd been killed. And the words *Semper fidelis.*

That was Ben. Always faithful.

It had been Robin's idea to come out here to Arlington while on his first six-hour pass from the rehab center.

The pass was part of the reintegration process. It gave the recovering substance abusers a chance to slowly reenter a world that was filled with bars and liquor stores. Six hours for the first pass. Nine for the next. Then Robin would be given a full overnight.

Jules was looking forward to that.

And okay, so here he was, standing at Ben's grave, thinking about spending the night with Robin. That seemed wrong. But at the same time, Jules knew that Ben would've understood. It was a topic they'd discussed frequently via e-mail—the importance of physical attraction in a relationship. It was, to Ben, the most important part of a romantic pairing.

But attraction, Jules had argued, was also cerebral. He'd had friends who dated men who looked like Chippendale dancers, but who were dumb as stones. Jules had never understood that. Stupidity was, for him, a total turnoff.

I hear you, Ben had written back, *but don't you want the total package?*

And it was then that Jules had known that, for Ben, *he* was that package. He should have had the courage right then to confront that unspoken message. He should have admitted that he just didn't feel the same way about Ben.

Because for Jules, it wasn't just about finding a guy who was both smart and cute.

It was about . . . connection.

He put the flowers that he and Robin had brought in the vase that sat next to Ben's gravestone, and turned back to Robin.

Dressed in jeans and a T-shirt, with his hair growing in, dark roots showing beneath the still-blond ends like some intentionally crazy yet eye-catching dye job, he looked much younger than he was.

He looked like some piece of candy Jules had picked up for a pleasant afternoon of no-strings sex.

Except for his eyes. His eyes were anxious as he searched Jules's face. "Are you all right?"

"Yeah." Together they walked toward Jules's car through the warmth of the early afternoon. "Thanks for suggesting we do this. I've been meaning to come out here for a while."

"I know." Robin took his hand. "I'm glad you waited. I wanted to come, too. Ben was . . . an inspiration. And not just the way you think, either."

Jules laughed. "What way do I think?"

"You know. He was ready to give up everything for love. If he could do it, yada yada. I mean, sure, that was inspiring," Robin told him. "But you know when I think of him most?" He didn't wait for Jules to answer. "When it's the middle of the night and I can't sleep and no one else is awake. And I get scared because of what I've done. I can't go back—I don't want to go back, but it's dark and I'm alone so I start to doubt myself. And you. I even start to doubt you, and . . . that's when I think of Ben."

Jules stopped walking. "You know, you can call me," he said. "Anytime. Day or night."

"We're not supposed to leave our rooms at night," Robin said. "If I break the rules, I won't get these day passes and— It's okay anyway. I chill out pretty quickly when I think of Ben. I think of that photo you showed me, remember?"

Jules nodded. Ben in his flight suit. It was a nice picture. In it, Ben was laughing, his eyes lit with amusement.

Robin tugged him forward, the last few steps toward the car. "I think of how perfect and smart he was, and then I remember that you didn't want perfect and smart. You wanted *me*. So thank you, Ben. What time is it?"

Jules looked at his watch. "We still have almost five hours before you have to go back."

"Well, come on, then," Robin said, opening the passenger-side door. "Let's go find a bar and get shit-faced."

Jules stared at him.

"What?" Robin teased. "Too soon?"

"Uh, *yeah.*" Jules laughed despite himself as he went around to the driver's side. "I'm definitely not ready to make jokes about that, thanks."

"Let me know when you are, babe," Robin said, climbing in. "Because I've got a lot of them." He sobered as Jules closed the car door behind him, too. "Seriously, Jules, I've got to be able to laugh about it. It's . . . This is the hardest thing I've ever done. And it's not anywhere near over."

"It's never going to end," Jules told him.

"Promise?" Robin asked, and Jules knew they were both remembering his words when he drove Robin to the rehab facility, weeks ago.

I'm right here. I can't do this for you, but I'm right beside you, however long it takes.

"Yeah," Jules told him quietly now. "You fight this battle, I'll be there. Right beside you."

Forever. He didn't have to say it. He knew Robin could see it in his eyes, the same way he could see it in Robin's. They had that kind of connection.

Jules leaned over and kissed him, and Robin's mouth was warm and sweet. For the first time, he didn't taste like rum or whiskey or wine. Jules could have sat right there and kissed him for all five of the hours they had left.

But Robin started to laugh. "I got fucking Julie Andrews in my head," he said. "That song from *Sound of Music.* The movie version. The one she sings to the captain with these perfect Julie Andrews vowels. You know, *Here you are standing there loving me. Whether or not you should . . .* Except we're sitting down and I'm not exactly a nun wannabe."

It was a beautiful song. Sappy, true, but when Julie sang it in the movie, it was heartfelt and almost unbearably romantic.

Unlike "Hooked on a Feeling"—the song that was stuck in Jules's head. Gee, he couldn't *begin* to guess why.

Robin kissed him again. Harder. Hotter. "Oh yeah," he breathed. *"Somewhere in my youth or childhood,* I definitely did something mega-good." He pulled back to look at Jules. "Did you know that I've never made love without being at least a little drunk?"

"Really," Jules said.

"Really." And there they were, sitting in Jules's car, staring at each other. "So are you going to invite me back to your place or are we going to waste the rest of this afternoon singing each other songs from *The Sound of Music?*"

"I can do a mean 'I Am Sixteen Going on Seventeen,' " Jules said, and as Robin laughed and kissed him again, his stomach did a slow flip. "I just . . . I wasn't sure . . ." Jules started again. "I didn't want to push you before you were ready—"

Robin pointed to his chest with both hands. "Three very long weeks of ready."

But unfortunately it wasn't that simple. "The paparazzi have staked out my condo," Jules said.

"Since the alternative is getting arrested for jumping you right here in the car, I pretty much don't care," Robin told him. "Drive."

Jules laughed as he put his car in gear. It was nice that Robin knew what he wanted, but still . . . "We could go to a hotel."

"No." Robin was certain. "I didn't go into rehab to hide from the press."

Which was what some of the tabloids were saying, despite the statement he'd made before going in.

"I'm out," Robin continued. "So let's just . . . be out. Eventually they'll get used to seeing us together, right? Might as well start today."

Jules nodded, unable to squeeze even an *okay* past the lump in his throat, let alone a full *Golly, I love you.*

"Can you maybe drive a little faster?" Robin asked. "We only have five hours. Tick tock."

Jules laughed. *Only* five hours? But when he glanced at Robin, when their eyes met and heat sparked, he realized just how inadequately short five hours could be.

He turned up the a/c in the car. And burned rubber.

Pierre greeted Ric enthusiastically.

Well, it was enthusiastic, considering it was Pierre, and considering it was Ric that he was greeting. Still Ric got a few whole seconds of tail wag and an actual lick on his hand.

But the kicker was Pierre leaping up onto his office couch to settle beside him, his head on Ric's thigh.

"Don't get up," his mother said as she followed the dog into Ric's office. She leaned over to kiss him hello. "How was California?"

"It was great," he said.

"Where's Annie? Her car's not in the drive."

Nothing got past his mother. "She ran out to the drugstore," Ric said as she sat down across from him in the new leather chair he'd gotten to replace the one that the forensics squad had drenched with blood. "She needed, you know . . . Drugstore stuff. Did Pierre behave himself?" he asked.

"He was very good," she said. "Although I'd prefer babysitting grandchildren without fur."

"I'm working on it," he told her, then laughed at the expression on her face. No doubt he'd nearly stopped her heart.

Eyes wide, his mother leaned forward, no doubt intending to grill him further. But Annie came home, opening the outer office door.

"Hi, Karen!" she called to Ric's mom, and Pierre shot off the couch and scampered out of the room. "Hey, puppy boy." Annie's laughter floated in from the other room. She appeared in the door, cheeks flushed and eyes sparkling, Pierre in her arms. "Hey, Ric. Did you tell your mom about the Troubleshooters job offer?"

"Not yet," he said.

"You were offered the job? In California?" Karen said it with such a mix of pleasure and dread, Ric had to laugh. His mother wanted him to be happy, but she definitely would have preferred he be happy here in Sarasota, twenty minutes from his parents' house.

"Yes and no." Annie sat down beside him on the sofa. "Tom Paoletti— he's this former SEAL who runs Troubleshooters Incorporated out in San Diego—he wants to open a Florida branch, and he wants Ric to run his personal-security division."

"It's an excellent opportunity," Ric said. And it meant no more investigating cheating husbands and wives, although his mother might not have known that that was where he'd gotten the bulk of his income, so he left that part out. "There'll be some travel involved at first," he told her, "until the division gets up and running. After that, we'll be working mostly in Florida."

"The office will be here in Sarasota," Annie reassured her.

"Annie'll be doing some extensive training out in California," Ric said. "That'll be one of the longest trips we take. I'll be going with her."

"Will that be before or after you're married?" his mother asked.

The silence that followed was painfully awkward. Ric risked a glance at Annie, who was suddenly preoccupied with Pierre.

Thanks, Mom. Way to go. He was still working out the exact wording of his response—*You see, Mom, I told Annie I'd give her some time, so she probably doesn't appreciate being pressured by my* mother—when Annie spoke.

"I don't know," Annie said, answering his mother's question. "That kind of depends on whether Ric's going to ask me. I mean, he asked me once, but it was . . . under somewhat . . . unique circumstances. It seemed almost accidental, so . . ."

Ric's mother laughed. And she kicked his foot. Hard.

"Ow!"

"Did you actually ask Annie to marry you while you were having sex?" Disbelief dripped from her voice.

Ric looked at Annie, who looked back at him.

"I was vague," she said.

Unique circumstances was apparently not vague enough.

Karen was shaking her head in disgust. "And you expected her to take you seriously?" She turned to Annie. "He is so much like his father, it's as if my genes had had nothing whatsoever to do with it." She sat back in her seat, crossed her arms, and told Ric, "Try it again."

"Not with my mother as the audience." Ric stood up. "Let me walk you to the door."

Karen gave him heavy attitude as she stayed glued to her seat. "Your *mother* as the *audi*ence is one way to guarantee that you won't *accidentally* ask her again while you're having *sex*."

Annie was laughing, her eyes sparkling with a mix of embarrassment and amusement, and as Ric looked at her, he realized exactly what she'd said to his mother. *That kind of depends on whether Ric's going to ask me . . .*

Was it possible . . . ?

Ric got down on his knees, right there with, yes, his mother as audience. "Marry me, Annie."

She was already nodding, her smile lighting the room. "Just say where and when, and I'll be there."

"That's a dangerous thing to say in front of my mother." Ric turned, expecting to see Karen unconscious from glee, but the chair was empty.

She was already gone.

Annie put Pierre down, and as she kissed Ric, he could hear the sound of his mother's car in the drive as she pulled away. No doubt racing off to buy the latest issue of *Mother of the Groom Monthly* magazine.

Of course, maybe, just maybe, she knew when it was time to make herself scarce.

But as Ric kissed Annie again, losing himself in her sweetness and heat, all he could think was, *Thanks, Mom.*

ABOUT THE AUTHOR

Since her explosion onto the publishing scene more than ten years ago, SUZANNE BROCKMANN has written more than forty books, and is now widely recognized as one of the leading voices in romantic suspense. Her work has earned her repeated appearances on the *USA Today* and *New York Times* bestseller lists, as well as numerous awards, including Romance Writers of America's #1 Favorite Book of the Year—three years running in 2000, 2001, and 2002—two RITA awards, and many *Romantic Times* Reviewer's Choice awards. Suzanne Brockmann lives west of Boston with her husband, author Ed Gaffney. Visit her website at www.suzannebrockmann.com.

Don't miss

SUZANNE BROCKMANN'S

first ever holiday novella!

ALL THROUGH THE NIGHT

When an FBI agent and a Hollywood heartthrob tie the knot, what was supposed to be a low-profile ceremony for family and friends snowballs into a thrill ride featuring a nosy reporter, a dashing personal assistant, and a stalker determined to claim the object of his obsession.

In *All Through the Night* Brockmann delivers another passionate and electrifying classic, this time featuring an unforgettable Christmas wedding, a reunion of many familiar and beloved characters from SEAL Team Sixteen, the FBI, and Troubleshooters Incorporated—including Sam Starrett and Alyssa Locke—and an unexpected romance.

"The reigning queen of military suspense."
—*USA Today*

Available in hardcover for the holidays